Not who they were e

A feathery hand touches the back

the wispy feeling goes away.

I cannot . . . It's the faintest whisper.

It's not Ana. I know Ana's voice inside my head, and this wasn't hers. I spin around, but no one looks at me like I'm crazy. Hex and Vera quickly separate, startled.

. . . *This place* . . .

"Holy crap. That sounded like Cy. Did you hear that?" he says.

I freeze, waving my hands at him to be quiet. But the touch that's not Ana's, and the voice—they're both gone.

"I heard it too," Vera says.

We all look around, confused at Cy's voice in our midst, when a loud pounding echoes from the main door upstairs.

We all freeze. No one ever knocks on our door. No one.

Thump, thump, thump.

My heart jumps a mile. Cy!

"He's here! He's back!" I scream. I tear out the door and up the stairs. I can't see where I'm going, all I can think is, it's really happening. He's really back! Marka, Vera, and Hex follow me, barely able to catch up. As soon as we career into the common room, tripping over the piles of pillows on the floor, a voice yells from behind the door.

"Open this door!"

We all freeze, the excitement on our faces melting instantly.

It's not Cy's voice.

OTHER BOOKS YOU MAY ENJOY

CaTALYST

by

LYDIA KANG

speak

SPEAK
An imprint of Penguin Random House LLC
375 Hudson Street
New York, New York 10014

First published in the United States of America by Kathy Dawson Books,
an imprint of Penguin Group (USA) LLC, 2015
Published by Speak, an imprint of Penguin Random House LLC, 2016

THE LIBRARY OF CONGRESS HAS CATALOGED THE KATHY DAWSON BOOKS EDITION AS FOLLOWS:
Kang, Lydia.
Catalyst / by Lydia Kang. pages cm. Sequel to: Control.
Summary: When their foster home is invaded, Zelia, her sister, and a band of
outcasts with mutated genes go on the run, trying to find a safe place and
make sense of what seems to be a larger conspiracy against them.
ISBN: 978-0-8037-4093-8 (hardback)
[1. Science fiction. 2. Genetic engineering—Fiction. 3. Survival—Fiction.
4. Conspiracies—Fiction. 5. Love—Fiction.] I. Title.
PZ7.K127644Cat 2015
[Fic]—dc23   2014019238

Speak ISBN 978-0-14-751604-6

Printed in the United States of America

1 3 5 7 9 10 8 6 4 2

FOR BENJAMIN, MAIA,
AND PHOEBE

CONTENTS

CALIFORNIA SENATOR ALEXANDER MILFORD IS DEAD AT 64

9.6.2151

(STATES NEWS PRESS)—Alexander Milford, Senator from the State of California for twenty years, died Sunday morning.

Senator Milford had been diagnosed with cancer only three days before his death, after passing a health screening one month earlier. Test results have strongly suggested a biological attack, and a subsequent homicide investigation has been opened.

"Preliminary reports show that foreign, altered DNA was found in the senator's tissue samples," said Dr. Meerhoven, Chief Pathologist at Sacramento's state hospital. "Every cell type in his body had become cancerous."

Senator Milford spent the last few years of his life rallying against HGM 2098, which outlaws genetic manipulation of human DNA. While not a direct proponent of the practice of genetic manipulation, his concern was for the human results of such experimentation. Others, however, have strongly disagreed.

"Human DNA must remain pure," said Dr. Meerhoven, a vocal advocate for HGM 2098. "Those carrying aberrant DNA—who are capable of poisoning the gene pool as they did with Senator Milford—cannot be allowed to exist. We will find the source of this altered DNA. We will find this person and others like them. And we will purge them to protect our society."

State lawmakers are already pushing for amendments to strengthen the law, calling for mandatory population screening to prevent possible deaths. Quarantines are already being prepared in every State.

"There will be no judge or jury. By federal law, anyone with artificially altered DNA should not, and cannot, exist," said a U.S. marshall at a CDC press conference.

Many elected officials are now having their own blood tested for signs of the abnormal

DNA. Thousands of citizens across the States have lined up at local clinics for testing, and orders for CompuDocs CancerClean screening programs have risen exponentially.

PART I
NEIA

CHAPTER 1

ALONE IS A FOUR-LETTER WORD.

Of course, no one in our crazy makeshift family at Carus House will ever admit this, especially while setting up for our nightly slumber party.

"Hex, get your Bomb Bed out of my corner." Vera is stomping around our common room, a blur of gesticulating green arms. Blankets and pillows are piled everywhere.

"Stop calling it that." Hex pushes his bedding back against the glass wall. He likes to sleep with his four arms splayed out, so he laid an extra mattress across the top of another and piled on countless pillows, giving it a mushroom-cloud shape. Hence "the Bomb Bed." It's also a convenient reference to the fact that Hex gets bomb-tastically gassy after dinner from Vera's fiber-rich meals.

"Anyway, you don't even need to sleep in here. The temperature in your room is perfect," he says, dodging a swipe of her green hand. Vera and her skin-embedded chloroplasts thrive in warmer temperatures, yet she loudly complains about her hot room anyway. But she just doesn't want to be alone. Same as the rest of us.

Since we lost Cy over a year ago, everyone finds all sorts of reasons to be in each other's presence, as if the world and our fear are cramming us closer every day. Dyl doesn't complain when I insist on brushing her hair before bed. For a whole hour. It's a miracle she has any hair left. And I say nothing when she and Ana sit reading on the floor by me, each leaning on one of my legs, fixing me in place while I work on my e-tablet. My legs get all hot and claustrophobic when they do that, but I can't bring myself to tell them.

We've been sleeping in the common room because the environmental controls have stopped working in parts of Carus House. Our home is growing decrepit, in bits and pieces. Wilbert, who had all the know-how for fixing things, went back to Aureus. And after our battle in the junkyards last year, we lost access to parts and equipment anyway. Even before the assassination of her senator uncle, Marka's allowances outside Carus were limited. Were it not for Vera's wicked gardening skills, we'd have gone hungry a long time ago. Even so, there's a clock ticking down in Carus. We can feel it in our bones.

The common room is one of the only rooms left that doesn't feel like Antarctica or the Sahara all the time. We could spread out to different corners of the room. It's big enough. But instead, we end up sleeping like a big egg yolk in the middle, within arm's reach of one another.

In the middle of the night, I sacrifice sleep to simply

watch them, hugging my arms to myself. Savoring the hours we have together. I watch Hex and Vera hold hands all night long. Ana curls into Dyl's arms, even though Ana's the tall one. It pains me that Cy can't witness this sweet evolution of our family.

Marka, the only adult at Carus, sleeps at the center of our human galaxy. She takes turns resting with her hand on Hex's ankle or Ana's wrist, as if afraid they'll disappear before dawn. Last night, when her blind search for my hand came up empty, she found me sitting against the glass wall.

She came over and started combing her fingers through my frizzled hair. I'd have stayed there in silence for hours, but Marka knows when I'm playing chicken. She always knows.

"You miss Cy," she whispered, matter-of-fact.

"I'm fine."

Marka wrapped her arms around me. "You're a lousy liar."

And that's when I cried.

No one brings him up anymore, and I don't talk about him. I don't want to be a downer, so every day I wear my plastic happiness like a suffocating, form-fitted skin with no cracks.

It's been over a year since he sacrificed himself to Aureus, so that they'd let Dyl go and take him instead. Aureus is like the opposite of Carus House: Instead of being a safe house, it's an exploitation factory—if you are traited. They'd mistakenly abducted my sister looking for *my* valuable longevity trait, but wouldn't let her go for free. The price was Cy. His regeneration trait is as valuable as mine.

Cy's scent was gradually swept out by the vents, replaced by the unlovely, sticky air of the State of Neia. I used to burrow my nose into his worn-out shirts, knowing that every breath I took whisked him away.

"Earth to Zel!" Vera hollers at me, snapping me out of my reverie.

I realize I've been sitting at the common room table, staring into space like a neurodrug junkie. I was supposed to help Hex and Vera rearrange the bedding, but they've stopped fighting and it's all done already.

"I'm so sorry, what?" I say blankly.

"What is with you, *Quahog*? Dyl's been calling you. Didn't you hear?" Vera's using her pet name for me. She thinks it's adorable to compare me and my longevity trait with a clam that can live over four hundred years. Truth is, I try to forget I even have a longevity trait. Because it will mean that I'll outlive everyone I love.

"Zelia, I said, can you come to the lab please?" Dyl speaks to me through the walls, the transmission crackling with static. These days she's in the lab all the time, without me. Her virtual professor, a ringer for Marka, has stepped in to teach Dyl when I haven't had the time.

Hex has lifted Vera off the floor with her legs bicycling helplessly in the air. She's squealing and laughing, trying to escape his masterful hugging technique.

"It's no use. You shall never defeat me!" he yells triumphantly.

"All right! You win, insect." Her face is that brownish color that shows she's blushing through her green skin. I know the make-out session is about to happen, so I scurry out of the room, protective of their time together.

I head for the door. Before I exit, something catches my arm. It's like a soft hand, but no one is there. It's Ana, Cy's sister. I'm used to her ghostly touch from afar by now. Usually, she'll also whisper in my ear from another floor entirely, but this time she says nothing.

Maybe she's with Marka in her bedroom. Lately Marka's been focused on the holographic screen in her room, absorbing every detail about her uncle's death. Senator Milford brought her to safety and built Carus House for her. He thought she was a gift to the world and deserved to live, and fought HGM 2098 in public. And now he's gone.

We've all taken turns bringing her food because she's losing weight from stress. The silence in that room has been frightening, bigger than the room and Carus itself. We know she's not just in mourning.

Ever since I took Marka's bionic-smell-enhancing pills last year, I've had a lingering, watered-down sense about people I hadn't had before. Dad had warned me about long-term side effects of pharmaceuticals, and Marka's scent trait in pill form was no ordinary drug. Now when she's nearby, I can faintly detect a sharp, metallic scent. Fear.

The transport is humid and warm, and it gets stuck on the third floor, though Dyl's lab is on the fourth. I curse and kick the walls. Another casualty of the failing muscle and sinew of Carus. After a lot of huffing and two broken nails, I pry open the circuit board and override the door locks, then take the stairs to the lab.

Ana is in her pajamas, perched on a stool with a lit Bunsen burner before her. The yellow-and-blue flame wobbles when I approach.

I'm making beasts, Ana says in my head, waving her hands at a collection of tiny glass animals spread out in a menagerie. Dragons, unicorns, and mermaids, among other things. They aren't perfect. Pointy glass juts out from odd angles of each one. Only if you blur your eyes can you see the creature it's meant to be.

Dyl walks over, all gangly in a pair of shorts and faded T-shirt topped with an oversized lab coat. Her hands come to rest on her hips. I hang my arm around her shoulder and she leans into me. I love when she does that.

"We only have so many pipettes, Ana. Really. I need them," she chides.

I need them, Ana says in our heads. This is part of her trait. She can make us hear her without uttering a word. Though whether she's echoing or arguing now, it's hard to tell. The thin glass pipette is like a transparent straw with a tiny narrow end. She holds it over the Bunsen burner with a flameproof glove until a section of glass glows orange, then bends the softened section at an extreme angle and repeats the process. When she's done, she's got a prickly glass ball that resembles a sea urchin. After it cools, she presents it to me on a bare, outstretched palm.

Be careful. If you breathe, it breaks.

"It's pretty Ana, but don't—"

Ana squeezes the urchin and cries out like a stepped-on kitten.

"Oh Ana!" Dyl rushes to her side to pluck the glass figurine out of her hand while I survey the damage. Luckily there's no broken glass embedded in her palm, but the cut is deep. Dyl hastily places the urchin on the table, but she's not careful. It skitters with a squeak and there's a tinkle of broken glass.

Ana pouts. *It died.*

Dyl retrieves a first aid kit from a drawer and I get to work cleaning the cut. When I wash away the blood, the wound seems far less deep than before. I blink several times. Huh. I guess the blood made it seem worse than it really is. Ana stares forlornly at the sprinkle of glass shards on the floor.

She is a wonder, even now. And a worry. Ana can make the kraken out of glass but doesn't have the sense not to impale herself on it.

It was beautiful, she says wistfully.

"Just because it's beautiful doesn't mean it can't hurt you," I say.

But I loved it.

Love is no guarantee of safety either, I want to say. I think of Dad. His lies, how he experimented on my mother, how she chose freedom over family and, in the giddiness of her new life, forgot her annual vaccine packet. Now she's dead. Dad was responsible for the creation of children destined to be nothing but raw material for Aureus products. Marka thinks there might be a hundred of us, in total, scattered around the States. Some in safe houses, some in not-so-safe houses. But no one knows for sure, except for Dad. And he's gone.

Sometimes I hate myself for missing him, for missing his love. That is, if he loved me at all.

Once she's bandaged up, Ana starts reading a holo book. A much safer endeavor than playing with fire and glass. I tilt my head to scan the book title. *Fine's Advanced Applied Mathematics.* Relaxing stuff.

"So . . . why did you ask me to come?" I ask Dyl.

"Oh. I just missed you. How are your med school lessons going?"

I shrug. "At a glacial pace." After Cy left, I took up the medical duties at Carus. Marka said someone had to take over his job. Since I was getting way too depressed rereading Dyl's poetry book and obsessing over Aureus's latest move, Marka put her foot down. Do something constructive, or else.

"Um. So how are you?" I ask guiltily, realizing that I haven't asked in a while.

Dyl brightens and shoves her hands into her pockets. "The Ana research is going well. My holoprof helped me isolate the protein she sheds in her skin. It's pharmacologically active. I think the only people affected are ones she's been around. Even at a distance."

"Really," I say, but I'm staring out the window at the darkening twilight of the city. The agriplane looms like a dull, chalky blue ceiling above the buildings. Tons of crops are grown up there in Neia and the Dakotas, away from the more toxic soil on earth. Directly in my line of sight is the building I climbed over to the day I lost Cy.

"Yeah. And what's more, it's exclusively for hearing her voice and touch, that's it. Not taste. That's good, right?"

"Right." I'm still staring at the building. The last time I tracked Aureus, they were in Arla, what used to be Arkansas and Louisiana. The patents for Cy's quick-healing elixirs had been emerging regularly, followed by the products hitting the shelves. The other products, like Accelerated Teggwear—thick, armor-like skin that can now be grown in a day—or ForEverDay—Wilbert's elixir that lets you stay awake for days without harmful effects (if you don't mind daytime dreaming)—they're still on shelves everywhere. The only reason they're not directly illegal themselves is that they don't alter the user's DNA.

It's ironic the way people scramble to buy these products, and yet are so quick to decry HGM 2098. They have no idea that these products come from us—the traited, the genetically manipulated. The illegal.

But in the last month, no new products have come out of Aureus. They've disappeared. Which means Cy has disappeared.

". . . because it would be bad if we tasted what she might dream about. Like wasabi-flavored scorpions."

"I'd eat that," Hex says, sailing in through the doorway with a cookie in each hand.

"Eat what?" I ask, totally out of it.

"You"—Dyl points a pipette at me—"aren't even listening to me. And you"—she points it at Hex—"are *not* allowed to eat in the lab! You'll get radioisotopes in your food!"

Hex hides two cookie-laden hands behind his back and shoves the other two in his mouth. "Who faid I waff eating anyffink?" He ambles over to me. "Marka wanfs to talk wiff you."

"Why didn't she call me herself?"

He swallows and picks a piece of raisin out of his teeth. "She says you don't respond to her calls."

I've been avoiding her since last night's cryfest, but tuck away the truth and smile brightly. "Oh. The wall coms must be worse off than last week."

Hex points to the door. We make our way down the stairs to the first floor of Carus, which is the ninety-fifth floor of our building. Marka's bedroom is insufferably hot. I don't know how she can bear it.

She sits on her bed in a tank top and shorts, her sleek pixie cut revealing delicate cheekbones and concerned eyes. Vera's beside her, nibbling her fingernails. Also not a good sign. With this much floor space, she's usually in some joint-twisting yoga pose.

"What's going on?" I ask.

"You're right on time. It's starting."

On the holographic wall screen, a woman stands behind a podium. She's got a lab coat on and wears glasses. Only people who don't trust technology wear glasses.

"The recent attack on Senator Milford was a wake-up call to the illegal and unregulated genomic crimes in the

States. We have located several sources of tainted DNA produced in direct violation of HGM 2098." She stands aside and holo photos appear beside her.

The first photo shows a dead toddler boy with eerie grayish skin. He has no eyes, just plain, bald skin over where the sockets would be. The press corps gasps collectively. The photo is replaced by a baby-sized lump beneath a white sheet. A fuzzy halo of brown hair peeks out from the top. A plastic-gloved hand reaches toward the body and tugs the white sheet away.

The baby is a dull, dead green. He could be Vera's baby brother. Or son, someday.

My stomach folds in on itself and I touch the wall, steadying myself. The press corps buzzes with frantic exclamations of horror.

Vera's face is frozen, but only for a second. Something horrible takes hold behind her eyes, widens, explodes. She bolts off the bed and out the door. Hex runs after her, his face harshly carved with concern. I can hear Vera hyperventilating as Hex murmurs to her in the hallway. Marka switches off the holo screen.

"Oh my god," I say, my hand shaking over my mouth. "They killed those children."

Marka's face is all grief, but there are no tears. Maybe she saves them for later, when no one can see, like I do. "I could have rescued some of them," she says. "New Horizons hasn't let me adopt anyone in a year."

New Horizons is where Dyl and I ended up last year after our father died. It's where Marka found us; an insider from New Horizons would call her whenever abnormal blood tests came up with new residents.

"No, Marka." We're all thinking it, so I might as well say it out loud. "It's not your fault. It's mine."

"Zelia, it's not that—"

"It's okay," I whisper. "You don't have to make me feel better."

Though the assassination happened a month ago, the media has been swarming with panic over the existence of altered DNA. Until now, altered DNA has been "an issue" and a "credible threat," rather than real walking, talking people who might sneeze mutant DNA in your face. Today's news conference is epic, in the worst way.

The day that news bulletin came out about the assassination, I wanted to die. The elixir I made was meant to turn regular DNA into the kind I had, the kind that might never degrade and might allow people to live forever. But when we tested it on Wilbert's guinea pig, Callie, she'd erupted in horrible tumors within hours. It ended up causing cancerous cells that grew out of control until she was dead. SunAj, Aureus's two-faced leader, had mentioned weaponizing my elixir. But when Dyl and I returned to Carus, I forgot about my trait-in-a-bottle that failed. In the blur of losing Cy, it was an afterthought.

"Somehow, the elixir I made got into the bloodstream of your uncle, Marka. I am responsible for his death, and we all know it." I've told her countless times already how sorry I am, but she's brushed the apologies away like errant table crumbs.

Marka moves over to touch my arm. Her nose does that tipping-in-the air thing she does when she's reading my scent signatures. I wonder what a murderess smells like. Blood, maybe. She opens her mouth to say something, when Hex and Vera return. They both look shaky and wrung-out.

"Are we going to talk?" Hex says. "We need to start planning, like, a month ago."

"Plan what?" I ask.

"Our evacuation," Marka says quietly. "My contact in New Horizons warned me that the police have been poking around their database. They'll decrypt my uncle's personal records. We can't stay here for much longer."

I take a huge breath after the dizziness sets in. My Ondine's curse. I put my necklace on quickly. The black box pendant dangles at my throat, triggering an implant within me to make my lungs expand and contract. It pushes and pulls my chest wall in that odd artificial way I don't like. Once my fuzzy brain gets enough oxygen, I start talking again.

"How long do we have?"

"I don't know, but we can't wait for someone to knock down our door. We'll prepare as fast as we can, and get out of here."

"Where can we go?" Vera asks.

"There's a safe house in Chicago."

"Okay," Hex says, two of his four arms crossed, the other two waving about. "I'll grow some fake F-TIDs. Every fingertip-ID is registered, but we can generate some black-market ones in a pinch. I have enough of that retinoic acid growth medium to make one for everyone. Vera, you get our provisions ready. Something that will keep for weeks, high protein and carb stuff. We need to load up more ethanol to run the chars. Dyl needs to destroy our DNA samples in the labs. We may even need to torch the rooms, to get rid of any lingering evidence. And Zel, you get medical kits ready to take on the road. Everyone's gotta pack their own clothes and disguises."

Vera, Marka, and I gape at him.

A small squeak issues from Vera's unbelieving mouth. "Since when did you become so . . . *responsible?*"

Hex reddens. "Is that a problem?"

"Hells, no. It's hot!" she coos. I smile and Marka laughs quietly, when a feathery hand touches the back of my neck. I grab at it, but the wispy feeling goes away.

I cannot . . . It's the faintest whisper.

It's not Ana. I know Ana's voice inside my head, and this wasn't hers. I spin around, but no one looks at me like I'm crazy. Hex and Vera quickly separate, startled.

. . . This place . . .

"Holy crap. That sounded like Cy. Did you hear that?" he says.

I freeze, waving my hands at him to be quiet. But the touch that's not Ana's, and the voice—they're both gone.

"I heard it too," Vera says.

We all look around, confused at Cy's voice in our midst, when a loud pounding echoes from the main door upstairs.

We all freeze. No one ever knocks on our door. No one.

Thump, thump, thump.

My heart jumps a mile. Cy!

"He's here! He's back!" I scream. I tear out the door and up the stairs. I can't see where I'm going, all I can think is, it's really happening. He's really back! Marka, Vera, and Hex follow me, barely able to catch up. As soon as we careen into the common room, tripping over the piles of pillows on the floor, a voice yells from behind the door.

"Open this door!"

We all freeze, the excitement on our faces melting instantly.

It's not Cy's voice.

CHAPTER 2

IT'S A GIRL'S VOICE. MY SKIN DROPS ten degrees from disappointment and fear. I turn back to Marka.

"If it's not Cy, then who—"

"They're here," Vera cuts me off. Her body is poised to run in five different directions. Running wouldn't do any good anyway. We're totally unprepared.

"No. It's too soon," Marka says.

Hex unfreezes quickly. "Don't open the door. We'll try to get to the chars by the transport—"

"The transport is broken," I say. I neglect to say that I'm the one who broke it.

"The medical room can't be opened from the outside without a verbal order from whoever's inside," Marka says. "It's the best we have for a panic room. Vera, can you—"

"I'll get Ana and Dyl in there." She gallops off in a blur of green. Hex ducks into the side door to the kitchen, emerging with a knife in each hand. I want to cry at the sight of him. I don't want anyone in my family to fight. Knives are no match for neural guns carried by the police.

I run to the window. On the ground, there are no flashing lights that warn of an imminent, violent takeover of Carus by law enforcement. Just the normal midday magpod traffic. Strange.

Thump, thump, thump. The last thump sounds more like a child's knock, it's so weak.

"Open up! Please!" the voice behind it cries.

"That doesn't sound like cops," Hex murmurs. "Too polite. And too girly."

"How could anyone even get up this far, without bypassing the mirror password program?" I wonder out loud. We gather around the image on the door's scanner pad. A blur at the bottom tells us the person out there is lumped on the floor and unmoving.

Marka passes her elegant hand over a scanner pad. There is a silky stuttering of clicks of multiple bolts receding into the doorframe. Hex takes a step forward, readying his knives. With one smooth movement, Marka tugs the door open.

Outside in the hallway, a girl is slumped on the floor. Dirty skin is stretched over too-thin arms and legs. Her hair might have been white once, but is now dishwater gray, matted with dreads and debris. Tired, strangely scarred and wide-open eyes search us, barely focused.

Marka feels it before I do. She staggers back, stumbling, holding her hand to her neck in a protective gesture. A soft wave of an invisible, anesthetic cloud hits my face and hands, along with an unmistakable wave of nausea. I'd go blind if I didn't stagger backward as well. The horrifying numb sensation is spreading over my skin. I'm not sure which is stronger—the numbness, the nausea, or the hate boiling in my chest.

"What is she doing here?" Hex asks. He rubs his face, irritated and grunting as she affects him.

It's Caliga. From Aureus. The girl who stole Dyl away without an ounce of regret. The first person that might be able to tell me where Cy is.

"Where is Cy?" I almost scream at her. "Where is he?"

"Not now, Zel! Everybody, get far back!" Marka orders us.

I gesture to Hex, who's still clutching the knives. "Give me one of those." Hex hands it over, but Marka shakes her head at me.

"No, Zelia, don't," she says.

My hand grips the knife handle so hard my palm hurts. I want to throw it with all the force I have, right into her face, because I can't see Caliga anymore. All I can see is Dyl, and all the horrible things that happened to her because of Caliga. My knuckles crack sharply from squeezing the knife. I'm shaking with fury.

"He said you'd help me," Caliga mews, hardly a whisper.

"Wilbert left this family a long time ago," Hex fires back at her.

Caliga twists her scrawny neck and her eyes converge on me, pinning me in place. The last time I saw those eyes, they had multiple pairs of eyelids, thanks to Hex's duplicative tissue serum. Now the whites of her eyes are bloodshot, the lids scarred and stretching her eyes open.

She takes a gasp before letting her head gently touch the ground, unable to keep it up.

"Not Wilbert," she rasps. "Cy. Cy said you'd help me."

Her body sinks to the floor as she passes out.

WE MANAGE TO PULL CALIGA INTO THE common room far enough to shut the door. It takes us minutes before we have normal sensation in our hands and the nausea subsides. Vera, Ana, and Dyl have since emerged from the infirmary.

We stand at a healthy distance in an arc around her. Just staring.

"How did she even get up here?" Hex asks.

"Wilbert must have hidden access for Caliga in the mirror password program," Marka thinks aloud.

"What are we going to do?" Dyl whispers. Her face is pale. She's not close enough to feel Caliga's effects, but not far away enough to forget her memories of Aureus. Caliga abducted her, and Micah expertly played with her mind and heart, just as he'd done with Ana. He'd impregnated her. Then he'd coldly and brutally ended Dyl's pregnancy because it was useless to him, and to Aureus.

Micah makes me sicker than Caliga's trait ever could.

As if thinking the same thing, Vera growls, "I'll tell you what I'd like to do to this piece of—"

"No." Marka tilts her head, studying Caliga's body. "None of that. We need to know what happened. I don't think it's a trap. I'd have smelled the deceit on her by now."

Caliga's so thin that her knees and elbows are disproportionately huge and knobby. Wherever she's been lately, there hasn't been much food. One shin sports a three-inch wound oozing pink liquid and resembling raw hamburger.

"Let's put a watch on her. She'll need to be searched, and scanned for any tracking implants," Hex says.

"And she needs medical care," Marka adds. "Zelia—"

"No way!" I grit my teeth. "Hell no."

"You have more training than anyone else."

"But—"

Marka stares helplessly at me. I'll do anything for Marka, but this? She serves me a look that tells me there's no choice.

"We'll all take turns watching her at night," she reasons. "In the meantime, Hex, bring her to the med room. Take a few swigs of that No-PuK and we'll make a stretcher so you don't have to touch her directly."

Hex drops a large sheet on the floor and rolls Caliga onto it. What a trouper. It takes him three breaks and a bout of projectile vomiting before he gets her up the stairs to the med room.

Hex is too depleted of bodily fluids to lift her onto the table, so he leaves her splayed out on the floor. By then, Dyl pops in.

"Let's get a blood sample. We need to reverse this numbness-nausea thing."

"Why, so she gets to be normal?" I scowl.

"No, so *we* can be normal," Dyl says. "You're the one working with her the most. Also, if she's waiting to pounce on us because she's still working for Aureus, we'll be able to neutralize her."

"Oh." My eyes fall closed for a second. I've been thinking with my heart. All red-hot blood and not a single brain cell. Survival has to come first.

"We only have seconds before we succumb, so a blood draw isn't going to happen. Let's just cut her skin, get a quick sample, and scoot away."

Caliga is so out of it, she doesn't flinch when I cut her. Dyl stares at the vial of blood while I recover.

"You okay?" I manage to ask. "With her being here and all?"

"I don't know. It's not so much her, but everything else. You know. *Him. Micah.*" She crosses her arms and stares at the floor. "There are things . . . I can't remember. But I remember Micah's smile." She shuts her eyes and tilts her head, as if listening to sweet music. "He made it so easy to fall in love with him. I was the center of his everything. Even if I was drugged half the time, I remember that so well." Her eyes snap open. "And then I remember him hurting you and me. I was in love with an actor." Her eyes are dry, though mine aren't.

I still have the scars on my arms from where Micah used his electrical trait to burn me. The scars are a landscape of puckered skin. Unlike Dyl, I remember everything. And I imagine a hell of a lot of what happened to Dyl when she was captive. Particularly where Micah was involved.

After Dyl leaves, I try to check my anger. If Cy sent Caliga here so that I would help her, then fine. I'll help her until I can figure out what happened to Aureus and Cy.

"After that," I say to her motionless body, "I owe you less than nothing."

NO-PUK AND I ARE THE BEST OF friends. I've been chugging it so regularly over the past twenty-four hours that the essence of spearmint and ginger oozes out my pores.

I've cleaned Caliga's cuts and put a dressing on her gaping leg wound. A transdermal patch the size of a small plate is now on the floor. It was supposed to infuse a giant bag of liquid vitamins, calories, and protein, but Caliga is so sick and confused that she's ripped it off twice.

I hook up the liquid bag of nutrients to a new patch, and peel away the backing. The sticky side has a million microscopic needles. It itches, which is probably why she keeps yanking it off.

"If you touch this one, I've no problems with tying you down," I say, taking a breath and readying to jump into the anesthetic field around her.

"If you try to tie me down, I'll kill you."

My hand twitches. Caliga hasn't moved, and her eyes are still closed. I drop to a squat, many feet away, watching her with narrowed eyes. Her skin color has grown less pasty in the last several hours, and her cheeks are less sunken. The button lead I've stuck to her chest reads out on a wall monitor. Her vital signs are almost normal.

"Well," I say at last. "It speaks."

Caliga groans, and props herself up on her elbows. Her stiff eyelids blink and it takes nearly a minute for her to focus on me. She licks her cracked lips. "Water."

"Say please."

She delivers me a withering glance.

I stand up and back away. "I can throw you out the window without even touching you. Really, I've been rehearsing it in my brain. It involves a pole, a knife, and a homemade catapult. Want to try me?"

Caliga's eyes bore into me. Her shoulders start to quiver from the effort of holding her body up. Finally, she gives in to her exhaustion and lies back down, shutting her eyes.

"Fine. Do what you want."

I turn to leave, when a voice chimes into my head.

Wait.

My hand goes to my chest. It's Cy again.

"Wait for what?" Caliga groans.

God, she heard it too, so I can't be hallucinating. I know it was Cy. I'm absolutely positive. Of course, Ptolemy was sure the Earth was the center of the universe, but still.

"Where are you?" I cry, spinning around to face the wall.

"I'm right here, idiot," Caliga mumbles from the floor.

I'd love to step on her face to shut her up once and for all. Why doesn't Cy speak again? Something brushes against my cheek, and Caliga and I swipe away the sensation simultaneously. It's as if Cy's broadcasting to everyone. I don't understand. I thought only Ana could do this.

Ana's voice whispers to me. *I heard him too.*

I've got to find out what Caliga knows about Cy. I turn to her, crossing my arms. "How would you like a hot bath, a glass of ice-cold water, and a sandwich?"

Caliga cracks open one scarred eye. It's the hungriest-looking eye I've ever seen.

"Okay." She stretches the word out, making room for the question silently embedded within it.

"And then we talk," I say.

"Maybe."

"That was not a request," I snap. Caliga turns her bony shoulder to me as a response, and I leave.

In the hallway, I gingerly touch my cheek where Cy had brushed my skin. "Marka," I call.

Marka wall-coms me back immediately, crackly but clear enough. "I heard him too, Zelia. Come to my room so we can talk. How is Caliga?"

"She's a royal bitch."

"I mean, how is her health, Zelia."

I roll my eyes. "She's up and ready to eat. The sooner we get some information, the sooner she can leave."

"We'll see."

Great. What is it about parents? They never give the answer you're looking for. *We'll see* is definitely Marka-speak for *We've just adopted a new Carus member.* Ugh.

In the empty kitchen, I punch in an order for a tomato sandwich from the food efferent. I grab the full plate and a glass of water, then return to the infirmary, where Caliga abandons her dignity and crams big bites into her mouth. She makes little *umf umf umf* sounds when she chews.

"Easy," I warn. "There's been enough puke in this place because of you. I don't need more to clean up."

Caliga stops chewing. Her eyes travel up and down my

body, as if she's scanning for a good holo channel and finding nothing to her liking.

"You're not what I expected." She puts the sandwich down, only half-eaten. "Between Cy and Wilbert talking you up, I thought maybe you'd be wearing a nun's habit. Saint Zelia, you're not."

"If you want your bath, follow me. Saint or not, I'm not carrying you."

"Fine."

It takes Caliga a few minutes to stand on her spindly, wounded legs and get to the door without falling over. We make our way downstairs to Dyl's room, ever so slowly. Once, she stumbles and nearly falls. Without thinking, my hands go out to catch her, forgetting for a moment who and what she is.

"Don't touch me!" she snaps. Her body twists away so fast, she nearly goes down on her knees from losing her balance. I back off, hands splayed in the air. You'd think I was the one with the poison touch, not her.

Finally, we get to Dyl's room. I start filling up the bathtub, popping in a few tablets of self-bubbling soap.

"Normally one tablet would do, but you stink," I explain.

"You were probably looking forward to telling me that."

"Well! Looks like we're starting to understand each other."

Caliga doesn't hide the longing in her face when she sees the tub full of iridescent foam. After a second, she leans over and tugs at the dressing on her leg. The edges are bonded to her skin, and she pants from exhaustion after several useless pulls.

An irritable hiss escapes me. "Ugh. Let me take off the dressing."

Caliga straightens up and lifts her chin in the air. I guess that's a yes, so I dart in as fast as I can. I force my quickly numbed hands to pull away the edges of the dressing, peeling it in one fluid motion. I back away and fall against the far wall, slapping my palms together to revive the deadened nerves.

When I turn around, I find Caliga's scarred eyes on me. Her face is pained, which surprises me. I'd expected she'd be all smiles.

"I hope you don't need help getting undressed," I say.

"I don't."

"Hooray for small miracles."

Caliga makes a soft hooting noise. It's nearly a laugh.

CHAPTER 3

MARKA AND I HAVE NO EXPLANATION for the Cy hauntings.

Everyone's been distracted by stray words and touches from Cy. A fingertip on our wrist, a confusing babble of words.

Absences

The same sky

Quarters and halves

I don't understand them. None of us do. But they're happening more frequently.

"Whatever it is, it's real," Marka says. For once, she's turned off the news and focused on me. Sitting on the bed with her legs tucked beneath her, she seems tinier than her six-plus feet, and younger than usual. Fragile.

"It's like he's got Ana's trait. But I've never heard of people carrying more than one trait," I say.

"It could just be Ana's memories, playing tricks on us." She stands up. "So how is Dyl doing with the sample?"

I tell her I'll check. Marka does this sometimes. She takes any hope lingering around, wraps it under thick layers of worry, and puts it on a shelf. I know she's protecting me, but it's irritating. I need straws to grasp. Twigs. Anything.

When I arrive at the lab, I find Dyl wasting the liquid nitrogen in the lab. Which she never does, so she must be frustrated. One by one, she takes a miniature hothouse peony, dips it into the liquid nitrogen tank (our last), and shatters the bloom on the floor. Shards of melted fuchsia, yellow, and orange petals form a kaleidoscope around her feet.

"Caliga antidote working?" I ask.

"It's . . . I need more time, Zel. I can't do this in five days. I even used some of Wilbert's leftover ForEverDay, to stay awake longer. Must have expired, though. Didn't do a thing," she says, disgusted.

"What do you know so far?" I ask.

Dyl shows me everything she knows. The open vial of Caliga's blood has the same effect on us as she does. When my hand strays too close, the fingertips go numb. When I withdraw, the effect goes away. Dyl wraps the sample in a sealed plastic baggie and the effect goes away. We put a drop in water, in liquid nitrogen, burn it, vaporize it, and boil it, trying her limits.

"She's fascinating," Dyl says, taking off her safety glasses.

"Yeah. That's nicer than what I'd like to call her." Dyl throws me a look and I roll my eyes.

Dyl goes to Cy's old desk and points out a protein electrophoresis. "She's actually a lot like Ana. They both shed abundant amounts of a protein particle that affects other people."

"So can you make an antidote? A reversible antagonist, maybe?"

"I tried. And failed. It's so annoying. *She's* so annoying. It's like her body chemistry doesn't want us to figure it out."

I grimace. "Ha. I'm sure Caliga's loving that."

"Loving what?" Caliga mutters behind us.

Dyl and I whip around, beet-faced and twitchy. Caliga limps in, white hair in a tidy ponytail and clad in a skirt and shirt that I know are Dyl's. I'm sure she didn't ask, just took. How typical of an Aureus member. She leans heavily on a makeshift cane I gave her.

"Nothing. Just talking about boring lab stuff," I explain. We haven't told her we're making an anti-Caliga medicine. The less she knows, the better.

"Huh." Caliga pauses to glance at the screen on Dyl's desk. It's covered in tiny scribbles of formula and calculations. She squints to read the writing, and then shakes her head, as if it's too complicated to understand.

She takes another few clacking steps toward us, when Dyl and I reflexively jump behind the table, putting distance between her and us. Caliga stops moving.

"How afraid you are. Like little birdies." She takes a small step closer. We squeeze ourselves farther back. I can already feel the cottony nebula of her atmosphere against my face. "I know what you're doing here. Playing scientist." She waves her stick directly at the computer screen. "Nice try."

Dyl nudges my foot with hers, and I look down to see that her hand is an inch away from the canister of liquid nitrogen. The top is open, still spilling clouds of cold nitrogen gas onto the floor and obscuring our feet. We could use it as a weapon, if necessary.

Caliga's eyes follow mine to the canister. She takes a halting shuffle backward and rubs her arms.

"I'm cold enough as it is. No need for that." She turns around and heads back to the door. "I came to tell you that you're probably doing it all wrong. A protein antagonist will never work. It's too short-acting and unstable." She takes a folded piece of paper out of her pocket and tosses it on the table.

As she hobbles out the door, Dyl picks up the paper, reading the handwritten formula covering every inch. Our expressions mirror each other.

Surprise. And shame.

THE NEXT AFTERNOON, I'M HELPING DYL IN the lab. Caliga's instructions are perfectly detailed. I'd compliment her, if I didn't hate her so much. We're so close to a final anti-Caliga product, when a rosemary scent breezes by. Vera pops in from the door with a tray of golden cakes in her hand.

"How goes it, my little lab squeaks? Just wanted to tell you that your patient is in the common room. She's freshly bathed, waiting to be fed."

"Like a dog," I mutter under my breath.

"And her leg smells rotten." Vera makes a face. "Can't

you do something about that? It's tainting my vanilla biscuits."

I blow out a raspberry of annoyance and make my way downstairs. Caliga sits by the window. Ana's perched on the end of the big dining table, and she and Caliga seem to be having a staring contest. Neither of them moves, but Caliga's eyeballs bulge more with each passing second. I wonder if Ana can make other people's head's explode. I certainly hope so.

Caliga slams her hand down on the chair.

"Get *out* of my head!" she yells.

Ana's mouth twitches, and she tilts her head, as if trying a new visual perspective. Caliga squeezes her eyes shut and clamps her hands over her ears. That's as effective as cleaning your hands with spit. But I'll let her figure that out.

I sigh. "C'mon, Ana. I have to work on her leg. You should be packing, anyway."

I have everything. Ana jumps off the table and leaves, after gifting me with a whispery kiss on the cheek.

Ana's cryptic words are either meaningless or so insightful that I'm too stupid to understand.

Caliga cautiously uncovers her ears. I stop three feet away, the farthest reach of her effects.

"How are you?" I ask. Actually, I don't care, but it's part of the job.

"I've been better. And worse." She shifts uncomfortably, watching me with her pale blue eyes. There's a box of wound care stuff sitting next to her on the couch. I get to work cleansing, squirting on antibiotic salve, applying a new bandage, all the while darting in and out of her circle of anesthesia.

The doors to the kitchen open, and Marka strides in. "Here's our patient," she says, stopping at the imaginary line surrounding Caliga. Her voice is gentle. I swear, Marka could make rabid dogs go all Zen. Caliga tilts her head up and gives a small smile—the first I've ever seen that wasn't suffused with malice. Marka refrains from overtly sniffing around Caliga (we've been working on getting her to tone down the bloodhound behavior), but her eyes glaze over as she reads her. "Ah. You are better today." The concern on her face intensifies. "Caliga, dear. Can you tell us what happened?"

Caliga nods. I stop putting away the medical supplies.

"They came when we were sleeping. We were in northern Arla, by the border of Ilmo and Okks. Everyone was sleeping, except Wilbert, of course. He sounded an alarm, but it was too late."

"Who were they?" I ask.

"They were like us. They had . . . traits. One guy was like strangely tall, and there were others, the guy with no eyes—it was crazy. We fought back, and they killed SunAj." Caliga swallows and tries to catch her breath.

"Wilbert and I ran into Cy's room. There were single evacuation pods in some of the rooms. They made me take the first one and said they'd follow soon." Caliga stops staring at the floor and her eyes find mine. "Cy said if he didn't catch up, to find you in Carus. He said you'd help me. I waited in the woods for them. I waited for days. But they never came." Caliga's stoic face trembles and she breathes frantically, unable to speak for several seconds. "I didn't want to come here. I wanted to be with Wilbert. I wish they'd never put me in that pod."

Marka extends her hand to reassure her. Caliga eyes the gesture hungrily, but Marka pulls back when her fingertips deaden from getting too close.

Marka takes a breath. "How did you get here, Caliga? All by yourself?"

"I traveled along the refuse pipelines. Wilbert told me how to hack the codes a long time ago, so I accessed the pipes to cross State lines."

"What happened to the other kids?" I finally manage to ask. What I really want to know is, where's Micah? Did he burn to a crisp, like he deserved?

Her scarred eyes won't meet mine, or Marka's. "Micah left a month before. I don't know where he went. And Wilbert, well, I just don't know. I saw the whole house go up in flames from miles away. The others, who knows?"

Gone. Which is why I couldn't track down Aureus for the last few months. Aureus doesn't exist anymore. Cy could have been captured by someone even more powerful than Aureus.

"They could come after us too," I tell Marka.

Her eyes cloud over. "Them, or the police. My contact in New Horizons stopped talking to me last night. We should get ready to leave sooner. Maybe tonight, or tomorrow."

"Marka? Zelia?" Dyl calls from the walls. "Can you bring Caliga to the lab?"

"What's wrong?" Marka asks.

"It's Caliga's vaccine. It's done."

EVERYONE COMES BY TO SEE THE RESULTS. Ana sits in the corner staring unabashedly at Caliga, who returns the favor with a narrow palette of evil looks. Ana must be chatting her up again.

Dyl draws up the two air syringes and places them on a tiny tray.

"They look like hors d'oeuvres. Not the tasty kind," Hex comments, and Vera slaps the back of his head.

"Okay. So who's first?" Marka asks calmly.

I step forward and roll up my sleeve. "I guess I should go," I volunteer. "Be nice to keep my stomach acid in my stomach for a change." Caliga throws me a dose of bitch-face for that one.

"Me too," Dyl says. "I worked on it hard enough." Caliga looks at Marka for a beat too long, then stares at the floor.

Marka nods. "That makes sense. We'll test someone with regular DNA, and someone with altered DNA."

"Vanilla or Freaky Flavor," Hex adds. Vera flicks his ear hard with her finger. "What? Keep your green paws off me, or I'm hiding a hot dog in your falafel."

Vera points to the door and Hex marches out. I watch them walk away. Seeing a happy couple is a bit like a screwdriver to the ribs. When they bicker, it hurts just the same, as if the screwdriver simply changed directions. They still have what I don't.

Marka holds up one syringe. She presses it to Dyl's arm, and then removes it quickly. "Okay. How did that feel?"

"Fine." Dyl turns to Caliga. "How long will it take to start working?"

"Fast. Within the hour."

"So did everyone in Aureus get this shot?"

Caliga's eyes avoid everyone's. "No. Just SunAj."

"I don't get it," I cut in. "Not even Wilbert? Why?"

"Well, SunAj is dead and Wilbert is gone, so you can't really ask them, can you?" she snarls.

The silence that follows is glassy and sharp. Marka clears her throat, picks up the second syringe, and approaches me. "Here you go." She presses the round tip of the air syringe against my biceps. Before long, prickles and stings begin to spread over my arm.

"Well. There's only one way to find out if this works," Dyl says.

"It'll work," Caliga says, but she sounds more nervous than angry. Dyl nods at me, and together we approach Caliga.

We take one step, then another. Caliga's hands grip the sides of the lab chair as we approach. I let my hand rise ahead of me, testing the space between us. A slight tingle hits my fingertips. It's a whisper of numbness, but not strong. I squeeze my hand in a fist and then wiggle the fingers. The numbness melts away.

I'd put my necklace on before, just in case. I lean forward, braver now. Caliga's eyes are wide with something—fear, or worry. They watch my fingertips as they close the distance to her hand.

I touch her. The skin of her hand is warm and soft. So human. I thought it would be like ice.

"Oh my god." Caliga covers her mouth with her other hand.

"Zelia!" Dyl cries out behind me.

I turn, but not fast enough. Dyl crumples to the ground, her eyes seeing nothing. Marka and I grab her under her arms and drag her ten feet away. She's not talking or moving, but only for a few seconds. Her mouth moves strangely as she tries to talk, but her words are too slurred to comprehend.

"I thought it was working. How could that be?" Caliga says, standing up.

"Get away! Don't go near her!" I practically spit at her. Caliga stares at us, shocked.

"Dylia. Dyl!" I whisper. She blinks and stares right through me.

"Gonna be sick," she slurs. We turn her over, but mercifully she holds it down.

"I don't understand," I say to Marka. I can't even look at Caliga, not after seeing Dyl like this. "Those were identical doses."

"Yes, but you aren't identical people," Marka says. "Maybe it only works on those with traits."

Caliga rubs her hands together. "No. It should on everyone."

"Well, you were wrong!" I say it with a viciousness that makes Caliga recoil farther away.

"You know," I say to Marka, "Dyl told me Wilbert's ForEverDay didn't work on her either. I don't get it."

"Maybe we can try it again," Marka says, ever the peacemaker. "We have time."

Hex and Vera burst in through the door. At first I assume it's just another fight, until I see Hex's face. His eyes are wide with a ferocity I've never, ever seen. It's terrifying.

"We gotta go. Now!" Hex yells.

We all stare at him. We have a millisecond to register what he's saying, when the explosions throw everyone to the floor.

CHAPTER 4

THE FLOOR BENEATH US SHAKES.

I use my body to smother Dyl, trying to shield her from I don't know what. It feels as if a mighty giant is wrenching the building's foundation from the ground. Marka tries to stand but loses her balance when another explosion hits.

"Where are they?" Marka shouts.

"They're coming down through the agriplane," Vera says quickly, helping me lift up Dyl. "Come on!"

"Who is it?" I yell, trying to hook Dyl's arm around my neck.

"Does it really matter?" Hex roars. He pushes Vera aside and scoops up Dyl's limp form with his lower arms like she weighs nothing. "We have to get to the stairs. The transports are toast."

Overhead, the noise of thumps and shouts follows us as we head for the stairs down the hallway.

"Where's Ana?" I scream. I turn around, but Marka already has her by the waist. Ana is scrunching her face in terror, her hands clapped over her ears. Marka has to practically drag her along.

"Wait!" Caliga. We forgot all about her.

Plaster is raining down from the ceiling. By the time I retrieve Caliga, they'll be here. It will be too late.

"Please!" she cries. "Please!"

I stop at the top of the stairs, watching Vera fly down ahead of me. Caliga could be killed if I leave her. And there's no one else who can touch her now.

"*Dammit!*" I spin around and gallop back to the lab. Caliga's on the floor, her bad leg twisted in the bent rungs of her chair that's fallen over. Her eyes are fierce and desperate at the same time.

"I can't . . . I can't get it loose. I can't . . ." Her hand scrabbles at her leg, trying to pull the metal loose. I tug on it, but it won't budge. I search around frantically. Where's a freaking crowbar when you need it?

A few feet away, the cane is partially covered by debris. I pull it out, and shove it between the two rungs that catch her ankle in a vise. My whole body weight pushes down and the wood creaks under the pressure. Caliga grabs her leg and tugs. I live a million years in a few seconds as she pulls it free.

"Come on, let's go!" I wrap my arm around her bony waist. She puts her arm over my shoulder and we exit the lab like we're in a three-legged race for our lives. The stairwell is only ten feet away, but a galloping rumble comes from our left.

"Stop! Everyone in this place is under arrest. Hands on the wall."

There are two uniformed police, and they're as tall as Hex.

One of them has bio-armor covering his skin—Teggwear, courtesy of Aureus's SkinGuard. They're both wearing helmets with dark shields covering their faces. Each is armed with a stumpy black stick. Neural guns. Caliga unwraps her hand from my shoulder. She takes a shaky, hobbling step forward.

"Oh god, you've come! They kept us prisoner here. They've been hurting us. Thank you!" Her voice quivers with gratitude. I almost scream at her for being the worst turncoat ever, when her hand makes a tiny gesture behind her back. She flattens her palm and stiffens her fingers, paddling the air between us.

She's telling me to wait, and keep calm.

"My leg. I can't—" Caliga crumples to the ground. Her face scrunches in pain. Fine, I'll play along. It's this or get fried with their guns. I crouch over her, feigning concern and make a show of touching her leg, covered in bandages.

I gesture to the nearer officer. "She's hurt. Please. We need help."

The far guard speaks into his helmet. "We need medics up here." He turns to us. "Keep your hands where we can see them, and we'll get help."

"They were awful. They're monsters." Caliga starts to cry, and I'm amazed to see real tears. The nearest guard holsters his gun and kneels forward to put a hand on her shoulder.

Excellent.

Caliga grabs his hand, and pulls him into a bear hug. "Oh thank you!"

Only I can see what the other guard can't—that her victim is now drooling, unable to speak, unable to see. Soon, he crumples over and I grab the gun from his holster. I aim, but it doesn't fire.

"Put the weapon down!" the other officer shouts. "I need backup on floor ninety-eight. Now! We have an officer down!" He takes several steps back and fires at us. A sizzling noise flies over our head and hits the wall.

"Holy sh—" I start to yell, when Caliga hisses at me.

"The gun! It's F-TID activated. Put his hand on it!"

Another neural bullet hits the guard draped over Caliga. His body is so numbed up now, he's barely breathing. He didn't even jerk when the shot hit his bare neck, one inch below Caliga's face. I grab his hand and press his fingertip to the trigger.

I'm not aiming, but the effect of shooting crackling neural bullets has the right effect. The officer balks as a shot bounces off his Tegg-enforced skin. He curses and backs away, still shooting at us, still hitting his comrade, three, four times.

I manage to hit him in the back of his knee, by sheer luck. He goes down like a fallen tree, helmet bouncing on the floor.

"Come on, get this guy off me." We push two hundred and fifty pounds of dead weight off Caliga's body and cling to each other as we take to the stairs. I let go of her suddenly.

"Wait!" I run back up, tugging the helmet off the officer and putting it on. Inside the helmet, I see a flash of listing red words, floor plans of Carus with a dozen moving, labeled dots. Suddenly, it goes blank, and the darkness is replaced by flashing, angry red letters.

Error: R-ID mismatch

I tug the helmet off and toss it. Doesn't matter. I got what I needed. Caliga and I stumble downstairs and careen down the hallway to the medical room. I pound on the door.

"It's Zelia! Let us in!"

The door flashes open and we're inside with everyone.

"Oh my god, Zel! You're okay!" Dyl exhales, taking me into a hug.

"*Okay* is a relative term," I say, panting hard, beyond relieved that she's recovered from Caliga's effect.

She cracks a smile.

Hex has a huge backpack on him, and he's fitting Vera with one too. We all have one, for our escape plan. The plan that is now an emergency plan.

"They have neural guns," I say.

"We know. My shoulder got nicked," Hex says. His left arm hangs uselessly at his side.

I close my eyes, remembering the images from inside the officer's helmet. "There's half a dozen guards upstairs, on the agriplane. More outside the building, and four inside trying to find us now."

Marka's eyes darken. "The agriplane was our way out. It's that or somehow get into the transport shafts."

Vera shakes her head. "There are other transports working in the shafts. We'll get crushed along the way."

"We'll go out the front door," Hex says, nursing his arm.

"That's suicide," Vera moans.

"There's one other place we haven't tried," Caliga says. We all spin around to stare at her, where she's crammed herself into the corner. She's only been here a few days; how would she know anything? "Wilbert's room. He's always made a secret exit in his closet. He's done that since he was a kid, in every place he's lived in. That's how he used to visit me at night."

"Wilbert doesn't have a room anymore. It's the library now. We redesigned it after he . . ." I nearly say *screwed us over*, but I refrain, just in time. "After he left. I saw every square inch of those walls. We popped holes all over them, installing the new holo screens and shelves. There was no door, no exit."

Caliga's face wilts with disappointment. "I wish I could ask him where it is. It's got to be here somewhere."

That somewhere is our only hope. And we have no Wilbert to ask. Unless . . .

"Maybe we can try to ask Wilbert." Everyone stares at me like I'm nuts. "The library. The old one, with the holo teachers. It's worth a try."

A *boom* resonates from the ceiling. They're coming, more of them, from the sound of stomping above us.

"They'll be on this level in a second. Let's move now. It's our only chance," Marka says.

"We have no weapons! We can't just toss Caliga at everyone who comes near us," I say, exasperated. When Caliga stares daggers at me, I hastily add, "I mean, what you did with that officer up there was awesome, but they'll never let themselves get that close again."

"I've got a couple of kitchen knives. That's it," Hex says, producing his supply of cutlery. Marka takes one, and so does Vera. I'm sure I'll cut off my own ear by accident, so I stay close to Caliga to help her walk.

"It's time. We need to leave, now," Marka says, reaching for the door.

For a fraction of a second, I see them all there, poised on the threshold. My family, sewn together with the threadbare illusion of safety. God, I never wanted this. Then again, I never thought I'd lose my father, lose my sister, and find my sister again. Fall in love, know pain worse than I've ever felt, then gain the weirdest and most wonderful family I could ever have imagined. And then at the end of it all, I find myself here—on the verge of losing everyone I love, all over again.

I know something terrible is going to happen after we cross that threshold. And I can't stop it from happening.

Marka opens the door and Hex charges into the empty corridor holding Vera's hand. The other three pour through after them. Caliga and I bring up the rear from a distance. The library is only one floor down, right below us. After all the thumping we'd heard before, our short journey is unexpectedly quiet. I can't believe we didn't get caught.

"That was too easy," Vera comments as she touches

the library door. As she pulls it, Marka sniffs hard, and screams.

"Vera! Don't!"

Three officers jump forward from inside the library and the center one points a neural gun straight at Vera.

It slugs into her chest, her torso shaking jerkily from the impact. Her lovely hazel eyes roll upward and she falls backward into Hex's two right arms.

"Where's the list?" The largest officer yells at us, aiming the gun at Marka's face. The other officers have them pointed at the rest of us.

"What list?" Marka responds calmly.

"The list of all the freaks you guys made. The codes to all the illegal genes. Don't play games, we know you have it."

We all exchange expressions of sheer confusion. Our unrehearsed surprise isn't lost on the officers. The officers don't move their guns from us.

One of them says, "They don't have a clue. Shoot first, interrogate later."

I squeeze my eyes tight, waiting for the shot.

CHAPTER 5

IT'S OVER. I KNOW IT.

I imagine that neural bullet in my forehead, almost feeling it blazing through my nerves and paralyzing me. When it doesn't come, I open one eye. Something is wrong with the officers.

Their heads tilt slightly, listening to something. The tips of their blunted guns sway away from us. They cannot hold them straight. One of them crumples to the ground and drops his weapon. Another falls, until there's only one left standing. As soon as he takes a step toward us, he starts to claw at his ears, yanking off his helmet. His face is bright red, eyes scrunched tightly in pain.

"Stop!" he screams. He can't point his gun at us because something unseen and vicious is hurting him.

"Ana!" Dyl is crouched over Ana, who is balled up, hands over her head. Her face is carved in agony. And then I understand. She is screaming, a hundred and fifty decibels straight to their eardrums. I have only ever heard the soft sadness of her wakeful dreaming, or the chatter of her usual nothings. I've never known Ana's scream.

The guard is with it enough to understand what's going on. He takes a giant step toward Ana. Dyl lunges at him but he knocks her aside and punts a well-aimed kick at Ana's head. She falls backward, almost airborne from the force of the blow. Her thin body hits the ground, blood pouring from the angle of her jaw.

"Take her, Marka!" Hex drops Vera into Marka's arms and lands a powerful kick across the officer's face with a sickening crack, and he collapses into a heap of black uniform. Caliga launches out of my protective grasp and plants her hands on the guy's face. He grabs her wrists, but only for a second before his grip melts limply away.

"Quickly," Marka says. "We'll be dead if more officers show up." She drags Vera into the library, and we follow after I help Caliga get up.

"Wilbert," she gasps, looking at the holo shelves of fake books. We all look around, waiting for something. Anything. But there's nothing but silence.

"Maybe the program isn't working anymore?" Hex says.

"Dad," I shout, barely able to form the words with my dry mouth. "Professor Benten!"

Dad shimmers into existence at my elbow. As always, his holo image is crisp, clean, and startlingly unperturbed. It never fails to shock me. His expression is sterile.

"Greetings. I'm Dr. Benten. I teach—"

"Okay, okay, it works. Try again!" I yell.

"Wilbert," Caliga whispers to the bookshelves. "Love. I need help. We need help. Please."

In a frenzy of glowing green particles, Wilbert appears. We all exhale in relief, except for Caliga. She reaches for the sparkling hologram, gasping as it shimmers from her touch.

"All you had to do was say the magic word, Cal." Wilbert smiles and Caliga beams at him through her tears. As if a boy with an extra, faceless head were the most stunning thing in the universe to behold. He points to the bookshelf on the far wall to the left. "There. It will only read your neural signature."

Caliga walks to the shelf and touches a few different books. They're not real, like the holoprofs. Her fingers graze the fake Brontës and Wildes when the holo image of bookshelves snaps, as if the whole wall got a rubber-band jolt. A crack opens in the image, unzipping it top to bottom to reveal a small door, only about four feet high.

Dyl hoots. "Okay, if there's a white rabbit involved in this scenario, I'm gonna—"

"Come on." Hex cuts her off, picking Vera up gently, and motions to us.

Caliga waves her hand and the door opens to a dark space within the building's infrastructure. There's a crude metal elevator that looks like it will hold two people. We look up the shaft and see that there are more waiting. It looks like an ancient service transport, but Wilbert must have tweaked it to work.

Hex and his verdant, sleeping Vera go in first. They zoom down, the darkness swallowing them. Ana, Dyl, and Marka squeeze into the next one.

When the third lift shows up, I stop. "Wait a second." I turn to my holo-dad. "I didn't think about downloading you. I can't take you with me."

"I am not a portable program. I must stay here."

He's not Dad. He's just a holoprof. I'm desperate for more of him, the real him. "There's no time. I'm leaving and I'm not coming back."

Holo-Dad crackles with electricity, and the sterile expression is replaced with an uneven smile. My heart falters and I gulp a gallon of air. It's *him*.

"When lost, I find my way to Wingfield," he says kindly. "Find your north there. I always do."

I shake my head, full of frustration and anger. "Wingfield? What is that? Why should I believe you? You never tell me enough of anything, when I—"

"What I didn't tell you, she can tell you now. It's time. She's ready, and you're ready."

"Who, Marka?"

"Not Marka. Your mother."

"What?"

Dad told me my mother died after Dyl was born. She's dead. *She's supposed to be dead.*

The floor shakes, and shouts issue from down the hallway, outside the library.

"Oh no." I glance over to Caliga, who's saying goodbye to her Wilbert holo. Wilbert disappears suddenly, and

Caliga covers her mouth. I grab her wrist and cram myself into the lift. Holo-Dad waves politely.

"Thank you. I look forward to seeing you at our next lesson."

My eyes blur with stinging moisture. I hate him. Still playing these games with my life. I wish with all my heart that I could slap him, but there's no part of him that's real anymore. And Wingfield? *My mother?* What the hell?

"Come on!" Caliga pulls my hands inside the elevator, which is disturbingly like a vertical metal coffin. Inside, there are no buttons, just bumpy, rusted metal. We hold on to the walls as it plummets down at a stomach-churning speed.

"Wilbert, tell me you put brakes on this thing," Caliga moans. Suddenly, the lift jolts to a stop, and Caliga and I knock heads.

We chorus in pain. "Ow!"

"Look." Caliga points to the door, which opens to a dark room. It smells of water and concrete, but there's definitely an organic whiff of rosemary and Hex sweat. Dyl's voice splinters the quiet.

"Here! We're over here!"

Caliga and I gallop into the darkness. A light breaks ahead of us, and we turn in to one of the holding spots for the big char, the one we took to the Argent nightclub over a year ago. Dyl's face is smudged and dirty on one side. She keeps her distance from us because Caliga is still with me. I let go of Caliga and run over.

"Are you okay?"

"Yeah, my face kind of hit the lift on the way down. It's quiet as a tomb here. No sign of the police or anything."

I snort. "Please don't use the word *tomb* today."

"Right. Good point." She pushes her messy hair out of her face, the way she used to when she was a toddler. Marka and Ana, who's acting more herself, walk in.

"Good. We're all here. All three chars are ready to go. We'll have to split up."

As soon as she says it, I grab Dyl's hand and squeeze. Marka's eyes fall to our clasped hands, and she frowns, turning to Caliga.

"Caliga, do you know how to drive one of these things?" She shakes her head.

Oh. Oh no.

"But. Can't we . . . Can I . . ." My words can't keep pace with what's going on in my head, and my heart is already breaking. No, no, no. I can't be separated from Dyl again! Not from Hex, and Vera, and Ana and . . . no. I won't. Tears pool in my eyes.

Marka speaks quietly. "We can't all fit together, not with our supplies. Dyl will go with me. You can drive Caliga. Vera, Hex, and Ana will go together. We'll meet at the safe house in Chicago in twelve days."

"Twelve days?" I squawk. Marka and I proceed to heatedly discuss the separation plan, when Caliga pipes in.

"I can't go to Chicago."

"What do you mean?" Marka asks.

"It's time for me to find Wilbert."

"Where are you going to go?" Marka reasons. "We can't

leave you here. You don't know where to go. And we're not just going to drop you off in the middle of nowhere." I peep out a sound and Marka shoots me a look that says *You are NOT going to drop her in the middle of nowhere!*

"I'll manage," Caliga says, standing on her good leg.

"How? In the sewer pipes again? Your wound will get worse before it gets better without Zelia's help, at least for another week. You can barely walk with that bone infection. You'll snap your leg in half."

I sigh. She's so right, and everyone knows it.

"Okay, Chicago." Hex hands out holo studs for everyone to put in their earlobes. It's been so long since I wore one of the thick, barbell-like earrings that projects a holographic screen. Normally, it would have communication ability, access to every piece of information you'd ever want, but ours are sorely limited because we're illegal.

"Access to the address is voice activated," Hex tells us. "And here are your F-TIDs. We matched them with unclaimed IDs we bought a year ago. Active accounts, but very inactive humans, so—"

"You mean dead?" Dyl asks.

"Not quite. They're all in care facilities."

I make a face. "You stole F-TIDs from sick geriatric patients?"

"Just borrowing them! Anyway, your artificial F-TIDs should work two or three times before the account holders realize they've been compromised. Here."

He squashes a small, warm bundle into my hand. I should be prepared for this, but still. There are a pair of separate fingers, each with a soft fringe of skin hanging from the base, like a skirt. The fingers are warm and pink, and pulsate slightly.

"One for you, and one for Caliga. Take this too." He hands me a packet of white powder. "Soak them in this solution every twelve hours, for nutrients. The digits have self-contained vascular systems, so they should stay alive for a while. Oh, and they sort of pee, so watch out."

One of the fingers twitches and tickles my palm. Oh lord. This is going to freak me out forever. I stuff them into my backpack, which is crammed full of food, clothes, and medical supplies, along with my e-tablet with all my research on tracking Cy down. Thank goodness Hex nagged us into keeping them at the ready. Before I can finish zipping it up, Hex has me in a two-armed hug, which is so sad and incomplete that my eyes sting. I choke down a sob.

"Zel, we're all going in different directions, just in case. We'll go west, Marka north, and you should go east. See you soon."

I can't bear to let go. Hex bends over a bit to whisper in my ear. "Remember when I chased you on the agriplane the first day you showed up at Carus? I knew you were tough. Tougher than I am. You're going to be okay. You can do this." He clears his throat, but I still don't let go. I'm going to ignore all social cues and glue myself to Hex for as long as he'll let me. "I know I'm jokey all the time and I never say what I—" Hex's voice breaks and something in me breaks too. He pushes the words out. "I'm so glad Cy got you back to us."

"Tell Vera I said good-bye," I tell him, sniffling. "Tell her I love her and to stop picking on you so much."

Hex gives me one last squeeze and nods before abruptly walking away. He doesn't want me to see his face. I'm glad of it. I couldn't stand to see him cry.

I jog over to Ana and an unconscious Vera in the backseat of the char. I lean over to embrace Ana, but she doesn't hug me back.

"Take care, okay?" I say gently. Her blue eyes turn up to me, swallow me whole.

My heart hurts. Her words inch around in my skull, quiet and fearful.

"Mine does too."

Take this. She pulls out a tiny glass figurine. It's one of her irregular glass unicorns. My fingers clasp the cool and pointed glass. *Poor little fellow. He'll be lonesome.*

Forget the unicorn. I'm going to be the lonesome one. "Thank you, Ana. I love you."

She says nothing, just stares. As I walk away, I feel her ghostly fingers curl around my shoulders, a whisper of an embrace.

Marka finds me as I walk to her char, and hugs me firmly. "Stay on the back roads, far away from the mag lanes. Hide the char during the day and travel at night. There will be plenty of places to hide in the Neia Deadlands. There's enough food and fuel in the trunk to last you for the trip."

"Marka? Before I came down here, Dad's holoprof said something about Wingfield. Do you know what that is?"

"Wingfield?" She looks past me into the darkness. "Wingfield," she mutters to herself.

"What is it?"

"Your father said he was born there."

I frown. Dad told us he was born in Minwi, but he never mentioned the town. I pinch the holo stud in my ear and Hex's pre-loaded map pops up in a glowing green rectangle in front of my face. I touch the image to find Minwi and do a search. Wingfield doesn't exist, just like countless other things about Dad he wanted us to believe. How he pretended to be an ordinary traveling doctor. Or how he cared for women when he was actually poisoning the children in their wombs with gene-altering meds. And now, he's lied about my mother.

I try to imagine her. Frizzy hair. Long fingers, like Dyl's. But her face . . . I can't see it, no matter how I try. Marka's warm hand lifts my chin, and she reaches to turn off my holo. I've been zoning out.

"Zelia? What is it?" She noses the air around me. She knows I'm hiding something. It infuriates me that Dad can drive a wedge between me and Marka with just two damn words. *Wingfield. Mother.*

I stare at Marka's face. The only real mother I've ever known. And then I decide: I'll figure out what I can. Until I have evidence, I've no room for any other parent in my heart but Marka. Dad's left enough of a bitter void, and Marka is everything I've ever wanted.

"It's nothing." I smile bravely and launch myself into her arms. "I'll miss you, Marka," I whisper. "So much."

"I'll miss you too. It's only twelve days. We'll be together in Chicago soon."

I take her words as truth. I have to. Marka pulls out a handful of little silver buttons from her pocket and pours them into my hand. "Stick these on your char. It's as close as we can get to a cloaking device." I remember how Wilbert used these to camouflage his extra head during our trip to Argent. Caliga scoops them from my palm and starts applying them to the char. As Marka walks away, I stare hard at her retreating form, trying to imprint her in my memory forever.

When Dyl walks up to me to say good-bye, Caliga pointedly turns away. Dyl crushes me so hard in a bear hug that I can't breathe for several seconds. The cold edge of Dad's ring hanging around her neck clinks against my black box pendant. A million thoughts go through my mind. My love for her, my bottomless worry, the tiny things I want to say, and the ones so big, they can't be contained in syllables.

We say nothing, because we don't have to.

I SINK INTO THE DRIVER'S SEAT. THE door to the back of the building opens.

Ahead of me, Hex's and Marka's chars ease out of the velvet darkness of the building. The cloaking buttons work well; the setting sun's light bends over their chars and causes a strange halo of light around them. Once there's a little distance between us, they're far more difficult to spot.

A few emergency magpods sit at the far corner of the building. The guards glance at the door, ready to investigate, but look away when no one seems to emerge. I drive slowly so our engine stays quiet. The rough street takes us along heaps of garbage and the ugly back sides of buildings.

Within minutes, Marka's and Hex's chars are completely lost to our sight. Buildings become sparser and the true ground shows itself—tufts of stubborn grass growing on dirt poisoned by chemicals used on the soil decades ago. Caliga faces her window and curls up in her seat, collapsing into her own thoughts. Before long, she falls asleep.

I am utterly alone.

"Cy," I say aloud. But of course he doesn't answer.

CHAPTER 6

HEX'S HOLOMAP KEEPS ME FAR FROM THE small towns. Unfortunately, that means driving off-road, slowly across swaths of filthy and uninhabitable Deadlands. After six hours, I'm exhausted. I pull over next to a decrepit, feral farmhouse riddled with toxic vines and weeds.

"Caliga." I nudge her thin arm. She's cold as ice.

She mumbles, turning over to rub her eyes. "Where are we?"

"Just past Des Moines. It's been six hours."

"That's as far as you could get?" Her tone is infused with irritation.

Ungrateful piece of dirt, I want to say, but don't. I reach into my satchel to grab a bottle of water and one of Vera's traveling biscuits, which I cram into my mouth. It's chewy and sweet. Caliga turns her nose up at the food. Fine. I don't bother to ask how her leg is, and she doesn't bother to tell me. When I offer her water, she drinks it greedily until the whole bottle is gone.

I leave the char to stretch my legs, suppressing a yelp

when a disfigured rat scuttles by my feet. I can smell the decay from the ground and the faint chemical signature that won't go away for another century. The tepid wind rustles my hair and I bend my neck to stare at the agriplane's bland underside.

I am here, in the same sky.

I will wait for you.

Cy's voice doesn't come with the breeze. I sense it in my blood, where it pulses in my arteries, down to my fingertips. Cy's voice is so much clearer and louder than when we were in Carus. I spin around, eyes wide open, but see nothing but the Deadlands. Miles of abandoned homes and the distant glow of Des Moines.

I remain, fixed in memory

Dead on a living sphere

Too weak to rise, and you, too strong to fall

The softest touch follows the words, right in the middle of my palm. It's like he's tracing the lines embedded there, showing me the way on my own map. I curl my hand closed, and the whispery sensation disintegrates. It's like he's right here. Except he's not. If it's a dream, it's the closest thing to reality I've ever concocted in my lonely brain. I squeeze my eyes shut, daring his voice to come into my head again. Hoping.

"Are you going to ask?" Caliga sits with her legs hanging out the open backseat. Sitting up must be a supreme effort, because she's breathing fast. An unnatural flush covers her cheeks.

"Ask what?" I say, unhappy at her intrusion.

"The obvious. I mean, I can hear him too. Feel him. Creepy as hell."

I hate needing Caliga for info, but I force myself anyway. "Okay. Did he ever do this in Aureus?"

"Yes," Caliga admits. "Not at first, only in the last two months. He'd be thinking inside his head and broadcast it to everyone. How he missed you. How he hated us." Her tone is mocking and I'd be more pissed, if I weren't so relieved. It isn't my imagination!

"What else did he say?"

Caliga shifts deeper into the backseat. "Not much. Blink told him we could hear everything. She got burned by Micah for that one."

"What, Micah punished you guys?"

"Not me. I did what I was supposed to do. But everyone else? All the time. Micah was damn good at it too." She says it like she almost admires his cruelty. "Anyway, after that, Cy would say things in fits and bursts, but later on, he just started reciting random stuff. Books he was reading, and poetry."

Poetry? Cy's words jostle against a totally different memory. When Cy was in Carus with me, I showed him Dyl's poetry book. I know those words—Cy's words. They're from a poem in Dyl's book entitled "Luna," by some hopeless, dead poet who fell in love with the moon. But why would he recite this, instead of calling for me?

The answer is so obvious. He wants me to follow his voice, but he can't say so outright. I know it. I run to the char and turn on the engine.

"I thought we were stopping to sleep," Caliga says. She tries to shut the door but isn't strong enough to pull it closed. I huff in annoyance and shut it for her, like a chauffeur.

"Why do you care? You were sleeping anyway." I don't need to tell Caliga what has to happen. I need to find Cy. He must be closer than ever before. I hit the gas and Des Moines grows smaller in the rearview mirror. When I hit a fluttering bat with my side mirror, it doesn't slow me down.

Caliga snickers. "I like it when you're annoyed. You drive like a lunatic."

DURING THE NEXT TWO DAYS, CY'S WORDS are crumbs leading me on a trail. Every phrase is a message. I change my direction slightly north or east, depending on the strength of his voice, but it's not long before I realize where he's leading me. Dubuque—a bustling city where Ilmo, Winmi, and Inky all converge on a single point on the map. It's the only legitimate way to get to Chicago, which worries me. Dubuque will be smothered with law enforcement searching for illegals eager to switch State citizenship. I've no idea why Cy would lead me there.

Caliga sleeps fitfully in the backseat, waking up less and less often to eat or drink. She mumbles through her dreams, and her breathing grows more rapid by the hour. I stop to check on her a few times, but she swats my hands away. When dawn hits on the second day of our drive, I look for a safe place to park, since the cloaking buttons don't conceal the char well during the day.

In the shadow of an abandoned factory, I turn off the engine and open the back door. Caliga lies there like a puddle, struggling to focus on me when I examine her. This time, she's too weak to push me away. I have trouble finding her pulse and when I do, it's a faint flutter. After a few tugs, her bandage falls off with a wet plop and the smell of her infected leg rises like a miasma. It's worse than Satan's outhouse.

"Ugh, ew!" I pinch my nose quickly. Her wound is puffy and purple. It didn't even look this bad when she arrived at Carus. "Geez, why didn't you say anything?" I chide her, scrambling for my medical supplies.

Caliga's scarred eyes barely stay open. "Dunno. I think . . . I got hurt again when we were attacked."

"Stupid," I mutter, rifling through the medical kit. "Stupid, stupid, stupid." I'm not sure if I'm talking to myself or to Caliga. I was supposed to take care of her. Marka's disappointed face pops into my head and I wither inside. I pull out some flat pouches filled with liquid antibiotics and pause at the open char door. Inside, Caliga has drifted back into unconsciousness.

I could leave her here and just go. She's already a skip and a stumble away from death. After what she'd done to Dyl, it would be a just ending. Lying askew on the backseat, her body is painfully thin and her white hair splays in oily strands. She looks like something that got tossed into the garbage yesterday.

"Damn it."

The universe owes me a million karma points for this. I

clean off her belly and peel the backing away from an antibiotic pouch and slap it on, giving it a yank so the swath of microneedles sink into her skin. I count the remaining pouches—three. Caliga's infection has definitely spread to her blood. She'll need at least a week's worth, and I only have enough to last one more day. How am I going to get to Chicago if she's this sick? Without more supplies?

I sit in the driver's seat, resting my head on the steering wheel.

We'll never make it.

I DRIVE ANOTHER FEW HOURS BUT STOP frequently to check on Caliga, who sleeps most of the time and barely moves. When I move her limp arm to feel her pulse, I notice how fairy-like her hands are. The nails are symmetrical ovals on slender fingers. She has the hands of an innocent girl. I wonder if hands can lie.

I must be getting lonely and desperate, because I start talking to her and asking ridiculous questions. Things like, "Tell me what Cy used to eat for breakfast," or "Did you kiss both of Wilbert's heads, or just the one with lips?" She never answers me.

As we approach the outskirts of Dubuque, Cy's voice is louder than ever, and the quality has changed. It has clarity now, as if freed from the confines of a thick blanket. When the edge of the agriplane comes into view where the scythe-like skyscrapers of Dubuque appear, I start to hear the poem in its entirety. He's close, so close. I know it.

The agriplane ends abruptly and I'm blinded with sunlight that hasn't warmed my skin in months, ever since Marka made the agriplane off-limits. I imagine how Vera might feel right now, yearning for light like water or food. What I wouldn't do to have her right here, calling me that stupid Quahog nickname again.

We pass domed metallic apartment complexes and pointed office buildings that resemble daggers. The city is denser now, and it's hard to avoid the mag lanes. I drive in the shadows and the back alleyways, but even so, it's nerve-wracking trying to avoid pedestrians and follow Cy's voice.

Finally, I round a bend behind some huge warehouses in the rougher, southern section of the city. Cy's voice is bell-clear, as if he were standing right next to me. As I pull up close to a pile of discarded building material, his voice hesitates. A few beats later, it resumes to finish the poem.

After a thoughtless twist, you return.
Keep your tides surging with their cold embrace
And I will rise to meet them
Drowning in our histories to come.

I turn off the char, listening to the engine tick and clank as it settles down. As soon as I shut the door, Cy's words stop again. I carefully pick my way around the small heaps of trash, heading closer to the largest pile. It's an A-frame shanty constructed of flat corrugated metal.

For a second, I feel his hand curl around my neck, sliding around my shoulder. It's comforting, yet unchaste—and I inhale so sharply that the noise I make echoes down the alleyway. His words stop yet again, but the hand stays where it is.

"Cy," I whisper.

A flap of plastic sheeting blocks the entrance to the shanty and it flutters in the scant breeze. And then I catch a scent of smoldering smokiness, like a warm autumn day succumbing to frost. A scent I've only dreamed of lately, because it disappeared from Cy's pillow months ago.

He's here. I can't believe he's so close.

In my arms, I think. *He'll be in my arms in two seconds.*

I push back the plastic, trying to see into the gloom within.

Someone lies on the roughly swept ground. I see the curve of the spine, the dark, shaggy hair. Filthy clothes hanging from a thin frame. But I know that skin. It glows almost preternaturally within the dark of the shelter—unmarred, if not for the smudges of mud.

My heart beats so hard, it bumps uncomfortably against my chest, making me dizzy. I take a tentative step closer, and my foot crackles on a plastic wrapper.

Cy stirs, his head twisting around to find the source of the noise. I'm shocked to see a short, patchy beard obscuring his jawline. His eyes squint in the scant light inside his shelter. He blinks painfully.

"Cy?" I whisper, sinking to my knees. "It's me."

As he twists to face me fully, something beyond him moves. Under the protection of his arms, a dark bundle sits up, and a pair of beautiful black eyes open to meet mine.

I've finally found Cy.

And he's not alone.

CHAPTER 7

THE DARK-EYED BUNDLE MURMURS SLEEPILY, HER TONE light and delicate. "*Qui est là?*"

"*C'est une amie,*" Cy murmurs back.

Cy is speaking French. To a girl he just had his arms around. I'd thought of a million things to say to Cy when I saw him again. Now I'm speechless.

Silence fills the little junk-shanty as I stand up, unsure of what to do. My buoyed heart just careened into the center of the earth, and I don't know how to retrieve it. Cy gets up shakily, his shoulders thinner, his cheekbones carved out with frightening severity. Dirt-caked pants hang on his narrow hips. He steps forward and reaches his hand out to touch my cheek, but hesitates.

"This might be the best hallucination I've ever had," he murmurs.

"Oh my god," I whisper. A sob escapes from me, shaking my whole body. In seconds, he has his arms around me, and I'm dissolving in his embrace. The scent of him is like mud and seawater and dying trees, but behind the dirty exhaustion, it's Cy.

He burrows his face into the crook of my neck. He's crying too, and we're both shaking and freaking out and I start kissing his cheeks—stubbly and rough with sharp angles that weren't there before. I find his eyelids and kiss them too. He's real. *This is real.*

He finally plucks my hands off him and holds my wrists, before releasing me. The action is gentle, but I recognize the movement. He's pushing me away and my eyes smart at the gesture.

"I can't believe it. You found me," he says softly.

I rub away my tears. "Your voice. I followed your voice. We could all hear it. How did it happen? And your touch—like Ana's. How? And who . . . who . . ." My words trip over themselves to get out.

"Is Ana okay?" he interrupts. "Is she safe?"

"Yes, she's okay. I think she's okay. She's with Hex and Vera, and we're going to try to meet up soon in . . . oh my god. How did you get here? How—"

"I'll tell you everything. But first, do you have anything to eat? Any water? We're starving to death." At the word *we* he steps farther away. The girl on the floor of the shanty sits up on her knees, swaying unsteadily.

Blink. The girl who could see in the dark. Micah, his sadistic colors on full display, had ordered her to attack us after I found Dyl in Aureus. Blink hit my leg so hard that I still have a lumpy scar. She's tiny, with dusted umber skin, a heart-shaped face, and full lips. Her cheekbones are sunken and match Cy's. She stares right back at me, as if she doesn't quite believe I'm here.

"You remember Élodie," he says awkwardly.

"Élodie," I murmur, parroting him.

"Yes, that's her name." He turns to Blink and smiles. "Everyone called her Blink because of how she reacts to the light."

I nod, but I can't get over how Cy pronounces her name. It's musical, sweet, lovely. Zelia, in comparison, is all angles. It buzzes, an irritant of a name. I try to sense what he's feeling, scenting around him. There's a peacefulness I'm picking up. But I sense an unmistakable scent of something tarry, black and sticky. What is that?

"I am pleased to meet you again," she says, her English heavily accented. "I am sorry for—I did not want. *C'était un cauchemar . . . trés difficile pour moi.*" When she looks up, she squints painfully at the light behind me. Her pupils are enormous. Big and wide and black within dark irises that might swallow a person whole. She fumbles for her pocket and digs out a pair of oversized wraparound sunglasses, putting them on with a relieved sigh.

"Water?" Cy asks again. His Adam's apple bobs as he swallows dryly.

"Stay here. I'll be right back." I run back to the char to dig up some food and water containers. I don't know how I manage, because I'm so distracted. I've imagined a million versions of how I'd be reunited with Cy. This was never one of them.

When I hand the biscuits and water to Cy and Blink,

they cram the food into their mouths, chugging water so fast that they cough and sputter. Soon after, they take turns groaning in pain as their empty stomachs react to the shock of real food.

Before long, I hear how they made it here. Walking on foot since the attack two weeks ago. Stealing food and water when they could. Hiding in abandoned houses and fighting off the malformed opossums, rats, and raccoons every night.

"We would have gone straight to Carus, but Élodie was convinced we'd put you in danger, so we came to the border instead."

"I followed your voice here," I say, wishing Blink weren't so near. I'm sure I'm blushing. "I didn't know you knew that poem 'Luna.'"

"If anyone could recognize it, it'd be you," he says quietly. He seems shy about the subject, so I take the opportunity to urge him to eat and drink some more. I realize why he feels so far away, even though he's right here, in touchable distance. His voice has stopped reciting the poem to me. I miss it.

I miss him, and he's right here.

"I didn't know anyone could have more than one trait," I say. "How could that be?"

"I don't know. Ana doesn't seem to have my trait."

I remember Ana's cut hand when she squeezed the glass sea urchin. "Wait. Maybe she does." I tell them about the accident, and Cy rubs his arms with a shiver. A waft of garbage-scented wind flows by, rank and overwhelming, when I need to concentrate. I pinch my nose, irritated by the intrusion.

"Could there be others like us? Have you noticed anything in Vera, or Hex?" he asks.

"No." An opossum slinks by the other end of the alley, its hindquarters raw and oozing from an infection. Ugh, it's putrid. I pinch my nose again.

"Why do you keep doing that?" He taps his nose.

"Too many smells. So distracting."

"Holy hell." Cy leans forward, his eyes roving over me like I'm a new lab specimen. "How long has this been going on?"

"Ever since I took Marka's pills last year. My dad said that some medications can have lingering side effects, so . . . I thought it would go away, but it's gotten worse."

"Zel. Marka's pills only have a twenty-four-hour half-life. I helped her make them. Tested them too."

"Wait. You think I have Marka's trait? For real?" I whisper. I can't hide the goofy grin expanding my cheeks, and Blink stares at me like I'm crazy. Why didn't I realize the obvious? "God, I wish I could tell her! She needs to teach me everything!" I'm giddy with excitement.

"Wait, whoa. But why? Why would some of us have more than one trait? Ones that didn't show up until we were nearly adults?"

"I don't know," I gasp. Blink can barely hide the disgust on her face. "What's wrong?" I ask.

"It's not a good thing, Zel," Cy says.

"What do you mean?"

"It's complicated." He waves away the topic, and anger simmers inside me. Cy never blew off the importance of our traits. I don't understand his dismissiveness. I steel myself to challenge him again, when he asks, "Where's Ana? How is Marka?"

My face must look awful, because worry suffuses his face. "What happened, Zel?"

"You don't know? About Senator Milford?"

"Marka's uncle? What happened?"

I tell him everything. About how he died, and how it must have been my DNA that did it. About how the police raided Carus and drove us to flee in different directions.

"Do you think someone in Aureus could have leaked the elixir I gave to SunAj?" I ask.

"I don't think so. SunAj had very specific plans to adapt that elixir."

"Very few people had access to it," Blink adds. "He didn't know how best to distribute it, even on the black market."

"But how could it have gotten to the senator?" I want so much to believe I might not be responsible for his death.

Voices sound close by and we all jerk to attention, cowering in the shadows.

"Come on," I whisper. "I have a char down the alley." I suddenly remember Caliga. "We have to go, quickly." I extend my hand to Cy, when Blink instinctively reaches for him at the same time, slipping her hand into his. Blink sees me staring, mouth idiotically open with surprise at their clasped hands, and she withdraws it with a jerk.

What the hell.

I spin around, smacking the plastic sheeting out of the way, and walk quickly back to the camouflaged char. I wipe my smarting eyes, and turn to see Cy and Blink emerging unsteadily from their shelter. There are a few seconds before they catch up. I've got to calm down.

Be reasonable, Zelia. They're hungry and they've been on the run. At least Cy had a friend in Aureus. She's probably like a sister to him.

I nod to myself. That's what I'll believe, for now. As soon as they get to the char, I hold my hand up.

"Wait here."

"Why?" Cy asks.

"Caliga's in there."

"You mean she made it to Carus after all?" He and Blink exchange glances. I feel stupid and left out and twelve years old, wondering what thoughts they're sharing without me.

"Yes, but she's sick. Cy, I need your help." I open the back door and lean over Caliga's sleepy body, when Cy yells out.

"Don't!" When he sees me unaffected by being so close, his eyes widen. "How can you bear to be close to her?"

I chuckle at his words. I'm surprised how well I've been bearing it, after all. "We made a vaccine to her trait when she showed up in Carus."

"You made it?"

"Dyl did, actually, with Caliga's help."

"Dyl did? Wow."

"I know," I say, my pride swelling. "But it didn't work on her."

"Why?"

"I don't know." I haven't had more time to think about why. Caliga was adamant that it should have worked fine on her. It doesn't make sense, and I've no answer as to why. I go back to examining Caliga. Her flush is gone and she's breathing more regularly. I replace her empty antibiotic pouch with a new one and feel her cheek. She's not feverish anymore. I add nutrient powder to another dermal pouch full of sterile water and attach that to the other side of her belly. After a quick change of her dressing, I step back.

"How did you learn to do all that?" Cy asks. Something passes over his face that resembles what I've been feeling. We've both been left behind in each other's life, and not by choice.

"I . . . had to do something when you were gone." I sigh. I can't explain a year's worth of my life in a sentence.

"Where are we?" Caliga mumbles, blinking slowly.

"We're in Dubuque," I say. "I found someone you know."

Caliga props herself up on one elbow and peers around me. As soon as she sees Blink and Cy, her hands frantically claw at my arms.

"Where is he? Wilbert? Wilbert!" Her mouth is so dry, she almost chokes on the words.

"Wilbert's not here," Cy says quietly.

Caliga's face is drained of color, and she had precious

little to begin with. I've seen her nearly permanent bitch face, and this new, hungry expression tears right through me. It's devastation and anguish all at once. I should know it well enough; I owned it when Cy volunteered his life for mine and Dyl's.

"He didn't make it out, Caliga. They took him."

Caliga lies back down and is mute for a long time. I think she's fallen asleep, when I see tears tracking down her temples into her white hair. "Where were you?" she finally says in a raspy whisper. She still won't open her eyes. "I waited for days."

"We came out on the other side of the lake, but there was a hoverpod searching the area for survivors. We had to run," Cy explains. His shoulders droop and he wears his exhaustion like a hundred-pound cloak.

"Cy, we should get going," I say.

"Where do we go?" Blink asks. Her accent is lilting and gorgeous.

"Caliga needs more antibiotics. We're trying to meet up with Marka and everybody in Chicago."

"Ilmo's not such a tough border to cross, last I heard. When are you meeting them?"

The last forty-eight hours have been an adrenaline blur and I've hardly slept. I think carefully. "Ten days."

"They will not let us in," Blink comments. I have to concentrate extra hard to understand her accented words. "None of us have working F-TIDs anymore."

"They might," Cy tells her. "Lots of States have an opt-out clause. They don't require an F-TID, but you're monitored and treated like a convict. Hard labor, crappy benefits, crappy pay, stuff like that."

"Then let's go. Caliga can't walk, so we'll have to drive as close as possible to the entrance registration areas."

Everyone nods, and Cy and Blink stand back so I can help Caliga get into the front passenger seat. With Cy and Blink crammed into the left corner of the backseat, they're just beyond the three-foot mark of Caliga's effect. Since I can't sit with him, I pile the biscuits and bottles of water on Cy's lap until he's blanketed in sustenance.

"Keep eating and drinking. You need your strength."

Cy smiles gratefully and hands Blink a bottle. As soon as I start the char, I glance at the rearview mirror. Blink leans her head against Cy's shoulder, her ebony hair clotted with braids full of twigs and leaf fragments. Cy's eyes are on me.

Part of me overflows with frightening happiness. I've found a puzzle piece that's been missing for too long. But as hard as I try to cram it into place, it somehow doesn't fit the same way anymore.

Caliga moans, and I take a minute to lean over and adjust her sagging bandage. As I tighten one of the bindings, her face is grim. For a moment, I wonder. She can make everyone else feel numbness, but does it affect her own body?

"Can you feel this?" I ask, tugging one last time.

"I feel everything," she says quietly.

I know exactly what she means.

CHAPTER 8

WE KNOW WE'RE GETTING CLOSER TO THE confluence of Neia's, Ilmo's, and Winmi's borders. Huge Neia-sponsored holo ads started popping up everywhere, begging us to stay in Neia, promising a lax morality code and lovely pale complexion, from the absence of harmful sunrays.

One of the cloaking buttons falls off our char after we hit a pothole, so we abandon it behind an old house and I grab my duffel bag. In the distance, huge, glowing blue plasma fences line the borders between Neia and Ilmo. There really is no good way out of Neia here except through the legal entrances.

Caliga leans heavily on me as we try to blend in with the crowds converging on the entrance areas. I recognize the building style of the Neia New Citizens Processing Center. It's all blue glass and silver metal, like a giant dewdrop fallen from the agriplane. We went through a similar building when Dad, Dyl, and I entered Neia from Okks.

They'd given us beautiful strands of sunseed flowers to

wear around our necks and hair. We'd pressed our F-TIDs into a tablet that outlined the rules and bylaws of Neia that we were required to obey. I hardly remember them now. Something about a minimum residence of one year; taxes; and morality codes written in a tiny, scripted font meant to be skimmed over with a hurried eye.

I never noticed the rules about HGM 2098, but back then I had no idea it would ever apply to me. And no idea that Neia would cause the worst pain of my life—after losing Dad, Dyl, and, later, Cy there.

We pass the Neia dewdrop building and try to look inconspicuous, but Caliga's tottering limp captures people's attention. Her trembling hands tell me she's more scared than unsteady. For once, I don't mind having her arms on me. Cy and Blink walk a good ten feet behind us.

Discarded, dissolvable flyers in various states of decomposition litter the ground. If we had legal holo studs on, our holo feeds would be inundated with ads. People crowd thickly at the Fast-Track lines, where previously approved people are set up with jobs and housing. The rest of the untested and undecided swivel their heads, reading the different holo signs and trying to magically extract the truth from the gossamer flyers.

I'm tempted to see if any of them offer a clue about Wingfield or missing mothers. I haven't told Cy about either one. It seems like I'll never get a moment alone with him, and the thought suffocates me all at once.

"Stay close," Caliga whispers, and I remember that I

need to be her human shield, so no one will feel her effects. But the crowds are too dense. When a few people clutch their faces and stomachs because of her numbing presence, I dig up a shirt from my bag.

"Hold this to your face and cough like you're losing a lung," I offer.

It works. People give us a wide berth. Fear of communicable diseases can be a good thing.

We're able to dodge most of the solicitors. They're all dressed in the State colors of Minwi, Ilmo, and Inky: green, blue, and gray, respectively. A few grays are clad in head-to-toe smocks and elaborate headdresses. They're all women, and one of them beelines toward me and Caliga. All that is human is concentrated onto an oval of pink skin, blue eyes, and rouged lips. She delivers a toothy smile.

"Inky has the lowest rate of State emigration! People never want to leave, because our quality of life is superb." When she comes too close, I push Caliga farther behind me and intercept the flimsy flyer she places into my hand.

"Inky?" I try to remember my geography. "Inky doesn't border Neia."

"We have an underground magtrain that will take you straight to the city of Coventry. We reach out to welcome women to our family."

She makes Inky sound like a spider with a huge leg span. We have no interest in going to Inky. I take the flyer to be polite. It's lighter than tissue paper and flashes words in gentle hues of pink and lavender.

INKY: WHERE YOU CAN BE QUEEN!
FULFILL A WOMAN'S GREATEST DESTINY
FULL VOTING RIGHTS
LOW TAXES; GUARANTEED SHELTER
FREE HEALTH CARE
NONEXISTENT UNEMPLOYMENT
FAMILY FRIENDLY

I give her a polite smile, then stick out my tongue after she scurries to hand a flyer to Blink. She can't fool anyone. The flyer should actually read:

INKY: WHERE YOU CAN BE A BREEDER!
FULFILL WHAT THEY CONSIDER YOUR ONLY DESTINY
FULL VOTING RIGHTS WHEN YOU'RE NOT KNOCKED UP,
WHICH IS NEVER
NO TAXES BECAUSE THEY STEAL THEM FROM YOUR
PAYCHECK ANYWAY
GUARANTEED SHELTER IN A BABY-MAKING FACTORY
FREE FERTILITY TREATMENTS
UTERUS FRIENDLY

I hand the flyer to Caliga behind me, where she rips it into tiny sparkling bits of trash, snorting. Plenty of women go to Inky for a few years, gather some money for themselves, and try to leave after they realize what a horror show it is. The sad thing is, you lose parental rights to your own babies if you leave, and half the time, they send the children to neighboring states whose own birth rates are abysmally low, in exchange for a State "donation" of goods or cash.

"Where's the Ilmo entrance?" Caliga asks impatiently. She's starting to limp more and her face is drained of energy. This is the most she's walked since we left Carus.

"There," Cy calls out from behind us. He's pointing beyond the crowds.

There's a blue crescent-shaped awning and a huge line to get in. Nearby, the Minwi line snakes in front of a green tree-shaped entrance. It's nearly as crowded. To the far right is the entrance to the underground magtrain to Inky. The line of women there is all but obscured by the crushing crowds from Minwi and Ilmo.

"How am I supposed to get into Ilmo?" Caliga whines. If we try to enter the crowd, people will start dropping like hail.

"How did you cross State lines before?" Blink asks. "When you came to Neia from Arla?"

"I went in the sewage tunnels. No people. But that's how I got this," she says, pointing to her ailing leg.

"Okay, we're not doing that," Cy says flatly.

"We could try the north border. Some of the plasma fences break down. We could sneak through," Blink suggests.

"But Caliga's going to need more antibiotics soon," I tell her.

"That's not an option, then," Cy agrees. Blink's mouth stays a flat line, like she doesn't care. Interesting.

I glance at the interviewing going on inside the Ilmo

entrance. "Look, once we get past the crowd, they ask us stuff across a partition."

Caliga already looks relieved. "Then I have a chance."

We're interrupted by blaring music. Caliga grabs my elbow and points to a flashing holoboard above the green-tree Minwi entrance. A bearded man wearing a tie and green coat smiles garishly.

"Minwi proudly offers the first screening procedures to ensure our citizens have the purest DNA! No need to fear harm from this new breed of mutant convicts in the States!"

I duck my head down and stare at my hands. Anything to take the focus off my fiery face.

"It's okay, no one's staring at us," Caliga says low, her hand on my back. "But look what's happening."

I let my eyes flick up quickly. The crowd around the Ilmo line sways and hesitates. The uncertainty spreads like an infection. Several groups of people break away to switch to the Minwi line.

The officials in the Ilmo entrance can't hide the disgust and jealousy in their faces. They start shouting over the loudspeakers about their imminent plans for state-of-the-art screening, but it's too late.

The crowd in front of Ilmo's blue crescent awning is no longer dense. Caliga and I could wriggle our way in without getting too close to anyone. I dip my chin at Cy and Blink, who nod back. We worm our way closer to Ilmo's entrance.

"How am I going to deal with the physical exams and everything?" Caliga mutters nervously.

"Maybe they'll have CompuDocs, instead of people. We'll see."

Caliga and I stay in the same line, and Cy and Blink go to another one. When we're nearly at the front of the line, her hand on my arm squeezes me painfully. She's staring at a huge holoboard behind the rows of cubicles. It's a news thread going loud enough for anyone to hear.

"On today's Inter-State Agenda news, the deadly DNA that killed Senator Milford has finally been identified, belonging to a Zelia Shirley Benten. Anyone knowing the whereabouts of this individual is urged to contact their local State officials."

Oh. My. God.

Caliga lifts an eyebrow and whispers, "Shirley? Really?"

"Shh!" I whisper.

My face appears on the screen, a school photo from two years ago. I hold my breath. Maybe if I don't move, no one will see me.

"Officials have been asked to take extra precautions, as Benten is a known flight risk from Neia. She is linked to a recent attack in Omaha involving other illegal individuals in which several police officers were injured."

Oh no. Carus House. Now that's on the news too.

The collective noise decrescendos, and my pulse rises in response. Heads rise above the cubicles. Both officers and the hopeful to-be citizens of Ilmo take a moment to scan their surroundings. I can't duck. I can't hide.

One small girl perched onto the hip of a frazzled mother ahead of us stares at my image on the screen, then twists about abruptly. Her mother groans with annoyance, trying to keep her child from falling off her hip.

"Mama. Look." The little girl points at my face. I freeze, as only the guilty can. Her mother turns to look, thinking to scold her child.

She doesn't.

When I hear her scream, I spin around. Cy and Blink are already bolting away from the entrance. Caliga grabs my hand, and the pain of her grip doesn't faze me.

We run.

CHAPTER 9

Four large, azure-clad police officers come forward, scanning the crowd. We calm our run down to a walk and dodge behind a holoboard kiosk, panting.

"What are we going to do?" Caliga whispers, her scarred eyes wide with panic.

"*Nous devrions retourner à la voiture,*" Blink says rapidly. She clutches at Cy's arm like he's a life preserver.

"No, we can't. The char's nearly out of fuel," he responds, still scanning the crowd for a way out.

"I've got an idea," I say hurriedly. "Inky." I toss my head toward the closest group of gray-smocked women.

"No! We can't!" Cy is a decibel away from yelling. Blink hangs back too.

"Absolutely not!" Caliga enunciates the words like they're infused with needles. "Are you insane?" she hisses. "There's got to be a better choice."

"This is our only choice!" I reason. "We're out of fuel. We don't have enough food for four people. And you'll be septic in two days if we can't get more antibiotics."

Cy pinches his eyes shut. "She's right. Everyone knows Inky takes in the dregs of society. The only other thing to do is to turn ourselves in."

And never see Dyl and my family again? "We are NOT turning ourselves in," I whisper fiercely, and Cy starts with surprise at the aggression in my words. We all scan the carnival-like environment around us. Guards are peppered throughout the crowd. One pair is only twenty feet away, and they're walking toward us.

"We're screwed," Caliga says helplessly.

"Exactly," I say, and we turn collectively to the group of Inky women. The nearest one's eyes narrow when she sees Cy. She quickly replaces her disappointment with happiness. I can actually see her molars, she's smiling so hard.

"Well hello, ladies! And . . . gentleman." She tips her head with artificial graciousness toward Cy. I don't like the way she says *ladies*. "Are you interested in entering Inky?"

"Yes!" We all say it a little too fast.

"We have a magtrain leaving momentarily. Why don't you join us and we can discuss it on the way?" She takes a few steps toward us. Reflexively, I slide in front of Caliga.

"She's not yet vaccinated. Wouldn't want you to get what she's got right now," I warn her. Caliga coughs loudly for dramatic effect, and it works. The Inky woman steps away with haste.

We start walking forward, but she holds a hand out, stopping Cy.

"However. We are not accepting males at this time," she says.

"Just looking for manual labor," Cy says quickly. He motions to me. "She's my sister. You said families could stay together, right?"

Caliga pinches my arms, because the officers from Ilmo are getting close. It's now or never. The gray lady studies us. *C'mon!* I want to yell. *We're young! And kinda, sorta, not really fertile, but we look like it, right?*

"Very well. Since there are three of you ladies, we should be able to work this out. Follow me."

She leads us to a simple, unadorned white awning. Underneath, there are no cubicles and no officials. The walls pulsate in shades of pale pink and blue, like some sort of disco baby womb.

"Here you go." She ushers us onto a long, silver escalator leading down to the magtrain. As we descend into the claustrophobic depths, the woman waves a cheerful good-bye from the top.

"There's only one escalator," Caliga says. Great. There's no backing out now. Caliga leans into me. "How am I going to hide this?" She waves at her body. "And I've heard the stories about Inky. No one's going to force me to be pregnant." I'm thinking the exact same thing, but I stay quiet. I may have promised Marka to care for Caliga's leg, but her emotional well-being isn't my responsibility.

At the bottom of the escalator, a white magtrain hums and hovers on its tracks. Oval compartments connect like giant glossy beads on a string. A cloaked guard points to an open compartment.

"Ladies, please take the near one." He turns to Cy.

"You'll be down there, in the men's pod." He points all the way to the other end of the magtrain. We all glance nervously at one another.

Blink complains before I can even open my mouth. "But—"

"No exceptions. You can apply for coupling requests later after we arrive."

"It's okay. I'll see you there," Cy says to Blink. Not me.

"Wait." I step quickly and reach for Cy. I don't even know what I'm going to say or do. At this point, I'm even afraid to give him a kiss on the cheek, but it doesn't matter, because the guard stops me.

"Public contact between the sexes is forbidden."

"It's okay, Zel. It's only a train ride," Cy says to me. With an obedience that surprises me, Cy heads quickly down the platform. I stare at him so long that Caliga yanks my arm.

"Let's go," Caliga says. She limps toward our compartment, and Blink and I follow her. Inside, there are four holo screens along the short wall with seats in front of them, some reclining chairs, and steps to an upper room. Blink sits herself on a corner chair, gathers her knees to her chest, and turns to face the windowless wall. A garish welcome sign flashes across the holo screens. Caliga watches the doors close. Her hand goes to her chest.

"I can't breathe."

I roll my eyes. "Believe me, you can." I wonder what Cy is doing in his compartment. As if on cue, his voice enters my head in a faint whisper.

I hope you're all okay. There is a pause, and then: *I'm alone in here.*

I wait for Cy to speak to me. For me only. One line of the poem, maybe. But his voice stays silent. Suddenly, words blare out from the walls.

"Welcome aboard the magtrain to Inky, the State that creates tomorrow's hope! Our journey will take forty minutes! We will be serving a beverage and meal shortly, followed by our entrance procedures! Please follow the holo screens for more instructions! Thank you, and welcome to Inky!"

The voice sounds a little bit like Dyl, except on a gallon of caffeine. Every exclamation is a fork in my ribs. Our good-bye seems years ago, not two days ago. And Cy hardly seems happy about being reunited again.

I could ask Blink why. But that would mean admitting that I need a map to a place I used to know by heart.

So I head for the stairs, relieved to find a chaise where I can lie down. Oblivion would be nice, even if only for a few minutes.

"Where are you going?" Caliga stops her anxious pacing to stare at me.

"Nap."

"How can you sleep at a time like this?"

"Easy. Watch me."

I flop down on a spotless cream chaise. A clicking sound heralds the emergence of a tray sliding out of the wall with a sandwich, orange juice, and vitamin packets. I put on my necklace and squeeze my eyes shut. I hope that I'll dream of sweeter things.

"HEY. GET UP. IT'S TIME."

Caliga prods my arm and I bat her away. My limbs are heavy and asking for a dozen more hours of sleep. The concept of being conscious is coldly depressing.

"Time for what?" I mumble.

"For our evaluation," Caliga says. "You should eat something."

I wake up enough to gobble down the sandwich and juice. I push the vitamins away after sniffing them suspiciously.

Downstairs, the lights are dim and Blink still sits in the corner. Did she move at all? Her black pupils are big and doll-like. She holds my gaze for way too long before dropping her eyes to her lap.

"I know why you don't talk with me," Blink says quietly. There's an edge to her words. Gritty bits of anger within the lilted vowels. "I am no thief, you know. I will not take anything that is not willingly given to me."

My hands clench at her words. The threat is so sharp, it cuts the silence and sits there, a real thing in the room. Even Caliga feels it. She coughs to break the stillness.

"Uh, Blink. Why don't you go upstairs for your eval."

"*Avec plaisir,*" she says simply, walking up the stairs.

"Yes, go far, far away," I whisper. But my angry words don't make me strong. I feel petty. I feel weak.

Caliga waves her hand to the row of monitors. "Sit down. The instructions are starting soon."

I take off my necklace and put it back in my pocket, then take a seat. A detached voice enters the room as *Basic Information* scrolls across the holo screen.

"Welcome to the Inky registration process. Please place your F-TID on the pad, so that we may download your existing information."

"Oh! Hex's fake fingers!" I yelp, and run to my duffel bag. I totally forgot to soak them in nutrient water like he said. I almost retch when I find the two disembodied digits. One is rolling over and over like a gray elliptic worm, and the other is bluish and looks dead. Gross, gross, gross. "Hex is going to kill me!" I wail.

The holo screen asks for my F-TID again and I break out in a sweat.

"What are we going to do? They'll know we've been off the grid," Caliga moans.

The holo screen voice speaks calmly. "To start your new life in Inky with a clean slate and decline an F-TID download, please say, 'New ID.'"

"Oh, for freak's sake. New ID!" I almost yell.

"New ID process has begun. By declining review of your previous F-TID, any accounts and positive moral credit are void. You will be started as an entry-level citizen."

Huh. "Entry-level citizen" could mean I'm licking toilets in the near future. I wonder how many young women chose to enter Inky because they were morally bankrupt.

I glance to the right, and Caliga is patiently answering

questions. She doesn't seem nearly as frazzled as I am. The holo screen asks more questions, like next of kin, family contacts, personal medical history, family medical history, sexual and fertility history. The lies come out of my mouth faster than Vera can yoga-cize into a scorpion pose.

"Please place your hand on our data pad for a blood test."

A small pad slides out of the wall. On it is the outline of a hand, where I'm supposed to lay mine down. There are holes in the pad where I'm sure needles are going to pop up to bite me.

"Are you doing the blood test?" I ask Caliga nervously.

"You have to," she responds calmly. As if she's entered Inky a thousand times before. "I tried to refuse, and it said we'd be returned to Neia if we don't comply."

I take a huge breath and lay my hand down. The hand pad grows warm. The monitor shows my vital signs being recorded, then tells me not to move. Suddenly I feel a pinch in my middle finger. Then another and another, in other fingers.

"Ow!" I jerk away from the pad and stare at the pin-pricks on my hand.

"Thank you. We will be testing your general health status; communicable diseases; fertility status . . ."

Oh no.

". . . any genetically inheritable diseases; your risk for violent mental instability . . ."

Are they kidding? No, they're not.

". . . and of course, prenatal testing, such as karyotype and drug susceptibility."

I should just walk out with my hands up as soon as the train reaches its destination. Maybe I should put the cuffs on now, just in case. I turn to Caliga, who's wiping the blood off her hand with an antiseptic pad.

"Just so you know," I say. "We're totally screwed."

"I know. Screwed to kingdom come."

I laugh, but it's the laugh of the almost-incarcerated. The holo screen changes to black and white. It asks me to read the full bylines, regulations, and laws of Inky.

What I'm looking for, hiding between the flagrant lying and horrible baby-making agenda, is stuff about HGM 2098. It's noticeably absent. I'm both relieved and worried. The holo screen dims to a pale yellow. Which is how I feel inside, after going through the process of becoming an Inkyan. Slightly fermented and impure.

"Thank you for completing your registration process. Please place your left hand in the designated opening for a welcome gift." A glowing orange circle appears in the wall next to the screen.

"Maybe it's optional," Caliga wonders, but I'm too distracted by the warning bells in my head. Sandwiched between *"Never talk to strangers"* and *"Never run with scissors"* is intuitive, new advice that says *"Never stick your limbs into dubious holes in the wall."*

So I just sit there, opting out. The orange circle flashes insistently. Stubbornly. After a full minute of this, the holo voice starts talking again.

"Please place your left hand in the designated opening."

"No."

"Please place your left hand in the designated opening."

"Dammit, I said no."

"Please place your left hand in the designated opening, or your application to Inky will be incomplete."

Oh. So there's the truth. It's not a gift; it's a requirement.

"Is it going to hurt?" I ask.

"The placement of your gift is painless."

"What does it do?"

"It is a State-sanctioned holo bracelet that receives Inky transmissions. Your previous holo studs will have no reception here. You will be able to tune in to our informational channels, communicate with your new family, and access crucial information needed for your transition to Inky."

"We don't really have a choice," Caliga says with a sigh.

I know she's right, so I put my hand into the orange circle, which switches to a pulsating apple green. The hole squeezes around my wrist, followed by a burning sensation. At the precise moment it becomes unbearable, the heat dissipates, leaving a cool heaviness around my wrist. The green light winks off and I take my hand out.

There's a red bracelet that weighs hardly anything adorning my wrist. The surface of it is carved with flowers and vines, and there's a single black dot embedded on the surface. I recognize it as a holo port. I try to look for a hinge or something, maybe a hidden clasp, but there is none.

I try to spin it around, but it's too tight. It's molded to

perfectly match the contours of my wrist. I try to pry it off. It won't budge.

"This is bad, bad, bad," I say, shaking my head. Caliga is studying hers, which is identical to mine.

The holo voice blasts back on, and I jerk back in annoyance. "Congratulations! You have now been accepted as a citizen of Inky, with a Level One pass. Please put on our regulatory gowns. A group leader will guide you to your new home. May your stay with us be bountiful and blessed! Welcome to the township of Coventry, State of Inky! You have been assigned to residential group Avida."

Blink comes down the stairs, fingering her matching bracelet. Caliga pulls open the closet where the uniforms are hanging. Once I wrestle one on, I'm as fetching as a slab of concrete. Caliga sits on a chair, swimming in her cloak. Her face is blanched and sweaty.

"Are you okay?" I ask her.

Caliga shakes her head. "Dizzy. And I'm feeling cold again, even with this thing on me."

"Hopefully they'll have antibiotics where we're going."

"That's one problem. What if they know about our traits already?"

"They know. Inky is Eugenics Central. They said they'd do a karyotype. My chromosomes scream 'freak' like no one else's. Believe me."

The magtrain finally comes to a stop. The compartment lock disengages with a slippery click and the doors slide open.

A cloaked figure stands waiting for us, blocking our exit. His hood is so huge, I can only make out a clean-shaven chin and unmoving lower lip. The cloak is bright red, rippling like a cascade of blood.

Caliga and I exchange uncertain looks.

"Um, we're supposed to be with . . . Avida, right?" I say.

The man pulls his hood off to reveal short brown hair. A pair of amber-brown eyes engage mine.

My mouth drops open.

Caliga isn't stunned like I am. Her hands cover her mouth, then fly away, unable to contain her joy.

"Micah!"

PART II
INKY

CHAPTER 10

OH HELL NO.

What the *hell* is Micah doing here?

"Oh my god!" Caliga says in a burst. "What are you doing here?" She takes an eager step forward, but Micah thrusts out a hand to prevent the embrace.

"Oh, I'm sorry," Caliga falters. "I forgot . . ."

Micah's eyebrows rise. "You forgot?" His observant eyes travel from Caliga to me, standing close and unaffected. He registers this, internalizes it. He sees Blink too and he pauses on her as well. Blink immediately drops her eyes as if she's been scolded.

"Why are you here?" I growl. The last time we were in the same room, he was burning his handprints into my arms. He'd brutally attacked Dyl. I'm one breath away from punching him.

"I was sent here to check on one of Avida's R&D labs a month ago. After I heard about the attack, I stayed."

Caliga narrows her eyes at his answer. "Why do you get to meet us here?"

He shrugs. "I'm a favorite."

"*Oui.* You have that effect wherever you go," Blink says softly.

I narrow my eyes. "It's convenient that you skipped out on seeing Aureus destroyed."

"That was pure luck. I had no idea that would happen. But I think I know who did it."

"Who?" I ask, trying not to sound desperate for information.

"We'll talk soon. But not here. In the meantime . . . welcome." Micah holds his hand out to shake mine.

"You try to touch me, you'll be missing body parts soon," I reply evenly.

"Please, allow me." Cy steps to my side in his white cloak. The gold flecks in his eyes sparkle, aflame with anger as he lifts a fist. As his sleeve slips down, my eye catches something streaky and pink on his arm. He rubs it absently.

Micah isn't fazed. "Go ahead and hit me, Cyrad. Show them how unstable you are."

We all glance over to where Micah gestures. Several guards in purple cloaks stand only twenty feet away, carefully watching the passengers disembark.

"If you want to be safe, you'll have to come quietly," Micah says. "You need to learn how to survive in this place."

And then head to Chicago as soon as possible, I think. I turn to Cy, who stares at Micah with a fury I've never witnessed before.

I am going to kill you, Cy says, *and I'm going to enjoy it.*

Cy's lips don't move, and everyone around us exchanges worried glances. A raw, awful scent of burning plastic emanates from him. Rage. He's holding back, but barely. I put my hands on his fists, trying to calm him.

"Cy," I whisper. "Not here." Micah puts a possessive hand on my shoulder. I try to shrug him off. "I said don't touch me!"

And then I feel it. A light-headedness that grows rapidly worse. I quickly find my necklace in my pocket and put it on, but the dizziness doesn't go away. I stagger with my arms splayed out, trying to steady myself, when I see Caliga's eyes unfocus. Her eyes roll back and in a second, her knees buckle and she's on the ground in a heap. Micah makes a useless grabbing gesture to the air and falls next, followed by Blink.

Darkness infects my field of vision. Suddenly, I can't feel the train platform under my feet. I can't tell up from down. The last thing I see is the passionate violence in Cy's features transform to utter surprise. And then my vision turns off, like a storm winking out the midday sun.

Everything becomes nothing as unconsciousness takes me.

FROM THE DISTANCE, A VOICE CALLS TO me. It's oceans away.

"Zelia!"

I blink to see Cy's blurry image hovering over me. I whip my arms up to shield my face. It's just a reflex.

But seeing that one gesture, Cy backs away and his face turns into despair itself. "It was an accident— I didn't—"

He drops his voice to a shattered plea. "Oh god. I'm sorry, Zel!"

I sit up slowly. A pounding headache blossoms, far worse than the hypoxia headaches my Ondine's curse has bequeathed in the past. My hand goes to my throat and my necklace is still there. Blink, Micah, and Caliga are all getting to their feet, clutching their heads and trembling. We're surrounded by three purple-clad guards, all pointing their neural guns at Cy's chest.

The fact that he hurt Blink as well as Micah tells me it was a mindless accident, as if he'd thrown a grenade when all he needed was a punch. The violence of it sweeps my reality away for a clear second.

Cy would never hurt me. But he did.

One of the guards barks, "Someone want to explain what happened here?"

What happened? There was nothing to see. No swinging bat, no arm following through on a hit. Only Cy, standing as guilty as can be.

"Shall we deport him?" One of the guards gestures at Cy with the silver snub tip of his gun. Cy's eyes are hollow, watching me. As if I'm the one to decide if he should be deported or not.

"Please. Don't. We were just . . . feeling a little faint. Right?" Caliga and Blink keep their distance from Cy and me. And because of Caliga, everyone is spread out even more. We're all afraid of each other, in one way or another. "It was nothing. Really." I spin around to catch Caliga's eye. She's rubbing her temple and her face is lined with fear.

Caliga nods reluctantly. "Yeah. We're okay now." Blink nods too.

The two guards step back. "Very well. I believe you have a mag waiting, sir."

Micah shoos the guards away. He points at Cy. "Keep that under control, or you're on your own. Got it? I can't protect you if you can't protect yourself. Or her," he says, glancing at me. Cy closes his eyes and steps away.

"Yes, Micah."

The meekness of those two words kills me. Is this what it was like the whole year in Aureus? I reach for Cy's hand, but he pulls away from me, crossing his arms and clawing his fingers harshly into his biceps. He won't look at me. He won't look at anyone.

Crowds of gray-cloaked people, with an occasional white indicating a male, are already funneling out the exit with their red-clad leaders.

"Look." Caliga points.

Two people lag behind the crowd. One woman is trying to pull her gray hood forward to cover her face, but it doesn't work. Her face is absolutely covered in hair. It's tawny-colored fur, short, and sleekly spread over her face and neck. She looks like some sort of missing link between humans and . . . lemmings or something.

Another girl is latched to her arm, but this one looks ready to faint at any moment. Thin, stringy blond hair sticks to her temples. Her skin—or what I think is her skin—is peeling away in papery, translucent sheets. Under the peeling skin, her hands and her face are cracked and bleeding.

Blood crusts the edges of her tightly dry lips. If she tried to speak, the words might tear her cheeks wide open.

Micah calls out to them. "Avida? Right here." The two murmur a few words, then slowly walk over.

Micah leads us all into a glass-covered atrium. People leave through various doors, accompanied by their new leaders. Out of curiosity, I hold my bracelet up to my face. "Show me a map of Inky."

"Uh, I don't think that's going to help," Micah says.

I ignore him. A pink holo screen pops up from the black port on my bracelet. The rose icon of Inky's holo provider, I-VIEW, appears. "Map of Inky," I order it.

A small octagonal area appears. At first I think it's a mistake. Inky isn't an octagonal State. It's supposed to look like a lumpy L shape. But there are flat lines that look like doors and windows, and a little island in the center.

"Wait a second." I scan our surroundings. This isn't a map of Inky. It's a map of this magtrain atrium. So Level One clearance only gets us to the doors of this stupid station?

Just then, a young girl with striped red-and-black braids breaks apart from a line of people waiting to leave the atrium.

"No. I can't. I'm going back to my mom," she says as the leader makes a grab for her arm. "I'll take the magtrain back. I don't care about the stipend. I'm goin' home." The guards smirk knowingly at each other but don't try to stop her. The girl dashes to the arched doorways leading back to the magtrain platform.

A muffled bang echoes inside the atrium. We all cower defensively, trying to dodge whatever caused the shot or explosion. The only person in our group who hasn't flinched is Micah.

The girl screams. Her shriek echoes so loudly that the building itself sounds like it's in agony. She hits the ground hard, her legs scrabbling and twisting in the heavy fabric of the cloak.

Two guards walk calmly over. "Not a normal day without at least one runner."

One of them speaks into his red bracelet. "Medical and sanitation to the atrium please." Together, they pull her back through the arch and into the atrium, leaving a trail of smeared red blood on the pristine floor. The girl moans repetitively, *Why why why why why.*

Blood pools by her body in shades of scarlet, coming from somewhere I can't see.

"Aren't they going to help her?" I ask. I automatically turn to Cy. He was the medic when we lived at Carus— I've had only a year of holo training. But Cy's still in shock. He seems terrified to do anything. When no one makes a motion to help her, I run forward to the girl's side. She's clutching her right arm, and crimson stains her cloak darkly.

"Oh geez, you're hemorrhaging." I bend closer. "Shh. Calm down. I'm going to try to stop the bleeding." I lift her arm and a thin spray of cherry-red blood shoots out. Instinctively, I grab her wrist and she howls in pain. It's squishy and hot, and bone shards meet my palm.

Her hand. It's gone.

"Oh god, oh god!" she screams. "It hurts!"

I immediately grasp her stump with both hands, holding pressure on what's left of her wrist. "Someone get some bandages! Rip a piece of clothing, anything!" I bark.

The guards don't even respond. Their lack of empathy is chilling. Cy finally jerks out of his shocked state and runs to the satchel I dropped. When he brings one of Caliga's cloth bandages over, I whisper to him hoarsely.

"Holy shit. What happened here?"

"Look," he says, and points.

Shards of shattered bracelet lay on the platform. In the center is a hand. A disembodied hand lying palm up, the dead fingers pointing to the magtrain, her failed destination.

I blink several times, but the vision of the grisly severed hand won't disappear. It merges with the memory of my father's hand, mangled on the street after his fatal magpod crash. With horrifying clarity, I can still see his gold wedding ring gleaming against torn flesh.

Red-clad medical techs arrive to whisk her away, leaving a garnet stain on the white floor.

"Messy way to enforce citizenship, but it works," Micah comments quietly, waving us to an exit. He's wearing a red bracelet too. He's as trapped as we are.

Micah touches his bracelet to a sensor at one of the arched ivory doors. One by one, we walk out.

Fancy new magpods in all different colors zoom on the road before us. The buildings are all oval-shaped and shades of pale—cream, buttery yellow, chalky blue. Like fancy Easter candies fell out of the clouds and embedded themselves into Inky. Not a single building has windows.

"Where are we again?" Caliga asks.

"Coventry. A small city near the border of Ilmo," Micah explains.

Before long, we're ushered into a sleek multi-compartment magpod. When Micah banishes Caliga to a back area by herself, her shoulders crumple, as if to say, "*So. We're back to this again.*" Cy is separated from me, but he says nothing to reassure me during our ride. Our ride is silent, with Micah watching me thoughtfully the entire time. When we finally exit, we're inside a dark garage. No wonder Inky loves the windowless mags and buildings. Disorientation is an easy way to keep its citizens powerless.

Fur Face emerges and Micah carries the sick girl out. She's already worse than ten minutes ago. Not just peeling and cracking, but literally dried out and crispy.

"We need water. Fast," Fur Face pleads.

"Will do." Micah nods. Finally, he opens Caliga's door. Her face is puckered and full of anger.

"About time."

Micah chuckles. This is the Caliga he recognizes. "Nice to have you back, Cal."

"Shut up." Caliga pointedly steps away from me, like I was responsible for her temporary magpod imprisonment. Great. As if we needed more tension in our group.

Micah leads us inside a plain room with a silver-lined chamber at one end. It feels wrong, like it's an elaborate, human-sized mousetrap.

"Each of you must be scanned. You'll enter the chamber, ditch your belongings in the empty receptacle inside, and put on the clothes provided in the other receptacle."

"There better not be any cameras in there," Caliga says, her surliness barely concealing her worry. When Micah doesn't answer immediately, she blanches whiter, which I thought was impossible.

Micah helps the sick girl into the chamber. Several minutes later, the door opens and she steps out wearing new clothes already stained with blood. Her eyes roll up into her head and Fur Face cries out in alarm. Micah catches her mid-faint, and hoists her into his arms.

"Next," Micah orders us.

Fur Face goes next, emerging wearing a wheat-colored cotton sheath dress. Then Cy. When he's done, he's got a matching khaki outfit like Micah's. I search his face for information, but he's a blank slate. Finally, after Caliga and Blink go, it's my turn. They both have stunned expressions.

"What?" I ask, my voice warbling with blossoming panic. Caliga won't answer, just shakes her head and keeps her eyes shut, as if trying to erase whatever just happened to her.

"You'd better just get it over with," Micah says.

Lovely. The words "get it over with" are never associated with anything remotely pleasant. I step inside the chamber with its tiny, arched ceiling. After the door closes, a small aperture opens on the wall in front of me.

"Place all your belongings in the space provided," a calm female voice intones. "This includes clothing, jewelry, holo studs, and any other paraphernalia."

"Fine," I growl. I put my duffel bag in the black space, and it's immediately sucked away. I pray that Ana's glass unicorn isn't shattered. I peel off my dirty clothes and shove them into the void. They stink anyway. The clothing disappears with a whispery whoosh. All I have on now is my necklace and the red bracelet.

Now I'm stark naked and the light is glaringly bright. I'm doing my best to cover myself with my hands. Where are the new clothes? I look for a drawer, but don't see one. An apple-green line appears at the ceiling, dropping slowly to scan me and the chamber. When it touches the necklace at my throat, it changes to red. Damn.

"Foreign material identified. Please place items in the receptacle."

"I . . . I can't get rid of that. See, I kind of need—"

"Foreign material identified. Please place items in the receptacle."

Perspiration leaks out of my pores. I try to breathe deeper to catch up to my accelerating heartbeat. "Look. I have to keep this. I can't toss it in your receptacle, okay?" I yell at the walls.

"If you play nice, you'll get it back." A very masculine, very non-digital voice suddenly enters the coffin-like space. My hands immediately jump off the pads to lamely cover my body.

"Who is that?" My voice sounds very squeaky.

"You're not in a position to be asking questions," the voice says. There's a slithery smile tucked into those words.

I don't trust whoever that is, any more than I can trust

Micah, or my body to breathe normally on its own. I hear a gusty sigh from the mystery man, and a deep chuckle.

"You can choose to keep your necklace, Zelia, but it means you'll stay in this scanner for hours. The view I've got is absolutely precious."

"Fine!" I yell, unclasping it quickly and tossing my necklace into the black hole. The man snickers faintly, but that's it. Soon, the scan finishes without a problem and a small door slides open, with clean underwear and a matching shift dress like the others. As soon I'm decently covered, the doors open and I bolt out of the tiny space.

"That took forever," Micah comments. He's still carrying the unconscious flaky girl in his arms.

"Your creepy, voyeuristic colleague was being ever so welcoming."

"I knew I was being watched," Caliga says. "I heard him breathing." Her arms are crossed, and I do the same.

"They took my necklace," I say faintly.

Micah smiles kindly and tries not to jostle the sick girl too much. "I can try to get it back for you. I may be able to pull some strings, explain your situation."

I don't get this guy. After what he's done to me and Dyl, he does this. Something that seems genuinely nice. I can't get a consistent read on him.

"Well, um. Thanks."

Micah almost beams at my response. He leads us away from the silver scanner and to a massive pair of ebony doors. At his command, they open wide.

"Welcome to Avida."

CHAPTER 11

WHEN THE DOORS OPEN, WE STARE IN ASTONISHMENT.

Tiles in burnished orange, fuchsia, and egg-yolk yellow pave a path through a lush garden. On either side, tide pools tremble with clear water, aglow with incandescent anemones. Darting jeweled fish zoom to hide under the lotus flowers at the surface. Every inch of space in the deep room is blanketed with plants.

Caliga whistles. "So this is where Micah's been hiding these last six weeks."

"Wish Vera could see this," Cy says sadly. Hearing Vera's name makes my throat ache. As lovely as this is, it's not our home. Wherever Vera, Hex, Ana, Dyl, and Marka are—that's home. And we still need to find it. I can't waste time being impressed with this pretty prison.

Right now, the only person I can ask about how to get to Chicago from Inky is Micah, which makes my stomach churn.

"Can we get on with this?" I try to move forward, but Blink is crouched on the path, blocking me. She's pointing to a small school of coppery fish that wriggle playfully near the surface.

"Look, but do not touch," a voice whispers from only inches away.

"*Dieu!*" Blink chirps, and scrambles back from the water.

A woman's face emerges straight out of the water, only a yard from Blink. Her skin is olive-toned but reflects light with faint iridescence, blending into the water.

Micah laughs, as does the water girl. Her hair is oily and black, spreading in a silky fan at the surface. She's totally naked under the water.

"You're late. They're waiting for you." Her voice sounds bubbly, as if she's got water caught on her vocal cords. Her black eyes scan all of us, but linger on the passed-out girl in Micah's arms. "Give her to me."

We all swivel to look at Micah and his heavy burden. Fur Face steps forward, still holding the limp girl's hand. The concern on her face turns to hope. "You'll take care of her?"

The water girl rolls her eyes. "No, I'm going to eat her for lunch." She waves an elegant, iridescent hand. "Bring her in. And take those stupid clothes off her."

Micah lowers the girl to the golden sand, then turns around. Fur Face carefully pulls off her new clothes, shedding huge flakes of dry skin crusted with blood. Blink has a horrified expression on her face, and Caliga averts her eyes.

"I'll help you." I crouch down to tug the girl's dress off, my hands growing slippery with blood. The metallic scent is overwhelming. This feels really, really wrong, stripping an unconscious girl of her clothes. "Are you sure this is okay?" I whisper to Fur Face, and she nods. Under all that hair, her face is squished together with worry. *Furry worry*, I think to myself. Then I mentally slap myself. *Stop it.*

Finally, we carry her to the water. The water girl envelops the sagging body in her arms. Inch by inch, they recede into the water. Bubbles flutter from their mouths and noses as they sink, the edges of their bodies blurred by the depths. And then they're gone.

Fur Face stares in the pool, as if they're still there. "When can I see her again?" she whispers.

"Soon," Micah says. He puts a strong hand on her shoulder and gives it a squeeze. "It'll be okay. I know what it's like to lose someone. At least you get to see her again."

I want to tell Fur Face not to believe him. He's a beautiful liar.

A few flakes of the girl's skin lie on the shiny cobalt tiles. They're the size of large coins and I pick one up, turning it this way and that. It's translucent, with the texture of a microthin polymer, rather than dry skin. I slip it into my pocket without a word. When I look up, I realize everyone has moved on except for me and Cy, who's standing a few feet away, studying a piece of her skin too.

"I wonder if she can breathe through it. Her skin, I mean," I murmur.

"I was thinking the same thing." He holds it up to the light and I take a step closer. "Maybe it's oxygen permeable."

"Maybe—"

"Cyrad! Come." Blink waves at us from behind a flowering plumeria tree, twenty feet ahead.

"Maybe later," I say lamely. To my surprise, Cy grabs my hand.

"Later. I promise." He looks toward the exit, where Blink awaits. "She's not our enemy, you know. You'll love her when you get to know her."

Cy lets go of my hand and walks forward, leaving me to follow in his wake. God, even Hex would hold my hand through this heartache. I already know Cy loves Blink. What I don't know is if he loves me anymore. A year is a long time. Maybe . . . maybe I wasn't worth the sacrifice. Maybe I wasn't worth the wait.

Through the door, everyone's standing around, ready to move on. When I walk in, I'm surprised to see it's an ordinary office, with two sad wooden desks, stain-proof industrial floors, and a holo wall broadcasting Inky news with the sound muted. The room is stuffy and stinks of emotionless business decisions.

"Who are we waiting for?" Cy asks.

Micah's mouth twitches. "You'll see."

His words are less than soothing. I remember my introduction to Carus: Two-headed, green-skinned, and four-armed kids—what could be weirder? I take a deep breath, steeling myself for a tentacled face, or possibly a bulldog's head on a human body. A creak issues from the corner of the room. A door opens, and we collectively inhale.

A short, dumpy woman emerges, her curly black hair

pulled back from her dusky cheeks. She's wearing a shape-less black skirt that nearly touches the floor, along with a pink silk shawl. She's heavy-chested and wide-hipped, which gives her the appearance of a floating apple. With-out a word or glance, she sits behind one of the desks and flicks on a holo screen and old-fashioned computer key-board. She cracks her knuckles and wriggles her chubby fingers.

"I need names, birthdates, medical history, what State you just fled . . ." She blinks twice as her watery eyes take us in. "Don't give me that rubbish you told the computers on the magtrain. Falsehoods are an irritating waste of time."

I wonder what this lady's trait is. Maybe it's being su-premely unpleasant. Micah waves at Fur Face, who steps forward.

"Tabitha Winesap. July seventh, twenty-one thirty-four. I don't know who my parents are. I've been hiding in Minwi my whole life, on the northern border."

Tabitha. I feel bad, not having asked her for her name before. I wonder if anyone calls her Tabbie Cat. *Stop.*

Office Lady waves a hand at her from head to toe. "Is that your trait? Anything else under all that fur we need to know about?"

"My blood doesn't freeze."

The lady is unimpressed, scribbling on her holo. "Any-thing else?"

"No."

The lady's eyes bulge. "No, *ma'am.*"

"No, ma'am," Tabitha repeats flatly.

"Cold up in Minwi," the lady says. "How perfect for you. You must be the reason for those Big Foot sightings in northern Minwi."

Tabitha doesn't bat an eye. I guess she's used to annoying cryptozoology rumors. She taps her foot impatiently. "What about Ryba?" she asks. "When can I see her?"

"Your girlfriend? When we say you can," the lady snaps.

"I heard we'd be safe here."

Office Lady dims her already grim expression. "You're alive, aren't you?"

Tabitha shuts up.

"How can we be safe? Every other State is out to get us," I say, before I remember I'm supposed to behave. Office Lady stares at me hard. Her eyes are like currants, but the intelligence behind them is needle sharp.

"The federal government isn't strong enough to enforce its rules within each State. Inky is very rich and its leaders do what's best for its own people."

She doesn't have to explain. Everyone knows the population growth rate in the States is abysmal because of contraceptive vaccines and Parental Examination Laws that must be passed before you're allowed to reverse your vaccine. Inky's birth rate is sky-high, and they export babies (for the right price) to all the State orphanages, where they can be brainwashed into staying put their whole life. It's all about money. More people in any one State means more taxpayers, more lifeblood for each government.

Office Lady smiles. "And Avida is good for its people. As long as Inky tolerates you here in Avida, you're safe."

"Tolerates?"

"Inky officials profit from our Avida-made products. They're well motivated to keep us secret and safe. Aureus created Avida and controlled every aspect of our lives. Now that they're gone—"

"You're free?" Caliga exclaims.

"Free?" Office Lady squeezes her hands together and a shrewd look enters her eyes. "The names have changed, but the game remains the same. No one here will ever be free. Not while HGM 2098 exists." She waves Cy forward. "Enough chatter. Back to work." She and Cy do the usual questions and answers before she moves on to Blink and Caliga.

"Caliga Jakobsen. I've heard of you." She swallows and hits her chest with her fist four times. She opens a drawer and pulls out a bottle of pink No-PuK pills, then proceeds to crunch a handful. "So, an orphan of Aureus now, are we?"

A shadow of that former cold Aureus persona takes shape in Caliga's features, but just as quickly, it disappears. Once again, she's just a scrawny girl with nowhere to go. "Yes, ma'am."

"Zelia Benten."

I bristle at hearing my name. Tabitha looks at me as if I'm famous. Not the good kind of famous, unfortunately.

"Your DNA signature is like no other," Micah says quietly behind me. "As soon as we received the information from the magtrain, there was a little celebration going on here."

"What?" I say, my mouth suddenly dry as chalk.

"In the quiet, hidden circles of our world, you're well known," the lady says, and not kindly. "We also know that it was your DNA that caused the death of Senator Milford."

"That wasn't my fault!" I protest.

"Perhaps you didn't administer the lethal treatment, but your DNA is screaming its identity from every cell in that man's corpse. You are a wanted woman, my dear." She cracks her lips and hatches a crescent smile. "So. Do you have it?"

I stare at her blankly. "Have what?"

"The list."

Again, with the list! I can still hear the yell of the police in Carus, demanding it. "I don't know what you're talking about."

"You're either lying or an idiot." When I don't say anything, she rolls her eyes. "The idiot category, then, I see. Pity." She pushes away from the desk and stands up. "Your father kept records of every traited child he made, and the code for their traits. How he made them. The. *List*."

"I don't have it." And if I did, I sure as hell wouldn't give it to this woman.

She sighs with irritation. "Micah, show them their room. Dinner is going to be served soon, and frankly, they stink to high holy hell."

"I have more questions," I say, not moving.

"I don't," she responds. "The answers I need are ones you clearly don't have."

A sprinkling of giggles and chortles sounds from behind us. I don't know what could possibly be so funny, so I whip around angrily to see who's laughing.

Two small children barrel toward us, scrambling in and out between our legs. A little boy slams straight into Tabitha. He swerves to hide behind her skirt. The boy wears a huge pair of wraparound sunglasses, comically held in place with straps going over his head and chin. Immediately I look over at Blink. She's already covered her mouth in shock at seeing another person wearing sunglasses the way she does.

"Victoria, I'm not it! You're it, she's the base!" he yells.

Victoria crouches on the floor in a frog squat. Her skin is chestnut brown, with corkscrew black curls over her head. She giggles and raises her arms—then a second pair—like a praying mantis ready to pounce.

Four arms and hands. My heart bounces a few inches inside my chest.

"Oh my god!" I say, unable to stifle my surprise.

Office Lady clicks her tongue against her teeth, and Victoria automatically snaps to attention. The boy scrambles from behind Tabitha, pink faced.

"Babies," she says patiently, "back to your nanna. Now."

"Can we play with Spork again today?"

"Leave that poor bot alone. No."

"Okay," they chime simultaneously. Before they disappear, she yells, "Victoria!"

The four-armed Victoria comes skipping back. The office lady crouches down and captures her chin in her hand, then feels her forehead. "Any more bleeding today?"

"Not much."

"Well then. Go."

"Can we have a sweetie?"

Tight lipped, she nods, and Victoria runs out, hollering, "Candy! We can have candy!" Out in the oasis, two whoops of unadulterated glee sound before their footfalls disappear.

I can't believe what I just saw. My heart feels soft and bruised, just at the memory of them. Caliga lifts her hand with a *what the hell* gesture.

"You're their *mother*?"

The lady barks, "Micah! I told you to take them out to their room."

He immediately herds us back through the arched door. I hardly see the beautiful trees or flowers in the oasis when we walk through. I hardly notice Cy, even though he's right beside me as we walk.

All I can see is the girl, Victoria. That heart-shaped face, the dark eyes, and her slender quartet of arms.

We are not unique. In here, and out there.

There are more of us.

CHAPTER 12

I CATCH UP TO MICAH QUICKLY. "Who was that lady? And what is up with the kids?"

"Her name is Renata. And she had those kids years ago, when Benten was still in charge of creating gene-altering meds to make the kids. Since then, no new births."

"But they have traits that are already out there. Duplicates."

Micah stops walking and spins to face me. "What, you thought you were unique?"

I don't mean to sound snobby, but . . . "Well, yeah. Are you unique?" I retort.

Micah recoils. "I don't know. I'd love to meet a little Micah someday, but who knows if I'll live that long." His words are haunting, but he shakes his head, forcing away the thought. "Your dad probably gave you all the answers."

"He never told me anything," I say, trying not to sulk.

"It's not about what you know. They think you *are* the answer."

I laugh. I'm probably the only eighteen-year-old girl

who doesn't have to complain about her monthly nuisance. "I'm not exactly a fertility goddess, if that's what they're thinking."

"You don't know that. Have you ever tried to get pregnant? Have you done it with an unvaccinated guy?"

Micah's earnest words are, at best, a violent intrusion into my intimate history with Cy. At worst, they're an invitation. I'm so pissed off, I can't even spew a retort. Cy stomps to my side.

"That's enough," Cy growls, but Micah doesn't back down.

"She has a right to know what Julian and Renata are thinking. I've gotten close to them—"

"You're good at that," Blink comments. "You work your way up, wherever you are. You were sent to Avida on an errand and never came back. Why, Micah? Did you know we were going to be attacked?"

"No." When we all stare at him, unbelieving, he almost yells, "I didn't know! I would have tried to warn you!"

"Yeah, right," Cy says. "You're so full of it. I wouldn't believe you if you said the sky was blue."

"You can ask Renata and Julian," he says defensively.

"As if we'd trust them." I don't know why I bother with another question. He'll just lie again, but I have to ask. "So. Who attacked Aureus, then? Was it people from Avida?"

"No. Julian thinks another group that Aureus had controlled broke off, got their own funds and weapons, and did that. I hear they're farther north somewhere."

North. *Find your north there.*

"North? Where?" Caliga asks, trying to hide her desperation but failing. If Wilbert is alive, that's where he is.

"I don't know. I heard rumors of someplace—Wing-something or other—but it's not on a map, that's for sure."

Oh god. Wingfield.

"Who told you this?" I ask.

"You can ask him yourself at dinner." Micah goes on. "He's the leader of Avida."

"Who?"

"Julian."

Micah refuses to answer any more questions, insisting he'll get in trouble if we're late to dinner.

We soon find that the inside of Avida is like a huge hollowed-out Easter egg, with concave outer walls and a central garden in the middle of each floor, like the oasis. And of course, no windows. Micah shows us how to wave our bracelets at the transport scanner, and tells us it knows to limit our access according to our schedules. Cy's room is on a floor with a perfectly manicured English rose garden and Micah quickly shows Cy his door.

"Unauthorized people in your room are forbidden."

"Or what?" Cy challenges.

Micah shifts his feet and doesn't answer immediately.

Cy bristles at the silence. "The building and the State have changed, but you haven't, Micah Kw. Still the high-and-mighty punisher, I see."

"Don't blame me for your mistakes, Cy. I've only ever been a messenger. Dinner is in two hours. Be ready."

Cy walks into his room and turns to say something. To me or Blink, I'm not sure, but the closing door cuts him off. Micah touches my hand, trying to guide me away. I expect a tingling jolt, but his hand is warm and gentle. "You'll see him later, I promise," he murmurs.

The kindness throws me off. With Micah on one end, and Cy on the other, my center of gravity is horribly off kilter.

Micah leads the rest of us to a level with a central meadow, with a holo setting sun in a holo sky. Holo birds fly by, snatching holo dragonflies out of the wheat-colored synth-grass. The sky above is blue mixed with milky clouds. The entire scene is straight out of a movie I've already forgotten, because this is so much better. A path curves around the garden where several identical doors line up, waiting for us. A shiny square of black is embedded in their centers.

"Here's your room," Micah says, and motions to Tabitha.

Tabitha waves her red bracelet near the ebony square and the door slides open. Cold air swooshes out of the room, hitting the warmer air outside and making a big cloud of icy fog. Hoarfrost quickly grows over the door's edges.

"You have a cold room ready for me?" Tabitha says warily.

"Yep. All the electronics and bots work at this temperature."

"Did you know I was coming? I mean, you can't get this stuff ready in a day." She steps into the room, running her fingers over the e-console and furniture. The fur on her arms and shoulder fluffs out on contact with the low temperature. She looks like she gained fifty pounds in a second.

"Julian ordered it a while ago. I had no idea anyone like you existed. You can ask him later. You've got all you need, but no food efferent. Renata and Julian arrange your meals on a schedule. They like us to eat together as a family when possible."

"Pfff!" I let the sound escape before I catch myself. Family, my ass. This isn't a family. It's Aureus, wearing a wig.

Tabitha shuts the door on us. I'm envying her solitude when Micah turns to me. "Whether you like it or not, this is your new home. You chose to be here."

I bite my lip. The only thing that matters is reuniting with my family. I will not lose everything I adore. I've got to get out of Avida with Cy, somehow. But "somehow" probably means playing nice with Micah. Honey versus vinegar and all that. So I fake a smile, but the effort is akin to stuffing a live chicken back into an eggshell. It's weird and unnatural and impossible.

"I'm so tired, Micah," I say softly. "I'm not on my best behavior."

"Of course. I understand." Micah points out my room to me. As I scan my bracelet, I carefully sniff the air between us. It smells clean, almost scrubbed with soap. "Get a little rest. I'll see you later."

My room is between Caliga's and Blink's. Blink opens her door and she sighs in relief to see it's pitch-black inside. Caliga enters hers without a good-bye. I start to enter mine, when Micah hooks my arm.

"Hey!" The electric tingle of his touch buzzes my skin, and I yank my arm away.

"I'm sorry, I'm sorry," he says, holding his hands up. "I'm just . . . It's good to see you. I got kind of excited."

"Don't you have an off switch for that?"

"Yes, but it usually involves somebody raining fire-retardant foam all over me."

I smile, hoping he can't read what I'm really thinking. Wish I could dump a bucketful on him, right now.

"Look, I know what you think of me. And I get it, you have every right. But this is a new place, and Aureus doesn't exist anymore. We can start over here."

"Start over," I repeat. What does he mean *we*? There is no *we*.

"I regret a lot of things, Zelia. But SunAj would have had me killed if I refused his orders." He takes a deep breath and puts his hands on my shoulders. My skin crawls underneath his hands. "I played the part, because I had no choice."

"There's always a choice, Micah," I say, forcing myself to keep my tone controlled.

"Of course. But some of us are too afraid to make the right ones." His amber-brown eyes are so sincere. I

hesitate, but then harden my heart. *He's playing you, Zel.*
Don't trust him. He finally lets go of my shoulders and
I turn to enter my room. I can't get away from him fast
enough.

"Only . . . one more thing. I just need to know. Dyl—is
she okay?"

My heart fires up at a million beats per minute. I use
every single breath and every neuron in my brain to keep
myself from strangling him. How dare he even speak her
name? I unclench my jaw to speak.

"Dyl is . . . fine. I think. I don't know where she is,
actually."

"Listen, I need to say something."

"Look, Micah. I'm really tired. Get my necklace back,
would you? I can't sleep without it."

"But I have to tell you—"

I reach for the button to shut the door. "I'll see you at
dinner." I retreat into the room, taking a glad breath. Just
before the door shuts, Micah spits out some hasty words.

"Zelia. I . . . I never slept with Ana. And I never slept
with Dyl either."

I whirl around, startled, only to see the door kill the
space between us.

THE DOOR STAYS CLOSED.

And I go a little crazy. What a liar! Why would he say
that, when it's so obviously untrue? I pace around, wishing I could walk in the garden and get some fake fresh
air. When I've waited long enough to think that Micah's

definitely gone, I wave my bracelet on the door scanner. Nothing happens.

"You are scheduled to rest, bathe, and prepare for dinner," the voice in the room states. How on earth am I going to get out of here with these kinds of restrictions?

"When can I walk around Avida freely?" I ask my room.

"You will be assigned duties tomorrow. Free play time is allowed if your behavior is satisfactory."

Play time? Good god. I'm in daycare.

I pace inside the small room, wishing I could throw or hit something, but everything is pretty much attached to the floor or upholstered in soft fabric, as if Avida expects its inhabitants to be suicidal on a regular basis. I couldn't get a hangnail in this room if I tried.

Finally, I sit down on the bed. I close my eyes and fall backward, letting my body sag into the silky ivory coverlet that catches the roughness of my fingertips. It's ridiculously comfortable, but I can't let myself fall asleep. I've got no necklace.

My whole life, I've never been without it. I still remember the conversation with my dad when I was twelve. Dad was determined to get me an extra implant. Not the one I already had that triggered when I wore my necklace, but one that would completely control everything. It would automatically switch on when I fell asleep, or kick in when my natural breaths weren't deep enough, but I'd refused.

"I don't want it in me. I want to be as normal as possible," I'd told him.

"Honey, it's not about normal, or not normal. It's about being safe."

"I can take care of myself," I'd argued. "I've never forgotten once to put it on. And Dyl reminds me all the time too."

"But—"

"I'm already weird enough."

"You're not weird. You're beyond perfect," he'd said, wrapping me in his arms.

Everything makes so much sense in hindsight. *Beyond perfect,* he'd said. My trait supposedly gives me a long life—longer than anyone, since my DNA won't degrade over time. But it also gifted me with my Ondine's curse. Dad wasn't a flawless architect.

A chime sounds from hidden speakers in the walls.

"Dinner will be served in one hour."

I push off the bed and head for the bathroom.

CHAPTER 13

THE GROOMING BOTS ARE GOING TO BE the death of me.

There's two of them. Squat and low to the ground, they scuttle out from the bathroom on spindly jointed legs. Their cantaloupe-sized bodies are black and shiny, just like an insect shell. I'd just stepped out of the shower and wrapped myself in a towel when one of them went straight for my face and the other, the crown of my head.

"Get *off*!" I yell, trying to fight them away. Their arms are thin but strong, gripping my body with gel-like suckers. One hovers over my face, extruding instruments from its belly tipped with sponges, sprays, and brushes. They're like giant bug mandibles about to eat my face off. The one on my head yanks painfully on my wet, unbrushed curls. I reach for the legs of the cosmetic bot. They feel like bendy chopsticks.

"Please do not damage the bots. They are only doing their job," the voice from the wall chides me.

"This isn't a job, this is assault!" I say, detaching the one on my face and tossing it to the floor. It performs a perfect ten-point landing. After only seconds, it crawls right back up my body with a little square patch extended on a mechanical arm. It tries to stick it on my leg, and I kick it away.

"What is that?"

The room voice chimes, "A sedative, to make your prep time a most enjoyable experience!"

"No, no, wait." I let go of the hairdressing bot and hold my hands in a gesture of surrender. "I'll be nice. Please. No drugs." I can't risk having a fuzzy mind; I need to know what I'm up against during dinner. And I can't be falling asleep, especially without my necklace. The bot withdraws the white patch into its body, and proceeds to head for my face. I sit calmly on the edge of the bed.

"Don't make me look like a circus freak," I beg. The bot bounces slightly and begins to hum contentedly as my face gets dabbed and sprayed to its little nanochip heart's content. The hair bot goes back to tackling my hair, but stutters a string of *tsks*, like it's highly irritated. I understand this language. I feel this way about my hair too.

Finally, they're done, even my nails. I've no ragged cuticles to chew on to assuage my nervousness. Darn. The hair bot spews a holo message.

A MaxInfuse hair conditioner will be added to your shower unit.

There's an insult in that statement. I sigh a thanks.

As they scuttle back to their wall units, I peek in the closet. A single peony-pink scrap of clothing hangs in front, with matching shoes and undergarments laid out on a poofy ottoman.

"Your ensemble has been chosen for tonight's meal," the voice says sweetly. "According to your measurements, it should fit appropriately."

So the house computer knows my bra size. Hooray.

I pick up the dress. It's a silk hanky of a garment, held together with thin strings around the neck. The pink is rich and saturated and the dress is floor length, but somewhere around the upper thigh area, the pink color bleeds away and transforms into transparent, shimmering spider biosilk. It's often used in costumes for shameless celebrities and performance artists.

And apparently, me.

After getting dressed and shoving my feet into the dainty silk heels, I sit stiffly on the bed. I contemplate wearing my bed coverlet to dinner. Sure, it would hide all the bumps and curves that this dress reveals and sure, I'd resemble a human soft taco. I start seriously considering it, when the room chirps at me.

"Please depart for dinner."

The door to my room slips into the wall and the meadow grass beyond dances a welcome. A handful of doors around the meadow yawn open and a few girls walk out, all in sleek gowns and dresses. Caliga stands blinking in the yellow light, dressed in an ice-blue concoction that makes her look like a post-modern Cinderella. She's got a cane and hobbles over to me. I immediately drop to my knees and inspect her leg. Surprisingly, she doesn't swat me away.

Her wound is covered in a biogel bandage with an antibiotic infusaport delivering meds straight to the wound.

"It looks good," I say. "How do you feel?"

"I'd feel better if we didn't have to do this song-and-dance dinner thing." She snickers. Her eyes scan me up and down. "Wow. You clean up nice."

"I can't stand it. I can't wait to get rid of this."

Caliga leans to the left so she can study my hair. "You'll need a crowbar."

My hand goes up to my head, where rock-hard loops of hair sprout from my crown. Caliga's hair is plaited to look like swirls of vanilla icing.

"I think my hairdressing bot despises me," I grumble.

"C'mon, let's go," she says, tugging my arm. After a day of sour attitude, she's being downright friendly. For once, I don't mind being close to her. In Avida, we're allies. For now.

"Where's Blink?" Caliga asks as we approach the transport. All the other girls have already left.

"I don't know. Maybe she went ahead with the rest."

I bite my lip. I have a feeling she was racing me to get to Cy first. But then I mentally smack myself. *Stop being so paranoid.*

We take the transport and hold our bracelets to the black monitor. Immediately, it shoots up to the top floor and opens to a roof patio. In the center, a long table is set decadently for dinner. Some smaller, one-person café tables are spaced farther out, like satellites to the main table. Wisteria vines hang down from a trellis over the table and all sorts of exotic plants and flowers surround the edges of the roof. Two curving pools of water flank the entire eating area like giant blue parentheses. The water girl from the oasis is there with another teen boy, talking in hushed tones. But the sick one, Ryba, isn't with them.

Overhead, the dome of our egg-shaped building encloses us. It's translucent, but I can't see the setting sun, or any celestial bodies. I long for the day when I can own the sky again.

Something soft brushes my arm. I reach over to rub whatever it is away, when a hand catches mine. It's Micah. I use every ounce of energy to mask my disgust and not snatch my hand away. He wears a charcoal-gray suit complete with dark tie, and every hair is perfectly in place. Micah squeezes my hand for a millisecond, before he lets go.

"I want to talk to you after dinner," he whispers.

"We don't have anything to talk about," I say. "I heard what you said."

"I'm telling the truth."

I turn just enough to see his earnest look. He reminds me so much of the Micah that Dyl and I met in New Horizons after Dad died. A simpler, sweeter guy. But he never really existed.

"There is no such thing as truth in this century," I say, quoting a common saying. You can always manipulate the truth, be it with neural implants or fake holo feeds or enough repetition of lies. I don't need to hear his plastic version of what happened.

Someone taps me on the shoulder. I spin around to find myself face-to-face with Cy. Micah is completely forgotten as my mouth drops with surprise. His scraggly beard is gone, revealing sculpted cheekbones from his hard days in the Deadlands. A sleek black suit is tailored perfectly for his slimmer frame, in a shade that perfectly offsets the copper glints in his irises. His tie is narrow and his hair is exactly as it usually is, a slightly rumpled, gorgeous mess of espresso brown. I guess his grooming bot realized he didn't need help there. Smart bot.

"Hi," I say breathlessly. "You're . . . you're in a suit."

"And you're in a dress," he says. He appraises me with an expression of curiosity.

"It's ridiculous," I say, waving at my dress and face with embarrassment.

"It is. You're far more stunning wearing my old T-shirts," he whispers. He warms my lower back with his hand and I grin stupidly, when thin fingers slip over his shoulder, pulling him away.

"Élodie!" Cy says. "You look beautiful." Blink stands there, her figure encased in a strapless sheath gown of iridescent black and purple. Her hair is in a perfect topknot and she's got a teeny waist with enviable cleavage. Cy smiles with a warmth that shows how much he's missed her. She's stunning and elegant. In my bright pink dress and makeup, I'm a child's finger-painting in comparison.

A loud cough comes from the center of the room.

"Please take your seats." Renata stands at the end of the table. Her unruly hair has been neatly plaited and she wears a brocade gown of gold with copper-colored paillettes.

For the first time, I spin around and look at who's

here. Not including Renata, there's only ten of us, varying in ages of about fifteen to twenty. Tabitha's hairy self is squeezed into a white cocktail dress, which is ridiculous. Besides her, there's another girl whose arms are covered in skin-colored tumors, like she's got mushroom caps glued all over. One teen girl with a long mane of black hair sports startlingly purple skin. I blink, wondering if I'm seeing what I'm seeing, when she laughs at something and suddenly she blanches orange, before going a pasty gray. She must have chromatophores in her skin.

No duplicate Veras here, and the little children, like the tiny Hex and the tiny Blink, must be eating dinner elsewhere.

Micah sits down between the girl with the bumpy skin and the one with the changing colors.

"Zelia, this is Daphne and Xiulan." They stare at me uncomfortably as I prepare to say hi, but Renata glares at us like we're not supposed to socialize, so I hurry to find a seat.

I end up one empty chair away from Renata, next to Daphne and across from a boy who looks about fifteen. Caliga finds one of the little satellite tables and sits down by herself. Her face settles into a pout of resignation.

Everyone's matching red bracelet vaguely looks like we've all got a bloody slash to the wrist. The whole thing—the fancy dresses, the crystal goblets, us—is a joke. A happy family, we are not.

The table is set with three forks, two knives, and a spoon. The salad glistens with dressing and rainbow-colored vegetables and edible blooms, fancier than those that Vera used to grow. I pick up a fork, then put it down when Renata glares at me.

Beyond Renata's chair, a door opens. A man walks in, wearing a relatively casual outfit in crumpled linen. People smile a welcome, and yet he doesn't meet anyone's eyes as he takes the seat next to me.

"Please, start eating," he says quietly, waving carelessly at us. I recognize his voice. It's the same one that spoke to me in the scanner, but softer and less confident. So this is Julian?

He completely ignores me and starts dissecting his salad. First he picks out the nasturtium flowers, then pitches the tiny heirloom tomatoes onto the other side. He eats the lettuce leaves one by one with his fingertips, like a child. A few wisps of gray hair lighten his mousy brown hair, and there are tiny crow's-feet at his temples. I almost feel sorry for him. He looks desperate to be alone and away from this huge table of people. Renata ignores Julian like everyone else.

After our plates are switched to synthetic beef tenderloin with morels drowning in butter sauce, Julian shyly catches my eye.

"Have . . . has your stay been okay?"

It's so polite, I'm too shocked to say anything at first. "Oh . . . um. Yes. My room is fine."

"Good. Good." He reaches for his water goblet and drinks so thirstily that I bet he guzzled it to avoid further conversation. This is the mighty leader of Avida? The other half of Renata? I don't get it.

Midway through dinner, Julian excuses himself (after three glasses of orange-flavored water, I'm not surprised). When ten minutes go by, Renata groans and leaves. I suspect she's gone to corral him back to the table. Everyone at the table relaxes a little and our plates are replaced with a dessert of cherry and brandy compote. I try to dig under the bracelet where it's chafing my skin, but it's no good. It's too snug around my wrist.

"Get used to it," a boy from across the table mutters. His tie is crooked and his hair is mussed up, as if he had a fight with a grooming bot.

"Excuse me?"

"The bracelet. Don't muck around with it. If you try to forcefully remove it, it'll blow." His left arm ends in a scarred stub, poking beyond the sleeve of his crisp shirt. He waves his stump at me. "I'm Tennie."

"I'm—"

"Zelia Benten. We all know who you are." At this, ten pairs of eyes stop eating cherry compote and stare at me. My skin rises with countless goose bumps. "We all knew Dr. Benten. You're like . . . Princess Freak here. Royalty."

I clear my throat. "I didn't have anything to do with any of this."

"Oh. Right, okay." Tennie nods at me, but disappointment coats his words, which frustrates me to no end. How could I disappoint anybody? I haven't done anything! None of this is my fault.

"Um, so . . . when did you lose your hand?" I mumble, changing the subject.

"Six years ago. I tried to leave. I thought they were bluffing about the bracelets. I was wrong."

"Why don't you have a prosthetic?"

He pokes his fork toward me. "That would take away the whole punishment aspect, don't ya think?"

Daphne pushes her macerated cherries around. They resemble bloody meat now. The bumps on her face glow with a faint phosphorescence in the twilight. "There's a beacon signal on the perimeter of the building," she tells us. "If you managed to jump off the roof, you'd take one step before your hand blew. They say even the ground is wired down to twenty feet below the building. You can't even dig your way out. Only Julian allows access to and from Avida."

"Anyway, what's the point? Feds would round us up and kill us anyway if we left Inky. At least we're protected in here. Hands and all."

"Are we? Do you know how many are in the infirmary right now?"

Cy immediately glances my way. "Who's sick?" he asks.

Xiulan's skin flashes blue. The blue disintegrates into tiny dots and disappears. "It was only one or two of us, at first. But more are getting sick. Sean's been trying to figure it out. But they're getting worse and we can't ask for help from any Inky doctors. No one knows us like Benten does." She sees my strained expression, then drops her eyes. "I mean, did."

I take a breath and gather my thoughts. "Wait. Who's Sean?"

"You just met Sean," Tennie says.

"I thought I just met Julian."

Daphne smiles. "It's okay, I was confused at first too. It's his trait. Julian and Sean—they're two conscious beings in one brain. Sean's a sweet guy. He takes care of all the technical aspects of Avida, basically runs all the security systems and stuff. He's been helping with getting meds for the sick kids. But he's a total wimp. It's Julian you have to worry about."

"I don't get it. So he's got multiple personality disorder? Last I checked, that was a psychiatric thing, not a trait."

"Oh no. It's physiological, not psychological. They share memories. They control who's the dominant consciousness. The non-dominant one is often just sleeping in the background. They have an overlapping neural network. Sean and Julian have been two separate identities since birth."

I stare at my plate. It reminds me of Wilbert, but the opposite. Instead of two brains and one being, it's one brain and two beings. It even reminds me of SunAj with his multiple beings in one person. I wonder if they could all be related.

"Does Julian—do they have any relatives?"

"Oh. Yeah. He's that Aureus guy's little brother. Whatshisname?"

"SunAj," I say, filling in the blanks. "He died when Aureus went down."

Tennie shakes his head. "Down, left, right. It's all the same, only with a new name."

"What are you talking about?"

He leans over, whispering. "They got rid of SunAj on purpose. New leader, same people. I heard they're in Minwi somewhere."

"Where in Minwi?" I ask, though I already know the answer. When he says it, my lips form the word simultaneously.

"Wingfield."

CHAPTER 14

WINGFIELD.

Why would Dad want me to find safety with those who destroyed Aureus?

I open my mouth to ask more questions, but the boy's open demeanor suddenly folds shut like a book. Renata and Sean reenter the dinner area, arm in arm. All the kids at the table abruptly sit up straighter, stop talking, and drop their gazes to their plates. Sean pulls out her chair for Renata to sit down; she complies with a simpering smile.

No, not Sean. This must be Julian. I try not to stare, but it's impossible. Sure, he looks exactly the same—same mousy brown hair with threads of silver, same linen outfit—but he's altered. Like someone removed a dying lightbulb from his body and replaced it with a solar-watted torch.

Julian turns to me. His pupils are so large and black. Not as enormous as Blink's, but they eat away almost the entire space of his blue irises. Their yawning void makes me uncomfortable, so I discreetly inch farther away from him.

"Welcome, Zelia. I feel like I already know you intimately. Your father spoke fondly of you when he used to visit."

My lips stay closed.

"Apparently you're quite talented in the lab. We look forward to seeing your gifts here." His eyes travel over the thin silk of my dress, and I cross my hands in front of my chest. Julian laughs at my clumsy efforts to conceal myself.

"You're a pretty young thing, Zelia. No reason to be ashamed."

"I'm not ashamed. I don't enjoy being on display like a hunk of meat."

Heads turn at my words. I've said them more strongly than I anticipated, but there's no reeling them back. Julian leans back in his chair to consider me.

"Interesting. Your father was far more docile."

"You're wrong," I retort, trying not to raise my voice. "He stopped being a pawn. He changed." I've been so angry at my father for so long that coming to his defense is entirely strange.

Julian smirks. "Change does not always equal rebellion. Sometimes it's just selling yourself for a better price."

Renata watches us jealously and gets up to fill Julian's wineglass. "Julian dear, you've had a busy day. You should relax."

"Excellent idea. Perhaps a walk? I need to show the newest member of Avida her new home." Julian stands up and offers me his hand.

Micah stands up suddenly.

"I was planning on giving them a tour after dinner. I promised Zelia."

I furrow my eyebrows. He made no such promise. He lies like he breathes air.

"Down, Micah. I know she's our crown jewel, but you've had your share already," Julian says, smiling.

My face boils with irritation. I'm not a freaking crown jewel, and attention is the last thing I need, when all I'm planning on is leaving this place as soon as I find a way. The faces in the pool and at the table fix their eyes on me yet again. Some seem intimidated by me, while others wear pure disgust. *This is because of Dad,* I think. *This is all because of him. I didn't ask for this. Is he responsible for creating everyone in this room? He can't be, Julian is too old.* I'll never have the answers I need—but then again, do I really want to know the full horror of what my father did?

Julian extends his hand again but I don't take it. I stand up and straighten out my dress, wishing I could fan my warmed cheeks. Micah immediately comes to my side. He looks freaked out and discomposed, which throws me totally off. He's usually Mr. Super Cool about everything.

He reaches for my arm and whispers so quietly that Julian can't hear him. "You don't want to be alone with him. Come with me."

"Micah!" Julian growls. "I said *sit down.*"

"But—"

"Sean. Do it."

I'm confused. Why is Julian talking to his other . . . self?

Julian's eyes suddenly flicker, the black pupils shrinking to pinpoints. He slouches ever so slightly, and I realize he's Sean now, touching a complicated holo image that emerges from his bracelet.

A strangled cry pierces the quiet. Micah's fallen to his knees and he's clutching at his bracelet. His face is bright red, eyes squeezed shut. He doubles over and stuffs his wrist and fist into his stomach.

"Ahhh, god! I'm sorry, I'm sorry!" he says, grimacing, before yelling out again in pain.

I can't believe it. This is what Micah did to me and to everyone he policed in Aureus, burning us with his electric touch. He deserves this. And yet, somewhere in my gut, I know that Micah was trying to protect me somehow. That he doesn't deserve *this*.

"Stop it!" I say, grabbing Julian's arm. Because it's Julian again, his pupils large and black, wearing that slippery smile. "What are you doing?"

"Sean disciplines everyone at my command. I will suffer no insubordination. Our lives can't afford it." He tilts his head, scrutinizing Micah's level of excruciating pain, and finally announces, "Enough."

Micah crumples to the ground, breathing heavily. I want to see if he's okay, but I'm terrified to touch him. Julian puts his arm out and I finally take it, my hands shaking uncontrollably. The entire table, including Renata and the teens in the water, watches us walk to the transport. Just as it closes, I see Cy stand up. My eyes plead with him.

Please, Cy. Say anything.

But his voice never enters my mind.

The transport door closes. Julian and I are all alone.

I HOPED FOR A TOUR OF THE gardens on each level. Maybe a peek inside an R&D lab. But this is the last place I ever wanted to see.

Julian's private quarters.

The doors open up to an octagonal library, decorated with gilt molding and plum-upholstered furniture. A holo picture window takes up one wall, with a view of eighteenth-century London. The rest of the walls are filled with books and a crystal display case at chest level on each wall. Inside are gold watches lying on a bed of black velvet. Some are wristwatches, but most are pocket watches open to show their delicate faces. My heart flubs within my chest from nervousness. I try to breathe a little faster to keep up, wishing my necklace was around my neck right now.

"What do you think of my collection?" Julian walks behind me and hovers a little too close.

"They're pretty." It's an effort to try to sound calm. I peer closer at the dials. None of the second hand sweeps are moving. "Are they broken?"

"No. But it took a long time finding an expert watchmaker who could make them work again. The right touch." He rests his hand on my shoulder and I quickly take a step away, clearing my throat.

"Are they all yours?"

"They belong to Endall."

"Endall?" I don't remember hearing his name at dinner.

"He's one of my sons. Obsessed with time, I think."

"You think? Don't you know?"

"He's not in Avida, nor is he a child of Renata. Another woman conceived him with my genes, thanks to your father. I tracked him down to Ilmo. He fled and left behind the watches."

"Why did he run away from you?"

Julian sits on the daybed and crosses his legs. "I didn't bring you here for an interview." He pats the mattress next to him but I don't budge, which is a mistake. Now he knows I'm afraid.

"If it's any comfort, Sean is awake and listening to our conversation. You have an ally in the room."

I stiffen. "If Sean is an ally, what does that make you?"

"A business partner." His face lights with an electric smile. Julian is handsome, there's no question of that, but it's a beauty so polished, it makes you wish for the imperfections.

"You mean my trait. I'm not comfortable making it again. After what happened to the senator—"

"Yes. A wild-type DNA can't handle your gene modifications. Mine could."

"Doesn't Sean have a say in this?"

"It's my body."

"It's his too," I counter.

"In our internal debates, I always win." He narrows his eyes. "I'd like to commission your skills for something else. Have you heard of suicide seeds?"

I think for a moment. "It's terminator technology. Genetically modified plants that produce fruit, but the seeds from the fruit can't grow a viable plant. It forces farmers to purchase viable seeds from the manufacturer every year, so they can't self-sustain their crops."

"Correct. Your father placed terminator technology into you," he says, pointing right at my breasts. *Ew.* "And every traited child born from Benten's tinkering. Even the older generation—myself, SunAj, your Marka—we are all suicide seeds. We cannot procreate, not without your father's key. Only he can unlock our potential."

"Wait. How can my father have controlled your and Marka's genes? You're all the same age."

"Excellent question." He stands up and walks to me, staring me down hard. "How indeed. Do you know how old your father is?"

"Yes. He's . . . he was forty-nine when he died."

"Are you sure?" He crinkles his eyes. "I have no way to really question this. I've researched him and found nothing to support my hypothesis. But I know that I'm sterile. I know that SunAj was too. I also don't know why there aren't more in our generation. From what I know, your father is the only person who could manipulate our genes to create children. Even SunAj didn't know how he did it. My own birth history is a mystery. Dr. Benten has answers he's never told me."

"Yeah, well. Get in line," I say bitterly.

"So. I believe the key to unlocking our fertility is hidden in something valuable. Something he held more dear than anything else." He reaches out and envelops my hands in his. It's everything I can do to keep from jerking them away. "I think he put the key in you. Will you help me find it?"

"No."

"That's very selfish of you."

"This isn't about sharing candy or something," I growl. "I am not a commodity." I pull my hands away and cross my arms.

"You know that we are genetically and biologically distinct from normal humans. We'll die out if we can't procreate. Would you commit our species to extinction?"

"Maybe it's meant to be that way."

"I am surprised, Zelia, that you would foster such primitive opinions. This is the same thoughtfulness that brought about HGM 2098. According to your argument, you should be dead."

I bite my tongue.

Julian steps away. "This has been quite entertaining. But a moot discussion, nonetheless. I will have my bots work on your sample as soon as possible, for both projects."

"But I didn't give you a sample," I say warily.

"We have it from your blood test on the magtrain. And Zelia?" He pulls out my necklace from his shirt pocket and dangles it in front of my face, the black cube pendant catching the light. My eyes must show how desperate I feel. "Don't try to interfere with me. You will regret it." He wiggles the pendant and I quickly snatch it away. "Come. Our tour isn't finished."

Julian walks me to the door, but the irresistible glint of rich gold in the nearby display makes me pause. I take a last glance at the exquisite watch nearby.

"It's a Hamilton 950b. An historic piece." He taps the case. "We are much the same as these watches, you know. A collection of unique qualities."

"You say that like we're things to be hoarded."

"There is nothing wrong with protecting what is precious. Just like your father kept the code for our genetic makeups. His recipes, so to speak."

"If you're asking about the list, I don't have it."

Julian smiles, like a sunrise after dawn. It's beauty, surrounded by darkness. "I'll bet you do. You just don't realize it."

JULIAN LEADS ME THROUGH EACH LEVEL'S LUSH, green center. An English rose garden, a Korean water garden with pagoda, the meadow, and a hedge maze. I'm barely listening to him brag about his non-poisonous flora ("So no one can intentionally kill themselves," he boasts).

All I can think of now is that damn list. My father never gave me anything on his deathbed, or before, that screamed "Guard this with your life!" Except my necklace, of course. But Avida scanned it before Julian gave it back. It can't be in there.

Dad's body barely made it through the wreckage. All we had left when it was over was his ring.

"Oh!" I say loudly. Julian stops abruptly beneath the pagoda in the Asian garden, staring at me.

"Are you all right?"

"I'm fine. Stubbed my toe," I say meekly, before walking on. As Julian takes me to the lowest level, my mind is whirring furiously.

Dad's ring. It has to be. He wore it everywhere, never took it off. It was a symbol of his marriage to a wife that, now, maybe still exists. Maybe this mysterious mother has the list. But knowing Dad, he probably kept his secrets even from her. He could have easily hidden nanochips inside that ring, and now it's hanging around Dyl's neck somewhere out there. I can't let anyone know. It's worth everything right now. Anyone holding that information could know the name and trait of every person my dad helped to create, and how he did it.

By now, Julian's taken me to the entrance to the laboratory. He says the lab takes up a whole floor. I'm dying to see what kind of equipment they have.

"Can we go in and take a look?" I ask, trying not to sound too eager.

"Ah. You're like a kid in a candy shop. Or should I say, a hunter in a weapons convention?"

I stare at him curiously, until I understand what he's trying to say. My mind and a lab are my weapons. "How did you know? About me?"

"Your father bragged about your skills in the lab. Working at post-doc levels at only sixteen? Impressive. But you're not getting into this lab."

I move to protest, but he interrupts me.

"Not until you earn your way in. It would be like handing you a gun, wouldn't it? Dangerous. Besides, there are other skills you'll need to learn that are far more deadly."

"Like what?"

"The fine art of prevarication," he says, grinning.

I give him a blank look, and he laughs, holds my hand up to twirl me in an awkward circle. "Politics, my dear! You're famous, you know. Our very own celebrity, the daughter of the famed Dr. Benten, and now the States' Most Wanted! You're the face of the traited everywhere, whether you like it or not. You'll get your first lesson soon."

I freeze as soon as I'm done spinning from under his arm. One of the last things Dad said before he died was that he'd wanted me to *stop* my lab work.

Life isn't about plasmid vectors and bio-accelerants. It's about dealing with people.

He'd wanted me to take political science courses and history. He was trying to tell me something. To prepare me for something he wasn't ready to reveal.

"I don't want to be anyone's spokesperson," I mumble.

"It's the legacy your father bequeathed."

"I don't want it!" I sound like a petulant child, but I don't care. All I want is to get out of here. Go back to my family. Figure out what's going on with Cy.

"Well. Perhaps it's been a long day. Sean, will you lead her back? She's exhausted me."

Under the cover of the pagoda, Julian's shoulders sag and the dark expanse of his pupils shrinks again. His eyes are a clear, pale blue now, and his face looks somehow faded. A shadow of himself. I immediately feel safer. That predatory aura of Julian's is completely extinguished.

Sean has no scent around him, though I concentrate hard. I realize that Julian didn't either. Maybe Julian is good at keeping his emotions under control, or maybe together they're too unhuman to give off a signature.

"I'll take you back to your room," he offers.

"I'm okay. I think I know what floor I'm on."

"I understand. I'm not as interesting as Julian." He smiles and shrugs. He looks like the last kid picked for holo kickball at school. "You must be tired too. I'll tell him you went straight to your room."

I feel so sorry for this guy. He's not frightening at all. I could probably knock him out with a withering stare. "It's all right. Actually, you can walk me back," I say. "So . . . won't he know?" I ask, curious. "Doesn't he remember what happens while you're the dominant consciousness?"

"Not when he's fallen asleep. And he falls asleep quickly. Julian burns brightly, and it exhausts us both, to share this one body. But he always asks me what's happened, and he knows when I'm lying." He steps into the transport and holds his bracelet to the black scanner. "Level four." It starts speeding upward.

I raise an eyebrow. "Can you tell when he's lying?"

"Julian is a living lie. He lets you see what he wants you to see. He has his plans and he doesn't share them with me." The transport stops and he walks me to my door.

"Sounds . . . lonely," I comment.

"I manage." He grins, but it's a watery version of Julian's megawatt smile. "I am glad you're here, Zelia. You seem like a nice girl. It's good to have some allies."

I open my door and close it, listening to Sean sigh on the other side and walk away. He's constantly bullied by the one person he can't ever escape.

I put on my necklace, hoping it still works. My chest wall automatically expands and contracts, and my head clears ever so slightly, a sign that I haven't been breathing as deeply as I should.

The bots waggle at my feet, and I sit on the edge of the bed and nod at them. Soon they're all over me, buffing off my makeup and releasing my hair from its ceramic stylings. After I put on a set of silk pajamas (it's that or a lace nightie, which I kick to the corner of the closet), I dive beneath the thick comforter.

As one bot gathers up my discarded clothes, the other one pounces onto the bed next to me and tucks the blankets around my shoulders.

There, there, it seems to say. *Let us take care of your squishy outsides.*

I think of Caliga in her room, unable to touch the one person she loves, unable to numb herself of her own pain. Of how a beautiful sunrise would agonize Blink, and how Cy used to tattoo himself daily, only to wake up to a new canvas ready for punishment. Even Micah isn't immune to the very electrical pain he produces.

And someday, with my longevity trait, I will outlive every person I've ever held dear to my heart.

What's the point of being created to be special when you've also been given a unique way to be tortured too?

"Thanks, Dad," I whisper into the gloom.

Despite how exhausted I am, it takes a long, lonely time to fall asleep.

CHAPTER 15

I TOSS AND TURN ALL NIGHT LONG, until my bracelet buzzes. I withdraw my wrist from the covers and a holo screen pops up.

"Good morning," it chirps.

"Not really."

"Your duty roster is as follows. Please arrive when prompted or you will be issued warnings."

Warnings. Ha. Why don't they just say that they'll zap us like cattle?

BREAKFAST: Rose Garden
MORNING and AFTERNOON ASSIGNMENT:
   Childcare Duty Group 2
LUNCH: Childcare Duty Meal Supervision
DINNER: Roof Gazebo
FREE PLAY TIME: One hour
CURFEW

After washing up and dressing in a slim purple tunic presented by the bots, I leave my room. The hair bot mercifully leaves my head alone, but the makeup bot sulks until I let it apply lip balm and moisturizer. When I leave, others kids are yawning and heading for the transport.

Out of curiosity, I try to explore a corridor behind the meadow. My bracelet buzzes uncomfortably, and a holo warning pops up.

Area not authorized.

I take a few more steps in the wrong direction and my wrist buzzes with very real, very electric pain.

"Ow! Okay, okay. I get it. Bracelet equals dog collar." I quickly walk back toward the transport doors. Caliga emerges from her room wearing a similar outfit but in dusky pink. The medicines for her leg must be working well, because she's not using the cane today, although she's still tottering a little. After hesitating, I give her my arm to lean on and she takes it.

"Where are you assigned to this morning?" I ask, yawning.

"The medic office. I'm supposed to help numb up any boo-boos that come my way."

"Well, that's a nice change," I joke.

"What, is it so hard to believe that Aureus members aren't pure evil?" Her eyes are bitter and angry, like when she first arrived at Carus. "When are you going to understand that you and your sister were a job that had to be taken care of. It was survival, and I wasn't ready to die. I'm still not ready to die."

I tear her hand off me and she winces at the violence of it. "So after we saved your ass, you'd still sell us out to whoever will save you the next time around?"

"I didn't say that!"

I wipe my hand across my mouth. "Get your story straight, Caliga. You either sell your soul to the highest bidder, or you don't."

Caliga turns awkwardly to limp to the transport. Our angry words hang heavy in the air, thicker and denser than the scent of the meadow flowers. As I stand there by the undulating grasses, I wonder. Is a stab wound such a bad thing, if the hand holding the knife is sorry?

I take the next transport down. The scent of blossoms is overwhelming when the door opens. The garden is covered in manicured shrubbery and artfully placed rosebushes of countless varieties. Clusters of cast-iron tables are grouped together and most of the Avida members are already halfway through their coffee, tea, and pastries.

None of them talk to each other. Caliga's again eating alone at a table. Correction: sitting alone. She's not eating a single crumb. Everyone else stares dully past each other at the too-perfect roses, chewing mechanically. It's nothing like the chaotic meals at Carus, when Hex would try to steal bites from everyone's plate, and we'd all pretend we didn't see while surreptitiously refilling our plates with his favorite foods. Ana and Dyl would have secret conversations over their latest poetry holo lessons and Marka would chide me for getting three new dreads in my hair because I'd forgotten to brush it.

"It's not like Carus, is it?"

I jerk in surprise to see Cy standing right next to me. He's got dark circles under his eyes, but seems less gaunt than when I found him in Dubuque. I find myself holding my breath, standing so close. It never fails to surprise, how easily he can unmoor me.

"No, it's not," I say, trying to keep my voice calm.

Cy clenches his jaw. Most wouldn't notice, but I see the telltale ripple of muscles along his cheek. He rubs his forearm absently. He did that yesterday too, after disembarking the magtrain.

"Is your arm okay?"

"Oh. Yeah, fine." He smiles at me, but it's a shallow smile that doesn't touch his eyes. "Where are you assigned?"

"Childcare." I slump my shoulders. "Julian told me yesterday he wouldn't let me near a lab with a ten-foot pole. Not until I've *earned* it."

Cy doesn't seem to be listening anymore, because Julian and Renata have entered the garden. They're having a heated argument that ends with Julian hissing, "Not in front of the children. We'll get more medicine when I say it's necessary." Renata's hair is in frizzled disarray and she's still wearing a powder-blue nightgown. Her brown cheeks are dulled, and dark circles shadow her eyes. She sits at a table next to Xiulan and grabs a cup of coffee, slurping it. Behind Julian's back, Renata pats Xiulan discreetly on the shoulder and her skin flashes green before quieting to a putty color. Renata's eyes brim with tears, and a single drop rolls down her cheek and salts her coffee.

Julian walks up to me and touches my waist. I sidestep him, but the possessive hand stays planted on my side. "Zelia. Sit with me. You too, Micah." I glance over my shoulder to see Micah walking slowly toward the garden. His skin is ashen and his hair messy, like he didn't sleep a wink. He holds his braceleted wrist at an angle, away from his body. Reluctantly, he sits down at his newly appointed seat at our small table. Cy joins Blink at another table.

Micah's wrist is raw and oozing beneath the bracelet. He can't rest it anywhere without cringing in pain. He pushes away the plate of pastries and just sits there, staring at his wrist. I've never seen him like this.

Julian didn't clip his wings; he singed them to ashes.

Julian sits down and takes a huge bite of an apple turnover. "He was hard to figure out, you know." He waves his bitten pastry at Micah.

"Excuse me?" I say.

"His trait. I make sure I'm immune to every person's trait in Avida. Took a page out of SunAj's book. Micah generates current, so I found a medicine that makes my skin nonconductive to electricity. Then I simply grafted immune-compatible artificial skin to his wrist, and his own protection against it was gone. Simple. Elegant."

I stare at the raw, burned flesh around his bracelet and lift my eyes, meeting Micah's.

"There's nothing elegant about torture," I say slowly.

"Discipline! There's a difference. Anyway, my next project is her." He slides a look to Caliga. She's sipping her coffee, oblivious to Julian's lecherous stare. "My lab is already working on it. Or you could help me. I understand you've already seen the formula."

"I don't remember it."

Julian laughs. "You need to work on your lying skills, Zelia! You're so absurdly obvious." He leans forward. "There's an art to lying, Zelia. Ask this one." He nudges Micah, who scrunches his face in pain. "Well, I'm off. We have a big day tomorrow, Zelia."

"Tomorrow?"

"I've arranged a meeting for tomorrow afternoon with several senior Inky officials. They're quite interested in meeting you. Your first lesson in politics! I promise, it will go swimmingly."

He grabs Micah's forearm, and Micah cries out in agony. Everyone at breakfast goes deathly silent. "You'll perform *perfectly,* because you already know the consequences if you don't."

Julian drops Micah's arm and leaves the rose garden. Slowly, everyone recovers except Micah, who sits trembling in the chair next to me.

My bracelet buzzes a warning, and a holo pops up to tell me I'm due to attend my childcare duties.

I get up to join a group leaving the garden, not knowing what to say to Micah.

"Zel." He grabs my wrist with his bad hand and gently pulls me back to the table. I don't have the heart to jerk away, knowing how much it would hurt.

"What?"

"I meant what I said before. I didn't sleep with Dyl. And I didn't sleep with Ana either."

Pressure rises in my chest and I fight the urge to yell at him. "I don't believe you."

"SunAj was obsessed with trying to figure out how your dad created traited kids. Dr. Benten didn't share the code with him, and SunAj was desperate to make new products. He took complete control of the entire process. They were both sedated and impregnated *in a lab*. It wasn't me. It was never me. I'm telling you the truth."

I lean closer and stare him down. "You manipulated innocent girls. Children! You victimized them. You're just as guilty as you were before."

CHAPTER 16

I'M WAITING AT THE TRANSPORT DOOR WHEN Blink walks up to me. We both enter it and scan our bracelets, but only one floor lights up: the lowest level.

"Oh. Are you babysitting too?" I ask, though inwardly I'm all *Please say no.*

"Yes," she says stiffly.

Oh joy.

The doors open to a gigantic, dimly lit underground cavern. A wetsuit-clad boy welcomes us—Tennie, the boy who lost a hand trying to escape. Two kids splash around the shallow end of the water, which glows with a faint blue-green phosphorescence. I'm surprised there aren't more.

"Welcome to Mutant Nannying 101," Tennie says, grinning.

"Tennie," I say. "Like Tennis?"

The boy laughs. "No. Like Tennessee Williams. Renata went through a playwright phase when I was born."

Blink stands there staring at us, until I clear my throat

uncomfortably. "Uh, Tennie, this is Blink." I flinch at my own mistake. "I mean Élodie."

"You may call me Blink," she says delicately.

I frown. "I assumed you'd hate the name Blink."

"*Oui. Je déteste ça.* But it defines me. So." She shrugs.

"How many kids are in Avida?" I ask Tennie.

"Twelve."

"Wow. Such a big place for so few people."

"Well, it used to be fifteen. Three have died in the last year."

Surprise stops me cold. Those are horrible odds. "What? Why?"

"We don't know," Tennie says. "A couple of the kids kept getting sick. They've been trying to figure out if it's related to their traits maybe . . . I don't know, making their bodies expire? It's weird."

That's so strange. No one in Carus ever got sick, except for Hex, from eating too many lemon bars in one sitting. Kids in Aureus were killed all the time when they were deemed useless or noncompliant, frozen in that blue ice wall I'd seen. But sickness? Then again, my dad did help when some kids weren't healthy. Vera mentioned having vitamin deficiencies that he'd balanced out for her particular physiology.

"Anyway. We've got way worse problems now, right?" he says, knowingly nodding at me. "No? You don't know?"

"Know what?" Blink asks.

"Didn't you hear the news?" He turns on his bracelet holo, and the scrolling news channel pops up. A headline about illegal products flashes in red. "See? Our products are being taken off the shelves and destroyed. Someone sent information to the press that proved that Teggwear, ForEverDay, and those skin-healing serums from that new guy—Cy?—were derived from people with altered DNA."

"But none of those products change people's DNA. They're just pharmaceuticals made from the same chemicals that traited bodies make," I argue.

"Does it matter? Anything associated with us right now is pretty bad. Some guy out there is leaking info and wants us dead."

"Who?" Blink and I say it simultaneously. She smiles shyly at me and I allow a tiny smile back.

"No one knows. I guess that's why Julian is desperate to meet with the Inky politicians tomorrow. Some of those products are made at our factory in Inky. The SkinGlow, and SkinChange."

I remember seeing ads for those. SkinGlow is a party drug that allows you to glow in the dark. And SkinChange is similar, but lets you flash rainbows.

"That's our money, our lifeblood."

"Does Julian have any idea about who's leaking the information?"

"I hope so," Tennie says. "Anyway, time to meet your charges." He cups his hands, hollering, "Hey, delinquents! Come meet your other nannies."

The two kids splash over to us, drenching my legs. The little boy with the wraparound sunglasses swims up to us, and another girl who looks totally normal, maybe seven years old?

"I already met them!" the boy yells, and flops backward into the water.

"So polite! That was Jensen," Tennie tells us. "This is Penelope."

"Hi," Penelope says, and then points beyond us. "Can I play with that mouse?"

Blink and I spin around, searching the ground for vermin. "What mouse?" I say.

"That one." She points again, to the far rock wall, full of dark crevices and moss.

"There is no playing with mice. Or rats. Okay?" Tennie tells her. At our confused faces, he adds, "She has superior vision. You've probably heard of her product, Visionite. The big game hunters in Utaz love it. She can see a fly from a mile away. You're lucky she didn't analyze your wrinkles."

"I'm eighteen. I don't have wrinkles," I say, frowning.

"According to Penelope, everyone's face resembles a dry lake bed."

Great. My face is already geriatric.

This underwater cavern is astonishingly real. The ceiling is covered in bone-colored stalactites that bare their teeth fifteen feet above eerily glowing water. I stoop down to the water, swirling it. The eddies and whirlpools flash with liquid foxfire.

"Amazing," I murmur. "How did you guys do this?"

"Ask Cela," he says, disgusted. Tennie points to where

a figure is swimming toward us beneath the water. Every inch of her naked skin is faintly aglow in blues and greens, the same ones throughout the cavern. When she breaks the surface, she spits water at Tennie, and not in a joking way. It's the same water girl who took Ryba into the oasis pool.

"What are you doing here?" she says to Tennie.

"I was assigned, okay?" He crosses his arms. Cela gives me and Blink the once-over and crinkles her nose, like we're yesterday's garbage. Might as well try to be civil.

"Hi. I'm Zelia," I say. Cela keeps frowning at me. "I love what you did with the bioluminescence. How did you do it?"

Cela bares her teeth. Her canines are sharp and shiny. "I spliced luciferin and luciferase genes into the natural bacteria of the water. Is that good enough an answer for you?" She turns around and then disappears into the depths.

Oooookay.

Tennie shakes his head. "Don't take it personally. She hates your dad almost as much as she hates me. She thinks of herself as being a victim of . . . let me see if I can get the words right." Tennie take a deep breath and in his best professorial voice, intones, "*The ultimate objectification of personhood down to the basest molecular level.*" When I give Tennie a blank stare, he shrugs. "Being created for the sake of her genes, rather than for the sake of making a human being."

I raise my hands. "Yeah, if anyone is listening out there. I had nothing to do with that!" I say, exasperated.

"I know. Like you had nothing to do with making me

like this," he says, waving his one good hand. I don't notice anything at first, and then I see that his hand is dripping water all over the rock he's standing on. It's like he's sweating water all over the place.

"You're gifted with excessive, voluntary sweating?"

"Ha. Not *perspiration,* but *precipitation.* I condense water out of the air by negatively charging the ions around me."

"Julian and Renata are your parents?" Blink asks. We both stare at her, surprised. She'd been so quiet, we almost forgot she was here.

"Yep." He smacks the moisture off his hand onto his shorts.

"But you tried to escape," she says, frowning.

"I never said we got along."

"You are blessed to have parents who love you." She takes off her sunglasses and she wipes her eyes with her sleeve.

I feel bad for her. I know what it's like to have a parent who seemed to care, even if Dad wasn't truthful with us. And I have Marka now.

"So . . ." I start carefully. "Did they abandon you?"

Her wide black eyes turn on me. "Abandon? No. I wish they had. They slapped me into silence when I cried in the sunlight. They locked me in a brightly lit room, trying to force my trait to go away. And when they realized how well I could see in the dark, they made me steal things, in the worst parts of Montreal." She stares at the cavern wall. "So much evil happens when the lights go out. I saw it all."

"Geez," Tennie says. "I'm sorry. Well, you're safe now."

Blink takes a step back from both of us. "We'll never be safe, as long as we're abnormal. We'll always be used as cattle. I wish we'd never been born."

Blink retreats to a mossy stone and puts her sunglasses back on. Tennie throws pebbles at the water when the transport door behind us opens. I'm surprised to see Tabitha walk toward us. She's wearing nothing. I wonder if that's still considered naked if she's covered in fur.

"So. They let the Wookie out of the freezer, huh?" Tennie says, smirking.

Tabitha ignores him and steps to the water's edge, far away from where the kids are splashing around, and taps the surface of the water. Tap, tap, tap, pause. She repeats the rhythm until Cela's lithe body appears, bucking beneath the surface toward the rocky shore. When she surfaces, she speaks in low tones with Tabitha. I catch a few words of it. Something about breathing, and turnover, or something. Cela twists back into the water, and Tabitha marches in, following her. They disappear into the depths in a few seconds.

"Where are they going?" I nudge Tennie.

"The other water rooms. They're accessible by underwater passageways."

"Wow. They really built this place to be pretty complicated," I remark. The grotto even smells perfectly real. Damp and mossy, with mineral-laden air.

"These caverns weren't constructed. They're natural. Apparently, the first person Aureus put in charge here was a water child. She had the building built over this place," he says, gesturing to the stalactites. "There's an underwater river in Inky, and a bunch of linked underwater caves too. I hear there are exits to the surface, outside of Avida and Inky, but none of the water kids ever leave."

"Why not? I'd be out of here in a heartbeat." Or a breath, if I could hold it for that long.

"Because there's no guarantee they'd be able to get to another body of water without drying out and dying. Their lungs don't work so well. Remember the Wookie's girlfriend, Ryba? I hear she was only out of the water for two hours. Nearly killed her." Tennie rubs his stump against his temple, thinking. "That's the thing with our traits. Sometimes they're like genetic handcuffs. I mean, can you see the Wookie—"

"Please call her Tabitha. Or I'll start calling you Luke Skywalker."

"Hey, that would be appropriate," he says wryly, holding up his amputated wrist. When I don't smile back, he concedes. "Okay, fine. Anyway, can you imagine Tabitha living in a fifth-world, tropical climate? She'd die. Or Cela living in a desert? We're trapped by our traits."

He's right. I think of this while we watch the kids, chatting about this and that.

Blink joins in and warms up to our conversation after a while. When Tennie walks to the far edge of the water to play with the kids, she blurts out, "He doesn't like me like that, you know."

"Excuse me?"

"Cyrad. We are friends. Nothing more."

"Oh." I have this crazy need to smile, but I suppress it.

"Micah and Tegg disciplined him almost daily when he first arrived. He'd heal quickly, but he would fight back the next day. *Tant et plus.* He was so angry. No one would speak to him but me. Sometimes we talked all night long about you, and your family." She picks up an ugly brown rock from the ground. It's like a rock potato. "You have nothing to be jealous about. It is I who is jealous."

I feel rotten for how I've felt about Blink. Élodie. "Well . . . I am jealous. You've spent a whole year with him. A year that I don't have."

She nods and we sit in quiet silence for a minute. Tennie bounds over and smiles. The kids are shivering, wrapped in towels and running for the transport.

"Lunchtime! Let's go."

We stand up and walk inside the transport. When the doors shut, it doesn't budge.

"Okay, who didn't scan their bracelet?" Tennie asks.

"Oh, me. Sorry." I wave my wrist against the black pad, and it indicates floor three, not the top floor where we're supposed to go to lunch. "Weird." I turn on my holo port and a new schedule message pops up.

LUNCH: Holo Room Six

"That explains it," Tennie says. The transport zooms up when a tiny, cold hand slips into mine. The little girl, Penelope with super vision, tugs at me.

"What's your trait? I can't see it," she says. I stoop down until I'm eye level with her. She's got stunning green eyes and crooked front teeth.

"My trait doesn't show," I explain. "My body won't grow old." I don't bother mentioning the scent trait—or that we can develop more than one trait—because I get the feeling it would be bad if Julian found out.

Penelope concentrates hard, trying to understand my words.

"Oh. So you'll stay here forever with us, right?"

Blink and Tennie immediately drop their eyes to me, waiting for the answer. I go hot in the face, wishing the transport wasn't so small.

"Well, I don't know. Maybe. Sort of."

"Stay, stay, *stayyyyyyyyyyyy*!" she sings, clutching my hands and bouncing with a vigor I'm not sure I ever possessed.

I'm saved by the doors opening up on my level. Penelope finally lets go of my hand and when she does, it feels far emptier than before she'd touched me.

MY BRACELET INSTRUCTS ME WHERE TO GO. It takes me to a boring, navy-blue hallway flanked by closed doors. There it is, room six. I walk in, expecting something interesting from the holo program. Maybe a lunar landscape? Or a bustling Paris city street?

That last thing I expect to see is Cy.

"Cy!" I gasp with surprise. Behind a table set with sandwiches for lunch, he spins around, crossing his arms in front of his chest. Like he's disappointed.

"What are you doing here?" he asks, quickly turning away and rolling down his sleeves.

"I should ask the same." I'm crestfallen at his reaction. But when he turns back around, he comes straight to my side.

"How was your morning?" he asks with a tenderness that makes my heart skip. It's a 180-degree turn from his frosty greeting, but I don't care.

"Good. I was with Élodie and Tennie watching the little kids." I bite my lip and decide to just spit it out. "She told me you had an awful time in Aureus. About what Micah and Tegg did to you." When Cy stays silent, I reach for his hand and he doesn't resist. "I wish you'd told me, though."

"I didn't want to worry you," he whispers.

"That's what girlfriends are supposed to do. They worry." And then with a horrible thought, I blurt, "If I'm still your girlfriend, that is. Because I totally get it if, you don't, you know . . . I would understand." I sound like an idiot. Cy pulls me closer and wraps his arms around my waist.

"You are so adorable when you're flustered."

"Sorry, it's just . . . a year is a long time. I don't know where I stand with you," I mumble, staring at his chest.

"You're standing in my arms, Zel," he whispers. "That's the only place you should ever be."

He crushes me into an embrace and for a full minute, there's nothing else in the world. No Avida, no Inky, no memories of Aureus. He finally loosens his hug.

"So what did you do this morning?" I ask, leaning my cheek against his chest.

"I was in the infirmary. I saw that little girl Victoria. The mini-Hex girl? She looked awful. Headaches, nausea . . . I started to examine her, when Renata whisked her away. It was weird."

"This whole place reeks of weird."

"I'm sorry about that," a voice intones from the door.

We bounce apart like repelling magnets. Julian stands in the doorway clothed in a simple outfit of head-to-toe khaki. They're like military pajamas.

"It's fine. Everything's fine," I say with stiff formality.

"You know I'm Sean, right?" He takes a step closer. Now I notice that his posture is droopy, his pupils are pinpoints and his eyes are full blue. "Hello, Cy. Julian's taking Zelia out tomorrow and he's been working nonstop preparing for it. He's sleeping very deeply now. I had to find you before he wakes up. But first, eat."

We sit down and Cy and I wolf down our lunches. Sean doesn't, just twiddles with his napkin. His nervousness puts me at ease.

"I have a proposal for you both. I need your help," he finally says. "I need to find a way to keep Julian under control."

Cy narrows his eyes. "You're the one in that body, not us. Can't you talk to him?"

"Julian has always been the dominant soul. He pushes me aside at his whim. As a result, his decisions dominate Avida."

I frown. "I'm sorry. That sounds awful. But that's not really our problem."

"It is if you wish to escape Avida. And Inky."

Cy and I immediately exchange surprised glances. Sean leans in closer and desperation transforms his face. "I set the programs for where you go within Avida, but Julian keeps the passkey that would get you out of Avida itself. But if there's a way to incapacitate him, maybe I could get it."

It's hard to shove the *YES PLEASE GET ME OUT OF HERE!* expression off my face, but I do my best. "So what are you suggesting?" I ask as calmly as possible.

"Our consciousness and memories are irrevocably intertwined with each other's. But maybe there's a way to make his side let go of the information he keeps. Or at least, fall asleep for more predictable periods of time. This is why I asked you both here. Cy, I need your neuroscience expertise. Your work on neural growth factors while you were in Aureus was wonderful."

Cy's face darkens. I know he started that research to try to fix Ana somehow, after she'd been hurt in Aureus, but it hadn't worked.

"And Zelia, I need you too."

"To work in the lab?" It's hard not to get too excited. Cy and me in a lab together would make Avida downright cozy.

"No. To keep Julian occupied."

"Are you kidding me?"

"Unfortunately, I'm not. And anyway, Julian wants to show you off. He covets your trait like I've never seen before."

Cy looks at me and we try to read each other's minds, but I shake my head, just the tiniest bit. The whole thing doesn't feel right. It's too risky.

I stand up and Cy stands up with me. "No. I don't think this is a good idea," he starts, before Sean puts his hands out.

"I need to show you one thing, before you decide."

"What?"

Sean pulls up his holo bracelet and touches several key lock codes. "Level Sub-One. You have twenty minutes."

CHAPTER 17

WE DON'T WAIT TO BE ASKED AGAIN. Cy and I immediately race to the transport and our bracelets grant us access to a floor we didn't know existed. Sub-One.

"Maybe this is below the grotto," I say. We feel the transport going diagonally, zipping left, then plunging down. My shoulder bumps into Cy, and he swings his arm around me. I wish there were more zigzags on this trip.

"Grotto? Sounds sort of romantic," he comments. When I give him a sideways look, he actually goes red in the face and clears his throat. "What is it? An Italian garden or something?"

I explain quickly about the water cave and Tennie. "There's so much going on here, Cy. Somehow, we've got to find time to compare notes on this place."

"I know." He reaches for my hand and runs his finger across my palm. My spine turns into a wet noodle and I grab for his hand. But I only grasp air.

"What the—" My hand is empty, and Cy's hands are

still by his side. "You touched me! Like you did when we were in the Deadlands!"

Cy curses and crosses his arms, stuffing his hands into his armpits. "I didn't mean to. I shouldn't have done that."

"But why—"

The doors slide open and what we see douses our conversation in a millisecond. It's a small infirmary, with rows of hover beds and a medical bot scurrying from bedside to bedside. Vital signs spill across a holo board above three occupied beds.

I recognize Renata hovering over one of the children—Victoria, the four-armed girl. Renata is stroking Victoria's bruised arm, and the movement elicits a deep ache within me. Marka would do the same thing to me, when I was awake at night.

"What's going on here?" Cy says.

Renata whirls around. Her eyes are bloodshot and her face is puffy. "Who let you in here?"

"Sean did," Cy says.

"Why?" She stands up with a face painted in defiance. Strength. It's an expression I've ever only recognized in Marka. The one that says she would stand against an army to protect what she loved best.

"I think Sean wants us to help," I explain.

"Does Julian know you're here?" she asks warily.

"No. We can't let him find out either. We only have a few minutes." The room is a stew of different scents I don't recognize. Bitter, salty mixes, and even floral. If only

Marka were her to teach me her abilities to smell diseases. "Why are they sick?"

Renata's lip trembles. "I don't know. I keep asking Julian to import medicines to help, but he won't." Cy and I exchange looks. "Sean keeps begging him to relent, but he hasn't budged."

"Why?" Cy asks as he starts scrolling through the lab tests on Victoria's holo.

"He's afraid that if the officials in Inky find out they're sick, they'll shut us down. Maybe kill us. He doesn't want them to think we have diseases. Julian's afraid the illnesses are caused by their traits. That somehow Dr. Benten . . ." Here she stares at me, venom in her eyes. "That your father programmed my children to die."

"No," I say. "He wouldn't do that!"

"How do you know?" she retorts, which silences me at first.

"How do you know he wasn't preventing these illnesses when he was alive? My dad was killed because he tried to hide children from SunAj and people like Julian, who were doing the same thing—using kids as products."

"Julian is trying to shelter more traited children. He wants to protect them."

"Because he wants more money, to keep Avida safe."

Renata's angry face settles into stony resignation. "Perhaps."

"Tell us what you know," Cy says. "I'm medically trained, and so is Zel. We'll try to help." Renata stares uncertainly between us before glancing at Victoria, who's counting her bruises now. She sighs in resignation.

"Victoria is five. She only started growing ill a week ago. She gets headaches and her bone marrow's been failing. Anemia, low white cells, everything." She leans over to give Victoria a kiss on the cheek and four tiny arms reach out and hug Renata.

"I'm better today," Victoria tells her. The bruises speckle her arms like purple roses, as if some silent, invisible thing has been relentlessly pummeling her. She struggles to sit up and points to a toddler girl, whose head is half bald. Clumps of blond hair litter her pillow and her skin is sallow. "That's Bianca. She can kolo—lokoko—"

"Echolocate," Renata corrects her. "You see what's happened to her hair. She can't keep food down—terrible nausea. Anemia too. Some of it's similar to what Victoria has, but some symptoms are different."

"And who's this?" Cy stands by the bed of an older boy, maybe eleven. Cy's face spreads with a gorgeous smile as his and the boy's eyes meet, and my heart liquefies like oozing butter. I miss those rare smiles so much.

"I'm Andy," he says in a whisper. He's wearing huge round suction-cup-like things around his ears. His eyes are yellow from jaundice, and his mouth is covered in sores.

"What are those for?" I try to smile as I point to his ear cups.

"Oh. I have hyperacute hearing. Without these, a whisper sounds like a scream."

"Wow, cool." I grin at him, and he grins, though the action appears to hurt him. I try not to flinch when I notice his gums are oozing blood.

"Can I run some tests on them?" Cy asks, turning to Renata.

"You can try, but Julian hasn't let me order the testing equipment I want. He's so paranoid we'll be discovered. We have an old CompuDoc program running, but it's very basic."

Cy spends a few minutes at each bedside, poring over the labs and carefully examining each kid. Renata is smoothing strands of hair from Victoria's face. I wonder if she loves her children more because they came from her body. I wonder about my mother in Wingfield. Did Dad keep her away from me on purpose, maybe so he could have total control over my life and Dyl's? Did she want to be in my life and have no choice?

Renata catches me watching her, and I look away. "What is it?" she asks.

"I'm sorry. I was just thinking." Maybe Renata knows about my mother; maybe she doesn't. But I've nothing to lose, since I had nothing to begin with. "My father told me once that my mother left us and died when we were young. And now, I think she's alive somewhere. Maybe with the people who took down Aureus."

"You came from Carus House, didn't you?"

"Yes."

"I thought there was a woman there in charge of the children . . ."

"Marka." I can't help but smile when I say her name.

"Yes, that's the name. Did you ask her?"

"No."

"Well, maybe you'll find the answers you're looking for. Maybe not. Maybe it will change you; maybe it won't."

Her answer is so noncommittal, I shake my head. It was stupid to bring it up with a stranger. But then Renata goes on. "You like science, don't you? It's kind of like cooking. When you add another ingredient to the mix, it changes the nature of the whole dish. Let me give you a word of advice, Zelia. You're not a casserole, or a beaker of chemicals. You can decide how things will affect you, if you have the strength for it."

Cy interrupts us. "We should go soon. I wrote down some treatments that hopefully Avida has. Not cures, but they might make them feel better at least."

"Thank you, Cyrad," Renata says with gratitude.

"We'll have to convince Sean to get us access to these rooms again," I say. I don't mention that I'd actually like to talk to Renata again. She's not Marka, but there's an earthy wisdom in her words that reminds me of her. I miss it.

"We'll be back," Cy assures Renata. She walks us to the transport door, turns to me and grimaces. Not really at me, but at the *idea* of me. "So Julian has his pretty little icon now. Now that you're here, I'll be in the outgoing garbage. You're the poster child for all these traited children now."

I gather my breath to argue, but all I can manage to say is, "I am not an *icon*." I wave my bracelet on the scanner and the transport doors open.

We step in and Renata says, "I have no power here in Avida. I'm as good as dead. And your father's no longer here to help us. So what are you going to do, Zelia?"

The doors thankfully shut before I can answer. Which is good, because I have no idea what to say.

AT DINNER THAT NIGHT, I TRY NOT to think of Renata's questions. She's not my responsibility, and neither is Avida, but when the small kids arrive in taffeta dresses and seersucker suits, I anxiously count them, hoping that no more have been relegated to the infirmary.

Cy sees me arrive and makes sure I sit beside him. He's so handsome in his slim black suit. I'm dressed in the bot's latest pick, translucent gown with sparkling gold embroidery that doesn't conceal my gray satin underwear. Cy leans over during our soup course.

"You look really pretty."

"I feel like all I'm wearing is my underwear," I whisper back.

"Works for me."

I try to conceal my goofy grin before slurping up more soup. Élodie is at the opposite end of the table, trying to teach her mini-Blink, Jensen, some words in French.

"You never told me that you could speak French," I say, nudging Cy.

"My mother was French Canadian, like Élodie."

"You never told me about your parents either." I realize that my statements all sound like accusations. I erase the pout from my mouth.

"We ran out of time," he whispers back. "But you've got more than a lifetime to make up for it, don't you?" Cy reaches under the table and squeezes my wrist. I flip my arm, and his fingers find my pulse. It's an automatic gesture for him given his medical skills, but it's far more intimate than a doctor's sterile touch. It's like he's letting my heart lean on him, by proxy. "We have a lot of catching up to do. And I intend to take back every minute I lost."

"Will this be before or after we incapacitate Julian?" I whisper.

"Shh."

Julian stands up at the front of the table, while Renata sits like a lump next to him. "As you know, several of us shall be traveling to the capital tomorrow. For those accompanying me, you must memorize the names and backgrounds of the senators in attendance. Sanctioned speaking points are listed, as well as taboo topics you will not discuss under any circumstances. Your grooming bots will start working on you at five a.m. Curfew is early tonight so you get enough sleep." He leans forward on the table and frowns deeply. "I can medicate you into good behavior, but what I'd prefer is authenticity. So please. Be good." He turns his holo on and flicks to a red screen. "The following will be accompanying me. Caliga Jakobsen. Micah Kw."

I turn to see Caliga slouch into her satellite table chair, and Micah, seated next to Renata, sags imperceptibly.

"Liu Xiulan."

Everyone turns to Xiulan. She pouts and her peach skin pulsates into a shade of azure.

"Zelia Benten. Cyrad William." Cy and I glance at each other, and his fingers on my pulse detect my heart fluttering with nervousness.

Renata watches Julian expectantly, but when he shuts off his holo and sits down, she catches my eye. Her head tilts as if to say, *"See Zelia? I told you. Out with the old, in with the new."*

Dinner resumes and eventually Cy releases my wrist so we can eat the carrot soufflé and lobster bisque.

"So I've been thinking," Cy whispers. "We'll need to get a functional scan of Sean and Julian's brain, to see how we can, uh . . ." He lowers his voice to the lowest decibel possible. "You know. Put him out."

"I know," I whisper back. "But how will we target his neurons? They're bioidentical."

We eat in silence for almost ten minutes. I'm seriously wishing that I could hear Cy's thoughts. Or feel his touch without anyone knowing. He hasn't used his extra Ana-like traits, except for the accident in the transport earlier. It makes me wonder what his brain would look like, lit up on a functional brain scan, when I almost choke on my food.

"Are you okay?" Cy says, patting my back.

"Tag him," I whisper, between coughs.

"What?"

I reach for the water pitcher and lean in close to Cy, filling his conveniently empty glass. "What if we map out what neurons are Julian-specific, and target them with 3-D ionizing radiation when he's asleep?" I whisper. "The beams turn on a heat-shock protein, HSP-71. That's the tag, and it'll last for a full day. Then we give him an HSP-targeted sedative and bam. Done." I put the pitcher down and lean back into my chair, smiling blandly into my soufflé.

"Holy . . . That was sexy as hell, Zelia. Damn, I've missed your brain."

My face flushes a hundred degrees and Cy coughs into his napkin. "Next chance I have, I'll see if we can cook up a portable ionizer in the lab."

Julian and Renata have stood up and the littlest kids run to Renata for a quick hug, before the older kids take them to bed.

"Those of you coming with me tomorrow have a curfew in ten minutes. Mind the time. I'd rather not have to hide your wounds if I don't have to."

Tennie blurts out, "Julian? How is Victoria? And the other two?"

Julian smiles silkily. "They're fine. Working on it."

"But—"

"They're fine!" Julian barks at him, and the entire table cringes. So much for caring. "Didn't I just say something about a curfew? Or is everyone going deaf?"

Caliga, Xiulan, Micah, Cy, and I quickly stand up and head for the transport. Blink follows. Xiulan's skin keeps flashing spots of gray, then orange.

"Have you been to one of these before?" I ask Xiulan.

"Yes." She shivers. "Hate them."

"What's so bad?"

"Ha. You'll see," she warns, before shifting to putty gray

and receding into the corner of the transport. She blends right into the walls.

That doesn't bode well. When we get to Cy's floor, I'm surprised to see that my bracelet and Blink's give us access here too, instead of buzzing a warning burn into our wrists. Xiulan goes straight to her room beyond the rose garden and I hear her cuss loudly at her bots before the door shuts. Something about not being a show dog.

Blink and I walk Cy to his door. Our bracelets give us a warning: five minutes to curfew.

"You know, I was thinking." I look to Élodie, hoping she'll support me on this. "It would be so much easier if you could talk to me. To us, in our heads. The way you did in the Deadlands. We could plan better that way."

"No." Cy's response is so flat and hard, I flinch.

"Why not?"

"It's too risky and it's too dangerous."

I shake my head. "But you touched me in the transport today. You didn't hurt me."

"*Non, mais je me sentais trop,*" Élodie tells him.

"Élodie, can you speak English please?"

She turns to me. "It is not controlled. He could spill secrets to everyone, including Julian, if he's not careful. It was a mistake."

"It's not a mistake!" I almost shout. Blink and Cy stare at me like I'm crazy. I lower my voice to sane levels. "Cy. Why don't you practice so you can use it the way Ana does?"

"No."

Blink nods in agreement, her hand on Cy's back in re-assurance. I don't know why, but her touching him drives me into berserk territory. Even though I know they're just friends.

"Cy. You always said our traits were good things. Why are you holding yours back?"

"Because I can't control it!" He hurls the words and they strike out, each one an attack on me, and only me.

"Goddammit, Cy! Then practice!"

"Why, so I can kill you next time? So I can broadcast how I feel to *them*?" He points a shaking finger beyond the garden to the unseen Renata and Julian. "So they know exactly how best to hurt us both?"

He spins around and opens his door, letting it shut behind him without another word. My bracelet buzzes a warning again.

One minute to curfew

"Fine!" I growl at my bracelet. The holo message dis-appears, for now. I stomp over to the transport in a huff, when Élodie catches up to me.

"Zelia. Please. If you love him, then don't do this. Don't make him hurt people."

I turn around slowly, so she can hear every single word out of my mouth.

"I do love him," I say fiercely. "That's why I will never stop trying."

CHAPTER 18

CY IS LETTING HIS TRAIT CONTROL HIM instead of the other way around. My frustration won't let me fall asleep, so instead I activate my bracelet to study the names and faces of the politicians we're meeting tomorrow.

Four men. All members of Inky's State senate. They're chairs of committees whose names make me bristle. Economic Development. Population. Aging. Health and Welfare. They sound like subcommittees of Aureus itself.

Politics bore the living daylights out of me, and I can't keep anything straight. I end up falling asleep with the holo shining above my face, dreaming of things I actually care about. Like sparkling laboratories, my family, and genetic codes embedded in circles of gold.

MORNING ARRIVES TOO SOON. THE BOTS POUNCE on me at precisely five in the morning, herding me into the shower. Afterward, I spy the little chip of dried skin that fell off of Ryba on our first day here that I'd left by the sink.

It's still translucent, like a slice of alabaster. I plunge it under cold water and it immediately turns into a jelly-like flap. I lay it on my inner forearm and it sucks right against my skin.

"Well, that's something you don't see every day," I murmur. I try to shake it off to no avail, so I shrug and leave it on.

After the bots twist my hair into a chignon and apply makeup (they pick a ruby-red lipstick that exactly matches my bracelet), I open the closet to find a pair of black patent high heels, a black pencil skirt, low-cut white blouse, and formfitting blazer.

I put it all on quickly, happy that it's not a bikini or something similarly outrageous. I clasp my necklace around my neck, tucking it beneath my blouse.

My bracelet tells me to head to the exit on level one, past the water oasis where we first entered days ago. Julian waits by the enormous doors, impeccably polished in a black suit that perfectly matches mine. Cy's wearing a similar suit but in charcoal gray, like Micah's.

"Where's Xiulan and Caliga?" I ask, when Micah points behind us.

Caliga walks over in a low-cut, gold sequined gown that barely covers her chest. It conceals her leg wound perfectly, and her hair's been ironed into a sheet of snowy white that cascades over her shoulder. But she's not the one we're staring at.

It's Xiulan. And she's completely nude.

Or at least, I think she is. Her skin's flashing a million different spots and splotches and solid colors, changing almost with each footstep. Her hair is in a sleek black top-knot, and I can't read her expression at all, though I can guess what's she's feeling. It's obvious now why she was dreading this trip. Cy and Micah decently look away, but Julian smiles broadly as he offers her his hand.

"Beautiful. You are otherworldly, my dear." He grabs her chin and stares her down. "You'll do just fine. But no tears this time, do you understand?" He releases her chin and Xiulan hangs her head. Julian doesn't notice, or doesn't care.

Renata hands out cloaks. Red for the men, and gray for the women. Xiulan hurries to put hers on. Julian walks ahead.

"A little advice?" Renata offers as I take my cloak.

"Sure."

"Play the game, Zelia. But make sure you're on the right team."

I raise an eyebrow, but there's no time to ask more. We pass the silver scanning chamber to a waiting magpod in the garage. After an uncomfortably silent ride, we reach the magtrain station.

It's not the same one we arrived in when we entered Inky. This one is far grander, with multiple tiers inside the atrium. Purple-cloaked guards usher us quietly and discreetly to a single black bullet of a train. There are three compartments. Caliga gets her own. Cy and Xiulan are put into the next one, and Julian insists that he and Micah accompany me in the first car.

"This is different," I say, noticing the full bar with different-colored drinks and a multi-tiered efferent that's already been serviced to provide a table full of food. I can't bear to touch a single bite. I take a seat on a corner chair and Micah stands against the wall, his hands deep in his pockets.

"It's the fastest magtrain in the country," Julian boasts as the train begins to accelerate. There is a single, narrow window on each side. The egg-shaped buildings of Coventry speed by in a blur. "We'll be in Indianapolis in five minutes." He downs an emerald-green cocktail. "So Zelia. Did you read your information about the senators?"

"I did." I neglect to tell him that I can't remember a single name or what committee they're on. A contact lens holo would be super-handy right now.

"Excellent. We have two tasks today. You may have heard about how Aureus's products are being stripped off the shelves already?"

"Yes."

"Well, Avida controls the factory in Inky that produces about a third of those products. There's another factory in the Carolinas, and one in Utaz. Since Aureus fell, we no longer share the profits with them, but now with the product recalls, our lifeline is at stake."

Micah withdraws one hand to rub his injured wrist. He looks up to listen, but stays quiet. I can almost imagine the invisible leash Julian has on him.

"What can I possibly do about that?" I ask simply.

"They all know the details of Senator Milford's death. They know it was your DNA that killed him. You're here to prove that you had nothing to do with his death, and that they have nothing to fear. And most importantly, that you possess what they covet—a young body that will never grow old."

"Covet," I repeat, but the word feels unclean when I say it.

"Yes. If they see you as a commodity, it will be insurance for the safety of Avida. For all those children your father made."

Julian's now standing right before me. He holds out his hand and I'm loath to touch him, but I take it anyway. Play the game, as Renata advised. He stands me up and spins me around, his eyes traveling over the curves of my body. I force down the nausea rising in my throat. Even Caliga never made me this brand of sick.

"Ah, you are lovely, Zelia. Listen and learn from me. Politics all boils down to manipulating three of the simplest human emotions—greed, sympathy, and fear. We're going to use them today. Like weapons."

"You make it sound like we're going to war, Julian."

"You were born in a world that says you don't have a right to exist," Julian tells me as the train begins to slow down. "You've been at war since you took your first, imperfect breath."

I reach for my pendant automatically, and the motion isn't missed by Julian. Out the narrow window, there are more egg-shaped buildings, far more than in Coventry, and some are enormous. Glassy connecting bridges span the structures in interconnecting lattices. The effect resembles a spun-sugar web over the whole city.

When the doors open, Julian leaves first and Micah waits for me. When I'm close enough, Micah whispers, "Don't drop this." He slips something into my hand. It's cold and angled. I turn just a little bit away from Julian to see Ana's glass unicorn in my hand.

I'm speechless. Not a single, irregular edge has been chipped. The tapering horn is still perfectly twisted. Flashes of Ana sitting on her hoverstool in the lab and crafting her glass trinkets flit through my brain.

"Where did you get this, Micah?"

"It was confiscated from your bag of belongings. I found it in the trash." I try to imagine Micah digging through the garbage of Avida, especially with that injured wrist.

"Thank you." I keep it in my hand. My suit is too fitted to put it in a pocket without accidentally breaking it.

Micah smiles just a touch. "C'mon. We shouldn't fall behind."

I'm not used to walking in heels, so I'm pathologically slow compared to everyone else. Cy and Xiulan are lagging behind us, because he's helping to adjust her cloak, which is too long. Caliga notices me walking like I've got rubber for ankles and makes a beeline for me. Which is surprising, because the last time we talked, I was telling her off at the top of my lungs.

"Looks like for once, you need my arm," she says, offering. I hesitate, but take it since my center of balance is so screwy.

"I'm no good with height. I'm perfectly happy being

vertically challenged," I tell her. Caliga snorts. She's at least five inches taller than I am. "So. How's that leg?"

"Really good. Cy's been checking it every day. There's a huge scar, but it's already fading with his serum. Avida had a supply here."

We leave the platform, and the main station opens up. It looks like a huge beehive from the inside—all silver beams and glass windows, with different magtrain platforms entering like bicycle spokes all over the hive. Another purple-cloaked guard leads us outside, where a luxurious, candy-apple-red magpod awaits.

Within minutes we're at our destination. Inside a black egg building, we're led to a tiny room. No fewer than five guards are stationed outside the door. Their neural guns are prominently held at chest level as we walk in. As soon as the doors close, Julian peels off his cloak.

"Ah, that is much better. You're all welcome to disrobe," he says. We all take off our cloaks, except for Xiulan, who tightens the fabric around herself. She's kept her skin color close to normal since we got off the magtrain. "Xiulan, you can wait until the senators are here. It will certainly be far more dramatic to unveil then, won't it?"

Xiulan presses her lips together. Fury washes over her face and she squeezes her hands together so tightly that her thumbs send rings of violet across her flesh.

Barbaric. Julian's basically brought her to be eye-candy for them. Well, maybe it won't be that bad. Maybe—

The doors swish open. Four men cloaked in bright red

enter. Two look well over sixty, with gray hair, but the other two are much younger. Middle-aged, with dark brown hair coiffed in that flawless style that senators always have. They must all own the same brand of grooming bot. They immediately start shaking hands with Julian, their eyes glancing over to our group. When they see Caliga standing apart from the others in her molten gold gown, their mouths open like fish.

"Gentlemen. May I introduce Zelia Benten. Cyrad William. Micah Kw. Liu Xiulan."

One by one, we take turns shaking their hands. Each one seems apprehensive to be close to us, especially Xiulan. Her face is flashing bright pinks and purples.

"And Caliga Jakobsen. But with our lovely Caliga, you may look but not touch."

"Indeed!" the oldest senator notes. The other three gawk unabashedly. "Well, we have a lot to discuss, don't we? Let's all have a seat."

One by one, Julian asks us to explain our traits. Micah is asked to do a brief demonstration of his electrical trait. They laugh good-naturedly when he surprises them with a buzzing tingle on the hand.

"Imagine having a concealed weapon at all times. Micah has already installed his own version into our bracelets," Julian boasts.

"Excellent!" Two of the men clap, but two don't. The least excited one leans forward.

"What can stop him?"

"I'm not invincible," Micah explains. "It works poorly

in high humidity climates. And it works on me as well. There's always a way to take us down." He smiles charmingly, but the senators don't seem to notice the deadened look in his eyes. When they turn their attention to Cy, Micah holds his breath and looks for affirmation that he didn't screw anything up. Julian gives him a little nod, and he exhales silently with relief. The senators are remarking on Cy's already well-known healing serums.

"How about a demonstration?" Julian offers brightly.

"No!" The word blurts out of my mouth before I can stop myself. Cy shakes his head at me and turns to the men.

"It would be my pleasure." There's a buffet with food and drinks in the corner. Cy picks up a carving knife next to a small roast beef and brings it over. He rolls up a sleeve and hands the knife to one of the older senators. "You may do the cut, to see that there are no magic tricks."

I'm puzzled by how okay Cy is with all of this. The senator grips the knife, tests the edge for sharpness with his thumb, then draws it across Cy's muscled forearm.

At first it seems like he didn't cut anything. Seconds later, a crimson line appears. I fight the urge to rush to his side and mop up the blood. Cy's squeezing his wrist, but his face is strangely Zen. In fact, he's calmer and more focused than I've seen in a while. Cy wipes the blood off with a wet napkin and shows the already healing wound to the senators.

"Excellent. Now tell us about this young lady in the gold."

"Caliga? Brand-new to Avida. She produces an anesthetic effect several feet around her. When I said look but do not touch, I meant it. But it is possible to be immune to her effects."

"Is that so?"

Julian stands and reaches for my hand. "Zelia, dear. Show them."

I stand up and take a few mincing steps in my heels. I sit next to Caliga. Her hand is right next to mine. She's trembling.

One by one, the senators feel her bubble of numbness with cautiously extended hands, before stepping back. "Fascinating," one says. "So it would be possible for a man to have a wife whom no one could touch but him. A key to his own property!"

Caliga bares her teeth at this, and I inconspicuously grab her hand to calm her down. Julian is laughing with the men. There are hands clapping his back, congratulating him on his newest acquisition, when Caliga's hand squeezes mine back.

"No, no," she mutters. "He can't. I'll never let him touch me."

I don't know what to say. He's already started working on a vaccine. It's only a matter of time before Caliga's cage—or defense, depending on how you see it—is open to him.

"And Xiulan. Our lovely peacock. Limitless applications for espionage, warfare . . . entertainment. I believe a different group of senators saw her charms at our last visit, but she was asked to return, just for you. Show them, Xiulan."

Xiulan is still tightly wrapped within her cloak. She doesn't budge, only tightens her crossed arms. Julian goes pink in the face with slow-rising rage.

"Xiulan. Our senators are waiting for their demonstration."

"I will not," Xiulan says with a quiet, firm tone. She might as well have screamed it, because it has the same effect. Her face is pulsating in deep pinks and oranges as Julian stands and towers over her, slowly lifting his hand. I let go of Caliga's hand to squeeze mine into a fist. In my other palm, Ana's glass unicorn is still hidden, cradled carefully.

Exquisite and unique. So breakable.

So worth saving.

I stand up abruptly. "Color and flashing lights. Is that what this is all about?" Every head swivels away from Xiulan to stare at me. "She's just smoke and mirrors. Let's be honest. It's not what you're really interested in, or what you came here to discuss." I step forward, praying that no one notices the slight warble in my voice.

"Maybe I ought to introduce myself again." I put my hands on my hips. "I'm Zelia Benten. And I can make you immortal."

CHAPTER 19

THE ROOM IS SILENT. EVEN JULIAN, which means I've either done something very good or very stupid.

"Really?" The oldest senator pivots in his seat and focuses on me with his green, slightly metallic eyes. Holo implanted. "Last I heard, your DNA killed Senator Milford. Don't see how that amounts to anything but trouble."

"Someone very eager to make a statement used an old prototype," I explain in my best bored voice. "That formula was slated for more aggressive purposes."

Julian finally gathers himself and comes to stand by my side. "Zelia is living proof of the longevity gene at work."

One of the younger senators points at me. "Are you saying that you could truly bottle your trait? Keep a person alive far beyond our life expectancy?"

The four men watch me carefully. They're trying to stay professional, unemotional. But there's a shiny, dark thing behind their eyes. Greed. And fear of death. That's when I realize the brilliance of Julian's words.

Greed, sympathy, and fear . . . use them . . . like weapons.

Julian walks around the senators, like a cat circling its prey. Oh, he's in his element, loving this. He puts his hands on two senators' shoulders and leans between their heads. One of Endall's beautiful watches gleams on this wrist. He sees me looking at the timepiece and winks at me. "Let me ask you, gentlemen. What's the one thing no one ever has enough of?"

The senators look inwardly as their focus blurs. I can imagine what their thoughts are. Money. Sex. Power. I sit down in front of them and cross my legs. Ready to deliver the final blow to make or break our meeting.

"Youth. Stamina. Beauty." I tick them off on my fingertips, then thread my hands together and smile. "Those are nice things. Small things. We're offering what you truly can never buy—that which is utterly priceless." I lean closer. "Time."

The senators sit back and consider this. Julian's eyes twinkle at me with approval. Micah and Cy watch us carefully and Xiulan's face has blended in with the couch beneath her. But there's a tiny camouflaged smile of relief on her face.

"What good is immortality if you can still be killed from an injury?" the younger senator asks.

At this, Cy stands up and plants himself by my side. "That's where I come in. You've already seen my regenerative serums."

The youngest senator claps his hands together. "Long life, and an invincible body! What I wouldn't do to see a child born of you two. It'd be a god, wouldn't it?"

Cy and I look at each other, startled. Kids? Us? Not that it's possible, since neither of us can procreate. But I never considered it. You'd think I'd be excited about the thought, but instead, it sends a chill into my heart. Humans weren't meant to be gods. We're too greedy, too afraid, and too emotional. Maybe we weren't meant to play god with genes either, but it's far too late for those kinds of regrets.

The senators are practically salivating at the thought. They start talking among themselves. I hear one of them say, "We could change history with this. At the right price on the black market, the profit could be beyond anything we've considered."

"Indeed, gentlemen," Julian replies. "The black market has posed quite a demand already."

Everyone in the room relaxes. One of the senators chats with Cy and Micah, while another pats Xiulan on her covered shoulder and she shows him her hand camouflage trick on a bowl of fruit. He smiles, then sits a safe distance away from where I'm sitting next to Caliga.

"So, young lady. Do you really think you can make this elixir of life?"

"I do," I say with a confidence that I don't actually have. His eyes light up and I can almost see the dollar signs in them. "Senator. We owe you our gratitude for protecting us."

For the rest of the hour, we mill around as Julian begins to outline a plan for exporting our goods and creating new products. I eavesdrop on the latter subject. Julian talks about surreptitiously welcoming undiscovered traited kids to Inky and funneling them to Avida.

The eldest senator sips his martini slowly. "It would be so nice if we could expand the market. I haven't seen a new product since that boy's serums came out," he says, pointing his olive-speared toothpick at Cy.

The brown-haired politician next to him shakes his head. "Too bad they only have one trait. Can't you just make some more? We are in Inky, after all. Shame if no more children could be produced. If you need pro-conception hormone treatments, we can certainly supply them by the bucketload."

"Ah. That's a work in progress." Julian's got a sheen of sweat on his forehead. Without an ability to unlock Dad's suicide seed terminator technology, there can be no more babies. "But we appreciate the offer."

"Well, can't you just . . . make mutations?" The youngest senator looks around the room and motions to me. "You. Come here." I walk over in my heels, which are now rubbing two spectacular blisters on my heels. It's an effort to not grimace. "Can you make a mutation?"

I fudge my answer. "It's complicated. And boring science-talk, to be honest," I say, smiling. I pray he'll drop the subject.

"Surely you could make it happen. There's a variety of dangerous chemicals out there." He snaps his fingers at Cy, who's crossing the room. "You! Name me some chemicals."

"Excuse me?"

"Chemicals! Ones that cause mutations."

Cy looks taken aback. "Uh, phosgene, I suppose. Ethylene oxide?" He shrugs his shoulders and walks by, pretending to be interested in a horrible abstract painting of an egg, of all things. Cy's losing his patience for these guys, as am I.

"There you go!" the senator says, ordering another martini from the bartending bot in the corner. "Can't you just see if they work?"

"On regular people?" I say, incredulous. "That would be like using a shovel to do surgery." I think I'm being clever, when I see Julian frowning deeply at me. Uh-oh. My playfulness strayed into disrespectful territory. I try to backtrack and apologize, but the senator gets up to leave with the others.

"Well, that's our cue. We'll leave the lab tinkering to you, Julian. We expect a report in two weeks."

We put our cloaks on to leave. When we enter the magtrain, Julian has Cy stay in our compartment. Julian is positively glowing when he brings us sapphire drinks in tiny glasses.

"A toast. To our jewel, Zelia. I had no idea you had it in you. Your father really hid your talents well, didn't he?" He grins broadly. When Julian raises his glass, Cy and I don't. He's halfway through his drink when he sees we haven't taken a single sip. "Don't you want to celebrate?"

"But the negotiations aren't done yet." I put my glass down and exchange nods with Cy.

"What negotiations?"

"We made a lot of promises today. We've done our part. Now it's your turn," Cy explains.

"What makes you think I need to negotiate with you?" he says, with an expression of surprise. As if we were three-year-olds demanding a billion dollars.

"Because of fear. Avida will be destroyed if you don't deliver what we've just promised the senators. And greed, because it will give you more power in Inky than you've ever had."

"What happened to sympathy?" He almost sneers at me.

"Sympathy is for children. They're for the masses, aren't they? Not for people like us."

He touches his red bracelet, considering this. We both watch his movements, and Cy says, "Of course, you could just torture us into doing what you want, but that would be the messy, slow way."

"Very true. So what is your request?"

"Zelia needs full access to the labs," Cy starts.

"Oh, that. Consider it done. But I expect progress reports."

"Of course," I agree, smiling. "We need our schedules relaxed and my door access throughout Avida relaxed as well. I work best when I'm on my own clock. Cy is going to help me work out the kinks."

Julian puts his empty glass down and laughs out loud. "You don't fool me for a minute, but very well. I'll grant you access."

"And one last thing. About the children in the locked infirmary," I begin.

Julian hoots. "I thought you said that sympathy was for the masses! Who told you, Renata?"

"We found out ourselves," I say quickly. I don't want Renata to get into more trouble than she already has. "Why are they sick? I have a stake in Avida now. I need to know what's going on, in case it affects my research," I say, walking up to him.

"That is not your business," he says.

"It's all my business, Julian!" I say firmly. He blinks hard at me, as if seeing me for the first time. "You've made it my business by bringing me here today. I need to *know*."

The train comes to a stop and the doors begin to open. As we exit to head for the magpod, he waves Cy ahead and pulls me back so we can walk alone.

"I don't want people to panic," he tells me in a low voice. "But it's complicated."

"I can handle complicated," I said. "Why are they sick, Julian?"

He inhales a huge breath, holding it for far too long before he lets it out. "They're dying, Zelia."

"Why?"

"Maybe you should have asked your father when you had the chance."

"Because he could have helped them?"

"Or not. Did it occur to you that some of Benten's creations had a kill switch built into them?"

"That makes zero sense. Why create something that's destined to die too early?"

Julian stops walking and stands close to me. Too close.

His hand reaches out to grasp my black box pendant between his fingers. "Why do you have your Ondine's curse? Why would your father make you, knowing you were so . . . breakable?"

"It was a mistake," I explain, pulling back until my pendant pops out of his fingers and nestles back against my throat. "The PHOX2B gene damage was an accident. My chromosomes had to lose some DNA to be made into those loops."

"Are you so sure, Zelia, that your father ever made mistakes?"

He waves me inside the magpod and gets into a different compartment. Only after the doors shut do I realize— Julian didn't answer my question. He just created a hell of a lot more.

THAT AFTERNOON, CY AND I TOUR THE labs after a dizzying ride through the transport. The rooms in every direction around us are visible through the plasticleer walls. The machines lining the walls are pristine, made of shiny composites that don't age or break.

It's the most beautiful lab I've ever seen. I might as well have micropore filters stuffed into my mouth, because I'm speechless. Cy is less impressed.

Bots float about doing their work. They're headless and legless, but one in particular bobs forward as if expecting us. Like the other lab bots, he's headless, but there's a half spoon, half fork sticking comically out of his torso. Some Avida child has scrawled the crooked letters *SPORK* on his torso.

"Welcome. I will assist the supreme in this lab. Happy to come orientate with me."

"Uh. Okay."

"Happy to come orientate with me."

He starts to lead us to a new room, when I ask, "Um, Spork? Why are you talking so weirdly?"

"The children alter my language chips. Pig Latin last week. This week, blessed normal!"

It's so not normal, but I don't have the energy to tell Spork the truth. We follow him around as he points out the different rooms, the sequence analyzers, replicators, and chemical storerooms.

"What's this?" Cy asks. There's a wall of holo boards in one room, and at the bottom, we recognize one name.

Jakobsen, C.

"The protocol for shiny Jakobsen C vaccine," Spork says emotionlessly.

"Is it correct?" Cy asks me.

My eyes scan the information. "It looks pretty correct. I wonder if they're done making it."

"Not possible. If Julian could have showed off his ability to touch Caliga today, you know he would have already."

"How many people can you treat with this vaccine?" I point to Caliga's protocol.

Spork answers, "Lonely single human dose."

"Why so few?" I say, starting to get used to Spork's odd way of speaking.

"Only uno requested," he responds.

One dose. What a sicko. He doesn't want anyone else to have Caliga, and meanwhile he can still use her as a weapon.

"Onward! Tissue bank arrives on our marvelous agenda." Spork whizzes to another room.

Long white storage tables line both sides, and a holo screen shows names listed on a central square.

"Please to squeeze one," Spork tells me. I touch Cela's name, and immediately a row of choices light up next to her name. Saliva. Urine. Hair. Plasma. Whole blood. Skin. Ova.

I touch the square labeled SKIN and the table hums. A clear window slides open on the surface to reveal several boxy containers filled with flakes of skin, like slices of opalescent glass.

"Oh, I just remembered." I lift up my sleeve and show Cy the blob of gelled skin that I attached there early this morning. "It's Ryba's. It rehydrated in a snap and stuck on like glue."

"Like this?" Cy pulls up his sleeve and he's got a blob attached too. "Great minds think alike." He gifts me with one of his rare smiles, and my heart flutters like he's just kissed me. "Cela's and Ryba's skin must pull oxygen directly out of the water to their tissues."

I turn to Spork, getting tired of the tour. "Listen. Julian says he's working on finding the key to the terminator technology in our genes. The thing that makes us all suicide seeds. Do you know how far the research has gone?"

Spork hovers by the holo screen. A few lights flicker on his torso, beneath the scrawled *SPORK*. "Benten Z juicy extracts have not resulted in viable embryos."

Phew. Well, that's what I assumed.

"Uh, Spork. You're going to assist us, right?" Cy says, clearing his throat.

"Amen," he bleeps at us.

I try not to choke on a laugh. "Um, we need neural maps of the members of Avida. To test my elixir on, for brain function purposes," I add hastily.

Cy adds, "Oh, and an ionizing gun. A big one. To denature some DNA."

"Will start now, perky immediately." Spork spins around and retreats to work on our commands.

Perky indeed.

I hope that Julian isn't well versed in lab techniques, because everything we just said is molecular hooey.

CHAPTER 20

DINNER IS INSUFFERABLE. FORGET MY LONGEVITY GENE; my life may be cut short by the tight, unforgiving gowns every night. The only thing that buoys my mood is my new, full access all over Avida.

Which means, for the first time in a year, I can spend the night with Cy again.

At dinner, he's much quieter than usual and we're separated by Élodie, who asks for updates on all the day's activities. After dessert, Cy leaves with Élodie so abruptly that the transport door closes before I catch up with them.

"In a hurry?" Micah says from behind me.

I try to extinguish my disappointment before I face him. "Not really."

"I heard that you and Cy are . . . working on something." He pauses for a long time, but I don't give him an inch.

"I'm tired, Micah. It's been a long day."

"If you try to leave, you have to take me with you."

I give him the rudest stare. "I don't owe you anything."

"I know. You have no reason to believe me, to trust me. Nothing. But I have to get away from Sean and Julian." He rubs his still-raw wrist. The bracelet is so tight that the skin beneath hasn't yet healed, and along the edges are red skin and scars in different stages of healing.

Cy's floor comes up and we both exit, but I plant my feet. I can't seem to leave Micah behind. I feel sorry for him, though my anger still simmers beneath it all.

"What are you proposing?" I ask him, arms crossed.

"I know you and Cy have ideas. I do too. And I know Avida much better than you do. I can tell you what won't work, what's already been tried. And I know Sean and Julian better too. You're playing Julian really well, but it won't last much longer."

This may be a huge mistake, but . . . "I'll talk to Cy about it," I tell him.

Micah closes his eyes, exhaling. "Thanks, Zelia."

I leave Micah behind and find Cy's room, pausing outside, wondering exactly what he'll think of Micah's proposal. From behind the door, I hear a grunt, and a sigh of release. Is Élodie in there? I could walk right in, but I'm worried. Should I go in, or not?

This is Cy. Your Cy. You've risked your lives for each other. Open the freaking door.

I knock anyway.

"Élodie, I said I'd see you in the morning," he answers, irritated.

I smile with relief. He's alone after all! I wave my bracelet over the scanner embedded by the door, and it swishes neatly open.

"Cy! It's me. I tried to catch up—"

My breath catches painfully in my throat. Cy is on the bed, hunched over and stiff. Rivulets of scarlet blood snake down his forearm, the drips caught on a white towel on the floor, like poppies on snow. He starts in alarm, and a small knife bounces on the carpet. Its sharp edge is blurry with blood.

"Oh my god!" I shriek.

Cy doesn't answer me. He snatches the towel from the floor and hastily wipes off his arms. His skin smears with pink before the towel absorbs the evidence. Cy used to tattoo himself as punishment for what happened to Ana, as if he were responsible. But it didn't occur to me that his habits hadn't stopped, just taken another form. He hid this from me. Vaguely, I remember seeing faint pink lines on his skin before. How he'd rolled down his sleeves, hiding the last traces of his cutting.

"*Why?* Why are you doing this?"

"Come here," he says, and offers me a hand. I take it, letting his fingers envelop mine. Cy's other hand guides my waist so that I'm sitting on his lap. "Look at me. No, don't turn away," he commands, weaving gentleness and strength together irresistibly, something I haven't witnessed since he told me that sacrificing himself was the only way to save Dyl. "I didn't want you to worry about me."

"But I could have helped you. You should have told—"
My voice cracks and I swallow the rest of my words.

Cy sighs so deeply, I rock on his lap, almost tipping
over. He catches me and we both fall sideways onto the
bed, cradling each other. For a few minutes, we say nothing. He lets me cry. So this is what happens when you
blend horrible and wonderful together.

Finally, the tears stop. I trace the rapidly fading marks
on his arms, asking through my stuffy nose, "It hurts,
doesn't it?"

Cy says nothing, only nods into my hair. He begins to
murmur into my ear, as if no one else in the world is allowed to hear.

"When I was in Aureus, they had me working constantly. Micah and Tegg took turns disciplining me, and it
was . . . hard to keep it together. I missed you so much, I
couldn't handle it.

"Some people in Aureus seemed to be laughing at me
at times, but I had no idea why until Élodie told me I was
transmitting my thoughts to everyone—my most private
thoughts. I tried to stop, but I had no idea how. And then
once, I almost killed Tegg."

"How?"

"I don't know how. He was beating the crap out of me,
and I just . . . I wanted to push him and hit him, but I could
barely lift my arms. And then . . . he passed out. And Renn,
and Wilbert. Their bodies went white, as if their circulation
had been cut off everywhere. It was like Ana's trait, but
instead of tricking people's nerves into feeling a soft touch,

I tricked their bodies into massive vasocontriction. No blood supply to anything. Micah found us and managed to rush in to zap me. If he hadn't, they would have died."

"So that's how you found out?"

"Yes. Élodie helped me train myself, to keep my trait contained. I don't know how Ana does it, limiting her touch or words to specific people if she wants to."

"I heard her talking once when she was with you," I confess. "The same night I went to the junkyards. I could hear her too."

"When Ana was tired, everyone could hear her speak."

"So now you can contain it? After we found each other in the Deadlands, you never spoke into my head anymore. And then on the magtrain platform—"

"I'll never forgive myself. I could have seriously injured you."

"But you didn't. It was an accident!"

"An accident that will never, ever happen again. I've been suppressing it for months now. Only when I'm really emotional, or lose my focus, do I let it slip."

"So . . . it's either all on or all off?"

"Yes."

"And the cutting?" I say gently.

"It hurts so much, but it's so liberating. The pain is something that's mine, and only mine. I can control it and own it and it doesn't hurt anyone but me. And afterward . . ." He closes his eyes and peace floods his face. "I'm calm and focused, in a way I can't seem to get doing anything else. Like this megaton weight is off my body and there's nothing left but clarity. It's helped me control my trait too."

"But all you're doing is suppressing it. I could help you practice. Not squashing it down, but using your trait selectively, the way Ana does. This"—I squeeze his arm gently, where the recent cuts are now completely gone—"is not control."

"It is. I don't want to end up hurting you or someone else!"

"Then you're going to have to try harder."

Cy crumples against my squeezing hands. "I don't know how. Not without a knife in my arm."

I pull back. Because, crap. I don't know how either.

There's a knock at the door. Cy hides the bloody towel and opens the door, where Élodie stands, her mouth open at seeing us together.

"There's an hour of free time before curfew," she says. "I was checking on you."

Cy reaches for her wrist and pulls her inside. Part of me doesn't want to include her, but the better part of me says to be a grown-up. The better half I sometimes hate.

"*Qu'est-ce qui se passe?*" she asks Cy, taking off her sunglasses.

"We need you," I tell her. When Élodie gives Cy a puzzled look, he explains rapidly in French. She frowns deeply.

"I don't think that is a good idea. You could hurt someone. You could give away your thoughts. You'll give your enemies a weapon."

"Enemies? You mean the police, or Julian?" I ask.

"I mean everyone," she says. She puts her hand on Cy. "We worked so hard to keep it under control. You probably shouldn't have even used it in the Deadlands."

"But that's how I found you both!" I raise my hands up, disbelieving. "Cy has a gift and he needs to practice, so it won't hurt him or anyone else."

At this, Élodie's eyes immediately drop to Cy's forearms. The faintest pink line remains from his last cut and she sees it.

"You knew about his cutting, didn't you?" I point at him.

Élodie crosses her arms. "*Oui.* I knew it. It was my idea."

Oh, I'm going to *kill* her. I walk up to her with a barrage of cusses ready to fly, when Cy grabs my arm.

"Zel. This isn't helping me. Let's all take a few breaths, okay?"

It's the right thing to say, because my necklace isn't on and fury is pumping blood through my shallowly breathing lungs. I take several huge breaths, and the rage begins to soften.

"So what do we do?" he asks.

I wipe my hands on my tunic, as if I could rub away the distraction of Cy's last kiss and the festering jealousy I have for Blink. "We work. All night, if we have to."

"But curfew's in less than an hour. Élodie will have to leave."

I turn on my holo and ask for Julian. "Julian, I need another favor."

Cy and Élodie nearly choke when they realize what I'm doing.

"Hi Zelia," a voice answers, but it sounds limper than usual. "And it's Sean. Julian is dead asleep."

Everyone exhales in relief. "I need Élodie to have door access in Avida."

"Why?"

"We need her to work on the elixir to make Julian sleep."

There's a wretched silence for a half minute, when I'm petrified that he'll reject my request. Or worse, that Julian woke up. "Okay. I can't guarantee it every night, though. Only when Julian's asleep."

"Thank you." I shut the holo off. "Let's start."

We practice until we can barely keep our eyes open. Cy alternately tries to whisper words to me only, then to Blink. Hopefully everyone in Avida is asleep and won't notice his muffled practicing.

Blink's beautiful face is guardedly neutral. At least she's not arguing with us over how this is a terrible idea. After almost a hundred tries, we make progress. He finally manages to whisper to me, and me only, the following words:

My toe itches

When Blink shakes her head, not hearing it, I squeal in delight.

"You did it! Does your toe really itch?"

"No," he says with an exhausted but triumphant smile. "I was running out of things to say."

"I am so tired." Blink yawns like a cat.

"Me too. It's almost three in the morning. Let's go to sleep," Cy says.

Blink doesn't move, and it takes her a few seconds to realize that I'm not leaving. Cy walks her to the door, even though it's only a five-step distance. They whisper a few words beyond my range. When Cy returns, he waits for the door to shut to scoop me into his arms. I giggle at the momentary weightlessness, and he unceremoniously plops me onto the bed. His hands start running over my clothes, searching my body with insistent impatience. My skin hides no secrets, radiating heat as I pull him closer.

"Cy," I murmur, trying to nuzzle his neck.

"Whoop. Found it." Cy triumphantly holds up my necklace.

"Pickpocket!" I accuse him. "Thief!"

He rolls me over and puts the necklace around my neck, watching my chest swell and fall regularly, with a clock's precision. His eyes skip over my body. "Did you know you're taller than last year?"

"No," I admit. "Am I?"

His fingers trace over my arm, then belly and hip. "You've changed." He pushes the edge of the fabric up to expose my stomach. "Your center of gravity is here." His fingertips touch my shivering belly, between my hip bones. "Instead of here." His hands skim upward to the area below my rib cage, letting his knuckles softly brush the underside of my breasts. "I can feel it when I pick you up." He's trying to be clinical about this, but the effect is anything but clinical. It takes all my strength to not pounce on him.

"I haven't changed," I whisper between regimented breaths. "It's still me."

"We're both different." He curls my body against his. "And the same too."

We lie there on his bed, listening to our breath. I just want to keep Cy to myself like this, to not think of Avida, or Julian, or anybody for hours and hours. But I can't. Not yet.

"Cy. I ran into Micah before I came here." I tell him his proposal, how he wants to help us escape Avida. His desperation to get out. "I don't trust him."

"No, I don't trust the bastard either. But I believe he wants to get out. He's reached his ceiling of power in Avida. We've seen evidence of that already." He thinks for a few minutes and says, "I think we should let him help. But once we're outside of Avida, all alliances are off."

I nod. It's a tenuous decision, wrapped in uncertainty and Micah's past betrayals. After several minutes, Cy's breathing slows down and he falls asleep. But I can't shut my mind off. My legs get antsy. I uncurl Cy's hand from mine and head to the door. A walk in the garden alone will be just what I need to settle my brain.

The smell of the rose garden is a little too strong, so instead I head upstairs for the meadow. The flowers aren't as cloying and the holo stars and sickle moon soothe me. I take my shoes off and walk barefoot in the soft grasses, when I hear a sound of sobbing. I stop, listening. It's coming from one of the rooms surrounding the meadow. My bare feet take me from door to door until I find the room with the crying.

It's Caliga's. It's probably not my business. I'm sure she wants to be alone. But then I remember Caliga's trait.

She's always alone.

I raise my bracelet to the door and it swishes open. Caliga's on the floor by a wall, hugging her knees and rocking herself. When she sees me, she puts her head right back onto her knees. I wait for her to yell at me to leave, but the acid remark never materializes. So I sit down next to her and wait.

After a long silence, she whispers, "Julian says the vaccine against my trait will be done tomorrow." There's another silence, followed by a sob so acute, it brings tears to my eyes. "I don't want Julian to touch me. I want . . . I want it to be Wilbert. Oh god, Zelia." She starts weeping in earnest again, and my arms reflexively reach over and envelop her in a tight hug. She wraps her arms around me with a strength that takes my breath away, and I find myself crooning a quiet *shhh* and rocking her softly.

She lets me hold her until there are no more tears left and her spasming hiccups finally disappear. It must be dawn, but I don't care. Finally, I release her and she wipes her eyes clumsily.

"Tell me about Wilbert," I whisper. "Tell me how you met him."

And so she does. From the first time they'd met in Aureus as pre-teens, to the barbed insults she'd hurl at him when he wouldn't leave her alone, thinking he was mocking her. Until she finally understood that all he wanted was to listen. To give her the companionship that no one dared to offer.

"We fell in love. Even when SunAj joked that we'd never consummate the marriage, we didn't care. He was the only person who loved me. *For me.* I love him so much, Zelia, you have no idea." She shakes her head, and laughs a little. "Well, I guess you do." She wipes her eyes again. "For a long time, I hated Aureus and your dad for creating me. But it brought me to Wilbert. He's so sweet. You know, every day he'd risk getting sick just to kiss me."

"There's a joke in that statement, but I bet you've already heard it."

Caliga bursts out with a genuine laugh. "You know I have." She sobers and withdraws slightly. "SunAj didn't like me. I had to prove that I was worth keeping and so did Wilbert. He betrayed everyone at Carus to ensure that he and I would stay safe in Aureus. He lied to you all, and stole your DNA for me." She stares at me with her scarred eyes. "I am sorry, Zelia. I'm so sorry I hurt you," she says, her tears flowing fresh.

"It's all right, Caliga." I put my arm around her shoulders and squeeze. "You are a prize bitch, but I totally forgive you."

Caliga snorts and we laugh together in the darkness. We end up lying on her bed, holding hands as we sleep the last few hours before morning. Like I had in Carus, with Marka and Dyl. You'd think that Caliga was the only person benefitting from me being vaccinated. But my hand holds on to hers just as tightly.

Our holos bleep at us at eight in the morning, so we sit up, bleary eyed and puffy faced. Caliga checks her bracelet.

"I'm on infirmary duty again," she sighs. "It's always a ghost town there."

"I know, because the sick kids are locked away downstairs." I clamp my hand over my mouth.

"What? Tell me, Zel!"

I can't bear to keep the truth from her, so as she gets ready quickly, I tell her everything I know. About Micah, and the plan to get out, and the anti-Julian elixir.

"Well, if someone is going to poison him with that elixir," she says, "it might as well be me. I'll be close enough not to raise suspicion."

"No, Caliga." I shake my head. "No way!"

"Can you make it today? Please! Because if you can neutralize Julian, tonight would be the best time ever for that. Wilbert and I would owe you . . . everything."

"I promise," I say. "I'll try to make it happen." I embrace Caliga quickly and run to the door.

"Wait, where are you going?" she yells.

"I've got to make a miracle happen!" I holler back, before running to my room.

CHAPTER 21

I'M SO TIRED THAT DAY, I WEAR my necklace constantly. I take a precious few minutes to grab breakfast. I even make Cy practice his trait, by asking him to touch my cheek. It's comical to see a half-dozen people wipe the fuzzy sensation away from their cheeks, until after a few swipes, they don't.

"You're making progress!" I half whisper, half squeal. Cy doesn't smile but he's hiding a glow beneath his cheeks. He sips his black coffee and leans closer.

"I was disappointed when I woke up and you weren't in my bed."

"I was with Caliga," I explain.

"So you've already moved on, eh?"

I jab him in the ribs with my elbow. "It's not like that." I tell him about Caliga's vaccine, and how we need to try to make the anti-Julian concoction. He shakes his head, eyeing Julian from across the long roof table.

"There's no way we'll get it done in time." When I

respond with a stubborn frown, he raises his eyebrows. "Well. I never said I didn't like a challenge, right?"

"Right. Let's go."

We meet Spork in the lab. He shows us Julian and Sean's neural maps.

"I can't believe you had these," I say.

"Sean headached Julian with marvelous pain in the parietal lobe butt. Five years ago," Spork explains.

"Oh. Thank you, Spork." But before he floats away, I ask, "Hey, one question . . . do you know if the vaccine for Caliga Jakobsen is done?"

"Very yes."

My face clouds over. "Where is it?"

"It is emigrated to a closed location by Julian."

I thank Spork, then whisper to Cy, "I bet a million dollars it's hidden somewhere."

"The secret infirmary, maybe?"

"Maybe, but it'll be locked up, even if it's in there."

So we throw ourselves into working on the anti-Julian medicine. Cy and I study 3-D scans of their brain biometrics. I don't know what I'm looking at, but Cy's in his element. Neuroscience is his specialty. I can sense his mind unfolding, seeing countless things I can't.

"I used to study Ana's brain like this. She's beautiful, even the parts that don't work quite right."

"Are you still upset that you couldn't reverse her damage?" I ask. Cy nods, turning slightly away from me.

"But she's exquisite, you know," I tell him. "The way

she is. I can't imagine Ana any other way, and if she were different, I'd miss her." I put my hand on Cy's.

Cy squeezes his eyes shut. "It's hard . . ." He swallows, and tries again. "It's still . . ."

It still hurts, Zel. So much.

His voice in my head is so pure, so clear. I glance around at a distant Xiulan working in a far room, but she doesn't seem to have heard him.

"I hear you, Cy," I whisper. "I hear you."

Cy lets go of my hand and collects himself. "Come on. We have some brains to analyze," he says, forcing a little brightness into his voice. He spins the image around with his finger, making the brain look like a flower on fire. "It's impossible to separate them anatomically." He points to the thick web of nerves between the hemispheres, now lit up in bright blue. "That's Julian. And here's Sean."

Sean's neural web is bright orange. When he flicks back and forth between colors, it's clear the tangled neurons overlap heavily, sharing multiple pathways. "It's not like you can slice Julian and Sean apart," I comment.

Cy crinkles his eyebrows. "Wait. Digitally subtract Sean's neural web from Julian's again," he orders the holo. We look closer and see that what's left is a pattern in the front. "This is it. The prefrontal cortex. These pathways are mostly used by Julian. That's our best bet."

"So we target this area with a few gamma rays, label some heat-shock protein specific tags with medicine."

"Which medicine?" Cy asks. "How long does Sean want Julian to be out of it? An hour? A day?"

"We need to ask Sean. And we need him here when Julian is asleep so we can gamma-blast Julian's neurons."

"That's so violent, Zel," Cy snickers.

"What can I say? He's not my favorite man in the world."

"I'll go find Sean. Or Julian, and get a reading on when he'll be asleep so we can do this."

"Okay." He leans over to me to kiss me softly on the lips. "I wish I could kiss you all day," he says as I finally step back.

"You can if you try." I wink at him. Cy's face goes rosy and I leave, hoping that he'll take me up on my invitation to keep working on his trait.

CY DOES TRY. HALTINGLY, AND CAREFULLY. IT must be working, since other people around me don't seem bothered by whispery touches on their cheeks, lips, and hands.

Luckily, he gives it a rest when I finally find Julian in an office down a hallway on an upper floor. The door is open and the holo image on the walls resembles twentieth-century Prague. The tawny rooftops and blue sky are beautiful, but I can detect the faint electric scent of the holo mechanism humming faintly in the background. Pretty, but fake.

"Hi Julian," I say, knocking.

"Zelia. Come in."

Above the desk, he's got several holo screens showing financials for Avida and business orders. A single small screen shows a girl sitting bored at her desk. I peer at it closer, only to realize it's Caliga, manning the infirmary office. I'm relieved that there's no sound or picture coming directly from her bracelet. At least we're not being monitored *that* intimately. But still.

Julian touches the screen and it disappears instantly. The lech.

"So. How's the research with Cyrad going?"

"Oh. Very well," I lie. Shoot. We didn't ever try to think up a good lie about what we've been doing for the last twelve hours.

"It's okay. I understand that you need a little catch-up time with your boyfriend."

It's positively gracious of him. I'm stunned into a "Thank you" before I can think of anything else to say. "Oh. And thanks to Sean too."

Julian makes a dismissive sound.

"What? Don't you like Sean?" I ask, truly curious.

"He's a part of my life that I tolerate."

"I'd think it would be nice to have someone always there for you."

"Always there to criticize." He scowls. "Believe me, I put him in his place, but he floods me with this . . . this . . ." Julian waves his hand like he's shooing away a fly. "Unnecessary emotion."

"You mean, a conscience."

"It's *irritating* as hell. If he ran Avida, we'd have collapsed long ago, even under the auspices of Aureus. You have ten times his spirit, Zelia."

"I see. Maybe I could talk to him. Get him off your back," I offer. "Maybe he's just lonely."

"He's a goddamned puppy. You're welcome to have

him as your pet. But he won't be around at least until tomorrow. I'm too busy."

"But don't you need to sleep?" I say, trying to hide my panic. *Tomorrow? That's too late to save Caliga!*

"Eh. I'll let Sean sleep for the two of us. I've too many things planned. Which reminds me. I need to prepare for the evening." Julian shuts all the holos off and walks me out of the office before locking it securely with his bracelet. Even the smallest action, like waving his bracelet, is replete with confidence and intimidation. Everything that Sean doesn't have.

He leaves me behind without a good-bye, as if I've already occupied too much of his time. I wait for the next transport, to warn Caliga. Cy's voice enters my head as I walk in.

I hope you found Sean. I hope you have some good news.

No. I don't. I have the unhappy job now of telling Caliga that everything I promised isn't going to happen.

When I find her in the upstairs infirmary, still sitting in the beyond-bored position I'd seen her in on Julian's holo, she hears my news with a dead-eyed expression.

"Cal, I'm so sorry. I tried, but unless Julian lets Sean take over, there's nothing I can do."

"I understand." She smiles, and that smile cracks my heart. It's pure resignation. "I'll survive. I'll get through it. It can't be worse than sludging through a hundred miles of sewer pipes, right?" she jokes.

I smile back, but don't respond. Because in truth, we both know it will be worse.

I DON'T LEAVE CALIGA'S SIDE FOR THE rest of the day, after Cy assures me that he can work alone. I hover close and occasionally put my hand on her shoulder. She never shrugs me off. Never throws a bitter word. I tell her stories about Dyl. About the poetry we'd read. She asks me to recite some of the poems I loved best. They seem to calm her down.

When it's time to prep for dinner, she gets dressed in a simple gown of black silk and her bots curl drooping spirals of hair around her shoulders. The whole process is awful and wrong, like she's dressing for her own execution. Afterward, she follows me to my room while I get ready. My personal bots go nuts. I'd been refusing their work for the last day. After my shower, they practically shake with bliss as they spray-paint my face.

"Enthusiastic, aren't they?" Caliga says, even giggling when my hair bot admires Caliga's curls.

"Yeah. I'll bet they've never had such a mess to fix before."

I wiggle into a low-cut dress of shimmering gold and emerald that tapers to white feathers all over the skirt. I'm a garish, nearly extinct bird with weak ankles. One good slip on the floor, and I'll fulfill my destiny. We leave my room and walk through the meadow, watching the holo butterflies alight on the blue columbine.

"We're early," I say, looking at my holo. "I want to go visit those kids again. It's been too long."

"My bracelet won't let me go," Caliga says. "I'm only

programmed for dinner." When she sees how torn I am, she smiles. "It's okay. I'd like a few minutes alone anyway. You go. I'll see you at dinner."

I head for the transport. Soon it's zooming down and diagonally to the hidden infirmary. When the doors open, I'm surprised to see Cy standing in a black suit, behind Renata. She's crouched over Victoria's bed, just like she'd been the first time we were here.

"Cy. Renata, I just came by . . ." My words disintegrate when Cy turns around, his eyes bloodshot. I walk forward, only to see Renata collapsed in misery. Victoria's eyes are half-open, dull and unfocused.

She's dead.

I cover my mouth. My eyes sting and brim with tears. Her four tiny arms are splayed out in an X, just like Hex does when he's deeply asleep. He never got to meet his little sister.

I hate Julian. I despise my father. And I hate myself, for not having done more.

"Is Victoria okay?"

Andy's sitting up in bed, his suction cups still covering his hypersensitive ears. He looks like he just woke up. He doesn't know. Renata won't move, still prostrate over Victoria's still body. I walk to his bedside.

"Oh Andy. It's . . . I'm sorry, but . . ."

Andy's face fills with horror and he rips off the protective cups over his ears. "Shut up, shut up!" he screams, throwing the cups on the floor. He splays his hands out. "Everybody, stop breathing! Be quiet!" His eyes grow wide and wild as he grips the edge of the bed rails and cocks his head to listen to the aching silence of the room. It only takes a few seconds. He lifts his shaking hand. "Victoria's heart isn't beating. It's not beating!" he wails.

He claws at me, so violently that I bump into the table next to his bed, knocking over his dinner and a glass of lemonade. I grab Andy's body and just smother him in my arms. He sobs into my chest. After a minute, he pushes me away.

"No. I want my mom," he whines.

Andy's voice seems to rouse Renata, who lifts her head up from where she's been soaking Victoria's sheets with her tears. She scuttles over to Andy's bedside and I give her a wide berth.

"It's okay, Andy. It's okay," she croons. "I love you, my darling. Mama's here."

My eyes take in the room with a hollow heart. The other girl, Bianca, looks like she's already in a coma. Cy and I try to comfort Renata, but we feel like outsiders trying to help a hopeless situation. As Cy and I leave to head to dinner, I collapse into his arms in the transport.

"What are we going to do?"

"I don't know," Cy says helplessly. "I don't know what we're up against. I have no tools."

But I know I have to do something. Bianca and Andy will die next. We're still stuck in Avida without a clear way out. And now Caliga's going to fall prey to Julian tonight too.

I've never felt so helpless in my whole life.

CHAPTER 22

CY AND I DRAG OURSELVES TO DINNER. The roof is resplendent with twinkle lights embedded in the domed ceiling, candles glowing on the tables, and place settings of gold-etched china and crystal. The forced gaudiness and decadence make me want to throw up, considering what we've just seen. My tight dress isn't helping any. Cy sees me clutching my ribs and leans close.

"Where's your necklace?"

I show him my wrist where I twined the chain as a bracelet, since I have no pockets. He clasps it around my neck and I relinquish control to the pendant. Victoria's death makes me so sad, I don't have the energy to breathe by myself. When someone touches my elbow, I cringe.

"Hi Zel," Tennie says. He doesn't seem upset, so he must not know about Victoria yet. He points across the room to Tabitha. "Check it out. I bet it's clogged-drain city in her bathroom." I hardly recognize her, because she's shaved all her fur off. She's wearing a skin-tight, flesh-toned strapless dress. The only hair left is a thick, wavy stripe trailing down from her head to the small of her back, like a horse's mane. Her face, without the fur, is heart shaped and almost elfin. Not what I expected.

Tabitha's talking to someone in the crescent pool at her feet. We walk over slowly. Ryba's in the water holding on to Tabitha's bare foot, like it belongs to her. Her skin glistens under the water like a pearl, and her yellow hair fans out, being tugged this way and that way by her head movements. Her eyes are nearly white, like moonstones.

"Zelia. This is Ryba," Tabitha says proudly. Ryba holds out a dripping hand and I stoop to shake it. It's rubbery and slick. She's healed so well.

"Hi Ryba," I say. "Wow. You're . . . beautiful." I can't help it. The golden hair and the pearlescent body are straight out of a fairy tale, if not for the lack of fish tail.

"Thank you," she says, her chin dipping into the water. "You look like a bird of paradise."

I nod in acceptance. "Not my choice, but whatever."

Julian's already sitting at the head of the table, a goblet of red wine in hand. His eyes are fixed on Caliga, who sits alone in the corner, swirling the lemon in her water glass. Xiulan walks to Julian, interrupting his line of vision. She leans over to whisper, her skin swirling in blue and orange, and he slams down his wineglass.

"I didn't authorize that."

Xiulan whispers hurriedly and her arms go black.

"I'll deal with it later." Julian waves his hand dismissively, but the irritation on his face remains. Xiulan slinks away and sits down, staring straight ahead of her. Micah comes to stand next to me.

"What's going on?" I ask him.

"I don't know." He and I sit down across from Xiulan. She looks too frightened to speak, but Micah asks anyway. "Xiulan, what happened?"

"Some of our newer drug samples got sent to Okks, of all places. It's all over the news."

"Who sent them?"

"I don't know. I'm in charge of shipping from the R&D lab, but I didn't do it."

We try to console Xiulan, but nothing we say makes her feel better. Micah whispers to me, "The police and Feds will put more pressure on Inky and Avida. They'll have to publicly show that they're doing something about it. This is bad."

"What a weird mistake," I say, but Micah shakes his head.

"This is no mistake. Places like Avida and Aureus— they don't make mistakes."

We all sit and eat our dinner with somber concentration. Renata never shows up, but the other kids seem afraid to ask about her absence. After dessert, the candles and lights wink out. They're replaced with black lights and music. Strange shapes begin to glow around us from the fluorescing clothes, nail polish, and makeup worn by everyone. I suppose it would be a fun club experience, dancing under a black light, except that nobody is in the mood.

"Let's get out of here," I mouth to Cy, who's several seats away. We head past the strange glowing lips, eyes, and bits of luminous clothing to the transport doors.

"Zel, what's that?" Cy points to a huge splotch on the feathers of my skirt. It's glowing eerily blue-green, and doesn't match any pattern on my gown. I reach for it and it's damp.

"Weird."

Micah and Élodie have also decided to leave. Inside the transport in the normal light, the wet splotch on my gown is bright yellow. It has a strange, chemical scent that's familiar, mixed with a sugary citrus note. My stomach drops and my heart starts pounding.

Oh no. This can't be what I think it is. Please. *No.*

The doors have opened to Cy and Micah's floor. Since it's free time, Élodie is allowed to step out with them, but I don't exit the transport.

"What's the matter?" Élodie asks. "Aren't you coming with us?"

"No." I try to smile, faking nonchalance. "I'll be back in a second. I forgot something."

Cy watches me with suspicion but lets the doors close. I scan my bracelet and head for the locked infirmary. Inside, Renata is gone. Victoria's body has been removed too, but Bianca continues to sleep under an oxygen mask, and Andy's playing a game on his holo.

His lemonade is still sitting by his bedside. I run over and smell it. Ugh, it reeks. I dump it down the sink in the corner of the room, before searching wildly by the beds and tables.

"God, where is it? Where is he keeping this stuff?" I say as Andy cowers from my frantic gestures.

I know what this smell is. Yellow color in daylight, fluorescing blue-green under black light. I used to use it in one of my first labs, for histochemical stains. Finally, peering through the glass of the far laboratory wall's transparent cabinets, I see the stoppered container. The liquid inside is bright yellow. The label is turned toward the back, but I know what it is.

Acridine yellow. A dye that's incredibly toxic. It causes mutations in animals and bacteria. And someone was hoping it would cause new mutations in Andy, by slipping it into his lemonade. I look frantically for a lock pad to scan my bracelet, but when I find it, the door won't open. And then I remember.

Caliga's vaccine is in here too. It has to be.

I look around desperately for a way to open the doors, but there's no hammer or anything I could use. A tall container of liquid nitrogen sits in the corner, along with oxygen tanks. I grab the liquid nitrogen container and detach the opening spigot. Holding it at eye level, I carefully pour the liquid nitrogen down the face of the locked plasticleer door.

"Julian really, *really* isn't going to like this," Andy warns me.

"Get back, Andy. Go to Bianca's bed, and push it as far away from me as you can. Cover your faces with the blanket," I order him. Andy's weak, but the hover beds are feather-light to push around.

"Okay, but I just wanna say . . . I had nothing to do with this!" he yells from beneath the sheets.

I have to work fast. The liquid pours down in serpentine rivulets, evaporating into smoky plumes so quickly that almost no liquid drips onto the floor. Soon, the room's floor fills with clouds of nitrogen.

"*Stop!*"

I spin around to see Julian standing in the doorway, livid.

"What are you doing, Benten?" he growls, striding forward and yanking my arm. The empty canister falls from my hands, banging onto the floor, hidden under the plumes of nitrogen clouds. Renata scuttles in behind him, her eyes wide with surprise.

"He's poisoning the children!" I tell her. "Ask him! Ask him about the yellow dye!" I turn to Julian and beg. "Sean. If you're awake in there . . . please. Open this door. If you're there, do it."

"Sean isn't here," Julian says coldly. He grabs for my wrist, but the floor is icy cold from the nitro, and water condenses to make it slippery. As he loses his balance, I grab the canister on the floor, heave it over my head, and bring it smashing down on the frozen patch of plasticleer door.

And just like that, the front of it shatters, raining down bits of sharp plastic onto my feet and the floor. The bottles are no longer locked away. No longer secret.

Benzene. Polonium-210. Arsenic.

They're sitting there like soldiers in a row, waiting to kill.

Julian's a monster.

He's been trying to cause more mutations, just like that senator had suggested. I'd compared it to using a shovel to do surgery. No wonder Julian had looked pissed.

He starts toward me, but my eye catches on a vial at the end of the shelf. CJ-001. A single vial with Caliga's initials on them. I grab it.

"*No!*" Julian yells angrily. "You idiot girl!" Julian rushes me and pins my shoulder to the broken wall of glass, but my legs are still free. I knee him in the groin, and he bends over in agony, gasping. It's all the time I need. I drop the vial and crush it under my shoe.

Julian yanks me away from the wall and twists my arm behind my back. I try to punch him, but he catches my hand easily.

"You stupid, stupid girl!" I don't even see the blow, I only feel it—his large, well-placed fist against my left cheek, before I'm falling. The hard, unforgiving floor ricochets against the back of my head.

I can't see. I can't move. I can't even lift my arms. Under my body, broken shards dig into the contours of my hip and spine. Julian's hand curls around my neck, not squeezing, but nearly encircling it. He's panting hard, and Renata whimpers in the corner. The air smells of burned plastic. The scent of fury.

"Get the solitary room ready," he barks at her. With a

cruel yank of my arm that threatens to pop my shoulder, he drags me out of the infirmary and into the transport.

Inside, I try to get up, but my face is crushed to the floor by Julian's shoe. I scream, but it's no use.

The door opens and he pulls me up and throws me out of the transport. Vaguely, I notice the English garden shrubbery whizzing by as I try to get my footing underneath me. My own yells grow hoarse and disappear in the space around me, replaced by a single voice.

"Zelia!"

Cy and Micah stand openmouthed at Cy's bedroom door. The sight of Cy renews my energy, and I kick and claw like an alley cat, but one swift kick to my kidneys takes my breath away. Julian drags me to the side of the garden.

"Let her go!" Cy yells, his voice full of fear and fury and terrible things. Micah's fighting to hold him back. For once, I'm thankful.

My eyes lock on Cy as I beg silently. *Don't hurt yourself for me. Don't do it.*

Julian kicks me into a hidden room behind the back of the garden. It's black and plain, with nothing but a drain in the middle, which horrifies me.

"You were right, Zelia. My methods are crude. I need to be using a scalpel, not a shovel, as you so poetically described it. You could be my blade. You could create, like your father did."

"I'm not like my father," I growl.

"Well. We'll have to change the balance of this argument, won't we?" Julian says, breathing hard into my face. His finger trails down my breastbone, before lifting away, hooking something. The chain of my necklace strains hard against my neck before it snaps off with a vicious tug.

"You've more spirit than I expected, Zelia. And you need to be broken."

Suddenly, without my necklace, my breathing is too shallow. I force a gasp to feed my body. I need my necklace, now more than ever.

If I fall asleep, I will die.

CHAPTER 23

MY BODY IS BATTERED. I'M GOING ON only two hours of scant sleep I'd snatched in Caliga's room last night. All I crave now is sleep.

And I can't.

Twelve times a minute, I force air in, gasping like a fish out of water. Seven hundred and twenty times per hour. My hands start to shake uncontrollably after six hours in my prison. My eyes feel gritty from lack of sleep, and my head is throbbing from Julian's blow and the hypoxia.

This room is a dimly lit, square box with a hard marble floor. Hours later (could it be morning now? Seven or eight a.m.?), the door opens. I shield myself from the biting light, while someone shoves a tray of food and water into my cell. I guzzle the water, but leave the food untouched.

Instead, I sit cross-legged in the corner, holding the titanium spork (of all things) way out in front of me. Watching it, never letting go. I count in fives, forcing a hard breath after number five. If I let go of the spork, it means I've fallen asleep. It clatters to the marble floor, waking me up. I rub my face, curse Julian, hold the spork in the same position, and go back to counting and breathing.

This is how I keep myself up.

This is how I stay alive.

For now.

IT FEELS LIKE MORE THAN A DAY goes by, although I can't be certain. I've lost count of the hours.

My hands tremble so much that I spill the water before I can drink it. At one point, I slip into a dream but wake myself up, only to find that I've jabbed myself with the spork. My arm bleeds with four tiny punctures. I can't remember doing the actual jabbing.

I cry for Cy, and for Marka, Dyl . . . for everyone in Carus, and Caliga. But even in my psychosis of seeing pink trees festooned with dead opossums, I never beg for mercy.

"Just say you're sorry," Julian says to me, appearing in the corner. He's covered in fur, just like Tabitha.

"Are you warm?" I ask.

"Just say you're sorry."

"I'd like to skin you alive. I'd chew you up. I bet you taste like petroleum," I say in a warbling voice. Julian's image shimmers away as the spork clatters to the floor.

This happens over and over. We have these conversations, and always, I end up chasing my dropped spork.

But soon, it occurs to me that the hallucinations might kill me anyway: bloody rodents, worms, and butterflies birth out of Julian's mouth and attack my fingers.

My spork clatters on the floor, and I hold it out again.

When my mouth starts to fill with blood from involuntarily biting my cheeks, I start to think.

Yes. Maybe he has gotten the better of me. Maybe it's time to give up.

"You should," Julian says casually. He looks normal for once, in a white suit. His pupils constrict, and Sean's worried face fills the room, expanding like a balloon so large, it squeezes me to the wall. "Please, Zelia. You'll never survive. Say you're sorry."

"I am sorry," I say, weeping. "Not for Julian. For everyone else." I have no tears, because my body is wrung out, made of Zelia jerky. Dry, sinewy, unreal.

I splay my hands open, and nothing clatters to the floor. The spork is gone. Where did it go? My dry eyes burn like they've been dipped in black pepper.

"Get her to her room. C'mon." Caliga's voice enters my head, but it must be another hallucination.

Strong arms scoop me up and I laugh, swatting at the butterflies that are dancing around my head. But instead of wings, they are shiny and edged with razor blades. One of them hits my cheek, and I touch the wound and look wonderingly at the red on my fingers.

"Beautiful," I say, and touch my tongue to the red smear. It tastes like death and metal.

"She's covered in blood," Micah's voice says, close to my ear. "Look what she's done to herself." I can't see him. I only see clouds of the flying razors.

Something touches my neck, and immediately my lungs

expand, almost painfully so. My back arches as oxygen floods me. The butterflies shimmer away, but within the darkness of my mind, shadows and sharp, unseen things continue to fly. And I cannot make them go away.

"Sleep, Zelia. You'll be safe now," Micah murmurs.

"Yes, sleep," Caliga says.

My old enemies are asking me to die. The two people I thought I'd never trust. But I can't fight anymore. My eyelids close as I surrender to unconsciousness.

WHEN I WAKE, I FEEL OLD. As if I've lost a life and gotten it back, only to find I've outgrown my own body. Completely disoriented.

"You're up. I was just about to leave."

Caliga's sitting on the edge of my bed. She wears a simple beige dress, her white hair pulled into a practical ponytail. The only color is the bright pink of her bottom lip, where she's just been biting it. My grooming bots try to fling themselves at me, but she shoos them away.

"God, they are so overprotective! I've been trying to convince them that I'm not going to secretly do your makeup."

My eyelashes are crusty and stuck together, and my mouth tastes like a sewer. "How long have I been out? What day is it? What happened?"

"Julian let me and Micah get you. You were in there for almost three days. He gave me your necklace and we brought you back here."

Three days. I mentally count the days since we left

Carus. That means we only have three more full days to meet my family in Chicago.

"Where is Cy?" I sit up in bed, rubbing my face. My brain feels bruised, like there's a loose sledgehammer swimming inside my skull. But my shaky hands and hallucinations are gone.

"You can't see him anymore. There's nothing I could do about that."

Nothing *she* could do about Cy? Does that mean she had something to do with getting me out of my sleep-deprivation nightmare?

"Caliga," I say slowly. "What did you do?"

Caliga stands and opens the door. "I should get going. I have to get ready." Micah walks in with a tray of food. He dodges Caliga as she darts out of my room.

"Hey. You look so much better." A warm smile softens his eyes.

I shake my head. "Wait. First tell me what happened."

"Eat first, talk later."

Micah leaves so I can wolf down my breakfast and shower. The bots apply a pain patch to my neck, and I start to feel more human. Even so, I keep my necklace on. It's worth the inconvenience of talking between breaths. I meet Micah outside my room, but the transport door stays shut when I wave my bracelet in front of the scanner.

"My access is gone," I say, stricken.

"That's no surprise. Julian was furious that you destroyed Caliga's vaccine. I honestly thought he wanted you dead. Sean would tell us, in moments he was let through, that Julian wouldn't listen to him."

"So Caliga's okay?"

Micah doesn't meet my eye. "She's getting ready for Julian."

"What? How is that possible? It's got to take at least another few days to make a vaccine. Longer, if she puts up a fight about giving another blood sample. Maybe there's time to mess with the vaccine—"

Micah grabs my arm so quickly, I stumble. "Wait. Zel, you don't understand. Caliga *made* the new batch. She volunteered, to get you out of there. To get your necklace back."

"What?" My recently swallowed breakfast threatens to rise up. "She can't do that!"

"It's done. She made her decision." He pulls me closer and his voice drops to a barely audible whisper. "She's doing this for us. We're leaving tonight, Zelia. Caliga's going to be with Julian tonight, and she's going to sneak him the sedative. Cy finally got Sean's help to finish it. As soon as Julian's unconscious, Sean is going to set us free."

"This is ridiculous. What if Julian doesn't take it? And Caliga gets attacked anyway? No way."

"This isn't your choice."

"What does Cy think of this? Blink? It's crazy."

"They agree with the plan."

"I want to talk to Caliga!"

"I'm telling you. It's too late. It's done." The helplessness in his expression tells me there's no point. I can push and yell all I want, but there it is.

Caliga's the bait, and we'll all benefit from her sacrifice.

MY ACCESS IS NEAR TO NOTHING. I'M stuck in my room and the meadow all day long, except for meals. I hope that I still get my one hour of freedom before curfew. I'll need every minute of it.

I want to talk to Caliga, but I can't. I'm desperate to see Cy, but I can't. Does he still care? Is he still slicing himself open when he's alone, when I can't be with him?

I wonder if he's been practicing his trait. Not once did he try to speak to me or touch me when I was being punished. He hasn't tried since I've been recovering, either. I think of the "Luna" poem, and wish I could recite it back to him.

Do you remember me?
I am here, in the same sky.
I will wait for you, ready to catch
The quarters and halves and broken hearts.

Micah says we're fleeing Avida forever after Caliga and Julian leave dinner. Sean told him that once Julian is incapacitated, he'll be granted access to disengage our bracelets so we can leave Inky. It's the price Sean is willing to pay for his own freedom. He'd never be able to silence Julian without our help. And then, when our bracelets shut down and fall off, we'll know we're free.

When.

If.

As I pace inside my room, everything here seems different. It already smells like a memory, like old things. The door swishes open and I jump up, eager for more information from Micah. A wide figure blocks the light and the door shuts.

It's Renata.

"I didn't think anyone had access to my room anymore," I say.

"Well, in Julian's eyes, I'm nobody. Being forgotten does have its privileges."

I drop my head. "I'm sorry about Victoria. Really sorry."

"I know," she says, sitting on the edge of my bed.

"How are Andy and Bianca?"

"Hanging in there. Now that I know why they're sick, it's easier to figure out how to treat them. Victoria was the only one who got radioactive polonium. We never would have been able to reverse that. The others might have a chance."

"How do you know Julian won't do it to other kids?"

"I don't." She turns and spies Ana's glass unicorn on a wall shelf. She picks it up, turning its prickly body this way and that. "He'll be at it again, unless he's stopped." Her eyes flick to me as she says this, waiting for me to fill the silence that follows.

"Do you know?" I ask. I'm not willing to say more.

"I do. Micah told me." She brings the unicorn over and I stretch out my palm, but she doesn't give it to me. I immediately want to snatch it from her grasp, but try to control myself. "I think your plan is going to fail."

"Why?"

Renata's bracelet buzzes. "I have to go," she says. "But I'm telling you. If you're relying on Sean to save you, then your plan has more problems than I do." She goes to leave but turns around quickly. "Oh. I almost took this." She hands me the glass unicorn. "Funny that you should own something that's not supposed to exist. Did you make it?"

"No."

"Hmm. But you'll take care of it anyway, won't you?" She smiles at me and her crinkling eyes remind me so much of Marka, I can't reply. When the door shuts behind her, I finally think of something to say. But I think Renata already knew my answer.

Maybe I started to know, that day that I forced the attention of the senators onto myself, instead of Xiulan. Or when Penelope with the super vision held my hand in the transport. Or when I saw Renata weeping over Victoria's lifeless body.

This isn't just about me, and escaping Avida to find my Carus family. Not anymore.

It's much, much bigger.

CHAPTER 24

DINNER IS REPLETE WITH POTENTIAL ENERGY LIKE a huge ball teetering on the edge of a step. On the rooftop, I can barely sit still in my smothering gown. When Cy, Micah, and Élodie arrive, they're surprised to see me sitting at the table. Cy almost runs to my side.

"I can't believe you're here. I thought Julian would keep you locked in your room for ages."

"I did too," I say. "I think he let me come to dinner for a reason."

"That doesn't sound good," Micah comments.

"Listen," I whisper. "We need another plan to get out of here. Just in case things don't work out with Sean."

"You think Sean is going to turn on us?" Micah asks.

"I don't know. But really, who's spent enough time with him to know what he's really like? Or even how he'll act when Julian's no longer around? I don't want to find out the wrong way that we've risked our lives for nothing."

"But there's no other way out of here," Cy says.

"There's one way out, but we can't do it without scuba

gear." I grimace. "The underground river. Only the water kids have used it. Tennie told me. He said that they go deep underground. But they can't survive outside, so they've never left."

Cy holds my hand tightly. "Maybe we can swim out of here."

"How?"

He lifts his sleeve. His forearm is now covered in slick blobs. I touch one. It's got that rubbery feel, like Ryba's skin. The skin flakes!

"But how do we know they'll work on our skin? How will we get enough to cover ourselves? All of us?" I ask, worried but excited.

"I can ask Cela if there are any more flakes from when Ryba first arrived," Cy says.

We jump to attention when the transport doors open. A few more kids arrive for dinner, but no Julian yet. We only have a minute more to talk.

Micah leans in closer. "Are the water kids going to lead us out? What if they want to come with us?"

"They can't survive on land without a dousing every few minutes," I say.

Everyone has the same panicked look as I do. There are too many cracks in a plan that isn't even whole yet.

The door to the transport opens and Julian enters with Renata trailing behind like a trained dog. We all scatter to our seats and concentrate on our food. No one talks about Victoria or the sick kids.

No one fights here anymore. No one is even brave enough to mourn Victoria.

For a few minutes, we all eat, or pretend to eat, pushing the soft dabs of purple potatoes around on our gilded plates. The transport doors open, and everyone turns to see who's bold enough to be late to dinner.

Caliga enters. She wears no makeup, and her white hair is messily tied in a knot. A simple day dress of crumpled linen hangs from her delicate shoulders. No gown, no jewels. Julian stands up at her entrance, and everyone braces for something—an acid comment about tardiness and hygiene, perhaps. Instead, he meets her as she approaches the table and extends his hand.

I hold my breath. No; we all hold our breath. Caliga flushes bright red. She hesitates, then tentatively touches her fingertips to his palm. When Julian's only reaction is to smile, then we all know. Caliga's vaccine worked.

Julian walks her to the table and sits right next to her. The other kids stare shamelessly. As the dinner goes on, Caliga doesn't eat a single bite. Renata is living misery in her orange silk muumuu, and Julian oozes contentment as he heartily shovels the synthetic filet mignon into his mouth. I haven't spoken to Sean in so long that I wonder if he's still inside that man.

Cy won't look at me at all during dinner. In fact, he spends the whole time staring at Caliga, as if he's angry with her for some reason. Finally, she stands up.

"I'm tired, Julian. I'd like to retire."

He nods and excuses himself, following her. As Caliga walks by us, she drops her napkin and Cy quickly reaches for it at the same time she does. He hands it back to her, but she says, "Thanks. Don't wait up."

Ugh. Such a flippant thing to say, considering. Everyone watches as Julian and Caliga retreat to the transport. I can't help myself.

I run to her, nearly knocking my chair over, only to see her frightened blue eyes swallowed by the closing doors.

Micah comes to me. "C'mon. Get back to your room and pack. Cy and I are going to stay here to try to work on plan B." I nod and enter the transport with several other kids, including Xiulan.

"We know you're trying to leave," Xiulan whispers in my ear.

"Excuse me?"

"It's okay. You don't have to lie. I tried to leave too, when I got here."

I don't know what to say.

"Xiulan—"

"It's okay." She forces a smile, a single curved line of disappointment. When the doors open to our floor, we walk together and I stop in front of her room.

"I'm sorry," I tell her. For what my dad did, for being here, for everything.

"Don't be. Nothing that's happened is your fault."

She's the only person to say this since I arrived. Her words make me feel light and airy, as if it were possible to unhitch myself from the earth itself. Because she's right.

None of this is my fault. But I can take responsibility for what I can and will do going forward. The sooner I get out of here, the sooner I can help the rest of them get out.

"Good-bye, Zelia. Don't forget us." She kisses my cheek and afterward, flashes optimistic spots of blue and yellow. "And good luck."

When I get to my room, I quickly change into the sturdiest clothes I can find. I order my bots to leave me alone, and they recede into their wall units so I can pack in peace. I put a change of clothes into a bundle, add some scavenged toiletries, and Ana's carefully wrapped glass unicorn. And then I wait.

My crimson bracelet has become a second thought lately, but now I stare at it with an intensity that would burn holes. When it falls off, we'll be on our way out of here. Anticipation tingles in my fingertips. I can't wait.

Five minutes go by. Then half an hour.

It should have fallen off by now. If Julian hasn't succumbed to the sedative, then Sean can't help us. And Caliga no longer has her trait to protect her.

I jump off the bed. I have to help her. Julian's a foot taller than Caliga and she's been so fragile lately. She'll never be able to fight him off. I touch my bracelet to the scanner on the wall and it bleeps at me.

Fifty-five minutes to curfew.

I close my eyes in thankfulness. I open the door and hear footsteps approaching. It's Micah, running straight to me.

"We've got to go. Now."

I grab my bundle and Micah practically pushes me to the transport.

"What happened?"

"I don't know. Caliga said that by eight o'clock, the deed would be done. And if it didn't work, to go on without her."

"*What?*" I stop moving so abruptly, my feet skid on the floor. "No. We have to get her!"

Micah grabs my hand again, buzzing my skin from anxiousness. "She's our only chance now! During dinner, Cy told her there was another way, to say the word and we'd abandon everything and come get her. But you heard what she said after dinner, didn't you? 'Don't wait up.' She *wants* to be the bait. She's trying to help us. Cy thinks we can actually escape from the underwater river. He talked to Cela and everything after dinner."

Before I can ask more questions, Micah drags me into the transport and we zoom down to the lowest level.

The doors open to the damp air of the water cavern. At the water's edge, Tabitha, Cy, and Élodie talk heatedly with Ryba, Cela, and another water person I remember seeing at one of the meals, a guy who looks twenty. Tabitha's skin is still fur free. She must need to be shaved at least twice a day to keep it that close to her skin. Her grooming bot must be exhausted.

"How do you know we won't need more?" Tabitha asks Cy, extending an arm.

"We won't know until we try." Cy picks up a container and opens it, showing a huge pile of opalescent, glass-like flakes. "Ryba's skin. Cela kept the pieces that fell off her when she was sick. They still exchange oxygen when reconstituted. Okay. Ready?"

"Yes." Tabitha picks up a flake the size of her palm. "Here goes nothing." She dips the crystalline flake in the water, and it immediately turns into a gel-like thing, translucent as milk glass. Tabitha lays it on her fuzz-free arm and Ryba's skin molds over hers, the way it did on me when I put it on.

"How does it feel?" Cy asks.

"Like I'm being kissed by a jellyfish," she laughs. Ryba's not as thrilled with the comments, and recedes into the water to glare at us all. With Cy's help, they apply the rest of the skin pieces, focusing on her cheeks and forehead, her neck and upper chest. "We need to put in on the places with the richest capillary network. The places where you flush."

After they're done, Tabitha lowers herself, shivering, into the water. "I wish I had my fur back," she says. As she slips under the surface of the water, Ryba holds her hands and stares in her eyes as bubbles issue out of Tabitha's nose. A minute goes by, then another. Maybe this will work after all.

"You're sure that our bracelets won't explode, swimming out of here?"

"Positive. The lowest caverns go well below the boundaries of the perimeters of Avida and Inky," Cela says.

"I still can't believe you didn't leave already," Micah says.

"We couldn't. Without another body of water nearby, or intermittent rain, our skin would dry out. We tried to leave for a few hours once, but we could barely handle it."

"Which is why I'm coming," Tennie says, walking up behind me. He already has his pack ready to leave, and is wearing nothing but swim shorts. The stump on his right hand waves cheerfully at me. "I can ionize the air around them every few minutes to keep them from drying out. Long enough to get to Lake Michigan."

"And you didn't think of this before?" My eyes are huge with disbelief.

"Well. We haven't actually spoken since—" Tennie touches his stump. He and Cela give each other measured glances. There is some sort of truce going on here that I'm not privy to. "And anyway, I can't hold my breath worth a damn. We had no idea this skin thing would work."

"So it's all worked out? What about Caliga?" I add.

Micah touches my hand. "Zel. We already talked about this. It's a done deal."

Cy bristles at Micah's words. I open my mouth to argue, when I realize that won't accomplish anything. Words aren't going to save Caliga, but something else might.

Me.

Suddenly, Tabitha bursts out of the water, blue-lipped and air-hungry. She coughs and sputters, panting hard. Ryba is right next to her, frantic with worry.

"What happened? You were fine for the first few minutes!"

"I don't know. I got so cold, and then it just stopped

working. I got short of breath." She's still breathing hard, and she pulls herself out of the water. She shivers and I touch her skin, which is cool to my fingertips.

"It's her skin temperature," I say. "The blood vessels in her skin are all constricted, and she's not absorbing enough oxygen. The water kids must already be adapted to the temperatures and have their own vascular network built for this. The only way this will work is if we make our skin flush like crazy." I squeeze my eyes shut, trying to remember my pharmacology holo lessons from Carus, several months ago. I turn to Cy. "What could we use?"

"Maybe a niacin analog, or a nitric oxide producer. I'll find something, and get the extra skin samples from the lab." He runs to the transport, and I go after him.

"You can't go. Stay here," Cy says.

"I know." I lean into him and kiss him on the lips. I wish I could kiss him for an hour. Maybe a whole day, but there's no time. So I thread my fingers into his hair, as if all future kisses were bundled into this one moment. Every night we won't spend together, every happy and sad moment. Just in case.

"What was that for?" Cy says, when he recovers from my embrace.

"For luck." I try to keep my tears back. "You know everyone has to leave before the top of the hour," I warn. "Our bracelets will start torturing us if we're still in Avida. We'll have to go, no matter what."

"I know," he reassures me. "I'll be right back."

After he leaves, Micah finds me staring at the closed

transport doors. I wave my bracelet, and an empty one opens up. He grabs my arm.

"Hey. Where are you going?"

I turn around to face him. "I forgot something. Something important," I whisper. "If I'm not back in time, then leave without me."

"What are you doing?" he whispers back. We look over his shoulder, but everyone's still discussing the plan, not paying attention to us. "We're this close to leaving. You'll be able to see Dyl again. Don't screw things up for yourself!"

"You mean for you?"

"No." He looks at me with more honesty in his face than I've ever seen. "The best thing I could do to make things up to Dyl is to bring her *you*. You're seriously ruining my apology plans."

I smile. "Dyl's not my only sister anymore." I shake my head. "Just promise me this. Leave if I'm not back in time. Tell Cy I said so. You owe me."

Micah nods, face distraught with helplessness, as I step into the transport.

CHAPTER 25

MICAH IS SMART TO NOT ACCOMPANY ME. It's a suicide run, and he knows it. It's obvious who inherited a self-preservation gene between the two of us.

When I reach Julian's quarters, the doors are locked.

"Julian," I say. "Let me in."

A few seconds go by. Julian coms my bracelet, sounding very far away. "Not now. Come back later."

"I have something that you want."

"It can wait."

"I'm talking about the list. Where all the traited kids are, and how my dad made them. I know where it is."

There is a pause in the air. It ends with the door sliding open, like a mouth inhaling. The octagonal library is lit with a golden haze that shines over the beautiful, glistening watches, all frozen in time. The door to his inner bedroom is open. I see Caliga sitting on an armchair, wearing her frumpy dress. Her bottom lip is swollen and split, and blood dots her dress. Her face is white with fear and she shakes her head at me.

She wants me to leave.

"Where is the list?" Julian says, mussing his hair, then folding his arms. He then quickly unfolds them to plunge his hands into the pockets of his pants. Oddly, he looks nervous. As if I'm the intimidating one.

I swallow. Caliga catches my eye and then looks pointedly at a huge grandfather clock ticking regularly to my right. Fifteen minutes until curfew. That's all I have.

"I want to speak to Sean," I say.

Julian walks over to the polished cherry table by the door. He withdraws one hand to touch an empty glass tumbler. The other hand stays in his pocket. He lifts up the glass and turns it over. Not a single drop left. "Zelia, the sedative worked."

I gasp. "You . . . you knew what that was for?"

"Zelia." Julian sets down the tumbler and takes a step closer to me, his face as puzzled as mine. "Who do you think I am?"

Caliga stifles a sob from behind him. I take a step forward, peering into his eyes. They're normal. No longer dilated, no longer pinpoint.

My eyes squint harder. "I don't understand . . ."

"It's me. It's Sean. The sedative worked. I tweaked it, though. I linked it to a selective neurotoxin. All of the Julian-specific areas have been targeted. Julian is dead."

My eyes travel from Sean to Caliga, trying to understand and failing spectacularly. Caliga sits filled with terror. Sean is in the room, not Julian. All of our bracelets are still on tightly, none of them disengaged as promised. Nothing makes sense. I pretend to smile a little, and clear my throat.

"So . . . um. That's great. Now you can take off our bracelets, right? Like you promised?"

"Julian's left me this mess . . . I have to look through his files first. See who wants to stay, and who wants to leave."

"But that's not what you promised," I say gently. "Micah said—"

"I know what I promised!" Sean shrieks, so freakishly loud that Caliga and I jump. Sean reaches out and then immediately slaps his hand against his leg, as if he's having a problem controlling his own body. "It's a mess. You left me this mess," he says, but he doesn't seem to be talking to me anymore. He starts crying silently.

It never occurred to me to consider the effects of separating Sean and Julian. It was never meant to be permanent. Maybe Sean can't exist normally without Julian? Maybe they needed each other as a means to keep each other balanced, especially after a lifetime linked together. I back up against the door, but my bracelet doesn't signal it to open. I'm trapped, and so is Caliga. I look at the grandfather clock. They'll all be leaving without us soon. As if to mock me, my bracelet buzzes a warning.

Ten minutes to curfew. Please move to a sanctioned area.

Caliga's eyes travel back to the grandfather clock again, as if it's her salvation. She must know that in ten minutes, we're all trapped here forever.

"Caliga and I should leave you alone." I use a nurturing, soft voice and soften the frown I'm wearing. "You need some rest, Sean."

"She's mine. Julian promised. It was a gift. It was his last gift," he says, and sits down next to Caliga. He rubs her shoulder, like a child petting a dog. Roughly, artlessly. Caliga winces and shuts her eyes. Sean's eyes open wide, as if remembering something. "You said you knew where the list was. Where?"

Say something, Zelia. Anything. "I know where it is, but it's not in Avida. It's in . . . Okks."

It's hard to concentrate on my words. My bracelet buzzes with increasing intensity. I clutch at it, digging my fingertips against the edge to rub the irritated skin.

"Liar."

I look up in surprise. Sean rushes forward, his arm coiled back and he punches me straight in the jaw before I can react. My body crashes to the floor and white star-bursts pepper my vision. I don't know which way is up. If it weren't for the necklace around my neck, I'd have stopped breathing from having the air slammed out of me.

"You know where that list is." Sean stands over me, frowning deeply, as if he might cry again. "That's one thing I was always better at than Julian. I know when someone is lying to me."

He rips my necklace off.

"I liked you, Zelia." Sean sounds like a hurt child. "You were supposed to be on my side."

No, I think. *You were supposed to be on mine.*

Sean lowers my necklace onto the round table nearby. He lifts a large glass paperweight and holds it over my pendant.

"No!" I beg him.

"Tell me where it is."

"I don't know. I just said that so I could talk to you," I say quickly. "I'm sorry. I just wanted to make sure Caliga was okay."

"She's mine," he repeats, raising the paperweight higher. His face is stricken with pain. "Julian promised she would be mine."

I cower on the floor. It's like I'm talking to a broken machine. There's no winning an argument here, no reasoning where reason has fled.

"Sean." Micah's voice comes from Sean's bracelet. "He's coming."

Sean's eyes stay on me as he holds the paperweight aloft. Clarity enters his eyes for a moment. "Where are the others?"

"All under control, like you asked. It went perfectly. You know who are the highest flight risks now. I'll have them locked in their rooms so you can discipline them as you planned. Cyrad got away, though. I thought you could take care of it. He's headed for your room right now. My hands are full at the moment."

I can't believe it. At the end of it all, I was wrong to trust Micah. He played me so easily.

"I'm not well, Micah. I'm not well," he whispers, barely concealing a sob. "Sedate them all for the night. Please," he adds. The paperweight bobbles in his hand. The other hand digs into his pocket, fumbling for something. "It was Julian's idea," he says, but I'm not sure he's even speaking to me. "Start a secret plan to escape and find out who the rule breakers would be. I told him no, they'd always obey him. But I knew no one would obey me. I have to know who my friends are. Everyone else can go away." He raises the paperweight over his head, aiming for my pendant. "Like you're going to go away."

Three things happen, almost all at once.

Sean crashes the glass orb onto my necklace, and the tiny metal insides fly apart, bouncing onto the carpet.

The door opens, and Cy sees me on the floor, too weak to fight, and Caliga, still frozen in her chair.

And the neural gun in Sean's other hand goes off with a hiss, aimed straight at Cy's chest.

Cy collapses to the floor, eyes wide open.

"Oh my god!" I push myself off the floor and drag myself over to him. He stares straight ahead, breathing comfortably, but he doesn't move. He doesn't blink. Neural guns work too well. They only paralyze the nerves that control your movement. So I know Cy can feel my hands on him, hear me scream. He can breathe. But he can't move, and he can't speak.

The sight of Cy's expressionless face fills me with so much hate, I can't contain the fire of it. I force my breath in and out, so hard, my throat burns. My bracelet buzzes painfully. Curfew is only minutes away.

Sean steps over Cy, as if he were nothing more than a fallen piece of trash, and grabs my face, squeezing hard. I push, but I can't get him off me.

"I could let you die on your own. It would take, what,

a few days maybe? A week? But I'm not as patient as Julian was." He lifts me up by my shirt, throwing me against the wall of the library. The holo shelves are fake, but the wall and watch cases are too real. I crash against them, skull and spine singing with pain, and my elbow smashes through a glass display full of watches.

Warm blood oozes over my arm, followed quickly by shooting pain in my elbow. Broken glass and watches and their cracked crystals surround my face. I try to crawl away but slip on the mess, chest down on the crackling glass.

And suddenly, my eyes open with surprise. Air forcefully spills into my lungs. My chest stretches wide as my body inhales—by itself. Without my effort.

The exhalation comes just as shockingly. Like a concrete block pressing down on my chest. The breaths are jerky, too long and abrupt, as if an ill-fitting iron lung has been crimped onto my body.

My back arches with each inhalation, and I lurch forward as the air leaves me. Confused, I turn my head to see Sean watching me curiously. How could my necklace work when it was shattered to pieces? Maybe the bits are still on the ground nearby? When I sit up more, the mechanical breaths stop abruptly.

And then Sean kicks me across my cheek.

The pain. It's everywhere. I catalog it, because it's all that lives in my consciousness. Head, arms, back, elbows. Skin, bones, teeth. I try to form a cry for help, but it issues out of my lips as a whimper.

A body cannot take more of this, I think. I'm already

broken. And for some reason, familiar words randomly enter my brain. Memories and sweet things, come to comfort me.

I cannot feel your light on my skin.
This place swells with absences
As you seep forward
And I remain, fixed in memory.

But they're not my thoughts. They are Cy's, and Cy's voice. Inside the pain, I smile. He's doing this for me, when I have nothing left to hold on to.

Through my closed eyelids, I sense Sean standing over me. I can smell his excitement. It's green, and there's the earthy, musky scent of passion too. He's giddy with it, swimming in his power. His foot pushes painfully into my ribs, rolling me over onto my back, onto more broken glass. My eyes open, and Cy and I lock onto each other. As his dark eyes stare unblinking into mine, I beg silently.

Make him stop. Cy. You can do it. I know you can.

I wait an eternity in a few seconds. But nothing happens.

Sean lifts his fist for another blow to my face. My bracelet relentlessly zaps me. I only feel it now that I'm not being bashed against the walls anymore. The clock chimes nine. The kids in the cavern are leaving. Right now.

"Wait, Sean." Caliga steps gingerly over the broken glass. She speaks with a tenderness that makes me want to vomit. "You're hurt."

Sean drops his gaze to his knuckles that are torn from punching me across my teeth. I want to scream at her to get away, but I'm too confused. After being paralyzed by fear, Caliga is now serenity itself. She lets his hands find their way to caress her cheek. He touches her, gently at first, then clumsily drops his arms.

"What's happening?" He stares at his hands, lurching his shoulders left then right to move them. It's no good; they flop down again, like he's got rubber flippers for limbs. His legs soon succumb, and he crumples to the floor, eyes wide open with wonder and fear.

How can this be? How could the vaccine not work anymore?

"You were going to take what wasn't yours," she whispers, crouching down to touch her hand to his face.

Sean tries to bat her hand away, but after contact with her arm, it drops again like a lead weight to the floor. Caliga lets her hand delicately touch his face, as if she were playing a sonatina on a piano. Her hands fold on top of his heart, and she waits.

"It will never be yours to take. From any girl. Ever," she says softly.

Cy and I wait, staring. Hanging back. We know this is no longer our fight.

In the space of a silent two minutes, Sean is dead.

CHAPTER 26

CALIGA LETS ME SCOOP MY ARM AROUND her thin waist. She helps pull me up.

"I don't understand. I thought your vaccine had worked," I say breathlessly.

"It did," she explains in a daze. "I used a vector with a really short half-life. It was only supposed to work for two hours, but I miscalculated. I was off by an hour."

Cy rolls over on the floor, groaning. "Thank god he only had a civilian neural gun." He manages to stand up, wobbling and holding on to the table for support. "We need to go." He stops in mid-lurch toward the door. "Wait. Your necklace," he says, turning around. "I though I saw it—"

"It's gone. Sean destroyed it," I explain.

"We'll find some way to help you. As I recall, I'm pretty good at CPR," Cy mumbles with a crooked smile.

But it's not funny. I hear Dad's voice in my head, asking me to assent to an implantable breathing pacer. But I remember something else too.

"Wait. Something in here forced me to breathe. Like a pendant made for another person." I gingerly step around Sean's inert body, crunching over the glass and overturned tables. A dozen or so watches, most of them smashed, lie amid the mess. I pick up one that looks intact. A gold pocket watch with a mother-of-pearl face.

I touch the cold watch to my chest. And my chest puffs out with a rough inhalation and exhalation. It doesn't fit me; it's like a bellows built for a different, larger fire.

"How . . ." Cy says. "Who made those?"

"It was Endall's," I tell him. "Sean and Julian's son."

We know what it means. Endall must have my genes. My longevity genes, and with it, my Ondine's curse. So Dad made a boy version of me too.

"Endall was here in Avida once, but he ran away." And he's out there somewhere.

"C'mon. Get as many of these as you can," Cy urges me, and we hastily pick through the mess to find three more intact watches that can make me breathe. After a minute, we're zooming down the transport.

"God, this bracelet is going to kill me," Cy groans. I haven't forgotten the pain. One pulse at a time, our bracelets are torturing us. The shocks were bad five minutes ago. Now they're pure torture.

With my head and back still throbbing from hitting the wall, Cy's recent paralysis, and Caliga's last hour, and all of us grimacing and gasping in agony over our bracelets, we are a trio of walking misery when we exit the transport.

Renata stands, blocking our way out of the transport.

"So. Is it done?" she asks me, ignoring Cy and Caliga.

There isn't an easy way to say it.

"Julian and Sean are dead," I tell her. "We tried to only . . ." It's so much to explain and I can't bear to rehash the story. "You were right, Renata. About Sean."

Renata nods. Her eyes take in my bruised body, Cy's weakened one, and Caliga's bloody lip. Her mouth twitches and she starts to cry. Her hand goes to cover her mouth as the tears drip down onto her dress.

"I'm sorry," I say. It's so easy to forget that they had a history together.

"Don't be," she sniffles. "I mourned losing Julian as a partner a long time ago. This is a relief, though I wish it hadn't had to happen like this."

Cy winces so hard next to me, his knees buckle. "The bracelets," he says. "Is there any way you can turn them off?"

"I can't," she admits. "I can't get full control of the security systems here until I report his death to the people who've protected Avida." She looks straight at me, and adds, "I don't think it would be wise for you to be here when I make that call."

Caliga nudges me. "We have to go, Renata. We can't stay here, even though Julian and Sean are dead."

"I'm not stopping you. I've already said good-bye to Tennessee. I knew my water children would be the first ones to go. A fish bowl is no place to live."

"It's time," Micah says gently. I step around Renata and slap his face.

"You bastard," I seethe. Micah stands up and approaches me, hands out.

"Now wait. You don't know—"

"I know everything! You lied. You set Cy up, sent him to Sean knowing he'd be attacked!" He only plays games to get ahead, no matter where he is.

"No," Micah starts, when Cy interrupts him.

"Zel. It's not like that," he says, his voice returning to normal. He's able to stand on his own now. "It was the only way I'd be able to get Caliga out without having Sean make all our bracelets injure us right when we needed to leave. I didn't know that you'd gone after Caliga. I thought you were safe in the grotto, waiting for me to come back."

"Tell me the truth," I whisper, staring at Micah. I step closer to him, stand too close so I can scent his behavior.

"I've been playing both sides, it's true. But my primary purpose has been to get out of here, not become the new king of Avida. I swear."

His face is nothing but earnest, but I can smell something on him. It's not the stench of a lie, but something more subtle. "You're holding back," I accuse him. "I can tell. So out with it."

Micah's face falters. He looks to Cy, who isn't giving an ounce of sympathy. "I . . . I've been wanting to leave Avida and Inky." He almost chokes on his words. "So I could find Dyl and Ana. And I wanted you on my side so they'd forgive me."

Cy's hand slips into mind and stiffens. I can't believe Micah. And even if he's telling the truth, which I think he is—the scent around him is something like a spring wind, without that spoiled-fruit scent I know to be lying—I can't handle what he's saying.

"Enough. We've got to go," Cy says, his face an abstraction of pain. Our bracelets are hurting us too much now.

"The bracelets should stop receiving the signals from Avida when you're far enough away. It won't hurt forever," Renata says.

Cela and one of her companions, the teen boy with white skin and light brown hair, emerge from the water. She waves her thin arm at us. "Zelia, this is James. The others are way ahead."

"So it's working? The skin samples?" I ask.

"It's not perfect. But you'll survive."

Huh. I'm not convinced by her confidence.

"Sounds good enough to me," Caliga says quietly. She's stooping by the water's edge, and glances at me with more energy than I've seen since she extinguished the life from Sean.

Cy hands out little capsules of niacin, and I dry-swallow the pill.

"When will this pill start to work?" Caliga asks as she starts peeling off her clothes. She seems eager to get out of her soiled and torn dress. I'm wondering the same thing when a warm flush flares over my face and neck. Perspiration dampens my forehead as I swipe my face.

"It's a rapid-acting formula and . . . it looks like it's working," Cy says, watching me.

My face and chest are on fire. I feel so hot, like I've been dropped into an oven and left there to roast.

"Your face is red," Micah observes, when I realize his face has gone beet red too.

Cela starts wetting the opalescent flakes of skin and I peel off my clothes in the cool, damp air. I'm too anxious to be self-conscious; and anyway, everyone else is nearly naked too. Micah retrieves a jiggling piece of skin and lays it on my cheek. It feels gummy and clammy, and it tingles in a pleasant, unexpected way. I put more everywhere I can reach, and Caliga lays some on my back.

Caliga reaches her hand up and grasps my hand. Her scarred lids make her eyes big and wide. "When we go in the water . . . don't let go of me. Okay?" she whispers.

After a few minutes, we're nearly done. The gel-like slabs of skin make us all look like we've bathed in gelatin goo.

My new pocket watches and belongings are safely encased in waterproof bags that Micah had brought. Cela ties weighted belts to our waists, so we can easily sink to access the underwater passageways. Seems like a sure-fire way to ensure we drown, but okay. Before we head into the water, Renata wades in to give James and Cela a hug. She whispers something into their ears, and they both blink rapidly and nod, hugging extra hard.

I let go of Caliga for just a second to say good-bye.

"Thank you, Renata."

She gathers me into a warm, fierce hug. "I'm proud of you, Zelia. I think your mother would be proud of you too."

"If I ever meet her," I say, laughing a little. Renata pulls away and puts her hands on my shoulders. "I meant Marka. I look forward to meeting her someday."

"Me too." And that's when I know—this will not be the last time I'll see Renata again, or Bianca, or Xiulan. I'm not really escaping. I'm fighting for them too; I just can't do it from inside Avida. "I'll do whatever it takes to keep you and the children safe. Not just prisoners, but really safe."

"I'll hold you to that," Renata whispers. "Now go."

Cela and James beckon us into the water.

"It's an hour's trip. There's two small pockets of air we'll rest in, but that's it."

I scoop up Caliga's hand and we inch into the shallow cave water. Goose bumps erupt all over me and my scalp prickles. My face and body pulsate with pain where water touches the wounds from Sean's beating. It's so frigid that I gulp air in surprise. Nervousness fills my chest like a hard knot. I breathe harder, but the knot only tightens.

We all submerge, letting the cold water swallow the tops of our heads. We paddle toward Cela and James, who wait patiently for us. Caliga's hand still tugs and clutches mine. After a few more kicks, I'm dying for air. But before I can surface for a gasp, something yanks at my ankle. Caliga is yanked too. We peer down through the water to see James with his hands around my ankle and Caliga's, and he's pulling us down with such strength that we can't resurface.

I don't know how to tell him I can't breathe, that the skin patches aren't working. The knot in my chest that was once anxiety is now savagely tight, telling me I'm running out of oxygen. My wrist screams in pain from the bracelet. Caliga thrashes next to me, clinging desperately to my hand.

Suddenly, the tugging on my ankle goes slack. Through the water, I see Caliga, blurry. Unmoving. James continues to pull us down to a dark, black hole near the bottom of the water.

Caliga's already passed out. I close my eyes and wait for the inevitable.

The pressure is intolerable. Inside my chest, the hunger for air is a living, dark thing. It claws without mercy, seeking air and failing. The water squeezes my eardrums and my body feels compressed, like a flower crushed beneath a shoe.

Just relax. Cy's voice enters my head. *Stop struggling. You'll be okay.*

My eyes open, expecting to see only darkness, but flashes of phosphorescent blue curl in waves around my body. Something solid and soft brushes my face and I capture it. It's Caliga's hand. She pulls me to her, eyes wide and alive, while electric blue and purple colors flash behind her in the undulating waves.

Her startled eyes say what I cannot.

We are still alive.

Caliga and I kick back to James to let him know we're okay. He lets go and waves us forward, urging us to swim on our own. There is a current in here and it gently urges us forward.

Without his two dead weights, James swims around us easily, like the water creature that he is. Caliga and I push and pull at the water with our hands, kicking ungracefully. We go several minutes before we both stop, fatigued and more air-hungry. The skin patches can only do so much to deliver oxygen.

So we continue this way, swimming in the underground passageway in short bursts, resting while James hauls us forward slowly. My fatigue grows to the point where I can't swim anymore and the cold of the water numbs my brain.

Finally, a dim light appears ahead and above us. James unhooks our weighted belts, and we surface like corks, gasping air as if we've just been born. We're in a tiny cavern, lit only by the water's surface bioluminescence, but the glow is weaker here. Cela is resting at the edge of the pool, along with Cy and Micah, who are panting hard too. Cy is utterly exhausted, resting his head on his hand.

"Oh . . . my . . . god," I say between forceful gasps.

"Save your energy. The next one is longer," Cela warns. "And we need to hurry. That pill you took is increasing the circulation to your skin, but it's also cooling you down too fast. You're not insulated like we are. You'll have serious hypothermia if we don't hustle."

Cy and I only get a chance to touch hands before we put our weight belts on again and dive. The next stretch nearly kills us land people. The passageway takes a deep turn into the earth, and we go lower and lower. The bioluminescence incrementally disappears, and the claustrophobia of the dark and constricted tunnel nearly gives me a panic attack.

When we rest inside another tiny grotto with a ceiling covered in monstrous stalactites, Cela grins at us. Though we're exhausted and bone tired, James manages a matching smirk.

"What's so funny?" Micah asks.

Cela's eyes are wide. "Don't you feel it?"

My mind is a blank, but Cela enlightens us by raising her braceleted wrist and jiggling it.

"It doesn't hurt anymore!" I exclaim.

"We are too far from Avida for them to affect us anymore," she says. "Far enough away that they didn't go off. So long as we stay away from the boundaries of Inky, they won't explode."

"But how will we get them off? Won't they explode if we forcibly remove them?"

Cela and James look at each other. No one has an answer for that.

We prepare ourselves for the last swim of the journey.

Hopefully it's just another half hour of swimming, but the current has gotten stronger, which means we'll be able to cover more distance with less effort. As we swim, the cold seeps into our bones, turning our legs and arms into cement limbs. After what feels like forever, we see a light in the distance and all start kicking and swimming, despite the need for oxygen that threatens to make our skulls explode.

The water churns around us, full of bubbles, grit, and tasting of dirt. My vision is obscured and I'm disoriented. Something pulls at my waist—James—and my weight belt is released. I let my buoyancy do its job, and warm air breaks over my face.

The light is blinding. I bob in the frothing water, rubbing the water out of my eyes. We're in a glade, with skeletal pine trees and blighted maples that surround the wreckage of houses nearby. Something taps me on my shoulder, and I turn to see Cy, Micah, Cela, James, and Caliga all bobbing along next to me.

"You did it!" Tennie yells from across the expanse of the stream. His hair is still spiky damp and Élodie sits next to him, sodden and shivering. Ryba is still in the water, but she's in an animated discussion with Tabitha, who's peeling off her used skin and chucking the bits of goo in the water.

I exhale everything—my fear, my air-hunger, the despair that hung on me, heavier than the weighted belt now residing in the subterranean river. My icy hand is caught by Cy, who smiles triumphantly. It's the most beautiful thing on earth. He lets go as Caliga bobs into my arms. Hot tears of relief start pouring down my face as she clings to me, weeping.

We are free.

PART III
MINWI

CHAPTER 27

"I AM SO WRUNG OUT!" TENNIE COMPLAINS.

It's the middle of the night. Chicago's upper city looms on the horizon in the north, miles away and aglow with lights. We've been traveling for two days. Well, nights really, since we can only travel in the dark, when Élodie leads us quietly. Tennie's been giving the kids who need hydrating a thorough drenching every half hour, but it's exhausting him.

"Just a little while longer, Ten," Cela coaxes. "C'mon. I'm getting crispy again. You don't want a potato chip for a sister. Let's go."

Tennie sighs. We're hidden behind a decrepit house in Ilmo, a few miles away from the border of Inky and Ilmo, which sports a ten-story, net-like plasma fence. Luckily, Chicago is due north if we follow the border. Otherwise, without a holo, we'd be lost. Cela, James, and Ryba surround Tennie. He concentrates hard, wrinkling his nose, and mist envelops them in a pale fog. Soon they're all covered in a sheen of water and the water kids exhale with relief, buffing the water deeper into their skin.

Cela and Tennie chat as we resume our hike to Chicago. They talk every chance they can. They must have used those last few days in Avida to work through a lot of crap. It makes me miss Dyl and the others that much more, watching them.

"A few more hours," I tell Cy. "Right on time. I wonder if they'll all be waiting there."

He holds my hand firmly in his. Since we left Avida behind, he barely lets go of me. Élodie leaves us alone, becoming more silent and withdrawn the closer we get to Chicago. Cy has tried to comfort her, assuming she's stressed out about finding the safe house in Chicago. During the daytime when we sleep, tucked into hidden places on the edge of towns, I find her awake. Staring out in the darkness, seeing what I can't.

I trip on a twisted root and almost drop my bag of belongings. Micah leans over to grab it.

"I can carry it, if you're tired," he offers.

"No thanks. I'm okay," I say, clutching it to my chest.

Did you lose any more since yesterday? Cy asks in my head. I shake mine back, and hug the parcel closer to my chest.

I've grown more paranoid since we left Avida. The first night after our escape, I told everyone about the pocket watches, and how Endall is out there somewhere—my genetic brother, maybe with my longevity trait too. The next morning, I awoke to find one of my watches gone. I had carefully wrapped each one and put them in different places. One in Cy's bag, one worn around my neck while I sleep (it's still crazy jerky and weird, but oxygen deprivation is not a good alternative), and one in my bag. Cy calmed me down when he pointed out a tear in the bottom of my bag.

"It's the rats. You kept your food in there. It was bound to happen," he reasons. I inwardly kicked myself for my stupidity, and agreed.

Until it happened again the next day. This time, it was Cy's bag.

"But you didn't have any food in your bag, and there's no hole in it," I notice. Cy and I share a glance of worry. I only have one watch left, which terrifies me.

Caliga and I talk when we can, but our discussions are always the same. Will Wilbert be in Chicago? How will we find him if he isn't? We discuss Wingfield, and consider how we'll get access to a holo so we can find out where it is. Micah tells us he knows it's in Minwi, while Cela, Ryba, Tabitha, and James listen on, uninterested. Their destiny is far closer.

We reach the shores of Lake Michigan just before dawn, standing among the wild tangle of plants at the water's edge. Stubborn, abandoned buildings still ring the shore, refusing to sink into the risen lake.

"You're really going?" I ask Tabitha. Her fur has started to grown back, dark brown and bristly.

"Yes. We're headed for Canada. You guys should come with us. There's a good chance we'll get refugee status there."

I shake my head and she doesn't try to convince me or the others. She envelops me in a quick, fuzzy embrace. We all take turns receiving squishy, damp hugs from the others. One by one, they do a triumphant dive into the murky lake water, kicking up splashes as they wave good-bye.

"Will they be okay?" Cy asks Tabitha, watching them disappear beneath the cloudy water. "I thought the lake water wasn't safe to swim in."

"They'll get sick for sure, but the water quality will get better the farther north we go," she reassures us.

Tennie sidles up to Tabitha and smiles sadly. "We should go."

"Tennie! I though you were coming with us," I say, disappointed. I'm already homesick for our group, even if we've only been traveling a few days.

"Nope. Tab and I are going north too." He points to the water kids dunking each other in the gentle lake waves. "We'll follow them by the water's edge. I want to stay with them. Cela's my sister, after all." He gives me a wet hug. "Good-bye, Zel."

Tabitha swings the group's heavy satchel onto her well-muscled back, grabs Tennie's hand, and leads him into the tangled, boggy foliage along the shore line. One last, large wave from a joyous kicking foot in the water, and the water kids are gone too.

Now it's only Micah, Cy, Blink, Caliga, and me. Chicago crowds the horizon ahead of us, buildings resting on enormous pilings ever since the lake rose seventy years ago. At the water level, the under-city is built upon a maze of decrepit, rotting boardwalks. Buildings are shabbily crafted of wood or scavenged plasticleer building materials. Some old warehouses still survive, their upper levels now the only available real estate.

The water just below us reeks with sheets of cobalt algae. Only the toughest, angriest animals skulk along the boards. We avoid the feral cats with huge, pointed ears, and brown rats big enough to fight back, and they avoid us.

Thankfully, Caliga memorized the address of the safe house when we were in the Deadlands.

"Four B and twenty." Cy reads the quadrant directions posted on the twenty-foot-wide pilings. "Four B and thirty."

"We're almost there," Caliga says.

It's been twelve days since I left Carus. We made it on time. I can't believe it.

We stay far away from other inhabitants peeking out from the doors of the shanties, who display open sores on their faces and fingertips. We've heard rumors of these people. Those who have chosen to live off the grid, because they needed to escape the law, or whose neurodrug habits dissolved their veil of normalcy.

"Here it is," Caliga says quietly. She points ahead to a structure of metal and concrete, with the lower floors flooded by lake sludge. The windows have long since been boarded up. It looks decrepit on the outside, but that could easily be a ruse. A makeshift front door cut into the wall is unlocked.

"That's weird," Micah says. He enters first, looking around and poking his head back out where we wait expectantly.

"It's empty, but there's an opening to the upper floors. Seems like the whole building is empty. Are you sure this is the right place, Cal?"

Caliga nods, but frowns. "Should we go in?"

"Why would it be wide open like this?" Cy wonders aloud.

I remember how intense the security was at Carus and Aureus, even Avida. It doesn't feel right. I wish I could smell something other than the toxic algae and the rotting rats floating under the decaying boardwalk.

"Let me go in," Micah volunteers. "Wait out here." Micah steps inside, dodges the soft spots of rust where water's weakened the metal floor. We keep the door cracked and I peer into the dim room, listening to the scuffle of rats. Micah looks around and heads for a crude ladder attached to the far wall and a window-sized opening in the ceiling.

He climbs it slowly and pops his head through the aperture.

"Seems empty—*oof*—"

Micah's feet suddenly dangle, as if he's been grabbed from above. His feet disappear into the opening. We hear a scuffle and a muffled yell.

"Oh my god!" Caliga nearly shrieks. "What do we do?"

"Micah!" I yell, running for the ladder.

"Zel, no!" Cy calls out, running after me, but I'm too

fast to catch. I scramble up the ladder and find Micah lying on the floor, with Hex on top of him. He's got one hand on Micah's neck and four fists ready to turn him into a mashed potato version of himself.

"*Hex!*" I scream out in joy.

Hex turns his head. He's got huge shadows under his eyes and he's far leaner than when he'd left Carus. His clothes are dirty and he looks exhausted, but his eyes have got that crinkly look he gets when he's about to break into a sunrise of a grin.

"Zel! Holy crap! Wait, are you with . . ."

"We're with Micah," Cy announces, his head sticking up through the opening. He looks at Micah, still being choked by Hex's hand. "Geez, Hex. Good thing I didn't come through here first."

"Cyrad!"

"Let Micah go, he's okay," I say.

"How do you know?"

"He's not shocking you, is he?"

Hex stands up from where he was sitting squarely on Micah's stomach.

"Thanks," Micah wheezes.

Hex points a single finger at him and yells, "Shut up." He turns to me. "What the hell's been going on?"

"It's a long, long story." I run straight to Hex and body-slam him with a hug. He squeezes me with all four arms so hard that my eyeballs bulge a little, but I don't care. He smells like sweat and dirt and a faint tang of worry. "Where's Ana and Vera?"

"Vera's on the roof, ready to unleash her green hell on anyone I can't handle," he says, letting go to give Cy a power hug too.

"What about Ana?" Cy asks.

"She's okay. She's with Marka and Dyl." His dark brown eyes light with excitement. "Guys. We've been waiting for you. We've got a new home. We're going to be safe."

"What? Where?" Cy and I yelp at the same time.

"Wingfield."

The word hovers in the air, but I'm not overwhelmed with happiness like I should be. Wingfield is a bucket of questions and worries, and there haven't been enough answers to appease me. When Élodie climbs through the opening, Hex's eyes widen.

He sidles next to me. "Long story, huh, Zel?"

"You have no idea," I say.

Right then, Vera swings through the sole window at the end of the room from a fire escape. She's wearing a long-sleeved shirt and pants, and her face and hands are covered in smeared makeup. In some spots, it's rubbed away and her green skin peeks through.

"Zelia, my little *Quahog* sis!" she yells, before screaming, "Oh my god, Cy!" But Vera stops her headlong rush toward us when she sees Micah and Élodie. "What . . . what are they doing here?" she asks coldly.

I suck in a deep breath. "Oh boy. Where should I start?"

MICAH, ÉLODIE, AND CALIGA STAY DOWNSTAIRS, EATING a dinner of very stale, stolen Avida food. Upstairs, Cy and I catch up with Vera and Hex, explaining how we found each other and survived the craziness of Avida. They stare at us like we're making all of it up.

"So Blink—that wench that attacked you in Aureus—is okay?"

"Uh . . . yeah." I nod.

"You have got to be kidding me. And we can trust Micah? I mean, of all the people . . . if you and Cy trust him now, then I guess we will, but . . . man. Really?"

Cy and I exchange uneasy glances. "I *think* I trust him," I say. I'm still reeling from the last-minute alliance-switch head-games he played on us.

Hex lowers his voice to a whisper. "He says he wants to make it up to Dyl and Ana. But how do you know he's only here to stick with the winning team?"

"I don't know if we'll ever know, unless he turns on us." It's the truth, as far as I'm concerned.

"Well, that Élodie girl seems nice enough," Vera comments. "Quiet, though."

"It's 'cause she's Canadian," Hex says, reaching for Vera's uneaten homemade travel bar.

She slaps his hand. "Stop stealing my food! And being Canadian doesn't make you quiet."

"She doesn't speak English, right?" he says, and Vera smacks his head this time. "Ow? What?"

"Canadians speak English! What is wrong with you?"

"Actually, French is her first language." I smirk, waiting for their reaction. Hex immediately points all four index fingers at me and glares at Vera in his defense. I stifle my laughter as he and Vera escalate their fight over Hex's horrible grade-school understanding of North American culture.

I interrupt their fight for more details on Wingfield. "What about Marka and Dyl? You met up with them?"

"We did," Hex explains. "They arrived before us. We snuck through the border to the Dakotas. Didn't realize it would be so lax there. Maybe because their population is so horrendously low that they want refugees. Anyway, we bribed a border patrol to get into Minwi in exchange for our char and the fake F-TIDs. We walked the rest of the way. When we got here, Marka and Dyl were already camped up on the roof."

"Would you believe they flew here?" Vera rearranges her legs into a knot that makes me uncomfortable just to look at. "They went west and found a tiny black-market hoverpod company that drained the money from Marka's fake F-TID account. Flew her and Dyl straight to Chicago to a landing strip with no immigration officials."

"Are you kidding me?" I slap my hands onto my legs. "We took the most direct route and ended up getting in the most trouble!"

"You never seem to take the easy way out," Hex comments, and nudges me with his elbow. I drape one of his arms around my shoulder and smile.

"So when Marka got here, it was empty. But she smelled something like lavender. It's her favorite scent, did you know? Because I didn't. I think it's something from her childhood. Anyway, she found a hidden message just for her, tucked into the wall. The people who had a safe house here relocated to Wingfield. They gave Marka explicit instructions on how to get there through Minwi and which border patrol house would let her cross over, unasked. So after we arrived, they left because Ana was getting weak from all the traveling. And here we are, waiting for you slowpokes."

Vera jabs Hex in the back with her big toe and I laugh. It's so good to laugh again. I was afraid I'd never remember how.

Cy stands up. "Look. Let's get some sleep. We need to start traveling in a few hours and I'm exhausted." We all nod and spread out our clothes into makeshift beds. I peek downstairs, but Micah, Caliga, and Élodie are already asleep, far apart from one another. They've barred the door with huge pieces of building materials scavenged from outside.

Cy and I make a place for ourselves in the corner. Vera and Hex turn their backs to us, tangled in each other's arms and whispering. I'd thank them for the privacy, but they're too engrossed in each other anyway. The floor is hard as concrete, but Cy's arm is my pillow, so I don't complain.

I snuggle into his shoulder. "You haven't used your other trait very much since we left."

"I know." There's a long pause, and he says, "I'm sorry. If I knew how to use the touch aspect properly, I could have kept Julian from hurting you."

"It's okay."

"No, it's not."

"Will you try to practice more? I miss your voice in my head," I whisper.

"I'll try. I promise." Cy concentrates, and recites the "Luna" poem to me in my head. When he's done, I spread my hand over his chest.

"That poem isn't right, you know."

"Hmm?" he murmurs into my hair.

"I never left you. I'm not some untouchable, heavenly body."

His fingers grasp my waist, pulling me on top of him. "I've always felt like you're too far away."

"Why? I'm right here. And when I wasn't, when you were in Aureus, I was always yours."

Cy closes his eyes. "I don't know if I'm ever going to feel like I deserve anything."

"Then I'll keep convincing you that you're wrong. I'm stubborn like that."

"Your faults are the best thing that ever happened to me," he says, guiding my lips to his. No matter how many times I kiss him, I marvel at how unreal it is. Each is our first kiss, and our last, and every one in between.

We don't sleep much. We're too busy missing each other.

CHAPTER 28

AT DUSK, WE ALL DESCEND THE LADDER QUICKLY. Leftover light from the sunset warms the western edge of sky as we stretch and get ready to leave Chicago.

"Let's go," Cy says, when he spins around. "Wait. Where is Élodie?"

"I don't know. I thought she was upstairs with you guys," Micah says. We all spill out onto the boardwalk, when footsteps approach.

"*Je suis ici.*" Élodie rounds the corner of a far shanty, wiping her mouth. "I'm okay. I got too close to Caliga and felt nauseated. I had to . . . you know." She pats her stomach.

Everyone exhales a group sigh of relief.

"So Hex, where do we go?" I ask.

"I have the coordinates on my holo. We'll go by the Ilmo border until we find border station twelve into Minwi. There's a guy that will let us through, according to the instructions Chicago House left us."

I'm glad to leave the stench of Chicago behind us. Soon the boardwalks are replaced by streets and sidewalks, crowded in by buildings. Their walls glow with holo ads that illuminate the evening with junk we don't want. Luckily there aren't many people around after dark. Caliga stays close to me, which keeps us separated from the rest of the group. I give Cy several meaningful looks, and he practices his trait while we walk the hours to the Minwi border.

He whispers things that no one else is privy to, and grows bolder with his touch trait. Sometimes, it's only an airy kiss on my cheek. Other times, a caress that leaves me weak in the spine. I love that these secret offerings are for me, and only for me.

Though he walks with Élodie, they don't say much. Hex and Vera walk with Micah between them, who's gesticulating and trying to explain everything that's happened since he left Carus. Hex keeps his four fists clenched behind his back and Vera doesn't even look at Micah.

Conversation alone can't make people forgive you. Though Caliga, Blink, Cy, and I still wear our red bracelets, Micah's got another burden he can't seem to shake. Maybe he never will.

When the sun rises, we find border patrol station twelve. Hex puts on his huge trench coat and Vera takes out a makeup compact to touch up the places where her green skin has peeked through. Caliga slips her hand into mine and I squeeze hers thankfully. We collectively shake off our exhaustion and enter the building. Hex veers us toward the office for unregistered Minwi applicants.

"We're looking for George Frederick," he tells the clerk there. "We have an appointment."

"All of you?" The lady looks at us suspiciously.

Hex nods, and she points to an office down the hall. Hex knocks and it's opened by an ordinary middle-aged man, with gray hair at his temples and dark brown skin sporting a few wrinkles. He frowns.

"You're late. Come in and keep the door open."

We all crowd into the room, with Caliga peeking in from the hallway. He says rather loudly, "Your paperwork is done. It was sent through last week. You passed your physicals just fine."

He puts his hand under the desk and pulls out a huge duffel bag and kicks it over to Cy. As he continues to drone on about our new housing assignments and jobs, a mellow, deep voice enters our heads.

These are provisions and camping equipment. Give me your holo. He gestures to Hex, who hands it to him. *I'll download a map. Stay away from the roads. When you reach the edge of town, it should be a two days' walk.*

We try not to make any squeaks or gasps of shock. He has Cy and Ana's trait! But it's dizzying to simultaneously hear his real voice lecturing us about Minwi's strict labor laws.

I wish you all the best of luck. Kria is looking forward to meeting you.

Cy steps forward and cocks his head. *Who is Kria?*

Mr. Frederick's eyebrows rise up and he smiles. *Look at you! Well!* he says with surprise. He's still continuing his audible list of the Top Ten Minwi Do's and Don'ts. Meanwhile, he's loading a map onto Hex's holo using a personal, thimble-sized holo adapter. This guy is seriously the king of multitasking.

Ah. Kria told me I wasn't the only one. She's head of Wingfield and has granted you safe passage. If all goes well, I might be there myself soon.

After his last lecture, he hands Hex his holo and gestures for us to follow him. He rubs his face when he gets too close to Caliga, but that passes after I shove her behind me.

He leads us out to the exit of the building, and points to a street where several new Minwi residents are loading onto huge, public magpods.

"Third magpod, leaving in half an hour," he orders us.

Take a left at the end of the block and keep walking. Your holo map will lead you from then on. Good luck. He gives us a genuine smile. "Good luck."

As we walk away, Cy twists around for one last look at Mr. Frederick. They lock eyes, and Mr. Frederick gives a slight bowing nod to Cy, before withdrawing back into the building.

Cy captures my arm in his as we catch up to the rest.

"I wish he could teach you. That was amazing, what he was doing," I say, trying to keep my excitement quiet.

"I know." Cy smiles but glues his eyes to the ground, as if afraid someone might see his enthusiasm. "I asked him if he would teach me, someday. And he said yes."

I smile and squeeze his hand. Cy squeezes back and lets a grin through.

The farther from town we go, the tighter the grasp the Minwi wilderness has on the land. Enough of the poisons that leached into the soil of Neia have hit lower Minwi too, and most people stay in the safe confines of the towns and cities. We hike along crumbling sidewalks and streets overgrown with spiky weeds and saplings. My scent trait tells me things I can't see—that the plastic trash inside the crumbling houses is still not decomposing; that the soil is too acidic. There are some good things, though. Ivy twines itself over feral buildings, swallowing them, and non-toxic plants erupt in tufts here and there. Life is reemerging lustily. It's nothing like the Deadlands.

We hide in a musty, abandoned barn when the ominous hum of hoverpods approaches, because we're too close to a bustling town. But after one day spent slumbering inside another abandoned house, we ready ourselves for the last trek toward Wingfield in the watery light of afternoon.

Cy checks on me by whispering in my head. Things like *Is your headache getting better?* or *Look out for that thorn bush.* It's all welcome. He even tests it by yelling *Look at the vampire woodchucks!* But none of the others bat an eyelash.

He also practices cutting off the circulation to my thumb, and my thumb only. Most of the time, he misses and everyone yells "*Thumbs!*" at Cy, holding up their universally white digits. He cusses, then tries again.

Élodie continues to lead us in the darkness toward our destination, but we're too tired to hike all night long. Micah is the most silent of us all. He's less talkative the closer we get to Wingfield. I know he's thinking of Dyl, and of the big, yawning unknown of what we're about to encounter. Here I am, with my Ondine's curse and all its breathing problems, and Micah is the one who's perpetually holding his breath.

Only ten miles away now, Cy says in my head.

"I know," I murmur.

"What are you talking about?" Caliga whips her head back at us.

"Sorry, Cal. We're getting really close." My legs ache from so many miles of walking and only shallow breaths to supply the oxygen they need. There was a time when Dyl would tell me I needed to put my necklace on. Those reminders to take care of myself seem like they happened in a dream. I miss her so much.

I pause to take the last gold pocket watch from my bag and hang it around my neck with a torn edge of a shirt used as a necklace. As soon as the watch bounces heavily against my rib cage, my chest swells and the air pours into me, lifting some of the cloudy tiredness in my head. Micah stops and stretches. The sun is turning gold just over the horizon. It'll be dark soon.

"What do you guys think about camping? Maybe we could get another nap in before we enter Wingfield. Just in case."

I'm dying to see Dyl and everybody, but I'm exhausted too.

We all look around, and no one makes a case to go forward. It goes to show you how fearful we are of the unfamiliar, that we're willing to put off reuniting with our loved ones for another uncomfortable and unshowered night on the run. Hex rummages through the duffel bag and digs out some water-purifying tablets. "I've got five left." He drops an azure tablet each into several water bottles. I grab three of them.

"I'll be back. I thought maybe I smelled a fresh stream nearby."

I leave the temporary camp, noting that Élodie and Cy are talking now. It's not a bad thing to give them a little space. They haven't had much time to keep their friendship going since we left Avida, and anyway, it looks like she's lecturing him on something I don't want to hear.

Here and there are traces of the old neighborhoods beneath the greenery that's taken over, like bits of broken patio furniture clad in shredded plastic and tough weeds. A brown rabbit with asymmetrical ears dashes ahead of me. Micah zapped one just like it yesterday for dinner, but nobody took a bite when the cooked flesh reeked of heavy metals.

Finally, I hear the rushing sound of bubbling water. Hidden behind a thicket, it's a tiny stream only two feet wide. I drop to my knees and fill the bottles one by one. I watch the purification tablets dissolve and the water goes from bright blue to clear, telling me that it's safe to drink now.

I tip a bottle to my lips, taking long, noisy gulps.

"Wow, that's good," I say to nobody, wiping my mouth.

A crackle breaks the quiet behind me. It's the sound of a plastic trash bag being stepped on. There's a warm breath on my neck, and a scent that doesn't belong to anyone in our group.

"Care to share?"

I whirl around at the sound of the unfamiliar voice and the smell. A large hand covers my mouth and strangles my cry for help. A strong arm half lifts, half drags me deeper into the forest as I struggle furiously.

I can't breathe. I can't even open my mouth to try to bite my attacker. I swipe the attacker's face and my nails rake against a stubbly beard.

"Ow. Stop that." His voice is gravelly, as if he hasn't spoken in years. "There's no need to fight me. You've got at least another two hundred years left to go. I'm not going to end that now."

My hands go limp. My attacker knows about my longevity trait? Before I can even wonder who he is, he throws me down in a ring of juniper trees and pins me to the ground.

Now I can see him. His hair is tangled and yellow, the color of dandelions. His skin is pale and almost greenish in the shadows. By the base of his neck, an inch-long ragged scar points to the hollow of this throat. Absurdly long blond eyelashes fringe plain brown eyes.

"Please don't scream," he says. He's still pressing his hand against my mouth.

Since when do kidnappers say "please"?

I force a tiny nod, and he releases my face. I gulp the air, coughing and clearing out the muddled sensation in my head.

"Goodness. So this is what it looks like to be a slave to one's imperfections."

"What?" I wheeze, coughing more.

"Your Ondine's curse." He narrows his eyes, centers them on the pocket watch hanging from my throat. "Ah. I've been looking for this." He puts a knife to my throat, sawing off the cloth necklace, and in seconds has my watch enclosed within his fist. My eyes grow wide with disbelief.

"Are you . . . Endall?"

"Yes." He smiles crookedly.

I can't believe it.

His clothes are dirty, but they're not old, nor worn. He doesn't seem insane, nor does he seem safe. I breathe carefully, trying to stay calm.

"How did you . . . What are you doing here?"

"I've come to take back what is rightfully mine." He releases one of my hands to pull out a tarnished watch from a hidden inside shirt pocket. "This one has fallen prey to the humidity. And time. Time is a slow-roasting hell for everything in the world but us."

Zelia! What's taking you so long? Where are you? Cy's voice is urgent, worried.

"Cy!" I yell.

Endall jumps off me and dashes into the darkness beyond the trees, his footsteps fading rapidly in the distance.

"Wait! Endall! I need that watch!" I scream. "Wait!"

Far away, his voice calls back to me.

"Where you're going, darling, you won't need one."

Crap. What does that mean?

Zelia! Where are you?

"Zel?" Caliga calls out, maybe twenty feet away. Feet

crash through the brush behind me as I slowly get to my feet, rubbing my arms where Endall held me down.

"I'm here!" I yell back.

Cy and Caliga see me from across the clearing, picking dead leaves out of my hair and stumbling into the light. I tell them everything—about the attack, Endall, the pocket watch that is no longer in my possession. And my imminent death without it.

Cy's face clouds with worry. "We've got to find this Wingfield place. Now."

So much for one last night camping under the stars.

We scurry to douse the fire and gather up our bags. As the darkness of the western sky starts to wipe out the blush of sunset, we start jogging southward, but I have to stop frequently because of the lactic acid cramps in my legs. After two hours, it's pitch-dark. Hex turns on the glowing green holo and points.

"It's only a half mile now. Just over that hill."

My Ondine's curse must be catching, because at the sight of the hill, we all take a huge, collective breath.

Ten minutes of walking later, we stop. Tiny pinprick stars twinkle above, and a sliver of moon rises over the eastern edge of sky. There's a plain, hard scent of mineral-rich water close by. Caliga blurts out in surprise, "Look. It's a lake."

"Not a lake. It's an old quarry," Élodie says. "You can see where they cut rock along the edges."

"Hex, do a search on mining companies named Wingfield in Minwi, will you?" I ask. Hex complies, searching his holo through the public info channels. After a minute, he stops.

"Here. Wingfield Incorporated. They mined granite, but the pit was abandoned and filled with water seventy years ago."

No wonder I couldn't find a town called Wingfield.

We peer into the gloom for signs of human habitation. In the twilight, the water resembles a crude oil spill extending half a mile into the distance. No buildings, no people. Nothing.

"No one's here," Caliga says. "It's a dead end."

Her voice quavers the tiniest bit, and I can read her emotions, even without scenting them. No safe haven means no Wilbert. It means no end to being on the run. Cy picks up a rough rock, throwing it ruthlessly into the water. We wait for the angry splash, but there is none.

"Hey. Hey! What happened to the rock?" I exclaim.

"I saw it go into the water. Look, there . . ." Cy points at a distance. We see the pinpoint stars reflected in the water, but oddly, some of the points of lights seem firmly fixed and unperturbed by the soft breeze blowing across the surface.

Caliga trembles as she clutches my arm.

"Something is down there," she says.

CHAPTER 29

"LOOK. LOOK!" CALIGA SAYS, UNABLE TO HIDE the hunger in her voice. She runs toward the water's edge, splashing noisily.

I grab for her arm. "Cal, wait!" I yell. But it's too late. She's up to her thighs in the water, slapping the surface.

"Wilbert! Wilbert! I'm here!" she cries.

I lunge for her again but Cy pulls me back by the waist.

"No. Wait. Something's moving down there."

Under the water, something big and glowing a ghostly blue moves only a few feet away from Caliga. A rounded pillar of translucence breaks the surface; its amorphous shape blurs and shimmers, rearranging atoms into a shell of something vaguely Y-shaped, yet human. And then, like a lens that suddenly drops out of nowhere to fix our vision, the blue thing sharpens into focus.

"Oh my god. Wil?" Caliga whispers, raising a soaking hand to touch the image.

It's Wilbert. He may be a blue digital image, but it's

him. His second, faceless head bobs quietly between his normal head and his left shoulder. He's crying.

"Cal. You made it. I can't believe it." He extends a hand toward her, and she slips her hand into the image of his. Caliga shivers at his touch. Wilbert blurs again, and refocuses. "Cal, it really is you."

"Are you here? Are you inside this place, somewhere?"

"Yes."

The water around Caliga's legs glows with the same eerie light blue. Like a giant amoeba, it starts to crawl up her legs and envelop her, as if she's being eaten by the reservoir water itself.

"Wait! Wilbert, is it safe? Are you okay?" I shriek at him, but the Wilbert water image won't respond to me. Caliga, now enveloped in blue shimmering water, lets the Wilbert image pull her into the depths. We all watch, stunned, as their blue lights wink out.

"Well. Count on Wilbert to create a dramatic passcode into this place," Cy murmurs. "Shall we?" He gestures to the water, and I hesitate. Micah does too. Drowning is not fun, particularly when you're volunteering to do the deed yourself.

We each gingerly step into the icy cold water. Within a minute, ghostly blue blobs arise from the deep to meet us. The first one to break the surface morphs and merges into the shape of Tegg—the tall guy from Aureus whose skin is thickened like bark. It's nearly impenetrable, though I managed to stab him in a weak spot when we battled in the underground club Argent. Tegg doesn't seem to see me or Cy, only Micah and Blink.

"Long time, no see, Kw," Tegg says. "Let's go." He offers a hand to Élodie, saying, "The Queen of Darkness. Welcome." Blink and Micah both grasp his hands with trepidation. Within seconds, they've all sunk beneath the surface of the water.

"I can't believe Tegg is here," I whisper, but Cy doesn't hear me. The blue blob that's come to welcome him is exactly Ana's height.

"Cy," she says in her girlish voice.

Another rises next to her, and it's tall and willowy. "Hex. Vera." The blob becomes focused to show Marka's pixie cut and gentle smile. Hex and Vera splash forward and each grab a hand. They collapse into one another's arms and the blue rises up from the water to envelop them, as Cy's and Ana's forms disappear into the depths.

One final glowing body rises up to meet me. Rounded soft lips form, then eyes—wide and beautiful, and unsure. Long, straight hair swishes like optical fibers behind the shoulders, and slender arms detach from the body to reach for me.

"Zel," it whispers.

I weep, and the scent of salty tears invades my thoughts. This is the scent of happiness, and fear, and relief, and yes, hope come to fruition.

"Dyl," I cry, and collapse into her ghostly blue arms. I know it isn't really Dyl, and that this apparition isn't really water. She's probably full of emulsified nanocircuits made by Wilbert.

I think these things to try to keep from completely losing it.

Blue phosphorescent water snakes up my legs, covering me like a wet, impenetrable skin. As it slithers over my chest, under my armpits, and twines up my neck, I take a huge breath.

"Relax," Dyl's apparition says. "It'll be over soon."

I grasp the mirage of Dyl as hard as I can, but she dissolves in my embrace. Just when I can't hold my breath any longer, a solid floor gathers beneath my feet. The liquid encasing my body breaks apart and fizzles into the air, dissipating like boiled water.

I'm in a painfully bright white room, spacious and plain. A lone holo panel with digital readings and numbers I don't understand blinks on one wall. The ceiling is waves of quarry water, somehow held back by an invisible barrier. Micah, Cy, Élodie, Vera, Hex, and I all stand in the room alone, not a smidge wet from the quarry water, just blinking confusedly in the bright light.

A door opens, and I nearly scream with joy at the person entering.

"Marka!" I rush straight into her open arms, followed by Cy, Vera, and Hex crushing us into a ball of Carus welcomes. Her laughs rings out, rich and full.

"You made it! God, I can finally draw a breath!" she says, and her eyes twinkle at me. "These last two weeks have felt like ten years!" We separate and Micah coughs uncomfortably behind us.

"Hi," he says to Marka, his face hung with shame and misery.

"Hello, Micah."

Micah doesn't make a move forward. Marka's eyes water. Micah lived at Carus before I got there, before he betrayed them and went to Aureus. Marka raises a hand to touch his shoulder, but hesitates. Fury and hurt and empathy flash across the features of her face, warring for precedence. Finally, she touches his shoulder and Micah's eyes squeeze shut. She pulls him into her arms.

He weeps.

More people crowd into the room, diluting the uncomfortable silence. Ana embraces Cy like she might never let go. Tegg enters and smirks, but welcomes no one. Caliga presses herself into the corner until she sees Wilbert enter.

"Wil!" she yells, and he runs straight to her, wrapping his arms around her rib cage and spinning her around and around like a carnival ride.

They're touching. And Wilbert isn't getting sick.

"Oh my god, oh my god! How? Wilbert!" she cries and blubbers. "How?"

"I made a vaccine according to your protocol as soon as I got here a month ago."

They're both crying so hard, I don't want to witness their impending very wet, very snotty kiss. I turn away when something smashes straight into me.

"Zel!"

Dyl sweeps me into a powerful hug. Relief unleashes within me like a living thing, too big to be contained. I burst out in tears, hugging her so hard, it hurts. We finally let go enough to laugh and look at each other, searching for signs that this is real and we're not dreaming, when Dyl freezes in my arms.

"What is he doing here?" She looks beyond me and I twist to see Micah watching us from ten feet away, where Marka's released him. He looks to Marka, but she keeps her distance, as if to say, "*No, Micah. I can't protect you from the consequences of your decisions.*"

"Dyl." I want to explain everything, my own worries and fears and everything he's told me, but she pulls out of my arms and marches straight up to him.

"I've waited too long for this," she seethes. Micah's face is so white, I think he might have just lost a pint of blood from her withering stare alone.

"Wait," Micah says, raising his hands slowly, but it's too late. Dyl slaps him hard across the face.

"That's enough, Dyl." Marka pulls her away and tucks her under a protective arm. "Everyone will have a chance to settle in. We've a lot to talk about. A lifetime's worth." The door opens again and an amber-skinned girl with lush, curly black hair steps inside.

"The exam room is ready," she tells Marka.

"Can't we put that off? They just got here, Jess."

"Which is why we can't hold off."

Everyone stops hugging everyone else. Funny how check-ins can break up a welcoming party.

"Very well. I'll see you all after you get cleaned up," Marka says brightly.

"Zel, let's start with you." The girl, Jess, leads us down the hallway and I wave a reluctant good-bye.

"I kept your unicorn," I tell Ana, patting the pack hanging from my shoulder. "She wasn't lonesome."

Ana pokes my elbow from afar and whispers in my head.

I knew you'd take care of her.

"We'll talk later, Ana. I promise," I call to her. I look back at Cy, and he shrugs. *What's the worst that could happen? Marka is here. Right?*

His words aren't confident. I mean, we should be safe now. But I can't dismiss my worry anyway. Because I know that even here, we're hiding. I wonder if we will ever be able to stop being afraid.

I'll see you soon, Cy says, and a whispery kiss touches my cheek.

The corridor ahead is bland and white. But around a curve, a veritable tree is embedded in one of the walls. Its branches curve and twist up to the ceiling, spreading out over another window where the quarry water shows darkly above us. The pale green leaves are nearly plastered against the invisible barrier, as if waiting to drink in the morning sun.

Jess waves me forward and leads me to a door with a thin willow tree arching over the top.

I part the drooping willow branches and enter. Inside is a medical room, not unlike the one from Carus House.

There's a white table, surrounded by walls of locked drawers and strange medical equipment I've never seen before. Everything is white and silver, cold and clean. Memories of my first day at Carus flood me—running away from Hex on the agriplane, having the shards of glass embedded in my skin removed by Cy, and his unexplained hostility toward me.

Jess walks in the door and sweeps by, turning on a holo screen.

"Hi Zelia. This will go by really fast. Hold out your hand." I extend my hand and she sees my bracelet. "Oh. That's from your stay in Inky?"

"Yes."

"Well, we'll have to see if someone can remove that without the explosive going off. And it's not going to be me," she says with a definitive nod. She takes my other hand and curls a silver band around my wrist. "This is a physiosensor. It's from a CompuDoc, but we changed the programming."

The holo screen immediately lights up with a huge list of blinking red statements. Jess peers at them, blocking my view.

"Hmm. Tox levels are moderate. We can chelate those out easily. Yep, demodex infestation. And a minor nematode infection." My skin crawls with itchiness at her comment. "Malnourishment levels aren't too bad. Hmm. Estrogen levels are normal, but you're anovulatory."

Hooray. It never gets easier to hear how unnatural I am sometimes.

Jess touches her holo a few times, and then proceeds to clean off my upper arm with a green liquid. Something beeps behind her and she removes a large patch, peeling the backing away.

"Wait, what's that?" I ask.

"I've infused it with the chelators and a few antiparasitic meds and vitamins."

I let her press it firmly to my arm. The microneedles attach to me, like a million ants nibbling all at once. It stops itching after a few seconds.

"Is that it?"

"Almost. Can you lie down for a second?" she asks.

"Why?" I say, reclining on the examining table.

"Because you're going to get dizzy. You need to sleep, and I'd rather you lie down than smack your head on the floor."

As soon as she says it, I feel the wooziness in my head. It's strong and sudden, and I have no pacer anymore. No watch, no necklace. And Jess doesn't know.

"Wait, wait," I say, realizing that my speech is already slurred. Or maybe my hearing is screwed up. I reach for the patch to tear it off, and Jess holds my wrist down.

"It's okay. She said it was okay."

"Who? Marka?" I say thickly.

"No. Your mother," she responds, looking at me like I'm stupid. She lets go of my arm, but it seems to weigh a thousand pounds and it falls limply by my side. I hear tubing and metal things banging against one another. A mask goes over my face, forcing air into my lungs.

Jess leans over me, patting my head. "When you wake up, you'll be right as rain."

With that my brain succumbs and slips into a dark, depthless sleep.

I HAVEN'T BEEN THIS COMFORTABLE IN A long time.

As I start to rise out of my deep slumber, little things make me smile. Cy is here. Marka and Dyl too. My fingers slip under the soft cotton sheets over my body. I feel clean. Did I take a shower? Who got me into this nightgown? I can't remember. My nose nuzzles the pillow, scented faintly of verbena and the ocean.

I stretch luxuriously, and reach for my breathing necklace.

It's not there.

What?

I slept a whole night without my pacer? My hand goes to my neck and touches a sore spot at the base of my neck. There's a tiny lump there. Flat, as if they'd slipped an antique dime under my skin. It's in the same exact place where Endall had a scar.

"Well," says a voice. "What do you think?"

I sit straight up in bed to see a woman on a chair, watching me. It would be utterly creepy, except for the uncreepy smile warming her middle-aged features. She's wearing a long shift the color of a spruce tree. Her brown hair is in braids, bundled up on top of her head, and her hands are clasped on her lap, as if anxiously awaiting something.

"I didn't ask for a pacer," I say, wary.

"Why wouldn't you?" she responds, perfectly surprised at my response. "And anyway, it was your father's wish that you have that placed as soon as you arrived."

"My father ordered this to be here?"

"Before he died. He said it was the first thing I should do, if you made it here. And here you are." Her brown hair is familiar. As are her eyes. They're wide and intelligent, self-conscious and stubborn, all at the same time. "Welcome to Wingfield," she says, standing up. She walks to the bedside and offers a hand to shake. "My name is Kria."

"I know who you are," I say evenly. "You're my mother."

CHAPTER 30

WE JUST STARE AT EACH OTHER, the unsaid things sharpening the silence between us.

Kria's eyes are shiny and pink-rimmed, as if she's on the verge of crying. She awkwardly approaches me, enveloping me in a warm, gentle hug. She smells of lavender soap and contentment. I'm stiff as a twig and don't hug her back.

"Why?" I ask.

"Why what, dear?" She raises her pin-straight eyebrows.

"Why *everything*."

She sighs and, thank god, goes back to her chair. I'm already suffocated by her proximity and the overwhelming lavender. A scent that I no longer like very much.

"We wanted to protect you. You wouldn't have understood what was going on with me if I'd stayed."

"I wasn't five years old anymore," I argue. "He could have said something. You could have."

"And for that, I'm sorry," she says, wringing her hands.

"But it was also important for your father to hide my identity. I had a trait that Aureus would have killed for. They looked for me, but your father kept me hidden and safe. He would have put you in danger, had you or Dylia known of my existence."

It all comes together at once. Julian's first conversation with me, and the damned list that everyone wanted, to find out who was made, and how.

How.

Kria *is* the how.

"You're the key?" I say, incredulous. "The key that unlocks the terminator technology. That keeps us from being suicide seeds, so we can procreate. It's in you?"

"Yes." She beams at me, as if I've just answered a prize question in a game. "Good for you, Zelia. He said you were smart!"

"Don't patronize me!"

Kria recoils. "I'm . . . I'm sorry." She takes a huge breath and tries again. "The key is in me. While I was away, I gave birth to so many traited children. Tegg and Caliga—"

"Caliga?" I inhale my spit and cough spastically.

"Yes. But your parent DNA is different. My own DNA isn't in all the children. Your father decided on the parentage and created the traits by altering the embryonic DNA, by design. But I was only one woman. So your father isolated the proteins in me that were necessary to create and carry traited children, and gave them to normal women to increase production of traited children. I believe you know Renata—she was perhaps the only woman who agreed to the process. Very prolific too. The other women never knew. They thought they were taking prenatal vitamins."

It's sick. She makes traited kids sound like products in a factory, and I'm staring at the walking factory in my room. All those women, who had no idea. Kria tries to smile, despite my expression of utter disgust.

"Why, Kria? Why would you let him . . . Why would you do this?"

"Your father said I could be part of something so much bigger than myself. Something historical, world-changing. He said that creation was the closest we could get to divinity. I believed him. I mean, look at you. How could I argue with his design?"

Her eyes are full of pride and love, but her words make me feel like a thing. A chunk of clay.

"But I am proud of you, Zelia. Your father told me all about your accomplishments, and Dyl's. He'd show me all your grades." She drops her eyes to the ground. "He'd even show me holo transmissions of you two sleeping at night. I missed you two. I hated being a lie in your life, but it had to be. It's what your father wanted."

"Is it what you wanted?" I ask.

Kria says nothing. For the first time in this whole conversation, I actually feel sorry for her. We do have something in common, besides being mother and daughter. We've both been masterfully manipulated by my father.

I rub my eyes. I can't believe all this. I can, but I can't. It's so much. And right now, all I want is clarity, and reason, and understanding. I want the familiar, and I want home.

I want Marka.

"I should get dressed . . . or something," I say, gesturing to my messy hair.

"Of course, Zelia." She walks to the door and pauses. "You know, we thought of you the whole time. Of your future and well-being. We planned on building a home here so that we could all be safe someday."

"Safe?" I cock my head. The word *safe* is so soft, so deceptively neat and easy. "We are still illegal. We're still being hunted. We're hiding."

"Zelia—"

"We may be standing still, Kria, but we're all still running away."

AFTER I GET READY, CY MEETS ME at my door. He's clean-shaven and looks like the Cy from Carus, from a year ago. Dark gray T-shirt, dark pants. Only, no tattoos and no piercings.

"Boy, are you a sight for sore eyes," I say, kissing him.

"You stole my line!" he says, smirking. "C'mon. Marka's waiting for us at breakfast."

Wingfield is built like a spiral snail shell beneath the quarry floor. We curve around a long hallway, occasionally encountering another tree embedded into the wall, with its leaves splayed against the flickering, watery light from the transparent ceiling. As we walk, I tell Cy about my conversation with Kria.

"Did she say anything about Endall?" he asks.

"No. We didn't really get there. I sort of spent the whole

time yelling," I admit. "But look." I point to the embedded breathing pacer. Cy runs his fingers over the implant and his lower lip drops in surprise.

"I thought you didn't want an implant."

"I didn't."

"They just stuck it in you. Without your permission?"

I nod. "Apparently, it was on Dad's pre-death orders." He's still making choices for me now, even though he's gone.

"Well, it's not like you have another pacer at this point. But we'll try to make one for you, maybe order one through the black market. And then you can take that one out later."

He's right. "Come on," I say. "Let's go find Marka."

We coil our way around Wingfield until we come to a large, central room. Inside, people I know (and plenty of others I don't) sit in groups of chairs here and there. In the center of the room is a huge, floor-to-ceiling cylindrical tank with all kinds of fish, from black-and-white striped to brilliant amethyst and burnt orange.

Dyl and Ana sit at a little table where Ana is tearing apart a cinnamon bun into a thousand pieces. When she sees me, Dyl walks over with a mug of coffee and a plate of toast in hand. She's cinching a thick book under her arm.

"Kria told me who she is," I say, frowning, taking her offering of coffee and toast.

Dyl nods, looking pissed. "I found out last week. Did she tell you about your genetic makeup?"

"Not quite. You?"

"No. She said she would, but she's been too busy."

"Yeah, right." I tip my chin to the book under her arm. "What is that?" I ask, sitting down next to Ana.

Dyl shows me the gilt letters pressed into the cover. *Twentieth-Century Poetry.* The one that Dad gave her years ago.

"You packed that?" I ask, sipping coffee and shoving toast in my mouth.

"No. I wanted to leave it behind. Marka brought it. She said I'd regret leaving it behind."

"But you've been reading it?"

"Yeah," she says, sounding like she almost regrets the fact. "You know, it's weird. I've been reading so much po- etry this last year. *This* book is really strange." She taps the tome in her hands. "All the poems are anonymous."

"So?"

"Well, there aren't a lot of poetry collections by anon- ymous poets. I never really though much about it until now. Poets may be dripping in creative mystique, but they certainly don't shy away from getting the credit they de- serve."

"Hmm." I take the heavy book from her and flip through the pages. "Luna." "Prayer for My Child." "The Memory Play." I'd been avoiding the pain of reading it again, knowing how it reminded me of Dad. But maybe it's time to try again. "Can I borrow this?"

"Sure. It's yours as much as mine," she says, smiling. When we look up, we see Micah watching us from across the room. Dyl immediately shrinks from his watchful gaze.

"He won't stop looking at me. It's super-creepy," she whispers to me. "So you guys actually got along in that place? Avida?"

"We did. Sort of. But I was a captive audience. He said a lot of things I didn't expect." When Dyl raises an eyebrow, I tell her everything he's told me. His actions, his punishments under Julian, and how he crossed Julian to ultimately help us escape. How he said he'd never slept with her or Ana.

"And you believed him?" she says, her voice rising above the din of other conversations. Half a dozen heads turn our way.

"I don't know. He was so good at lying. An artist."

"He is an artist," she says. "A con artist." Her eyes rise to meet his. He tries to smile, but wilts when Dyl pointedly looks away again. I wonder if she will ever forgive him.

"Zel, c'mon." Hex is standing behind our couch and claps a hand on our shoulders. "Kria wants to talk to some of us."

We stand up, and everyone but Carus members leaves. Caliga, Élodie, and Micah are asked to stay, since they're new too. Marka sits next to Ana, who leans her head on her shoulder. Kria stands by the fish tank column, pressing a button to release food.

"They're African cichlids, from Lake Tanganyika," she says. We all wait for something more than a biology lecture. "An interesting example of evolution. Every niche of that rift lake now has a different species. Human evolution has been staggeringly linear, in comparison."

"What are you trying to tell us? That we're fish?" Élodie says with a bitterness that we all feel.

"No. You are a species that has unnaturally evolved, with your father's help. You are precious, beyond words or money."

"*Personne ne croit que c'est vrai,*" Élodie murmurs. I don't know what it means, but I can guess. Kria does one of those *smiling-but-ignoring-your-comment* faces.

"So. Are you the one responsible for destroying Aureus?" I ask.

"Yes. But it took years and years to plan. Aureus was abusing its power and turning children into commodities. In the beginning, SunAj agreed to support Dr. Benten and his work. But back then when SunAj built Aureus, there was a different philosophy: Create products to sustain an income, so the traited children could be sheltered and provided for. But then the money and power became too enticing. Dr. Benten stopped bringing them children. So they killed him."

Visions of my dad in the hospital flood my memories. The missing limbs; the ventilator strapped to his chest. I shut my eyes and Marka grasps my hand. Kria continues.

"Through our contacts, we found a place in Minwi where we could hide children. And your father contacted Senator Milford for the money, weapons, and the hoverpod we'd need to take over Aureus."

"Senator Milford!" several of us exclaim at the same time. What? I immediately lock eyes with Marka.

Vera's green fingers curl onto Marka's arm. "Did you know?"

Marka stands with her hand wide open, as if she's dropped something she can't recover. "I didn't know. Why didn't my uncle tell me?"

"Dr. Benten expressly asked that it be kept from you," Kria tells her. "The plans were dangerous and he didn't want you involved until the very end, when you could be brought here safely. When he died, this place wasn't ready, which is why Zelia and Dyl went to Carus, instead. But we never anticipated that the senator would be assassinated, or that his death would set off that chain of events that caused Carus to be attacked."

"So you know who attacked him? Who poisoned him with my old elixir?" I ask.

"No. We still don't know," Kria admits.

Cy comes to stand next to me. "So. What do we do now? Stay here forever?"

"For the time being. Minwi was bribed with a good deal of money to keep this area uninhabited for a few years."

A few years. They could go by in a snap. And then what? I sit down on the nearest chair, exhausted. I'm so tired of being chased like an animal, always on the verge of becoming history.

"Now we have to fight to get you rights," Kria goes on. "Freedom, like every other human."

Marka, Cy, Kria, and Vera start talking heatedly, of which States might be willing to break federal law to help us, or how we're even going to manage to have a voice when we're in hiding. I hear them talk about supplies, and money, and how risky it will be to rescue other traited kids across the States.

I think of Renata, now alone with her children. She'll have to face those Inky senators by herself, without Julian's silky behind-the-scenes deal-making. They're still waiting on a promise for my trait to be made, and I'm gone. There's only so long before they'll demand what she doesn't have.

While the discussion heats up even more, I quietly get up and leave the room. In the hallway, the trees along the walls and the transparent ceiling of ice-blue quarry water don't feel ephemeral or unique anymore. They're just fancy walls to yet another cage.

The question is, how can we get out and be free, once and for all?

CHAPTER 31

WE SPEND THE DAY WANDERING AROUND WINGFIELD, built beneath the water-filled, abandoned mine of the same name. The curving vortex of hallways all share the force field that acts as a ceiling, keeping the water at bay.

We also meet the other members of Wingfield. There's about twenty of us in total. It's all so overwhelming that I can barely remember any names. There's a girl with bat-like wings, and an eyeless young boy who can navigate the vortex-like hallways easily, amongst others. I'm astonished by all of their varied traits. Traits I never imagined might exist.

That night, I curl in bed and Cy slides in next to me. When he wraps his hands around my waist, I take his hand and stare at it. Long, strong fingers and wrists so smooth, you'd never know he'd once regularly dragged broken glass across them.

"What are you thinking?" He breathes, rather than speaks the words.

"About practicing."

"What, mouth-to-mouth resuscitation? I'm ready," he teases.

I smack his arm. "I mean your trait."

He sighs in resignation. After a few more coaxing words, he starts. We use only our hands to experiment on. Cy tries to pinch off the circulation to a finger at a time, then a toe. It doesn't always go smoothly, though. I get really dizzy and my heart races when I realize my whole body is being constricted, like I've got a python wrapped all over me.

"Stub," I say, my speech slurring from the lack of blood to my brain.

"Stub?"

I gasp. "Ssss . . . *stop*!"

When he sees that I've gone red in the face, he releases me. "Oh geez! Zel, I'm not doing this anymore!"

Luckily, I recover in a few seconds. It takes forever before he's willing to practice again. By two in the morning, he can make any finger of mine turn white easily. Even my leg, or my arm.

I yawn. "That was really good."

"I almost killed you. That's good?"

"Yeah! A miss is as good as a mile, as they say." I snuggle closer and curl into his arms. Cy's body radiates warmth straight into my bones.

He soon falls asleep, his body sagging into the bed. I carefully unwrap myself from his arms, watching his effortless breathing. His face is so peaceful, so perfect. I wish I could bottle this—the feeling I get from being within his orbit. That's a product that Aureus could have made a killing on.

I can't sleep. There are too many unanswered questions fighting for space in my mind, so I leave and walk through the darkened, spiral corridor in my nightgown.

At the innermost coil, there is a single door. It opens to a staircase, and then to a huge, dark cavernous space. Something clinks in the distance. Sounds like a dropped screwdriver.

A distant voice huffs in annoyance.

"Hello?" I call.

Suddenly, the lights pop on. I try not to squeal in surprise. There's a huge hoverpod taking up a hangar barely big enough to shelter it. The hoverpod is shaped like a square pillow, with black metal encasing the structure. There's a shuffling sound, and Kria walks out from behind the hoverpod, wearing dirty work clothes.

"Zelia! What are you doing up?" she says, wiping her dirty hands on her pants.

"Nothing. Sorry," I say, immediately turning back to the door. I don't really want to chat with her right now. And anyway, she's busy.

"Please. Stay a few minutes. I could use your help."

"I don't know a thing about fixing hoverpods."

"Neither do I. We'll be ignorant together." She smiles, but a certain desperation lurks behind her eyes.

I've no idea how to help. Kria opens the hatch to the hoverpod and steps inside, and I follow. Inside, she squats by an open panel revealing a million wires and circuits, blinking in red, white, and green. "It's like a glowing Italian flag in here. I don't know what I'm doing," she confesses.

"Why don't you ask Wilbert? He's good at this stuff."

She scratches her head. "Wilbert is with his wife for the first time in ages. I'm not going to bother him for this."

Oh. The first time they've been able to be together. As in, *together*.

"So you made the vaccine for Wilbert?"

"Oh yes. It was the first thing we worked on after I got him out of Aureus."

"So that was really you? You attacked Aureus?"

She touches the frazzled braids over her head. "I don't look very fierce now. But it helped to have the right equipment and friends."

"So you killed SunAj?"

Her face clouds over. "It didn't go as planned. He attacked first when I arrived at their new base in Okks. I wish so many Aureus kids hadn't run away, it would have made things easier. But the kids are safe now, so it was worth it." There she goes again, with the safe thing. She's delusional, if she thinks hiding equals safety. She points to some flashing lights, and says, "The cloaking buttons aren't working on the starboard side. Everything outside is okay, so it's an internal issue." She wiggles a few circuit relays, then throws her arms into the air. "Ugh. I really should just wait for Wilbert tomorrow."

"Why'd you bother?" I ask, before I realize the question is a little rude.

"Why not? Funny, your father would have said the same

thing. It used to drive him crazy when I started something he assumed I couldn't finish."

Never start something where failure is likely. He used to say that to me too. I look at Kria, up in the middle of night, working on something stubbornly, despite the odds. It reminds me of someone.

Oh. *Me.*

"So." I stand up and back away a little, as if my upcoming question requires space. "So if you're my mom, are you . . . How much of me . . ."

"You want to know who you are?" She crinkles her eyes at me. "What you are?"

It sounds like I'm asking for ingredients to a pot roast. "Yes."

"You've grown into such a pretty girl." Kria barely suppresses a smile. "Well. That hair is mine, so I'm sorry about that. Your father designed your longevity trait, and your body has developed slower because of it. I added Marka's genes, as an extra gift."

I'm definitely feeling like a pot roast now. "Why the extra scent trait? Why is it showing up now?"

"Your father wanted some children to have two traits."

"Who made you?"

"A long as there's been gene manipulation, there've been scientists who wanted to experiment. Really, it could have been anyone."

"How could you want to give birth to these kids, to us, and not know . . . *everything?*"

Kria's lip trembles. "I loved him. He was a brilliant

man, doing great things. I didn't ask to be in charge of it all. He was supposed to be here. With us."

I feel a pang of sympathy, thinking of the year I had without Cy.

"Zel, none of this is easy. Time will help. Love does strange things to your internal chemistry. There's also so much anger, confusion, and bitterness—"

"Look, I don't need to know every detail of your relationship with my dad."

Kria stares at me. "I'm not talking about me and your father. I'm talking about *you*."

Oh no she didn't. "Don't make this about me! It's about him, and it's always been about him. About what he's done to us. How he's created us and left us to figure out how to fix this mess."

"He tried to be transparent with me—"

"Ha!" I bark.

"Zelia," Kria admonishes me. "Your father was trying to help."

"I might have believed that once. I'm not sure I can anymore, Kria." I turn and head for the door.

"Zelia, please." I turn to see Kria, arms out. "Don't leave Wingfield."

I cock my head. "You mean like Endall?"

"How did you know about him?"

"We've met." My hand goes to the implant in my neck. "So. What made him leave?"

"Would you believe that he's claustrophobic?"

"In this place, sure. Who wouldn't be?"

"Not just about Wingfield. About everything. There aren't a lot of others like him, with your longevity trait. Your father wanted to make sure that Endall had a breathing pacer."

"You can't alter people's bodies without their permission!" I say, pointing to my neck. My own words illuminate what I haven't been able to see before. "*Oh*. It's not that Dad feels responsible. It's like we belonged to him, like a collection. We're his little menagerie, aren't we?"

"Zelia, he wanted the best for you. For all of you. He dedicated his life to you. But Endall went . . . slightly . . . crazy after his implant. He actually dug it out with a knife before he left." She shivers and waves her hand. "He's out there. Our doors are always open to him, but I doubt he'll ever walk in again."

For an infinite moment, I envy his choice. But turning my back on my father's legacy would mean turning my back on everyone I love too.

I can't afford that flavor of freedom. It would kill me.

I FINALLY MANAGE TO FALL ASLEEP AFTER snuggling beneath Cy's arms, but it doesn't last. When morning light flickers in through the watery ceiling, I'm up, as if already loaded on caffeine. I inch out of bed to find the poetry book sitting on a chair.

I read a few poems, pausing over the *Anonymous* written under the titles. Why did Dad give Dyl a book full of ownerless verses? I flip to the beginning and read the front matter, where the publisher and publishing date are listed.

Lanier Publishing. 1998.

I freeze.

Lanier was my father's middle name.

I close the book shut and leave my room and Cy's sleeping self, running down the curving hallway to Dyl's room. Someone's sitting outside of her room.

Micah.

His skin is sallow and his eyelids puffy, as if he's stayed up all night sitting in this one spot.

"Micah, what are you doing here?"

"She said she'd talk to me this morning." His arms are crossed on the tops of his bent knees and he stares at the blank wall opposite him.

"So you camped out here?"

"I have to try."

I sigh. "Micah, I don't think you should force it. Stalking doesn't help."

His eyes rise wearily to meet mine, and he gets up and walks away without another word.

I knock on the door. "Dyl, it's me."

The door swishes open and hides half her face behind the doorjamb. "Is Micah gone?"

"Yes. I sent him away. I told him to dial down the creep factor and give you some breathing space."

"Good. Thanks." I walk in and we sit on her bed. A school of those fish are wriggling in arcs above her room, casting shadows onto her quilt. "I don't know how to handle him. He wants a nonstop rehashing of everything and I just can't . . . ." She shakes her head. I don't blame her. I make a mental note to try to keep him out of her space at least for a few weeks, until we can all settle in.

"I wanted to show you this," I say, opening up the poetry book. I point to the publisher name and she frowns.

"That's Dad's middle name."

"I know. Do you have a holo we can use?"

"Yeah. Kria gave it to me when I got here. It's just a general network one." She pinches the stud in her earlobe and the glowing green rectangle screen pops up in front of her face. She angles it so we can both see it.

"Search 'Lanier Publishing,'" she commands. No site pops up, but several books are listed under the publisher. Reprints of novels, textbooks, and other poetry. It's all random.

"Wait, look." I run my finger down the list of books. "These all have the same publishing date. 1998. Strange."

A few images accompany the books. Mostly cover photos and scraps of text. But one catches my eye. It's a fuzzy photograph of a young man with messy hair, holding a book that could be our poetry book. He's not smiling, nor is he looking at the camera. It's a true candid, and seems like he didn't even know the picture was being taken. The date is January 1, 1999.

"Expand that one." I point, and Dyl grabs the photo and stretches it out with her fingertips.

I grab Dyl's wrist and she says only two words.

"Holy shit."

It's Dad.

CHAPTER 32

DYL AND I RUN THROUGH WINGFIELD, searching for Kria and Marka. We find them along with the others eating breakfast.

"We need to talk," Dyl says, dropping her book on their table. Several heads turn in our direction, including Cy's. He and Élodie amble over.

"What is it, dear?" Kria asks. I wince at the *dear*, but try to ignore it.

"Dad had a trait. Did you know? Either of you?" I ask.

"No, he didn't. He told me he didn't," Kria says. Marka's face mirrors Kria's.

"What's going on?" Cy asks quietly. His hand touches my back.

Dyl turns on her holo and spins the rectangle around so Kria, Marka, and Cy can see it clearly. She expands the photo as large as it can go, until the image of our father is actual size.

"This is Dad, isn't it?"

Kria and Marka nod, still not quite understanding why we're so upset.

I point to the caption below the image. "This is dated 1999. According to this picture, Dad was alive one hundred and fifty years ago."

Marka's a sickening shade of green. "That's not possible," she whispers.

"That's just a fuzzy picture. How do you know it's real? How did you find it?" Kria asks, her hand planted firmly on her chest, as if trying to keep her insides from spilling outward.

Dyl and I explain how the book led us to the answer. There's silence for a long time, and Tegg sidles up to us, peering at the picture.

"How do you know it's really him? Could be his great-great-grandfather or something."

"He's right," Cy reluctantly admits. He pulls up his own holo, and after a few searches, adds, "There's no information on this Lanier Publishing Company. There just isn't enough data here."

A glint of metal catches my eyes. Dyl is touching Dad's ring hanging around her neck. The ring that I'd forgotten about in the insanity of making it to Wingfield.

"No. There's data. We just didn't know we had it." I reach over to Dyl and she gives me a confused look as I touch the ring. "Dyl, can I have this for a second?"

"Sure, why?"

"Because I think that Dad never meant to tell us anything. He left clues, but he didn't tell us because he never intended for us to know. He never intended to die."

I slip the heavy gold ring off the chain and hold it up. It feels like an ordinary ring. Round, with scuffs along the edges, the inside surface smooth and worn. He never took it off. It was that precious.

"Wilbert," I call, and find him seated next to Caliga in the far corner, where they're watching us, their coffee untouched.

"Yes?" he answers. Caliga's hand conspicuously grabs his under their table.

"I need you to find something for us. Inside this ring."

He lets go of Caliga and walks toward us, scratching his extra, faceless head. He holds out his hand and receives the circle of gold, turning it over in his palm. "What do you think is in here?"

"The answers," I explain. "To everything."

WE ALL GATHER IN WILBERT'S WORKROOM. CAL stands behind him (she hasn't been more than one micrometer away from him since she arrived). Marka, Kria, Élodie, Micah, and everyone from Carus stand around, watching Wilbert study the ring under a scanning microscope.

Wilbert's room in Wingfield looks nothing like ours in Carus. Half the room is his bedroom, and half a nanocircuit lab. It's tidy, and something's missing. The gallon of No-PuK, for one thing.

"The walls look pretty different in here," I say.

"Oh yeah. The posters of half-naked women in Carus?

Those were there to throw you off. They all changed to portraits of Caliga when no one could see," he explains, sitting at his work desk.

He goes back to his scanner, then he utters a noise of surprise. "There's a seam here. Hand me those chargers, Cal." She picks up something that looks like pliers, but with wires attached. "I'll charge the two sides with the same polarity and they should come apart." Wilbert fiddles with the controls on the holo panel to the side, and clamps the pliers onto two halves of the ring. There's a quiet buzzing sound, and the two halves of the ring split in half cleanly. "Voilà."

The inside of the ring is hollow. A tiny ring of black lies within, and Wilbert pulls it out with delicate forceps.

"Wow, that is a beauty! A polymer data unit. Non-volatile. This thing is indestructible." He loads the tiny circle into a slot in the wall, and the holo screen above starts to read it.

"It's not encrypted?"

"No. It's like he never had a doubt that anyone would access it but him."

How cocky of him. It doesn't surprise me, though.

Within minutes, huge lines of data begin scrolling down. There are formulas and endless lines of genetic code. So much that it's unreadable at first.

"Whoa. What . . . Who are we looking at?" I say, my eyes blinking rapidly, trying to catch bits of lines here and there.

"Wait. Let me find the menu." Wilbert touches the

screen in a few places, and the confusing jumbles of lines disappear, replaced by a single list of names.

The list.

Caliga, me, Marka, SunAj, Tegg . . . everyone I know, plus at least sixty names I've never seen before. All neatly laid out, with birthdates next to them.

"Oh my god. These are the traited."

The room is quiet as snowfall as everyone scans the list.

"So this is it. The name and genetic code of every child he ever made," Marka says quietly. "Anyone with this list could make others like us too."

"We can't let anyone ever find it," I say quickly. "Someone could use it against us. Maybe we should destroy it."

"But this is *us*. We can't throw it away," Hex argues. "We might need it for ourselves."

Marka's peering at the list, her finger running down the names, when it trembles by a cluster of all-too familiar ones.

Marka Sissum

Kria Weisberger

Julian/Sean Llewellyn

SunAj Agni

"It's you." I look at Kria and Marka. "Both of you. I thought . . . I thought . . ."

"You never thought that he'd made us too. I didn't know either," Marka says, and she hugs herself, shivering. I remember Marka telling me that she'd been attached to my dad, back when he was pretending to be just an underling of Aureus. It's eternally creepy, to think of how he created the women in his life. It's awful. I just want to peel my skin off at the thought.

Below are a list of other names and birthdates, but I don't recognize them.

"Who are they?" I point to the other names.

Marka opens up a file of a name no one recognizes, born a year after her. There's an error-type message stamped across their code. She opens several other folders, but gets the same message. "He made others in our generation, but they didn't survive. That would explain why there are so few of us. He tried, but he failed a lot."

"Wait . . . what? My name is on there!" Dyl exclaims. We all stop to stare.

Dylia Laura Benten

"That can't be," Micah says from behind me. "Aureus tested you. There's nothing in your blood that's abnormal."

"Look here." Wilbert clicks on her name and a triptych of files opens. Next to a creation protocol, there are two distinct genetic codes listed for Dyl.

"Two codes?" Dyl peers closer, her eyes wide and searching. "So . . . my blood and external body have a different code from my internal organs?"

"You're a mosaic," I say with wonder. "Someone with completely different DNA in different parts of your body. Why?"

"Oh god. She's like me," Kria says, astonished. "I didn't know there was anyone else like me. I thought it was lucky—if someone tests me by blood test or skin sample, I resemble a normal person. But internally, I'm not. I can carry traited children and not be affected by their traits. My internal codes neutralize the terminator technology that makes everyone else sterile."

"You've got to be kidding me," Dyl says, frowning. "He made me into a . . . breeder? *What?*" Her face is bright red. She's going to pop if she doesn't calm down.

"No. This will never define you and it's not your fate. None of these things define us. I don't care what he did!" I'm yelling, but I'm not yelling at Dyl. How dare he? How could he?

"Why the hell would he prevent most of us from having children?" Vera asks.

Marka's face is lined with pain. "So they . . . or he, somehow, could control the production of us."

"What else is on this list that we need to know about?" Cy wonders aloud.

Wilbert goes back to the master list. We scroll back to the top, and right next to Dyl's name is another, too familiar one.

Thomas Lanier Benten

"So. There he is," Dyl says softly. "He must have some sort of longevity trait too."

"Is it like yours?" Hex asks, peering at the thousands of lines of genetic code swimming across the holo screen.

"I can't tell by just looking. This list doesn't spell it out. But he's marked part of the code in red. We match that up with a normal DNA dataset and we'll have our answer."

We all stand there, numb. There we are, in one neat little list for anyone to see, and for anyone to decide that we're too abnormal to deserve to live.

"Wait. If this is the whole list, then . . ." I turn to Marka and Kria, hopeful. "Then we could find everyone he's made. We can bring them here, right?"

"I don't know. To find them would be to reveal them. Avida is firmly locked within Inky. You saw how hard it was to leave there. We may have a list, but we're powerless to do anything except keep bribing Minwi to keep our own border guards, like George, in place so that our own can come to us."

"So they can find *us*?" It's too passive. I shake my head, saying, "We have to do more."

"Like what?" Kria asks. "We are criminals. I don't want to risk the safety of everyone in Wingfield. I don't know that I *can* do more, Zelia."

"It's not good enough, Kria."

We break away into smaller groups. And we start doing what we do best. Hex, Vera, and Micah volunteer to pore through the past holo news to see how many children have already died since we were discovered, so we'll know who's still alive. Cy and I promise to devote plans to decode the traits of the children we're not familiar with. Dyl and Kria plan on piecing out the actual altered proteins and immunological quirks that make up the key to unlocking terminator technology.

"Because I am not going to be anybody's damned baby-making key," Dyl mutters as she sits down at the desk next to Wilbert, rolling up her sleeves. She looks like she's going to war on her own DNA code. I couldn't be prouder.

"Where's Élodie?" Cy suddenly asks. We turn around, but she's gone.

Hex shrugs. "Maybe the excitement of the list sent her to the bathroom?"

"Ugh, not everyone has to pee like you when you get excited," Vera teases him.

Cy leaves the room and I lean over Wilbert. Caliga's brought a hover chair next to him.

"We have to be careful that none of this data leaves this room. Ever," Marka says.

Kria nods. "Wingfield is a closed system and I'm the only person who has the ability to communicate with the outside world. And believe me, I'm telling no one." Her lips press into a thin line. "We'll make multiple copies so everyone can work on their share. There's two labs downstairs, next to the hoverpod hangar. You'll love it, Zelia," Kria says, almost shyly. "It's state-of-the-art. Your father wasn't crazy about getting you into the lab again, but I made sure it had the same equipment you've used at your last few jobs, so you'd feel at home."

Marka gives her a softened, grateful look and I can't help but feel grateful too. "Wow. Thank you, Kria. Before he died, Dad told me to stop working in the lab and start studying political science and history courses."

"You can do that too, if you want."

I hesitate. Part of me—the old me—wants to say *no way*. But I think of what it was like to talk to those Inky senators. Of what it means to be the ant under the boot, and having nothing but a voice, at best, to fight with.

"Actually, I think I might want to."

"Maybe we could learn together. I've a lot to learn too."

I nod. Kria's ready to launch herself at me for an epic hug, but I'm still not quite ready for more of those yet. So I just smile. She stays put, smiles back, then shuffles away.

"Kria, are you doing this?" Wilbert points to a green line buzzing up and down in zigzags on the corner of his wall screen.

Kria spins around. "What's that?"

"There's an outgoing communication from Wingfield." He spins around on his hover chair, his faceless head bouncing against his shoulder. "And it's not coming from your holo."

Kria's hand goes straight to her earlobe, but her silver holo barbell is still there. "All the other holos here aren't even capable of communication," she says.

"Wait." I touch the tight red bracelet on my wrist, holding it up. "What about our Inky bracelets? What if these tracked us here?"

"They didn't," Wilbert says with confidence. "You have no signal on those outside of a certain radius from Inky. And anyway, if they gave off a signal, I'd be able to pick it up."

"Did you screen people when they arrived for other devices?" I ask.

Kria frowns. "I'm no Aureus, or Avida. I assumed that we're all on the same side, so no, I didn't expect anyone here to want to escape."

"And Endall?"

"I let him go. No fight."

"Wait. What is that?" Vera says, her hands spreading out onto the table in front of her.

We all stop talking, stop moving. There's the faintest hum in our ears and beneath our feet. The holo images on the wall screens blur ever so slightly.

The door slides open and Cy runs in, his face ashen.

"We're in trouble. Someone's found Wingfield."

CHAPTER 33

WE YELL THE QUESTION SIMULTANEOUSLY. "WHO?"

"I don't know. Come look."

I grab the book of poetry, and we all exit to spill into the hallway. Above us, a coal-gray cloud shaped like a huge diamond darkens the watery ceiling.

Wait. Not a cloud. A hoverpod.

Kria shakes her head. "That can't be! I have an understanding with Minwi. They keep our airspace locked out."

"Maybe this isn't someone from Minwi," Marka says.

Kria wrings her hands again. "We need to prepare to evacuate."

"But we just got here!" Hex says, his four arms rising into the air in exasperation.

"Where are we going to go?" Vera says. She's already at Marka's side, holding her hand.

"Wilbert," Kria barks. "Go to the hoverpod and fix that broken cloaking panel. Now! Everyone else, grab only what's crucial and head to the main common room. There's a direct passageway to the hoverpod hangar from there. I'll call my contact and see what's going on." She immediately puts her hand to her holo stud, running down the hallway.

My heart and mind are a tangle of panic. I don't know what to say, or where to go. Cy rushes to my side. "I have a bad feeling," Cy says.

"Yeah, I hate those."

Dyl rushes to my side, clasping her necklace around her neck. "I reassembled Dad's ring again. We erased the data we just downloaded. It's ready to be torched if we need to."

"Where is Élodie?" I ask Cy.

"Yeah. That's where the bad feeling comes in," Cy tells us. "I can't find her anywhere."

"Do you think she . . . They said someone inside here transmitted a message."

"Why would she do that?" Cy says, more to himself than to us. "No. It can't be. She doesn't have a holo stud."

"Wait. Where's Ana?" I ask.

"She's still sleeping. C'mon, we have to get her."

In her room, Ana's staring at the dark shape above her room, spellbound. She's so freaked out that we have to pack her stuff for her. Together, we gallop to our rooms and gather a few scant belongings. The only thing I care about is Ana's glass unicorn, which I wrap inside several layers of clothes.

We race back to the main room, the one with the column of fish. All the kids in Wingfield are here, chattering away nervously, staring at the hoverpod still fixed in our watery sky. What are they waiting for?

Kria makes a motion for everyone to be quiet. "I've spoken to my contact in Minwi. It's not the State police. They said that officials from Inky and Neia have forced a federal warrant to search the area on a tip."

"A tip?" Micah asks. He looks around. "From who?"

"From me."

We all spin around, searching for the owner of that statement. Élodie steps from behind a broad chair, where she must have been hiding. Her sunglasses hide her expression as she holds out an emerald-green holo stud in her palm. It's a police holo. She must have snuck away in Chicago to contact them.

"Élodie. *Qu'avez-vous fait?*" Cy asks, his voice shaking with hurt.

"What I've always set out to do. It wasn't enough to kill the senator. I leaked the truth about Aureus's products, and sent the shipment to the wrong place in Okks." She curls her lips back in a grimace. "The momentum was never enough. But now, they'll recover the list. And it will all be over," she says, waving at the ring hanging from Dyl's neck. Dyl clutches it with fear, her eyes catching mine. I can read my own emotions in her face.

Run. We have to run away. Now.

"Why would you want them to have that power over us?" Marka asks. She tries to approach Élodie, who stops Marka with a bitter glance.

"They will always have power over us, because we weren't meant to be. Benten was evil and selfish for making us. What are we but slaves? That's all we've ever been since we were born. We aren't normal. We aren't pure."

Slick tears track down her cheeks from her covered eyes. Cy motions to Marka to step away, and instead he closes the distance between himself and Élodie.

"You didn't have to do this. You could have talked to me."

"You stopped listening a long time ago, Cyrad," she whispers to him. "You had a chance, but you let her"— she points at me, and the gesture is like a knife in my chest—"you let her convince you that using those . . . mistakes . . . was better than hiding them."

No one speaks.

"Forget this. Forget all of it," Dyl says. "Let's get out of here. We don't have to stay and be arrested and killed. We have a hoverpod, right?" she asks Kria.

"No. No one's leaving. Ever," Blink says, still standing by the door. She withdraws the long tool that Kria was using to repair the hoverpod, and with a swift motion, jams it into the nearly invisible panel by the door that controls the opening mechanism. Cy and Tegg lunge for her but she manages to stab the panel one more time before Tegg pulls her from the door and slams her against the wall. Élodie cries out in pain before she crumples to the floor, unmoving.

"Was that the only way out?" Marka asks Kria, and she shakes her head.

"No. There's a door in the far corner going to the hoverpod." Several of us rush over there, but the door won't open.

"Wilbert?" Kria calls into her holo. "Are you there?"

"Yes. Cal and I are in the hoverpod. I fixed the panel. Where are you guys?"

"You've got to come upstairs. The doors have been deactivated."

"We're on our way. I've a got a good nanocircuit liquid patch that should work."

Oh thank goodness for Wilbert and his liquid nanocircuits! We all breathe a sigh of relief, but we still know what hovers above Wingfield. Ana quivers in Marka's arms and Dyl won't stop squeezing my hand. Élodie comes to.

"Someone tie her arms together," Kria orders.

"I'm sorry," Élodie cries. Her face is turned to Cy. "I'm so sorry," she repeats, crawling on the floor to the center of the room. Soon, she's sitting against the tall water column as the gold-and-purple fish zing up and down by the glass, anticipating a feeding of fish food. Her hands splay on the glass as she cries. There's a little clink of her Inky bracelet against the glass.

Oh my god.

"Get her away from there!" I scream, pitching Dyl away and running as fast as I can. Everything happens in slow motion. My feet won't run fast enough as Élodie swings her arm back. Cy's eyes widen in horror when he sees what she's doing, but we're both too late.

Élodie slams her bracelet with brutal force against the glass and everything explodes.

Glass flies everywhere, along with a huge gush of impossibly strong water that pours from the broken column into the room. Screams fill the air as everyone flails in the white water. The surge is so strong that it knocks the closest people off their feet, and blood mixes with water as the huge shards of glass slice in the roiling, rising waves.

Marka's yelling for everyone to grab furniture, and Kria is screaming through her holo for Wilbert to get to the doors.

It's chaos. And the water is rising so fast, it'll be at the ceiling within a few minutes.

Élodie's half submerged in the water, her right arm now a ragged, torn stump. Cy fights the flotsam to get to her side. He squeezes her wrist hard with his hands, and she jerks away, crying in agony.

"No! Let me be!"

"I can stop the bleeding, Élodie. Please . . . I can help!" He squeezes his eyes shut, concentrating. He's using his trait to pinch her torn arteries shut.

"No! Let me go! God, if you ever loved me, Cyrad, please. I beg you. Let me go!" she screeches.

Tegg and Micah tumble off a table that's floating nearby, and Tegg's armored leg accidentally kicks Cy squarely in the face as he falls. Cy shakes his head, stunned. Immediately, Élodie's stump begins to bleed profusely again. She closes her eyes and sinks beneath the water.

"Élodie!" Cy screams, but it's impossible to see her under the churning debris.

"I can't get it open!" Wilbert's face shows in the holo floating above Kria where she's treading bubbling water. "The circuit board is drenched!" he yells. There's a hammering outside the wall, but it only sounds like a distant, quiet thud amidst the roar of splashing and hollers for help. Wilbert is trying to break open the door by hand, but there's no way he'll break through in time.

Dyl's face, cold and wet, presses against my cheek. Her icy hands cling to my waist, and she's hyperventilating, like I am. Ten feet away against the front wall, Micah stares at us both, but he doesn't carry that haunted look anymore. In fact, he doesn't look scared at all.

"Dyl," he yells over the rushing water. "I am sorry. For you and for Ana, and everything."

"Can we please talk about this later?" Dyl screams back.

"There's never going to be a later," he hollers. His eyes are bloodshot red, and though he's as soaked as we are, I realize—he's crying. He starts hyperventilating, gulping air so hard, I wonder if he's having convulsions or something. After one last look at Dyl, he squeezes his eyes shut and dives beneath the splashing waves.

"Micah!" I scream, but Dyl clutches me so hard, there's no way I can swim to him. The last we see are his feet kicking and propelling him down to where Élodie jammed the door shut.

The rising water forces us up against the ceiling now. I can touch the force field above that keeps the quarry water from penetrating the ceiling. It feels like vinyl and static electricity mixed together, but as hard as I pummel it, I can't push through. My legs are exhausted from kicking to keep my head above the water.

A huge, bubbling explosion sounds from somewhere.

Suddenly, our heads aren't bobbing against the ceiling. A strong undertow pulls us closer to the wall as water is sucked down into a vortex.

Micah's maimed body floats up like a cork, facedown in the water. Red seeps from his tattered, blown-off wrist.

Oh god. He detonated his bracelet to open the door. Dyl shrieks so loudly, the pain pierces my skull. I search frantically for Cy.

"Cy! You have to help Micah! His arm!" I yell, trying to gesture to him. But Cy is behind a berg of floating furniture, pinning him into a corner. The water continues to drain down and within a few minutes, we're able to stand chest deep in the watery mess.

"C'mon! Everyone to the hangar, now!" Kria yells. We all dive below the surface and let ourselves get sucked out through the broken doorframe. After a slide and a scramble to our feet, Dyl and I find each other, coughing and sputtering.

"Go, go, go!" Cy says, waving us down the corridor.

"What about Micah?" Dyl grabs Marka's sodden sleeve, but Marka's eyes say everything.

"We can't leave him," Dyl says, shivering so hard, her teeth clack.

Kria shakes her head. "Dyl, we have to go."

"No. We're all leaving together," I say, and I mean it. "It won't take long. C'mon. Cy, you get Élodie. The rest of us will bring Micah's body."

Grimly, we fight the gushing knee-high water. Micah's and Élodie's limp bodies are draped over the debris. I know exactly what to expect, but as soon as I fix on Micah's vacantly staring eyes and gray face, I burst out sobbing. Dyl's face is empty and haunted.

"Come on. We can't stay here. We have to go," she says, and we gingerly pick up his legs, while Kria and Marka lift his shoulders. Cy picks up Elodie's sagging body. She looks as if she's only sleeping. His lips are pressed together in a tight line. I don't know how he's keeping it together.

We rush as fast as we can down the slippery spiral hallway. I glance up to see the dark gray diamond of the hoverpod still there. I don't know how we can possibly escape with that thing out there, waiting for us.

The hangar is lit with blue lights everywhere, and the door to the hoverpod is open. We see Hex and Vera just inside it. Their faces relax with relief when they see us galloping in our soaked clothes, heavily burdened, and they run out to help carry the bodies aboard.

We all scramble inside and lay Micah and Élodie gently on the floor.

"Go sit down, quickly," Kria says, hitting a button to secure the hatch closed. I squelch wetly down on a seat between Cy and Dyl. Wilbert's already in the pilot seat and Kria runs past me to strap into the copilot seat.

The entire hoverpod begins to hum and there's a telltale lurch when we launch off the ground. All around us, the windows only show the hangar's lights. The huge front wall of the hangar begins to rise, and blue quarry water rushes in to flood the space.

"Uh, this thing is waterproof, right?" I ask nervously.

"It better be," Dyl whispers as the water level rises over the windows. This is too similar to our near-drowning in the room, so I stop watching the windows. I glance over to Marka.

"Where are we going?"

"I spoke to Kria. I don't think we have a choice. We're going to land in Canada and see if we can get refugee status there."

Dyl, Cy, and the others around us nod. At first, I'm relieved. Having protected status sounds like a great idea. But then I think of the thirty other kids on the list. If we're out of the country, how on earth can I help keep them safe?

"Wait. We can't go to Canada," I blurt out to Marka, and she stares back at me like I'm nuts.

"Zelia, we don't have a choice."

"If we leave the States, we've lost the war. Don't you see?"

Tegg leans over and gives me a rude look. "If we stay, we're dead. I vote for 'not-dead.'"

"We can't argue about this. Not now." There's a hard edge to Marka's words that nips at my heart. I don't like fighting with her, but I can't help it. Leaving the States is the wrong choice.

The hanger is now completely flooded and open to the quarry. The hoverpod glides through the blue water. As it rises and breaks the surface with sheets of water pouring down the windows, Wilbert steers away from the other gray pod hovering above Wingfield.

"There's a transmission coming in," Kria announces. "Hold your hats."

"We don't have any hats," Wilbert says.

"Shhh!" Caliga says. "Listen."

"PLEASE LAND YOUR CRAFT IMMEDIATELY. ANY ATTEMPT TO FLEE WILL BE CONSIDERED AN OFFENSIVE MANEUVER AND YOU *WILL* BE FIRED UPON."

Wilbert's hands are squeezing the steering mechanism so hard, his hands are half-white, half-pink.

"Kria, what do I do?"

She's gripping the dash of the hovercraft and not moving. We're all twisted in our seats to watch her. The other Wingfield kids are all murmuring among themselves. *Flee. Give up. It's over. Just make a run for it. Oh god* and *Oh my god. It's over.*

Her chin drops and she rests a hand on Wilbert's shoulder.

"Land it."

"What?" Wilbert croaks.

"Are we going to fight them?" Tegg asks, flexing beneath his armored skin.

"We can't. We'll certainly die if we fight. We need to be far more clever than that."

OUR HOVERPOD SINKS THROUGH THE AIR AND approaches the swath of wild grass by the edge of the quarry. There's a crunch as the landing gear gets a foothold on the firm ground. The other gray hoverpod floats close by and lands right in front of us.

For a moment, we all sit there. I memorize the faces of everyone around me.

So this is what surrender feels like, Cy says in my head.

CHAPTER 34

COME WITH ME, CY SAYS IN MY HEAD. *We can't let Kria and Marka do this part alone.*

I nod and unbuckle myself. Dyl gives me a questioning look of worry and panic.

"Stay here," I tell her. "Watch Ana, okay? Make sure she doesn't hurt anyone. She could get us in more trouble if she's spooked."

Dyl nods.

Kria and Marka head to the shuttle hatch with grim expressions. When they see Cy and me, they begin to protest, but Cy tells them firmly, "You're not doing this alone."

He threads his fingers into Marka's, and I marvel at how beautiful he is. This is what I fell in love with. In times like this, the strength of his love overshadows anything on this marble of a planet.

Kria turns to all the kids. "Everyone stay in here. Please don't fight. I don't want anyone hurt or killed. There's already been enough death today," she says.

Kria punches the button to open the hatch. The bright

light gradually fills our space as it lowers. The other hover-pod has already opened and spilled its contents—fifteen armed police in an arc around us. They wear gray uniforms and helmets that obscure their faces. Shiny, narrow black neural guns are pointed at us.

"Raise your hands," one of the officers barks at us. We comply, and for a second I'm irritated that Cy's no longer able to hold Marka's hand. "How many are in your hover-pod?"

"Twenty. Two are dead," Kria responds. "We need medical care for a few others. There was an accident in our home."

"Cy. Do you think your trait will work through their uniforms?" I whisper through my teeth. "You might be able to do something."

I don't think so. That would be a disaster. He's staring straight at the officers with zero expression, but his voice is impatient, nervous.

"We already are a disaster," I growl.

"Lie facedown, with your hands on your heads," the officer commands. Cy, Marka, and I carefully drop to our knees, but Kria hesitates.

"Please, may I have a word? We only want to—" she starts, when the nearest officer makes a tiny movement of his arm. A hissing zing sounds and the neural bullet strikes Kria straight in the chest. There's an eternity in a second, when her body hovers between control and oblivion, before succumbing to the shot and hitting the grassy soil.

"Kria!" I cry out, but immediately regret my word

when the same officer pivots to aim at me. "Never mind!" I yelp, hastily flattening myself to the ground and slapping my hands on my head.

"You're a smart girl," the officer says. "Let's restrain these four. Don't touch them," he warns.

My arms are twisted hard behind my back, and my wrists and hands are gummed together with something that feels hot and gooey, then cools immediately to a hard but rubbery material. Plasticizer cuffs. Nearly unbreakable and form-fitting.

"Hmm. Look, these are Inky bracelets," an officer comments. "You two are escapees, huh? Impressive. Hard to get out of there. They'll claim you, of course, if you ever get out of prison. Alive, that is," the gruff voice says.

"May I go to prison too?" a man's voice calls playfully from far away, beyond the clearing where our hoverpods are.

I twist my neck around to find the source of the brash voice. I barely make out a tiny blur of yellowish white beyond the brush. Someone tall, with blond hair.

"It's Endall!" I whisper to Cy.

The lead officer points to the woods. "I see him in my scanner. It's just one guy. Unarmed, and skinny too. You three, go get him." Out of the corner of my eye, I see the trio march toward the forest edge, holding their neural guns carefully in front of them. They disappear into the shadows of the looming trees. There's a telltale zing sound, followed by two others. A faint thump sounds, like a body hitting the ground.

That was quick.

"All right, let's get the rest rounded up," the lead officer says as they walk toward the hoverpod. But they don't get far. All the kids from Wingfield slowly exit the hoverpod with their hands in the air, like they've already been trained on how to surrender properly. Dyl and Ana are in the front, and Dyl blinks her eyes innocently.

"Can we go to prison too?"

What are they doing? Cy wonders. I have no answer for him. I suppose they're making it easier for the police, but still.

"All right. Everyone in a line. Facedown on the ground."

Everyone complies to form a long line behind us, keeping their hands over their heads. When they see Hex's four arms and Vera's green face, some of the officers shift their weight with discomfort. Wilbert isn't with them.

The police notice too. "There's another one inside. Go." Two officers obey their commander, and go around the line to enter the hoverpod. I count the remaining officers. Only ten now. Why haven't the three returned with Endall's body?

"I said facedown on the ground," the main officer yells, holding his neural gun higher.

The air is ripe with tension as none of the kids move. Slowly, they drop their arms.

And then, it's chaos.

Five kids drop to the ground, as if they'd been hit by guns. Another six scatter, screaming. The officers start shooting their neural guns and the air crackles with bullets.

I shriek when Hex tackles an officer and they land with a crunching thud only inches from my face. The officer's neural gun skitters over the grass.

"Caliga!" Hex yells, and they continue to wrestle. Hex won't punch him, just takes blow after blow to his abdomen as he wrestles with the officer's head. A well-placed boot kicks Hex hard and he rolls away, huffing in pain, but the officer's helmet is tucked away in Hex's arms. The sandy-haired policeman stands up, preparing to fire another weapon, when Caliga bear-hugs him.

"Hey! Sleepy time!" she says, breathing hard after running over. The officer falls to his knees. Caliga keeps her hands on his face for another ten seconds.

"Cal, don't kill him. If we kill anyone, we'll really be criminals," Cy urges her. Caliga lets go and nods, before searching his pocket. She pulls out a small lipstick-sized instrument.

"Aha! I saw this on a holo show once," she says. She twists the tube and presses it into the solid plasticizer around my hands and wrists. The material liquefies with the pulse from the device and falls to the ground in a wet glob. My hands are free. She helps Cy and Marka, before running after Hex, who's wrestling with another officer.

It's crazy. Some of the kids have been shot and are immobile on the ground. Others are trying to fight. Some, who faked being shot, are popping up and fighting. Vera lands a powerful roundhouse kick to an officer's head, and Tegg is disarming another one nearby. Three other officers surround the fighting pair. They keep shooting at Tegg, but the neural bullets ping uselessly off his hardened skin. Realizing their mistake, they take out knife-tipped batons and close in.

"Tegg!" I screech, but it's too late. He turns only to get a knife straight into his shoulder, where his armor is weakest. Tegg cries out and another officer dives forward to stab him in the neck. The brightest crimson sprays into the air as I shriek again.

"This is crazy!" Cy yells, checking the pulse of Caliga's downed officer.

"Tell everyone not to fight to kill! We've got to bring the police down without seriously injuring them." I look over my shoulder to where Hex and Vera have immobilized another officer, but Hex's face is a bloody mess now. "We're not going to win this one by one."

Cy kneels down and concentrates hard, shutting his eyes.

Listen, everyone. Do not kill any officers. It will only hurt us. Just disarm, or knock them out. And someone figure out how to open up their helmet visors.

Marka nods at us from across the field, where she's tending to the fallen. One of the kids is shocking one of the guards, who convulses and falls backward. He must have Micah's trait. Ana and Dyl aren't anywhere to be seen, but bodies of the fallen lie everywhere. We're losing.

A voice booms across us from the police hoverpod.

"Reinforcements are arriving shortly. We will be shooting to kill. You will not be hurt if you lie down with your hands on your head."

Everyone stops fighting. Marka looks around to the few left standing, and shouts, "Stop fighting! Everyone! Please, stop. It's over."

Hex wipes his bloody face and his shoulders fall, exhausted. Caliga takes her hands off an officer and drops to her knees, ready to surrender.

"It's really over, isn't it?" I whisper to Cy.

Cy closes his eyes, then covers his face. We both fall to our knees. Someone runs out of the doorway of the police hoverpod, face smeared in dirt and blood. He's wearing body armor, but doesn't look like an officer. He's holding a helmet in his arms, with wires sticking out the edges of the visor. Only his dandelion-yellow hair tells me who it is.

"Endall!" I gasp. I thought he was shot in the woods. What was he doing inside the police craft? He smiles over at me and Cy, before hollering, "I owe you for the watch, Zelia. Here you go." His hand digs into the helmet, and suddenly the face visor of every officer slides open with simultaneous clicks. Their expressions show surprise and shock at losing their face protection.

"Fire on them!" the lead officer yells, because he's lost communication inside his helmet.

Most of the Wingfield kids cower, covering their heads and diving to the ground. The only people standing are me, Marka, and Cy, who squeezes his hands into fists and concentrates so hard that the veins in his temples and neck bulge. Nothing happens.

Each officer takes careful aim at one of us. One of them

walks straight up to Cy. "We won, freak. It's over," he says with a grim face. The neural gun presses hard into Cy's chest as he smiles.

Cy says nothing, still trembling all over. He won't look anyone in the eye.

None of them aim at our faces, only our hearts. We've surrendered now, and they're still going to kill us. I see Marka's gaze travel over her children, helpless. Tears wash a thin path down her dirty cheeks.

The officer's face goes starkly ashen. His trigger finger releases, and his arms jerk once, twice, before his eyes roll into his head. The neural gun drops from his flaccid hand.

And then, as if an unseen person is cutting their invisible marionette strings, every officer collapses to the ground in a synchronized fall.

The silence that remains is so sharp, no one dares to speak or breathe at first.

Cy keeps his concentration for a few more seconds before relaxing. His arms and legs are shaking so hard that he stumbles to the ground. I run to throw my arms around him.

"Oh my god! Cy, you did it!" I shriek. The others yell and scream in triumph, and the entire collective breathes again.

"I didn't think I could," he says wonderingly.

"I did," I whisper.

Hex runs over and offers a bloodied hand to help Cy up. "We'd better go. They'll all wake up in a minute."

"Everyone, back to the hoverpod! Now!" I yell as loudly

as possible. Most of the kids are okay, but so many of them had been hit with the neural guns, they're hardly able to walk. We all carry the fallen with us as fast as we can. Wilbert's still unconscious where he was hit with no fewer than four bullets, so Kria takes the controls, even though she can barely walk.

"Wait! Endall! I need another minute. Please."

"Zelia, that other police hoverpod's going to be here any minute," Kria warns.

"I'll be quick." I run out onto the field, but I don't have to yell for Endall at all. He's standing right there among the fallen, peeling away his dirty flannel shirt. Underneath, he's wearing full body armor, the kind that's illegal in almost every State because it repels neural gun strikes.

"Clever, right?" he says, grinning. "I wear it all the time. It's easy to fake a neural gun hit. Law enforcement relaxes too much in the presence of an unconscious body." He laughs, a sound that's bright and unrestrained. I haven't felt that way in too long.

"Endall. Thank you for what you did. We'd never have escaped without you."

"What? For opening a few helmets?"

"It was more than that." I step closer and try to touch his arm, but he shrinks away from me. "Endall. Come with us."

"No. But thank you."

"But your watch! It won't last forever. How are you going to survive here?"

Endall only smiles, and it makes me distinctly uncomfortable. It's the closed grin of someone who holds all the answers you ever wanted to know, but won't share.

"Here, Zelia." He takes one of my hands, and with his other, digs into his breast pocket. He withdraws the pocket watch and lays it in my outstretched palm. It's blood-warm from being carried close to his chest.

I shake my head. "I can't take this!"

"That's your choice. This is mine." His face lights with a brilliant, mirth-filled happiness, before he turns and runs into the forest.

"Endall!" I yell. "*Endall!*"

He doesn't return. I'm left clutching the piece of anti-quated timekeeping that was the only thing keeping him alive.

I don't run after him.

Because I know I've just lost an argument that I was never meant to win.

I turn and run back to the hoverpod, which is humming loudly, waiting for me. I gallop inside and Cy shuts the hatch, just as the police lying on the field begin to stir fully awake again. We head to the cockpit and strap into chairs behind Kria and Marka.

"So," Kria says to us. "I'm heading to Canada, unless anyone else can give me a damn good reason not to. Because after this battle, no one is going to let people like us live in their State."

People like us. That's the problem. So long as we're considered people who aren't allowed to exist, we've got no future. We'll be extinct, before we even have a chance to really live.

Extinct.

The single word swirls inside my head, needling me.

Wait a second.

"Does anyone here have a holo I can use?" I ask.

"Sure," Marka says, unscrewing her holo stud. "But what for?"

I take the stud and screw it into my earlobe, turning it on and searching for a State law database.

"I think I may have found a new home. For everyone."

CHAPTER 35

WE FLY WEST, NOT NORTH.

The second we left Wingfield, we were quickly followed and now have six hoverpods trailing us at an uncomfortably close distance. As long as we stay in unregulated airspace and don't do anything offensive, they won't touch us. But the second we land, they'll arrest us.

At least, they'll try. We have other plans.

Vera's cleaned up Hex's bloodied face as well as possible. They steal a kiss when no one is looking and Vera sheds a few tears of relief into Hex's black hair. I told everyone to be camera ready and put on their best doe-eyed looks. Hands will need to be held. The smallest and weakest will be carried, even if they can walk.

Julian's political lesson plays back in my head on an endless loop. *Greed, fear, sympathy; greed, fear, sympathy.* It's time to play the sympathy card, and play it well. I've been writing a speech incessantly since we figured out where to land. I've run it by everyone, tweaking it here and there. When I'm done, I present it to Marka, but she shakes her head.

"You read it, Zelia."

"I don't know if I'm the right person to speak for everyone."

"I think you are."

I turn the speech off on my holo and sit down, staring out the cockpit where the hoverpod is now slicing through clouds that cover Sacramento. Marka stands behind me and starts to braid my hair, then thinks twice.

"Actually, I like it when it's frizzy."

Kria raises her hand. "My fault!"

I laugh. It is her fault. But I can't seem to hold the same stubborn anger against her anymore. She was as much a victim of my dad's manipulation as anyone. She'll never take Marka's place, but I suspect that a heart can expand in infinite ways that can't be measured by a cardioscope. I'm gradually feeling the stretch, and I'm okay with it.

The hoverpods have surrounded us in a perfect hexagonal formation ever since we entered the legal airspace of California. Kria steers toward the city hoverport.

"Get ready, everyone," Kria announces.

"Did you already contact the press?" I ask.

"Yes. I spoke to my personal contact in California, and Marka spoke to Senator Milford's prior press secretary. It's going to be a media circus, as requested."

"Good," I say, but my heart thrums hard against my chest and I'm hyperventilating without thinking. Hyperventilating! What a weird sensation. I touch the implant in my neck, and Kria sees me fiddling with my scar.

"I'm sorry. I thought I was helping."

"It's okay. I mean, I understand."

"So you still want it out?"

I almost blurt out a yes, but don't. The last day or so, it's been one huge thing I haven't had to think about as much. Granted, it's still weird to feel the slightly jerky push and pull of my chest wall expanding and contracting every minute of the day. I miss being in control. The funny thing is, most people don't wish for that level of control. Dad had always had his finger on the pulse of every part of my life. Getting a permanent implant was the only thing I'd resisted, even when I was the docile girl from over a year ago. It's hard to let go of that bit of rebellion. And yet . . .

"I think I'll keep it. For now," I decide. Kria nods and Marka winks at me. That one wink tells me that she'd rather I kept the implant too but was too wise to pressure me about it.

Smart mom.

Our hoverpod approaches the hoverport. Several emergency magpods are scattered in the area around us, and law enforcement are everywhere. There's a podium set up with a huge holo screen behind it, and a field of press corps waiting. We land.

"Ready, everyone?" Marka asks. "Okay. Let's go. Two by two, and head directly for the podium. Fan yourselves around it. Look serious but, uh, innocent." As I brush by, she shakes her head. "I'm not good at acting."

"We're not acting, Marka. We *are* innocent," I remind her. She nods and follows me out. Kria squeezes my shoulder.

It's a cloudy day, but a thin line of sunshine appears

at the edge of the sky. The police immediately surround us and escort us forward. I try to look alert, but not too spooked as I head to the sea of press ahead of us. The holocameras are everywhere, and there are loud murmurs over seeing Hex with his four arms cradling a young girl, and Vera's skin. More gasps erupt over seeing Wilbert's two heads, but Caliga holds his hand firmly, and even I have to admit that his blush is endearing.

Kria gives me an encouraging smile and I climb the podium. I clear my throat, and wait. Several police officers come forward. Kria told us to expect this.

"You are all in violation of HGM 2098, as well as in-filtrating the following States under illegal measures: Neia, Okks, Minwi, Inky . . ." He reads every single State and includes the attacks in Minwi and Neia. I keep my expression neutral, though I'm so annoyed that they're blaming us for what happened in Carus. "Following your statement, you will be escorted to the nearest police station for processing according to California State and Federal laws." He then reads us the long list of adapted Miranda rights, before pausing. I look to Marka, and she nods for me to go ahead.

"We're ready to make a statement," I tell the officer.

He nods and I walk up to the audio buds on the podium that resemble a cluster of clear fish eggs. I clear my throat.

"We would like to address the accusations made against us. Until now, our voices have been silent, not because we chose to be quiet, but because we have been relentlessly and cruelly blamed for that which we have no control over.

"HGM 2098 states that it is illegal to manipulate human DNA to heritable mutations that could affect the larger population's gene pools. It's true that each of us carries a mutation. However, this law is not in effect here. The law cites an action—the creation of a mutation. The person solely responsible for our creation, Thomas Lanier Benten, my father, is now deceased. We, as a group, are incapable of breeding naturally with humans with normal DNA. According to Ernst Mayr's Biological Species Concept, which is still the standard of speciation nomenclature . . ." I clear my dry throat, trying not to swallow my words. ". . . my family meets criteria as a distinct species."

I straighten my back and raise my voice. "On behalf of my family"—here, I turn to gesture to everyone behind me. Marka holds hands with Ana; Kria cradles a weak-looking Jess. Everyone has their innocent doe-eyes on full display—"we are seeking protection in the State of California under the 1973 Endangered Species Act, or ESA, that was amended to a Federal States law in 2077."

A huge gasp of surprise erupts from the police and press. Several of them begin to bark out questions, and I hold up a hand.

"According to the ESA, we are considered endangered. The ESA does not exclude hominid species from its laws. Which means that right now, any action that prohibits our free and natural existence is a felony."

The police are now huddling, wondering what to do as the slow roar of questions hit me left and right. But I'm not done.

"My name is Zelia Shirley Benten. I am eighteen years

old. I'm terrified that . . ." Here, my voice quavers, and it's not an act. ". . . that I won't make it to nineteen. I love poetry, and my mother and Marie Curie are my biggest heroes." I turn and smile at Marka and Kria, and they both have tears in their eyes, dabbing them with their fingertips. "Also, I hate peanuts and I love chocolate. I think high heels are torture and I'm sure I'm really bad at public speaking." Here, a few of the press snicker with amusement. I smile back. "My family and I are different, but we're also the same. We have sisters, and brothers. Our hearts can shatter when we lose the people we love. We bleed; we feel pain; we laugh and we cry." I take a huge breath and stare straight into the holocameras. "And right now, all we want to do is live. Freely. Just like all of you."

I exhale loudly and close my eyes. There's no applause. Cy comes forward and holds my hands. I'm aware that the entire press corps and cameras are watching us as I look into his steady eyes.

You were great. I think you scared the skin off the police.

"They're still going to arrest us," I say.

I know. You're going to look adorable in stripes.

He leans forward and kisses me tenderly on the cheek and a million holocameras catch it for the evening news. The police come closer to arrest us, and we all hug each other quickly. Marka whispers in my ear.

"This phase of the fight is going to go on for a long, long time. Are you ready?"

I squeeze her back. "I've got my whole long life to fight, Marka. I'm more than ready."

EPILOGUE

TWO MONTHS AGO, IF YOU TOLD ME I'd be best friends with Caliga and chatting daily with my birth mother, I'd assume you were crazy. If you said that I'd be doing press conferences every week inside prison walls, I'd assume you were beyond delusional.

Then again, my assumptions are often a hundred percent crap.

I am relearning everything I know about everyone. Kria makes time to spend with me and Dyl. Though it's awkward, it's getting better. Dyl says sometimes it's like living backward in time. We're rehashing our lives in reverse, so we can move forward. Meanwhile, Marka's also been schooling me on my scent trait. I have so much to learn, but thankfully, she's endlessly patient. I love that we have this to share together. It's icing on a gigantic, sweet confection that's already more than I could have wished for.

Dyl doesn't speak of Micah for a long time. Six weeks after we arrived in Sacramento, the States were ordered to gather evidence for the ongoing legal battle. Which meant that after everything was catalogued and scanned, our abandoned belongings from Wingfield's waterlogged spirals were delivered to us.

Among them were Micah's things, including a book of poetry from various poets in the twentieth century. He'd written Dyl's name inside, probably planning on giving it to her. The pages are so warped, the book won't shut. Dyl holds it for a long, long time.

"I might have forgiven him. I should have." Her shoulders start to shake with a sob.

"I don't think Micah could have forgiven himself," I tell her, and we sit there in silence, trying to figure out how a life could have become so broken, so quickly. Micah's loneliness and guilt still feel huge and real, though he's gone. Maybe somehow, somewhere, he knows that the slate is clean between us and he can be at peace.

Every night, I take out Ana's unicorn and polish its irregular and beautiful body, placing it back on the shelf in my dorm room inside the State of California's correctional facility. This place is super-low-security, more to keep people out than us inside. We're gaining tons of supporters in-State and from other countries, who offer safety and citizenship elsewhere. But we want to keep the fight here, where our home is.

The unicorn has become a mascot for our cause. It's on billboards and our holo site. Our lawyers tell us it's only a matter of time before we get our way. They've already planned to move us to a high-security residence next month that isn't technically jail. It can't come a day too soon.

It took a week for us to get our awful Inky bracelets safely removed. It took two months before Inky released Renata and the kids from Avida to California. Unfortunately, Bianca and Andy didn't survive long enough to make it. But we've no fear that any of them will suffer like that again. Renata is a different creature now. She has a sturdy, tough core that refuses to break. We've also since heard from Tennie, Tabitha, and the others. They're safe and healthy in Canada. As soon as it's legal, there's going to be a reunion.

In the meantime, we have epic sleepovers every weekend in the cafeteria. Even the correctional officers say we're the most charming convicts they've ever watched over. Once again, we always squash Marka in the middle of the Carus area. Only now, I never wake up in the middle of the night, worrying half the hours away. I sleep like a rock, tucked into Cy's arms and breathing in his woodsy scent, with my toes touching Marka's ankles.

Dyl and Kria work with federal molecular biologists on analyzing the genetic codes in Dad's list data. There's active talk of HGM 2098 being dismantled and dealt with on a State-by-State basis. Inky is pushing hard to make it happen, since it claims to own patents on all its Avida products.

Which means, in California, we may be free soon. Not free as an endangered freak species, but as people. Like everyone else.

There's hope that we'll be able to manufacture the medications to allow anyone with Benten Mutations to conceive children without Kria or Dyl being the surrogates. It's not easy, though. Dyl's passionate about keeping herself from being a trait breeder, the way Dad had designed her, but so far, her work hasn't turned up a good way to bottle her "key." But she's relentless, and I know eventually she'll find it. Every spare moment I have, I help too. It's nice to get my hands dirty in the lab world again.

Hex and Vera have been hinting that they want to be the first to try, in a few years. Hex wants to name their first baby girl "Katydid." It's too easy to imagine an adorable, wriggly, green infant with six limbs. Vera's already chosen their first baby boy name: "Hopper." Everyone approves.

Cy's started taking bona fide medical school courses on holo while I've been honing my PR skills. He's figured out that he has the ability to dilate and constrict even minute blood vessels with his thoughts. A career in neurosurgery is on his agenda now. He had worked up the courage to ask Ana if he could solicit real neurologists to help him work on a treatment to reverse the damage she sustained years ago, when Ana looked at him blankly.

"What makes you think I need fixing? I'm perfect."

And that was the end of that.

The whispers in my head continue, and the ghostly kisses, but he no longer recites the Luna poem, and I don't ask for it. He knows now that I'm not some celestial object that cannot be captured, that must be worshipped from afar. I'm just me, my faults, and I. And he is beyond content with that, as I am content with him.

I still read Dad's poetry book. I'm not haunted by him, nor do I want to shut the book on my life with him. He was, and is a part of me. I'll never have the answers to why almost a hundred and fifty years ago, he decided to create more people with traits like himself. Was it to make a family he longed for? To feel like God? Was he afraid of being alone? Did he feel his control slipping away when he couldn't bypass the laws, when Aureus felt that money was more important than keeping us safe and sound? There are so many questions without answers.

One thing is for sure: I'm content not knowing it all, which is more than I can say for my father. He likely lived unnatural decades full of discontent, trying to create a happiness that can't be manufactured in a test tube. That ring was never a marriage to a person. It was an idea, an obsession that outweighed everything that was truly important. I pity him, and the sentiment assuages my anger. Even for a life as long as mine might be, I don't want to waste time on hate anymore.

Yesterday, I was reading "Prayer for My Child" when I got a paper cut. I marveled at the little blob of red on my finger. I think of the DNA story hidden there, and the stories that aren't dictated by our genetics.

We are not simply a sum of our genes. We are not defined by the code within them. When Endall walked away from his watch, he showed me that I have the power to turn forever into yesterday.

Maybe we are destined to be extinct, before our generation has had a full chance to breathe.

But not yet.

Not yet.

APPENDIX

LUNA

ANONYMOUS

TWENTIETH-CENTURY POETRY

I cannot feel your light on my skin.
This place swells with absences
As you seep forward
And I remain, fixed in memory.

Tonight, silver will dilate on a bed of black
Leaving me askew, amid curves of water and atmo-
sphere.
Dead on a living sphere, I wait,
Too weak to rise and you, too strong to fall.

The sun will warm your skin
Touching your sickle waist
As I watch, jealous from afar,
Unable to offer one gifted breath.

Do you remember me?
I am here, in the same sky.
I will wait for you, ready to catch
The quarters and halves and broken hearts.

After a thoughtless twist, you will return.
Keep your tides surging with their cold embrace
And I will rise to meet them,
Drowning in our histories to come.

Acknowledgments

THESE BOOKS COULD NOT HAVE BREATHED and existed without the people who buoyed me up since birth. My sincere thanks to . . .

Bernie, my husband and best friend. You have always been my number one fan and always see the best in me, even when I have spinach in my teeth. I love you, dear.

My children, Ben, Maia, and Phoebe. You are the reasons why I smile so much. I am a proud mama. I adore you all.

Alice. I'm such a fan. You make everything beautiful. And to the Kwon boys: Eemo loves ya.

Richard, who invented fierce loyalty. I am so glad you'll be on my side when the apocalypse comes. And to the Kang family—buckets of love from Aunt Lydia!

To the wonderful Saak family—I love you all so very much! Your support has been priceless.

Mom, Dad, A-Ma, and Ah-Gong, who teach me about

kindness, generosity, and how to stretch your soul to love what matters the most.

Jenny and Aaron and the Saak girls, whom I love so dearly.

Dushana Yoganathan-Triola, who gets my frantic daily emails about subjects no other human needs to know about. I'm emailing you right now.

Gale Etherton, Julie Fedderson, Phyllis Nsiah-Kumi, Jennifer Hickman, Jean Thierfelder, and my other work colleagues who've become more than work colleagues. You're beautiful people and I bask in your radiance.

Sarah Fine, whose utter brilliance hurts my eyes. Thank you for being you, and being there for me.

My many author friends, a.k.a. the best career perks EVER—Carol Riggs, Paula Stokes, April Tucholke, Lenore Appelhans, Lynette Moey, and so many others!

Ellen Scott and the Bookworm Omaha for being so supportive of a local author, and being awesome in general.

Shelley and Zoe Colquitt, and the CCHS community. You guys are my idols. Thank you for being the real heroes.

My team at Penguin and Kathy Dawson Books! Endless thanks to Kathy Dawson (Editor Extraordinaire), Claire Evans, Jessica Schoffel, Regina Castillo, Danielle Calotta, Jenny Kelly, Mia Garcia, and Colleen Lindsay. Also, thanks to Alex Genis for spreading the word!

Dana Kaye and Anne Whealdon of Kaye Publicity. You guys rock. Thanks for getting me out of my hovel and into the presence of flesh-and-blood readers!

Eric Myers, my agent, who never runs short of excellent advice and thankfully believes that my nutty ideas are great.

Readers, bloggers, booksellers, librarians, and teachers I've met this last year—I would kiss you all, but I'm sure that would freak you out.

Steven Langan, for being perpetually supportive and shepherding new poets and authors into the world.

Amber at Me, MyShelf, and I, for the gorgeous swag designing!

My friends, both Omahaan and far away. There are too many to thank. I am always grateful for the emails, the hugs, and messages of support, and the book buying!

Anna, Leo, and PJ Monardo. Whether you like it or not, you're family. Let's make spaghetti soon.

Drs. Dan Lydiatt and Ali Mirmiran, who gave me advice on Latin and radioactive poisons. Thank you for letting me borrow your genius.

My brothers and sisters in the Lucky 13s. I need you guys like I need caffeine.

And finally, to my patients and their families, who show me every day what it means to live, love, and be brave; and to the staff and colleagues who care for them. You bring out the best in me.

TURN THE PAGE TO SAMPLE THE
FIRST BOOK OF THIS THRILLING DUET:

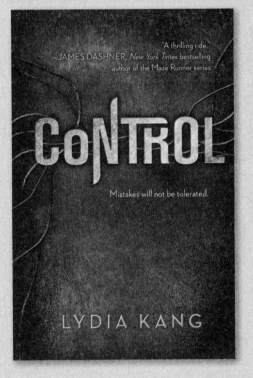

CHAPTER 1

MAYBE IF I MOVE A LITTLE SLOWER, I can prevent the inevitable. Time will freeze and it'll be easy to pretend we're not moving again. I don't want to budge from the roof of this cruddy building.

The door to the stairwell creaks open. Dad sees the lump of me at the edge of the roof, unmoving. Dark clothes, dark frizzled hair. I am depression personified.

"Here you are, Zelia. I told you to stay off the roof," Dad says, his voice scratchy with fatigue.

I jerk to my feet. "Sorry."

"Traffic is about to get bad. Let's go."

"Okay." I cross the gravel roof quickly, trying to catch his shadow slipping down the stairwell to our apartment. Our old apartment. This place is nothing to me anymore. Dust bunnies lurk in the angles of the hallways, kicked around by the maelstrom of moving activity. Inside my small bedroom, I push my duffel bag to the door. Just one bag, crammed to the brim. It's not much. After years of moving every ten months, you give up amassing anything larger than your fist. Basically, heart-sized or smaller is all I can take.

Around the empty room, remnants of the past haunt the surfaces. Rings from juice bottles cover the desk; pictoscreens glow in big white rectangles where photographs have been deleted. I still had eight weeks of rental left on those images—the latest telescope images of the M-16 nebula, beaches and mountains from the twentieth century untouched by humans. So pretty. So gone.

Down the hallway, I smell my little sister walk by. This month, it's Persian freesia. Dad says nothing about her pricey scent downloads. He also hasn't commented on the string of boys popping up with alarming regularity on her holo. Unlike me, he's not bothered by Dylia's flourishing teenage hormonal nirvana. In fact, she's chatting up one of her undeserving male friends as she skips down the stairs.

The glowing green screen hovers at an angle in front of her, a projected image from an earring stud that everyone wears. It's practically impossible to live without our holos. They're like a sixth sense, with limitless connections and information. Dyl got her first holo stud six months ago when she turned thirteen and barely turns it off now. Within the green rectangle, a boy's face is shadowed under a hoodie and he's wearing an oily smile.

I follow her downstairs and join Dad in front of our dilapidated townhouse. I tell myself I won't miss the building's crunchy gravel roof, or even the ancient ion oven that always zapped our food too much on the crispy side.

There's no point in getting attached to the good or bad of wherever we live.

Dad punches in an order for a magpod on one of the metal cones decorating each street corner. I drop the bag from my tired shoulder and massage my neck, looking up. Out here, the sky isn't sky but one continuous sheet of painted blue, as if the whole town were built underneath a gigantic, endless table. In Neia—what used to be Nebraska and Iowa—we get the fake blue underside of the agriplane; up above it's got grain fields of burnished gold and a sun so bright, it doesn't look real.

Moving from State to State sucks. In history class, we read about a unified nation hundreds of years ago where you could live wherever you wanted, with any lifestyle you chose. No intense border scrutiny and screening tests; no pledges to adhere to the morals and dress code mandated by each State. But after the country couldn't agree on religion or politics or how to wipe your butt the right way, they divided into clustered States. Alms, Ilmo, Neia, Okks . . . each stewing in their happy ideals, all of them unified under a federal government weaker than my left pinkie.

Dad thought Neia would be a unique place to live. Of all the States we've lived in, I almost looked forward to this one. He said we'd go up to the agriplane and have a picnic someday, but the picnic never happened. Now when I stare up at that false sky held aloft by synthetic, spidery supports and blockish buildings, I don't want to go up there anymore. They say it used to be sunny and bright here, but now the agriplane steals it from everyone.

There's never a moon to look forward to, or a dawn. At least it'll be a change to see the sun again, which reminds me . . .

"What State are we moving to?" I ask. Dad doesn't answer until Dyl pokes him, hard, on the shoulder.

"We're . . . I'm . . . maybe Alaska."

"Alaska's another country, remember? It seceded four years ago," Dyl points out. I wouldn't be surprised if he didn't actually know. He breathes and sleeps work. No matter the little consequences of State politics or geothermal catastrophes in what's left of California.

"Right, right," he mutters. We both watch him suspiciously. Usually we have one week's notice and a detailed to-do list for the move. This time, it was twelve hours, and Dad's more scatter-brained than usual.

"Well, as soon as we know, I'll see what labs I can work in," I say brightly. Four years ago, Dad decided I should take a holo molecular bio course. I was going through a poetry phase and balked. But as usual, he knew me best. I love my lab work now. He pulls strings to find me after-school work in each new town. I've spent all my free time running protocols alongside post-docs and grad students, learning all I could. Hungry for it. There have only been three constancies in my life—Dad, Dyl, and lab work.

"No more lab work," he snaps.

My body shrinks into a smaller space. "What?"

"You're too unbalanced. Life isn't about plasmid vectors and bio-accelerants. It's about dealing with people. You're going to take States history and political science courses. I'll reprogram your holo channels when we get settled."

History? Politics? Is he kidding? I wish I could argue, but Dad's face is stony and confident. My gram of rebellion combusts like pure magnesium. Well, he's probably right. He always knows what I like, even before I know myself. I thought I wouldn't like molecular bio, but it's a second language for me now. Or at least, it was.

"Okay," I mumble. I wait to see if he has new classes in mind for Dyl, but he stays silent. She never needs any nudging or fixing, academically or otherwise. I'm the imperfect one.

"Anyway, there's a worldwide excess of geeks," Dyl adds, trying to unstiffen the air around us. "Why add to that?" The guy on her holo chortles on cue.

"And there's a worldwide excess of brain-dead boys trying to get in your pants," I counter.

Dyl cups her ear, and the holo image disappears. "Quinn is not like that!" she whispers. The guy on Dyl's holo coughs. It's the guiltiest-sounding cough I've ever heard.

I mope aggressively, but Dad is too busy studying the metal cone's flashing display. With one touch, it accesses your info and account. Even if you can't afford a magpod, a nasty public pod will come pick you up. If you're a little kid, lost, a press of a finger brings a magpod that will take you to the police, your school, or home, depending on the time of day. They're more reliable than the sun rising and setting. On cloudy days, even the sun lets you down.

It won't be long before he confesses where we're really going. Maybe it'll be like Inky, where there's a women's uniform. Dyl will just love that to death. A neck-to-toe gray smock can't be easy to accessorize.

Other magpods of varying size and luxury float by, hovering over the metal lines embedded in the road. A flashing 3-D sign across the street tells me I need the New and Improved SkinGuard to harden my soft self, in case any projectiles fly my way. If only I wanted to look like I was part insect.

I yank my no-slip (yeah, right) bra straps back onto my shoulders for the third time today. When there's hardly anything up front to keep the bra in place, it defies the laws of gravity and rises up. Dyl, who's younger by four years, is already my height and is destined to sprout a larger chest. Maybe by tomorrow.

A dull-looking magpod slows down in front of us, the color of old teeth and sporting a triangle-shaped dent in the back. I've never seen this one before, but like all the magpods we get, it looks abused and stinky.

"Get your bags, girls. Let's go." Dad's eyes are hooded and dark. His late nights working have etched deep lines in his face. I toss my bag into the back compartment. Maybe with this next job, he'll have a better schedule. But who am I kidding? Doctors are always in short supply for those who can't afford personal CompuDocs, which is half of the population. So no matter where we go, he's crazy busy.

Dyl turns away from us, whispering to her mugshot of

a friend. "Don't forget your vitamins. And call me after the test. I want to know which poets they quizzed you on." She finally shuts off her holo.

"You're over your weekly holo hours anyway," I tell her. "And remember to switch sides. Your neck is already getting twisted. Look." I reach over to gently touch the tense muscles below her ear.

She straightens her neck and moves away from me. "I'm okay," Dyl says, adding a tiny smile to dispel any meanness. She does that little side-stepping dance all the time now—keeping her distance, owning her space more and more. I know it's normal for her age, but it hurts. She hasn't let me hug her in weeks.

I jump into the driver's seat before Dyl can protest.

"At least put it on auto, Zel," she whines.

"Why? I like driving." Most people put their mags on auto. Just punch in your destination and it goes. But going manual is so fun. It's a dying art. You really feel like part of the magpod and sense its personality. All the magic of technology disappears, and it's just you and the machine. No games, no illusions.

Thankfully, Dad's deep in thought and doesn't care about me driving today. Dyl tucks herself into the backseat and grabs a pen-sized styling tool from the mini salon stashed in her purse. She zaps a lock of dirty-blond hair into a perfect helix, then pauses to yawn, squeezing her eyes shut. When they open, she sees me still planted in the driver's seat and wrinkles her nose.

"You know, nobody in school drives mags."

"Well, L'il Miss Dyl Pickle, your friends aren't here, so I can embarrass you all I want."

Dyl's face pinks up. "Don't call me that. I'm not a kid." She goes back to curling her hair, but won't meet my eye. Her voice drops. "And you don't embarrass me, Zel."

I bite my lip. She's trying not to hurt my feelings, but I know the truth, with the same certainty that I know the atomic number of oxygen. I'm a total embarrassment. My refusal to wear makeup, nice shoes, or tight clothes. My penchant for getting excited over CellTech News, my favorite holo channel. My endless nagging about her flashy dresses and too-shiny lipstick. She's horrified of me.

I glance back at Dyl, whose head is now covered in romantic, drooping curls. She's daydreaming of meat-for-brains boys, I'm sure. I turn to Dad.

"Okay. So where to this time?" I say, feigning a good attitude.

"Let's . . . let's go north. No, west." I can almost hear the dice-roll of our future clinking in his brain. I don't like it. I like having a plan, and Dad always has a plan.

"I'm hungry," Dyl moans.

"We'll get food later. After we leave town." He looks behind us as we hover for a bit. I push the T-shaped steering bar forward and we zoom down the street, ensconced in our bubble of plainness. Inside the mag, there are no sweet treats, games, no mobile e-chef. Nothing. There isn't anything to do but curl your hair, drive, or ignore your imminent future, like Dad is doing.

The other mags zip around us. The hum from the

metal mag lines in the street is the only sound we hear. I'm concentrating so hard on swerving in and around the slower mags that my vision goes blurry around the edges. Dad touches my arm.

"Breathe, Zelia."

And then I remember, the way I must remember hundreds of times a day. I suck in a huge breath, and then a few more big ones to make up for my distracted moments. My stupid affliction. Dad says it's called Ondine's curse. On its own, my body will only take a few piddly, shallow breaths a minute. If I don't consciously breathe more deeply or frequently when I'm excited, or running, or doing anything besides imitating a rock, my brain won't reflexively take over enough to keep me alive.

Just add it to the list of other annoyances in my life. The non-fatal ones, that is.

"Why don't you just put on your necklace?" Dyl suggests. "It scares me when you don't wear it." She gives me a worried look, but it doesn't convince me. My titanium necklace is safely tucked away in my pocket. When I wear it around my neck, the pendant signals an implanted electrode in my chest to trigger normal, healthy breaths every few seconds. It's great for sleeping, since dying every night is quite the inconvenience. But during the day? It feels like an invisible force yanking the air in and out of my body.

"You know I hate that thing when I'm awake."

When Dyl was little, she used to fetch it for me all the time. As soon as she'd leave the room, I'd take it off. It was a cat-and-mouse game we played. Now that she's older, she respects my decision not to wear it when I'm awake, but she still brings it up every day. My heart dreads the day she stops reminding me.

"It would make life easier for you," Dad adds. His fingers comb through my hair absentmindedly. After two seconds, his scuffed wedding ring gets tangled in the mess. "Drat." After a tug, and a small tuft of lost hair on my part, he's free. Luckily, the subject has changed to how I inherited the frizz-fro that skipped a generation.

"You can borrow this, you know." Dyl taps my head with her hair-styling pen.

Deep breath, I tell myself, so I don't grab the pen and chuck it out of the magpod.

I twist the T-bar to maneuver around other mags, now that we're in the center of town. The 3-D signs are everywhere, poking out from the sleek metal façades of the buildings, beckoning us to buy their wares. We drive under a giant holographic arm holding a purple fizzy drink the size of a trash can.

Another mag swerves a little too close, and I veer to the right with a jerk.

"Can you please put this thing on auto?" Dyl squeaks. She braces herself against the inner walls of the magpod to maximize the drama, while her curls bounce erratically. "I don't want to break my arm if I'm going to join the fencing team in my new school."

"You'll be fine," I groan.

"You should join me," she says. "It's harder to hit a small target like you."

Before I can deflect her insult-as-compliment, Dad interjects. "Dyl, no more fencing either. Time to move on to something else."

"But Dad! I was getting really good."

"Balance is the key," he says. "And Zelia, no sports."

My hand touches the outline of my pocketed necklace. "But—"

"Never start something where failure is likely."

I shut my mouth. Dad's list of no's runs through my mind. No sports—you're too weak and delicate. No roofs—you'll fall off. No rule breaking—you'll get in trouble. No boyfriends—they'll give you a resistant form of disfiguring herpes. And now, no science.

Still, I understand. He's protecting me like he always has. He may not be around much, but I appreciate how he cares for me, every day. In every *No*.

Dyl steers the conversation away from me, knowing I'm upset and brooding in the driver's seat. She tries to convince Dad to let her buy $1900 morphs ("But the shoes pay for themselves! Fifty pairs in one!"), then chatters on about where to eat, when he rubs his eyes again.

"Let's just get beyond the city limits first."

I'm distracted by an octopus ad with tentacles curving toward me when Dad puts an anxious hand on mine. A bright red magpod far away in the opposite lane bobbles unsteadily, like a cork being dragged through water. People on the elevated walkways point at it and pedestrians scramble out of the way in anticipation.

"Watch it!" Dad yells.

I turn our mag to the right, to get as far away as possible. Still, it comes closer, its speed increasing, and I open my mouth in surprise.

"Oh *crap!*"

The runaway mag drives into our lane and smacks right into a yellow mag way ahead of us. The sound of the crash is loud, and the mag spins in a yolk-colored blur on the sidewalk, the metal squealing horribly. People nearby throw their arms up and scatter from the wreckage. The out-of-control red magpod changes direction again and heads our way.

This is like a horrible holo game I'm losing. I go left, the red magpod goes left; I go right and now it's too close. I can't get out of the way of this thing hurtling so impossibly fast toward us.

"Hold on!" I yell, making one last jerk to the right.

"No!" Dad throws his whole body over me and grabs the T-bar, pushing it hard to the left instead, putting himself between us and the oncoming mag. I see his other hand pull the emergency detach lever by my leg. In a second, we are all flying in different directions and my world is upside-down and I'm spinning so fast that the g-forces press my body painfully to the left side of the magpod. I can't see anything because white foam expands in milliseconds, surrounding my body and skull to cushion me from the inevitable impact. I spin, it seems, forever and ever, and pump the air into my lungs so fast, I'm dizzy from hyperventilating.

The crash.